AGENT OF ROME

THE EARTHLY GODS

Also in the Agent of Rome series

The Siege
The Imperial Banner
The Far Shore
The Black Stone
The Emperor's Silver

AGENT OF ROME

THE EARTHLY GODS

NICK BROWN

HODDER &
STOUGHTON

First published in Great Britain in 2016 by Hodder & Stoughton
An Hachette UK company

1

Map drawn by Rosie Collins

A CIP catalogue record for this title is available from the British Library

Hardback ISBN 978 1 444 77919 6
eBook ISBN 978 1 444 76274 7

Typeset in Plantin Light by
Palimpsest Book Production Ltd, Falkirk, Stirlingshire

Printed and bound by CPI Group (UK) Ltd, Croydon, CR0 4YY

Hodder & Stoughton policy is to use papers that are natural,
renewable and recyclable products and made from wood grown in
sustainable forests. The logging and manufacturing processes are expected
to conform to the environmental regulations of the country of origin.

Hodder & Stoughton Ltd
Carmelite House
50 Victoria Embankment
London EC4Y 0DZ

www.hodder.co.uk

For Matthew and Becky

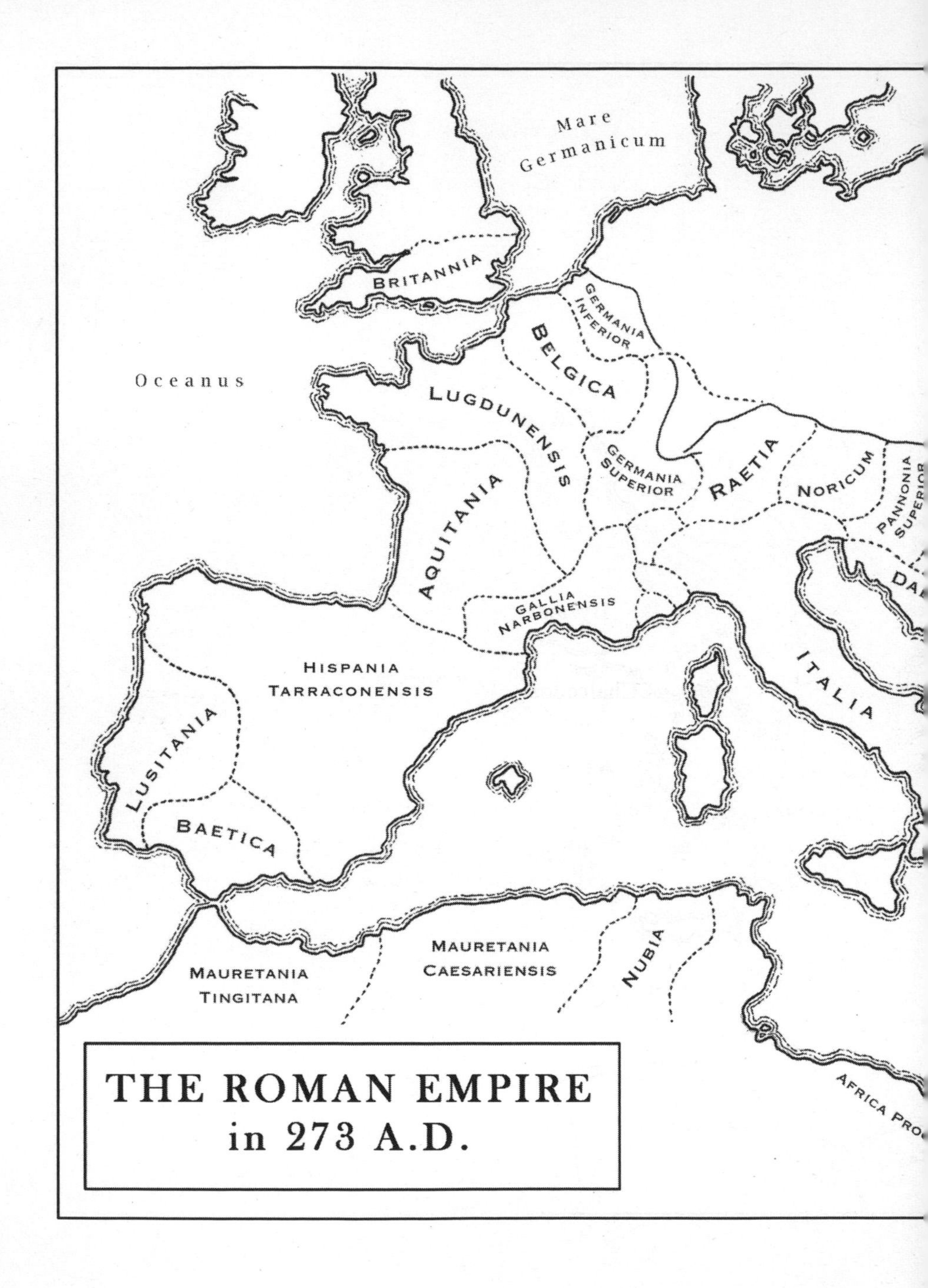
THE ROMAN EMPIRE
in 273 A.D.
Mare
Germanicum
Oceanus
BRITANNIA
GERMANIA
INFERIOR
BELGICA
LUGDUNENSIS
GERMANIA
SUPERIOR
RAETIA
NORICUM
PANNONIA
SUPERIOR
AQUITANIA
GALLIA
NARBONENSIS
ITALIA
HISPANIA
TARRACONENSIS
LUSITANIA
BAETICA
MAURETANIA
TINGITANA
MAURETANIA
CAESARIENSIS
NUBIA

N
W
E
S
DACIA
MOESIA INFERIOR
MOESIA SUPERIOR
Pontus Euxinus
Byzantium
THRACIA
Chalcedon
MACEDONIA
Ancyra
GALATIA
CAPPADOCIA
ASIA
Tyana
MESPOTAMIA
CILICIA
Antioch
Tarsus
SYRIA COELE
R. Euphrates
PHOENICA
Mare Nostrum
ARABIA
Desert
CYRENAICA
AEGYPTUS
Miles
0
200
400
600

August, 273 AD

Indavara had stopped praying after ten days. He wasn't sure how many had passed now: eighteen, maybe twenty. For the first of those days he'd been inside a building: gagged, blindfolded and with his hands and legs bound so tight that he'd been unable to stand when they tried to move him. The next day was spent inside a covered cart. Then they put him on a ship and after a few hours the blindfold and the gag were removed.

Warty – who he'd named on account of the bumps all over his nose – had told him there was no point screaming or shouting; they were at sea and would be for many days. Indavara asked where they were going; why he had been taken. Warty did not reply and neither did Narrow Eyes, the second guard who brought him his food and water.

The pair were always together when it was time for Indavara to exercise and they never took any chances. One was always armed with a sword: close enough to strike if needed, too far for Indavara to make a grab. The captive's hands were manacled at the wrist; his legs at the ankle. The manacles were never removed, only the chain connecting the bottom pair to a huge iron ring embedded in the ship's hull. For about half an hour every day, they would make him walk around the hold, which was no more than five yards from corner to corner. Even then, they hardly spoke. Indavara had been unable to pick up a single clue about who had taken him or why.

He and Corbulo had made the same mistake: assuming the men who had first attacked them in Arabia had been after the Roman officer, not his bodyguard. Indavara had foiled that first attempt, killing three of them, but they had struck with numbers in Berytus, surrounding him and catching him completely off guard. At least Mahalie had got away.

Indavara often thought of the Christian girl he had met in Berytus. He and Corbulo had freed her from her vicious owners and he'd hoped to help her settle into a new life. At least Simo was there to look after her. The Gaul would be praying for him, Indavara knew that. And Corbulo? Corbulo would be looking for him. And the fact that the resourceful army officer hadn't found him confirmed what Indavara suspected; these people didn't make many mistakes. But they had made one, and he intended to exploit it.

The nail had probably been there for years. When there was enough light coming through the holes in the higher timbers, he could clearly see the floor and had nothing much else to look at. The nail had been embedded in a thick mud-like substance between two planks. He had levered it out, then cleaned it. It was large, about two inches long with a rough, square head.

During his time as a gladiator, Indavara had occasionally spent time chained up with his fellow fighters. He'd heard men talk about how locks could be picked but he'd never actually seen anyone do it. It was physically impossible to try the manacles on his wrist and he made no progress with those on his ankles.

But the chain that connected the lower set to the iron ring was padlocked; and this was a different design. While working in daylight, he got nowhere. But when night came, he found that by focusing solely on the sounds of the nail pushing and prodding at the mechanism, he was eventually able to pry it open.

Yet the ship was still at sea, and there was therefore no reason to free himself and let his captors know what he had done. So he'd locked the chain and tried again. After three more nights of practice, he could now pick the lock in what he estimated to be less than a minute.

And on this day – when the ship seemed to have wallowed in the same place for some time and he'd heard unfamiliar voices – he reckoned his chance had come. The nail was safely wedged between two planks beneath his right thigh. Indavara was considering a return to prayer when he heard footsteps outside the hold.

Having unlocked the door, Warty and Narrow Eyes walked in. This time it was Narrow Eyes who had the sword.

'No walk for you today, boy,' said Warty. 'Quick stop for us – so you're going to have to stay nice and quiet.'

Indavara thought it best to persist with the impression he had been presenting for the last few days; that of a man who had given up.

'Water?' he said. There was none left in his bowl.

'Nah,' said Warty, adding a giggle. 'Actually, that's why we're here – now you know what it's like to go without. And if you make so much as a peep there'll be none for three days. Understood?'

Indavara nodded. He had occupied much of his spare time imagining how he would kill the pair of them but he presently had other matters to consider.

They left, locking the door behind them.

Indavara waited: until they had gone; until he heard more shouts; until ropes landed on the deck above him; until the hull knocked against something solid. In the distance he could hear vendors plying their wares. There were people close; people who could help him.

There was no time to start praying again. He shifted backwards and plucked out the nail.

He almost couldn't do it. The task somehow seemed more difficult in daylight and he had dropped the nail five times and rubbed two of his fingers raw by the time he finally heard the click.

Indavara removed the lock from the chain and quietly pulled it off, almost one link at a time. Now free to move, he manoeuvred himself on to his knees, then stood and stretched out his aching limbs.

With ankles and wrists still locked together it was difficult to walk without noise, but he turned and hobbled closer to the side of the hull. He put his eye to one of the wider holes in the timbers and looked out.

The view was limited. All he could see were a few masts and high land beyond wherever the harbour was located. He saw a cleared area surrounded by trees where a sparkling white temple looked out over a steep slope. It seemed familiar.

And when he moved his view to the right and saw the huge slab of bronze amidst a collection of houses he knew exactly where he was. The metal was the flank of the fallen statue – the Helios. He had been to this island the previous year with Corbulo and Simo.

Rhodes.

The thought of it brought on rapid breaths. Help – real help – was close. Annia, the girl who had accompanied them while they pursued her father's killer, lived just miles away. Here in the harbour were legionaries he had worked alongside for several days. They would know him. They would help. What was the name of that officer?

The sound of movement from the rear of the ship galvanised him into action. He had heard lots of men leaving when they first arrived; that's what always happened when you reached harbour. They might have left only a few to watch the ship and its secret cargo. He had to go now.

Like most hatches he'd seen, the one in the hold's roof was covered when not in use to prevent the ingress of water. This one was protected by a heavy, leather cover. Indavara shuffled over to the closest corner, grimacing at every clink from the manacles.

He immediately went to work on the panels stitched together to form the cover. By pushing the nail up and severing the threads, he soon had enough of a hole to push his finger through. And once he could get a proper grip, he could tear the panel open. This was loud; but so was the noise from the harbour, and nobody came.

Though his fingers and wrists and arms began to ache he kept going: pushing the nail up, breaking the stiches, pulling open the panels. Before long he could get both hands through.

Assuming that if any of the sailors could see him they would have stopped him by now, he grabbed the cover and hauled it downwards, tearing a hole big enough to climb through.

Indavara stepped into the light, gripped the edge of the hatch with both hands and swung himself upwards. Once his feet hit the deck, he levered himself up and rolled on to the timbers.

The light hurt his eyes. But once he could open them properly, he found himself sitting close to the bow of a small galley. The vessel was tied to a high stone breakwater to his left, some way from the main quay. He recognised the buildings less than a hundred feet away. He saw the fish market and remembered that the legionary way station was close. What was the name of that officer?

Now on his knees, he looked up at the breakwater and saw a gull land and peck at some morsel. A pair of sailors with coils of rope over their shoulders were walking towards the quay. Tied up in front of the ship was another vessel but it seemed to be unoccupied.

Indavara crawled towards the breakwater and looked back along the side of the ship. Some of the crew were gathered close to the stern, talking. He recognised only Warty but there were four others. The gangplank was roughly halfway between him and them.

'What are you doing?' said a refined voice.

A wealthy-looking couple were looking down at him from the breakwater. The man was wearing a fine cloak, the woman was holding a parasol over her head to shield herself from the sun.

'Must be a slave or something,' added the man.

The woman looked at Indavara with something close to pity in her eyes.

The man turned to the sailors. 'You there! You seem to have an escapee on your hands.'

The woman shook her head and cast a despairing glance at Indavara.

As the sailors came at him, he turned and hobbled towards the bow. The longer he could fight, the better the chance that someone might see him and help. He already knew who the best source of help was.

'Please, mistress, I'm a free man and a soldier of Rome. My name is Indavara. Please tell—'

What was the officer's name?

He passed the hatch and turned round. They were advancing from both sides. Warty was leading the way, a heavy cudgel in his hand. Indavara wished he had conquered his fear of water but he could not jump – it would kill him, manacled or not.

One of the sailors dived at his legs. He came down hard on his left shoulder.

What's the name?

'Very bad idea, boy,' spat Warty. 'Very bad indeed.'

His boot crunched into Indavara's knee.

Name!

'Mistress, it's Clemens! Optio Clemens!'

Warty's bulky body had blocked out the sun. He drew back the cudgel.

'Mistress, I beg you, I beg you. Please tell—'

I

Antioch, September, 273 AD

With every morning came a little hope.

It was the responsibility of the clerks at the basilica to collect all post received and hold it for those officers assigned to the governor's staff. Each morning, the administrators would place the letters and notes in the rack of pigeonholes mounted on the wall in one corner of the enormous main chamber. Technically speaking, Cassius Quintius Corbulo was still part of the governor's staff of Arabia – not Syria – so he didn't merit a pigeonhole. This meant that he had to ask the clerks whether any correspondence had come in for him the previous day.

'Anything?'

'Morning, Officer Corbulo,' said Vibius, the youngest and most enthusiastic of the clerks. 'I'll just check – I believe there was something.'

Cassius had sent letters to no less than forty officers of the Imperial Security Service and a similar amount of provincial governors. The missives described Indavara and the circumstances surrounding his capture. Cassius had also pestered the local governor for a week to ensure that the official stamp of his office went on every letter. They had been dispatched thirty-three days ago. Although the reliability of the imperial post gave him confidence that the majority would have reached their intended recipient, he was yet to receive a single reply. Just as he had found in Berytus in the days after the bodyguard's capture, Indavara seemed to have completely disappeared.

Vibius had already checked the box of scrolls (usually official correspondence) and had now moved on to the box of notes.

Tellingly, the former was constructed of a polished hardwood, the latter of wicker.

Cassius felt his spirits sink: it was highly unlikely that anything regarding Indavara would arrive via this route. He placed his helmet on the front desk and idly watched two other clerks trying to get ink out of a bronze pen.

'Ah, here it is. Just another of these, I'm afraid.'

Vibius handed him a tiny sheet of worn paper with the familiar note on it, scrawled in poorly rendered Latin.

For Officer Cassius Corbulo,

Sir, I need your help. Please meet me at the statue of Hadrian at midday.

Kabir, Alauran.

Cassius had received two identical notes in the last week. At any other time he would have complied with the request. Three years ago, when he had led the defence of the fort at Alauran, the contribution of the charismatic Syrian and his auxiliaries had been crucial. Kabir had lost many men, including family members. The last time he had seen him, the nomad chieftain had been riding north, to return at long last to his people. Cassius owed the man. But he could do nothing for him; not at the moment.

As he tucked the note into the money bag attached to his belt, he noted two tribunes standing by one of the basilica's colossal main columns. They had clearly been looking at him but now turned away. He had observed similar incidents before. Curiosity was to be expected. He was something of an anomaly – an officer of the Imperial Security Service without any assigned role who seemed obsessed with tracking down his missing bodyguard.

Cassius couldn't have cared less about what they said or what they thought.

Typically, he spent his mornings exercising. It helped counter the drinking later in the day and he somehow felt he owed it to

Indavara to keep up with his running and his sword work. The inn where he and Simo were staying was close to the Baths of Tiberius. He would practise his blade routines for twenty minutes, walk to the baths with his attendant, then run for forty minutes before entering the baths.

While he lay in the hot room, or swam in the cold pool, he would think: mainly about who could have taken Indavara and why. Sometimes he came up with a new angle or thought, which he would discuss with Simo while being cleaned and dried. Of late, he'd been considering the bodyguard's mysterious past. The man had suffered a blow to the head before being captured and made a gladiator. He could remember nothing of his life before. Was it possible that some event from his earlier years could explain why he had been taken?

When they returned to the inn, Cassius would go over his notes and consider anything promising from the day. Once he had eaten, he would then start drinking until he fell asleep. It was the only workable way he had found to get through his waking hours.

But today would be different: today he had a meeting to attend.

'Gods, you look terrible.'

Aulus Celatus Abascantius ushered Cassius into the room. Already inside was his attendant Shostra, who was leaning against the wall. As usual, the hulking ex-wrestler offered no greeting, merely an implacable gaze.

'Excuse the venue,' said Abascantius, 'it's the only empty space I could find.'

Antioch's legionary fortress was now flooded with troops returning – like Abascantius – from the Emperor Aurelian's campaign to put down a revolt in Egypt. Many, including the veteran agent, had arrived yesterday with a column containing hundreds of troops and other assorted personnel.

As they sat, Cassius glanced around. The room seemed to have been reserved for storage. Apart from the table and chairs, the rest of the floor was covered with wooden chests, amphoras and woven baskets. Shostra was standing between a pile of shields and a collection of damaged spears.

'Nothing to eat or drink either, I'm afraid. I thought perhaps you could come for dinner at my place tonight. Don't worry, Shostra's not cooking; I sent word ahead to my housekeeper.'

'Thank you, sir.'

Abascantius ran his fingers through his thinning hair, which was now more grey than brown. Weeks on the road had darkened his skin, which partially hid the pockmarks that were responsible for the nickname used across the eastern provinces: Pitface.

'Still nothing?'

Cassius shook his head.

'What about Pietas Julia – you thought there might be some connection to his time as a fighter?'

'Nothing yet. Sir, I'm glad you're here: we need to step things up. I would like a squad of men; eight will do. We can start back at Bertyus. Someone has to know something.'

'Your letter said that the magistrate and the army there did everything they could to help. The trail is cold now. What makes you think you'd get anywhere?'

Cassius tried not to let this response put him off. 'If we don't we can move on to Pietas Julia. It would be quickest to hire a ship – then I can stay mobile. If you're to remain here for a while, sir, you can monitor the post – see if anything comes in.'

Abascantius cleared his throat then aimed a thumb at the door. Shostra obediently left. Cassius did not consider this a good sign.

'Corbulo, even if there was money for that – which there isn't – I can't just remove you from your normal duties for an indefinite period. I am gathering all my officers here next week and I have urgent work for them all – including you. The Emperor made it very clear to me that he does not want to have to return to the East again. Apart from the Egyptians, there are the Palmyrans to keep an eye on, the Arabians—'

'I should have known.'

As Abascantius shifted backwards, the legs of his chair scraped across the stone floor. 'What?'

'I should have known you wouldn't care.'

Abascantius rolled his tongue around his mouth and held the younger man's stare.

Cassius could see no reason to hold back any longer. 'Do I have to remind you what he's done for the Service? For you? The flag, Africa, the black stone! By the gods, he and I have brought you victory after victory.'

Cassius half-expected Abascantius to spring at him; it wouldn't have been the first time. If the consequences weren't so dire, he would have enjoyed landing a blow on that fat, ugly face.

'Not quite.'

When he understood what his superior meant, Cassius simply shook his head in disbelief; how typical of the man to concentrate on his only failure to date.

'Indavara has risked his life time and again for me; and for you.' Cassius barely realised that he was leaning forward, pointing at Abascantius. 'Without him, we would have failed on every occasion. You know it as well as I do and now you just—'

A knock on the door.

'Sir?'

'What is it?' snapped the agent.

Shostra opened the door. 'Sir, Tribune Autronius is asking for you. He wants to go over the briefing before your meeting with the governor.'

'Very well. I'll be along presently.'

Shostra shut the door.

The agent drew in a long breath through his nose. 'This interruption might be propitious. I suggest you calm down, young man, and remember that it was I who recruited him. If there is anything we can feasibly do, we will do it. But I think we both know that the situation is not looking good. We have to be realistic.'

Abascantius stood. He straightened his tunic and adjusted the sheathed dagger upon his belt. 'We'll talk later. Let's say the twelfth hour. That's not an invitation, it's an order.'

Cassius picked up his horse from a nearby stable and rode back to the inn. The busy city was nothing but a noisy blur. With his crested helmet and cloak, he didn't even need to speak; anyone in his way got out of it quickly.

Throwing his reins to the lad on duty at the inn's courtyard, he removed his helmet and strode inside. He and Simo were occupying the hostelry's largest room, which was on the ground floor and had exclusive access to a flower garden. Cassius had spent hours there over the last few weeks and was currently interested in doing nothing else – as long as he had a mug of wine for company.

He found the room locked and cursed Simo as he fetched the key from his money bag. Once inside, he dropped his cloak on to a chair and pulled off his boots. He grabbed a pail of water, briefly dunked his aching feet then walked over to the jug of wine. Despite his later appointment, he filled his mug and did not dilute it.

Considering the central position of the inn, the flower garden always seemed remarkably peaceful. Cassius took a pillow from the bed and walked out to his favoured position in the corner. Well-shaded but warm, he could lie on the grass and see only the flowers, the ivy-covered walls and the blue skies above. He had come to consider the place a haven; where he found more solace than any temple could offer.

As he lay there, sipping the wine, he tried not to think about the meeting. But before long the thoughts crept in. As he recalled Abascantius's words, his fingers moved on to a red tile that had come loose from the wall. He gripped the edge and smashed it into the ground, leaving half of it in his hand. He continued to smash it until he was damaging only his own flesh.

'What have you done to yourself, sir?'

Groggy from the wine, Cassius looked up to see Simo standing over him.

'What?'

'You're bleeding, sir.'

The big Gaul always carried a handkerchief tucked into his belt. He knelt beside Cassius and gently examined his hand. 'You've cut it quite badly. I'll get a bandage.'

'I'm fine.'

'Sir.'

'Later.'

'How was the meeting?'

'Sit. Let's talk.'

Simo sat down on the grass. Cassius had never seen him so thin; and with a recent haircut that had chopped off most of his thick black hair, he looked five years younger.

At first, the attendant had been the one who had struggled to cope with the loss of Indavara. The two had grown increasingly close over the years and neither had a better friend. While Cassius had thrown himself into the search, Simo had become so desperate that he had even questioned his faith. He found it almost impossible to accept that poor Indavara could be put through so much suffering. But now, back in Antioch, with his father and old friends close by, he had rallied.

Cassius was relieved at first, but now he realised that Simo's renewed strength had allowed him to weaken. And he had seldom felt weaker.

It did not take him long to summarise the short meeting with Abascantius.

Noting that the top of the cross around his neck was showing, Simo pulled up his tunic. 'Perhaps you will be able to persuade him tonight, sir.'

Cassius sat up and leant back against the wall. He looked down at his hand; the trickle of blood had run all the way down his forearm and dried.

'Simo, he doesn't care. I doubt if he would be particularly concerned if I or any other of his agents went missing. He'll simply find some other poor bastard to do his bidding – risk their necks so that he doesn't have to.'

Simo cupped a nearby yellow flower in his hand. They had

both held out hope that the return of Abascantius would signal a change in their fortunes.

'However,' said Cassius, trying to somehow remain optimistic, 'I must do what I can. We need him. And we certainly need the power and reach of the Service. I know nothing's come in but I just try to think of all those letters we sent out: at least people know, they'll be keeping an eye out.'

'He is quite hard to miss,' said Simo, 'what with all those scars.'

'And that mangled ear. In a few weeks, I can send out more letters – keep it fresh in people's minds.'

'He has only us in the world, sir.'

'I know. I wonder what he must think of his precious Fortuna now. I wonder if he believes she has forsaken him.'

Later, Cassius accompanied Simo when he went to check on Patch. The durable, good-natured donkey had been with them since the hunt for the black stone in Arabia. Though Cassius had often mocked Indavara and Simo for the care they lavished on the beast, he now found that he had developed some affection for it too.

'Poor thing – I really believe it misses him,' he said as he stroked the donkey's neck.

'There's no question about it, sir. He only recovered his appetite in the last week or so.'

Simo lifted up the pail of vegetable offcuts he had obtained from the inn's kitchen. Patch sniffed it a couple of times then pushed his snout in and started chewing.

'Oh, sir – I didn't tell you. Some good news. Mahalie did very well on her first day. My father said Mistress Helena was very happy with her needlework.'

'Excellent. You've done well for the girl, Simo.'

'It was my father who arranged the job, sir.'

Cassius felt guilty that he had done little to assist. Mahalie had been so distraught in the days following Indavara's capture and their trip north to Antioch that he had kept his distance.

'Well, Indavara will be grateful. As am I. How is your father?'

'He seems happy enough, sir. The congregation has grown since I've been away. Elder Nura is very popular in the city.'

'Listen, I don't know how long we'll be here but if you want to continue your studies, you should.'

'Perhaps not now, sir. We might have to leave at any time.'

'True enough, I suppose. Simo, there was another of those notes. You do understand that normally I would meet with Kabir – I'd like to help. But we have to put all our energies into . . . into finding him.'

'Of course, sir.'

'Master Corbulo?' The innkeeper's son appeared outside the stable. 'Message for you.'

He ushered a young lad forward who handed over a small, rolled page tied with twine. While Simo reached into his money bag and gave the lad a coin, Cassius opened the letter and read it.

When he had done so, he tapped the page against his leg and considered its contents.

'Everything all right, sir?'

'I have no idea.'

II

Abascantius's villa – or rather the villa he had liberated from a Palmyran collaborator the previous year – was much as Cassius remembered it: secluded and spacious but rather basic and impersonal. The agent was, however, clearly determined to give his subordinate a pleasant evening. The housekeeper served spiced wine just after Cassius arrived and Abascantius asked about his current accommodation on the way out to the terrace. There were even some big soft cushions on the stone benches they sat on.

As the older man selected some dates from a bowl, Cassius glanced inside. His ceremonial spearhead – which marked him out as a Service agent – was lying on a table. Abascantius's note had asked him to bring it.

Fairly certain that some of the later conversation might be less than cordial, he thought it wise to build some bridges. 'I gather the campaign in Egypt went well, sir?'

'Exceptionally. The Emperor has run out of patience with these bloody uprisings dragging him away from Rome and the situation in the West. The leaders were caught and killed with some speed. Several centuries have been left behind to reinforce Trajan's Legion. There'll be no more trouble from that quarter for a while; or Palmyra; or Arabia. It is my job to make sure of it – I have been promoted to the position previously occupied by Memor, with control over the Service in all the provinces east of Byzantium.'

'Congratulations, sir,' said Cassius, holding up his glass and hoping he had hidden his true reaction well. He felt sure this development would not work in his favour; the man who had already sent him on four treacherous missions now had even more power over his fate.

Abascantius held up his glass too. 'Thank *you*, Corbulo. And not only for your sentiment. Whatever you may think, I am aware that your successes have done nothing to harm my reputation with the Emperor and Marshal Marcellinus.'

'Well, I'm sorry we were unable to deliver another success in Berytus, sir.'

'It seems this brother and sister were a capable pair. At least you disrupted their operation. You sent out the report as I instructed?'

'Yes, sir – though the information on them is still very limited. We probably don't even have their real names.'

'At some point I will assign a significant force to investigate properly. For now, we have other priorities.' Abascantius began munching through his dates.

Cassius almost pressed him further: if the agent was going to try and send him off on some other mission, he wanted to know now.

But it was the older man who spoke first. 'You're probably wondering why I asked you to bring the spearhead. It still identifies you as a member of the governor's staff in Arabia. We need to change that to Syria – you won't be spending all your time here but—'

Shostra appeared in the doorway. 'First course is ready.'

'Are you addressing me?' countered Abascantius.

'Sir,' grunted the Syrian.

Cassius had long understood that the agent did not keep him around for his skills in the domestic realm. Shostra was simply a loyal thug who never asked twice when ordered to do his master's dirty work.

'Come, Corbulo. I don't know about you but I'm starving.'

Cassius wasn't particularly hungry but he had to admit the housekeeper had done well. The first course was fresh sea bream, the second peppered lamb, dessert honey cakes and fig syrup. Cassius managed about half of each. When he finished his third glass of wine, he noted that his host did not request any more for the table.

Abascantius also seemed keen to avoid – or at least delay – the inevitable clash. He talked mainly of events in Rome and the current state of affairs to the West, where the usurper Tetricus had held sway for several years. The attention of both the Emperor and the Senate was turning in that direction. After three years in power, Aurelian had finally subjugated the East; Tetricus represented the sole remaining serious threat to his rule. Cassius knew that his father and everyone else back home would be revelling in these successes and the first prospect of genuine stability for years. It should have meant a great deal to him too; yet he had given the situation barely a moment's thought.

When the housekeeper removed the plates, Abascantius planted his palms on the table and looked across at his guest. 'I have made a provisional plan to promote you, Corbulo. You would be the senior man in Antioch, with command of all Service personnel in Syria. The role would keep you away from field operations and give you the break you need and deserve. Your pay will increase by a third; and you will be in charge of more than a dozen other agents, all of whom are some years older than you. Under the terms of your service, you have a year and a half left to serve. I would remind you – that is a fraction of what most of us must do. Unless a specific mission arose suited to your particular skills, you would remain here in the capital before returning home.'

Cassius considered his reply and took great care to remain calm. 'I thank you, sir, sincerely. The post sounds . . . ideal. But I could not possibly commit to it at the moment. I do understand that I can't continue the search indefinitely but I would ask for three months as a minimum.'

Abascantius leaned back in his chair. 'Six weeks have already passed. As you yourself admitted, there are no leads.'

Cassius tried to interject but the agent continued. 'Listen, if I honestly thought there was a reasonable chance of finding him, I would give you the time. But you're better off working here. If anything solid comes in, I'll let you go.'

What annoyed, what *hurt*, Cassius the most, was that Abascantius wasn't even using Indavara's name; as if he had already forgotten him.

'Sir, I simply cannot just *wait*. Indavara is out there somewhere. His only hope is that we find him.'

'Corbulo, I'm sorry to have to say this but I think that's unlikely. He was a gladiator. He killed, what, more than thirty men in the arena? And at least one other in Pietas Julia before I recruited him. There could be more we don't know about. In all likelihood, this was a case of revenge.'

'Then why not just kill him?'

Abascantius didn't give the answer, which was obvious: to torture him, punish him – slowly, painfully.

'Unfortunately, I have dealt with similar cases before. Those in our trade have many enemies, those in his many more. His face and name were well known from his time in the arena; he could have been spotted anywhere. We have to accept that Indavara is probably dead.'

Cassius felt tears forming in his eyes. The older man saw it and spared him by taking another drink. Cassius wiped his sleeve across his face.

'There is another alternative for you,' added Abascantius. 'One that occurred to me after seeing the state of you this morning. Return home now. You're due some leave, after all. You could spend a month in Ravenna with your family.'

The thought had never been so tempting. He had been away for three years. If not for Indavara, Cassius would have jumped at the chance. His last contact with his parents had been an exchange of letters a month ago; Cassius had confided that he didn't know exactly what the future held. He had mentioned the counterfeiting investigation. He had not mentioned Indavara.

'And after that?'

'Though he has not met you, Chief Pulcher is well aware of your achievements. We will now see far more operations in Gaul and the surrounding provinces as the Emperor prepares to deal with Tetricus. I'm sure Pulcher could find something for you. If it were field work, we would of course find another bodyguard.'

Not like him. There is no one like him.

Cassius doubted he would have survived any of the assignments he'd been given without Indavara beside him. Could he even countenance continuing in the Service without him?

Abascantius gave a half-smile, exposing his crooked, yellow teeth. 'Cassius, as I said, we are not giving up on him.'

That is exactly what you are doing.

I will not. Not ever.

'If we hear something – anything – worthy of investigation; you'll be excused duty.'

'Yes, sir.'

'Take some time to think about what you want to do – remain here or return to Italy. But don't take too long.'

Cassius did not go straight home. Having made his excuses soon after the meal, he called in at The Sea Sprite, a superior tavern which – oddly – was some distance from any body of water. Using a trick he'd often employed, Cassius removed his cloak and stuffed it into his helmet, which he then held by the crest. Inside the gloomy tavern, only the most observant would notice there was an army officer present.

The innkeeper had told him about The Sea Sprite, which was only a five-minute walk away. Cassius had made his enquiries subtly; he didn't enjoy the judgemental looks Simo deployed when he knew his master had been out drinking and whoring. He often wondered what the Gaul would think if he knew Cassius now spent more time talking to the girls than bedding them. In fact, Cassius had not felt such bodily urges in weeks. He put this down to a combination of his drinking and his mental state. Compared to his other concerns, it didn't worry him.

Apart from its proximity and the quality of the girls, The Sea Sprite also boasted numerous private booths. Once ensconced, Cassius ordered a jug of Falernian and gave the serving-girl three sesterces to sit with him. He guessed at least two of these would go to the proprietors: a husband and wife team who at least seemed less avaricious than most of their kind.

He had spoken to Isidora several times before. She was Thracian; a well-proportioned girl with a pleasant – if unexceptional – face. More importantly for Cassius, especially on this particular night, she was cheerful and knew enough of the world to make conversation worthwhile.

Isidora allowed Cassius to pour her some wine, even though she was supposed to take it with water. They sat beside each other on one side of a booth, well away from the other patrons.

'How was your day, Cassius?'

He was glad she'd remembered not to call him 'sir'.

'Not very good.' He swatted at an insect hovering close to the light. The oil lamp on the table was of a type he had seen before: bronze, with a well-rendered mouse forming part of the handle. It had been designed so that the creature appeared to have leaped on to the lamp.

'Why's that?'

'You remember I told you about my friend?'

'Yes. Any news?'

'None. And worse, a man I thought would help doesn't seem to want to.'

'Is he a friend too?'

'No. I don't think he has any friends, to be honest.'

'Is he a soldier?'

'Yes. My superior.'

'Soldiers usually come here in groups. Even officers.'

'Our work is different. We're not really soldiers at all.'

They drank.

Cassius put his hand on her knee and ran it up under her tunic until the flesh beneath his fingers became pleasingly soft.

'Will we go upstairs later?' she asked.

'I don't think so.' Apart from anything else, he couldn't really spare the money. Most of his last wage payment from Abascantius was gone and Simo had mentioned that they were running short. He would have to look into it in the morning.

He kissed her on the cheek then emptied his mug and refilled it.

Isidora picked up the lamp – by the mouse – and moved it closer to him. She leaned forward and examined his face.

'Most men have a better side. Not you.' She made a small adjustment to his hair, which had grown quite long, with an unruly tuft at the front. 'Taura says you are the most handsome man who ever walked into the Sprite.'

'Who's that – the leggy girl? No, the Carthaginian?'

'The owner's wife.'

'Clearly a woman of great taste. And what do *you* think?'

'Honestly, you're a bit skinny for me. But if we put a wig on you and fixed your nose, you'd probably make more money than I do.'

Cassius would have laughed if not for the mention of his nose. He pointed at it.

'Do you know how that happened? I was in Africa – a prisoner of a centurion, would you believe? I was tied up. He just held it and twisted his hand and broke it. Snapped like a twig.'

Isidora made a face then put down her wine and held his arm. She always wore the same pair of earrings – brass squares with a 'jewel' of green glass.

Cassius added, '*That's* the type of work I do.'

'What happened? How did you get away?'

'My friend killed him.' Cassius drank more. 'I wish you could see him. He is not very tall but he's as strong as an ox. I've seen him take on four men and win. I've seen him face down a lion. He never takes a backwards step, never gives in. And he's saved my life more times than I can count.'

Isidora gave Cassius his wine. He drank, forced a smile and put an arm around her. 'Last time you were telling me about your village.'

'Yes, a boy disappeared from there too. I must have been around ten. Nobody could understand it. His family didn't know anything; or his friends. He went to fetch water from a well and just didn't come back.'

She looked at Cassius. 'I . . . sorry.'

'It's all right. They never found him?'

She didn't need to reply for him to know the answer.

Having drunk nine tenths of the jug of Falernian, Cassius lurched out of The Sea Sprite and took two wrong turns off the Avenue of Herod and Tiberius before finding the right side street. Antioch was generally an easy place to navigate – with its copious street lighting and numerous landmarks – but what should have been a five-minute journey had already taken what he estimated to be . . . well, a long time.

He had just decided to relieve himself against a wall when two watchmen came around a corner. Cassius put his hand up to block the glare of their lantern. He could see nothing of their faces beyond the light.

'Where you headed, mate?' The man with the lantern stepped forward.

'Get that bloody thing out of my face!'

He reached for the man's arm but missed.

When the other watchman clutched his wrist, Cassius shook it off. 'Unhand me, you dolt.'

'You best calm down, mate,' said the first man, his accent as rough as Cassius had heard.

When fingers gripped his shoulder, he lashed out with his fist. To his surprise, he connected with something soft. The fingers let go.

He thought the clanging noise that followed must have been the watchman's lantern. Then he realised the light was still there, though now several feet further away.

'Right, you, my friend, are going to get a damn good—'

'Hang on, Plancus. Look there – what he dropped.'

'Shit. A crest. And a red cloak too.'

The lantern was at last lowered. Their faces seemed blurred and unclear.

'Sorry, sir,' said one. 'Centurion, is it?'

'Officer,' replied Cassius. He had to think quite hard to add anything more. 'Imp . . . Imperial Security.'

'Double shit.'

'Sincere apologies, sir.'

'From me too, sir. Here's your helmet and cloak.'

'Can we help you get home, sir?'

III

Cassius awoke on the floor of the inn's parlour.

When his eyes finally cleared, he spied Simo sitting on a chair, watching him, a mug of water ready in his hand. The Gaul informed his master that, late the previous night, he'd been summoned by the innkeeper to find Cassius slumped outside the front door. Between them they'd only managed to get him this far before he started vomiting. Once Simo had cleaned him up, they'd decided it was best to leave him there. The attendant had remained with him throughout the night.

Once on his feet, Cassius apologised to both him and the innkeeper. He spent the remainder of the day in bed and the only three notable events occurred late on.

The first was a check of the monetary situation. If all the accounts – including the inn and stable – were paid off, they would be left with less than fifty denarii. When Simo confided that he had not taken his allowance for that month, Cassius instructed him to do so immediately. He planned to ask Abascantius for an advance; he had used up his pay.

The other two events involved post. The first letter was from the agent – reminding Cassius to let his superior know his decision swiftly. The second was from the basilica: another note from Kabir, identical to the others. As the sun set, Cassius wrote a reply to Abascantius, requesting the money and asking for a little more time to decide.

He and Simo were awoken at dawn the following day, when the innkeeper knocked on the door and told Cassius that he had a visitor: and his name was Kabir.

'How in Hades did he get this address?'

'No idea, sir,' said Simo as he pulled on his tunic.

'Did you tell him I'm here?' demanded Cassius of the innkeeper.

The man shrugged. 'I told him I'd ask if you'd see him.'

'Gods.' Cassius put his head in his hands. He really didn't have the strength to deal with this now. Refusing Kabir's help face to face would be extremely awkward.

'Tell him I'm ill. Very ill. Close to death, in fact.'

The innkeeper sighed.

'Come on,' said Cassius. 'Can't be the first time you've lied for a guest. There's an extra two denarii in it for you if you get him to leave. Tell him I'm infectious. Very infectious.'

'With what?'

'Simo?'

The big Gaul was not one for deceit. He wrung his hands as he considered his answer. 'Er . . . '

'Just say I'm delirious,' said Cassius. 'And coughing up blood. With a terrible rash. And my hair's falling out. That should do it.'

The innkeeper shook his head, then left, closing the door behind him.

'Pitiful effort, Simo,' said Cassius as he got up, clad only in his sleeveless sleeping tunic. 'All that medical knowledge and you're as useful as a candle in a snowstorm.'

'Sir, excuse my impertinence but it might be easier to just see Kabir.'

'You really think I should get involved? With all I'm dealing with? Simo, I know you and your kind believe it is a man's duty to help every single person with every single problem but it's simply not poss—'

Cassius heard a loud thud from outside, like something landing on the ground. He walked over to the door and looked out into the flower garden. A tall, lean, brown-skinned man wearing a black tunic was walking towards him. Tucked into his belt was a long knife. His face was quite horrifying: a pale scar ran from his left eyebrow to the right side of his mouth. He didn't really have a nose: just a pink mess of bone and flesh.

His name was Idan; and Cassius had last seen him three

years ago. Though his Latin was not good, he made himself very clear.

'Enough lies, Roman. You will see Chief Kabir. If you wish to refuse him, at least have the courage to do so man to man.'

'Good morning, Idan. I see you haven't lost your powers of persuasion.'

The appearance of Kabir was, to Cassius, far more shocking than that of his lieutenant. His long hair – tied with twine like the others – was now white where it had once been as black as the tunics the nomads wore. Though still striking, the feline green eyes had also lost much of their lustre.

It was to the Syrian's great credit that, after all Cassius's efforts to avoid him, he still summoned a polite greeting and a handshake. He and Idan also greeted Simo warmly, with Kabir complimenting him on his loss of weight. The four had spent less than a week together but it had been under the most trying of circumstances. They had depended on each other and belonged to a select group – those who had survived the siege of Alauran. After losing virtually his entire force of auxiliaries, the nomad leader had pledged to never fight for Rome again.

With him were two younger men, who Kabir introduced as his eldest son and his nephew. Both offered nothing more than grim glares through the doorway. When Cassius invited Kabir inside, the chief instructed the pair to wait outside in the inn's main courtyard. All four Syrians seemed rather out of place in the city, with their long hair and the large, hooped rings they wore in their left ears.

While Simo put some chairs out in the garden, Cassius spoke to Kabir. 'My apologies for the lies. I would call my actions inexcusable but there *is* a reason why I did not reply. I have never forgotten what you did for me and for the garrison but . . . well, we've had some problems of our own. If you would allow me to explain?'

Kabir nodded. The garden darkened as the sun was temporarily obscured by cloud. The two nomads sat down opposite Cassius. Somewhere beyond the inn, a group of labourers were lustily reciting a work song.

Cassius described the events as swiftly as he could, making sure that Kabir understood what a debt he owed Indavara; and how his disappearance had affected both him and Simo. Shortly after he finished, the sun reappeared.

As light filled the little space, both Kabir and Idan clasped their hands and spoke a brief invocation. They worshipped a Syrian sun god that Cassius had only ever heard them refer to as 'The Glorious Fire'.

Kabir ran a hand across his hair, then hunched forward. 'Officer Corbulo, when I sent Idan over the wall I was angry. I know three years have passed but I felt I had the measure of you; and I was sure you would help. I could not understand why you would avoid me. Now I do.'

Kabir's Latin was flawless. Cassius recalled that his father had insisted he learn it, believing it was essential for trade.

'Call me Cassius, please.'

'Very well. I understand your situation because I face something similar and I too have been unable to think of anything else. My daughter was taken three months ago; along with two other girls. They had been sent to a market to fetch fruit. Our camp was less than a mile away from the town. We had dozens out searching as soon as we learned what had happened. For three days we remained there and I believe we spoke to every single man and woman. The town was not well known to us but we eventually learned that a gang of slave traders had been in the area. They were preying exclusively on young, attractive girls. The only name that we heard, and we heard it several times, was that of a man known only as Hood – because he always hides his face. The town was to the east, not far from Beroea. We knew they would most likely be taken west, away from those that knew them – to where they can be . . . used.'

Idan put a hand on his chief's shoulder.

Kabir took a moment to compose himself before continuing.

'We arrived here two weeks ago and paid another Roman officer we had fought with to look into it. He's only an optio but he discovered that this "Hood" is known to the authorities – his true name is Tychon.'

'Is that how you found me?'

'The optio told me to ask at the basilica. When you didn't reply, I paid a servant who works there to find out where you were staying.'

'It is fortuitous in a way,' said Cassius. 'I have only been back in Antioch for a few weeks. This Tychon – do you know where he is now?'

'We do. But we can't get to him. You are our last chance. He is in the prison tower. He will be executed tomorrow.'

Cassius ordered Simo to bring out some wine; and also to give mugs to the pair waiting outside.

Kabir explained that though Tychon's involvement in the illegal slave trade was known, his punishment was unrelated. He had been sentenced to execution on account of two charges of murder. Once back in Antioch, he had broken into the home of a long-standing enemy and killed both the man and his wife in their bed. Unfortunately for him, a dog had raised the alarm and he had run from the dwelling straight into a pair of watchmen. They came off best. Tychon still had the incriminating blood-stained knife stuck into his belt. The magistrate had been pursuing him for some time and the judicial prefect had taken only minutes to review the evidence and make his decision.

'Well, can you do anything?' asked Kabir.

'Probably. In theory, I should request permission from the magistrate but I doubt they'll put up much resistance at the tower if I want to see a condemned man.'

This would not be the first time Cassius had visited the place where Antioch's prisoners were held: during the affair of the imperial banner, Simo's father had been incarcerated for assisting the controversial bishop, Paul of Samosata.

'Do you know for sure that he and his associates took your daughter?'

'No. But this is all we have. With so much time having passed, Aikaterine could be anywhere.'

'How old is she?'

'Seventeen. The others too. My wife, her sisters . . . they . . .'

'I can imagine. Kabir, I am truly sorry that I did not answer you sooner. You do understand that they will not let *you* into the tower?'

'I do.'

'In fact, it's probably best if I go alone. You have to trust me – if there's anything useful to be had from this Tychon, I will get it.'

Kabir looked into his eyes. 'As you wish.'

Cassius wished he felt as confident as he sounded. There were not many ways to apply pressure to a man with only a day left to live.

In the year or so since he had last crossed on to the island that made up Antioch's north-western quarter, much had changed. Back then, the city had only recently been wrested back from the Palmyrans and the authorities had faced more pressing priorities than restoration work. The sixty-foot tower was attached to a long building now encased with scaffolding, where scores of workers were attending to the long-neglected brickwork. Other buildings had been demolished and many plots were now marked out with posts and twine for new construction. Cassius imagined the orders had come from on high; the area close to the river was both visible from the imperial palace and on the route to the city's largest structure: the hippodrome.

Today, thankfully, there were no races and he and Simo made good time. Cassius was glad Kabir had agreed not to come along. The outlandish appearance of him and his party – not to mention his desperate desire to extract information from the prisoner – would have made an already difficult task even harder.

As they approached the tower, with its small grilled windows and single doorway, Cassius spied the two legionaries on duty.

'By the gods, it seems an age ago since we came here to see your father.'

Simo looked almost as anxious as he had back then.

'You would prefer to stay outside, I suppose?'

'If you don't mind, sir.'

Cassius was actually glad to have something to focus on other than Indavara and the choice Abascantius had offered. He still felt immensely guilty about not helping Kabir sooner; he was determined to use every trick he had learned while in the Service to glean something useful from this man Tychon.

As he dismounted and put on his helmet, the two legionaries looked on curiously.

'I hope that miserable bastard jailer isn't still in charge,' said Cassius as Simo took control of his horse. 'What was his name?'

'Her . . . Her something.'

'Herminius. Well, I don't intend to take no for an answer.'

'Best of luck, sir.'

Cassius buckled his helmet as he strode towards the tower. The two legionaries put their arms by their sides at the position of attention.

'Good morning, centurion,' said the older man.

'Officer, actually.'

'Ah, sorry sir, I—'

Cassius kept his eyes fixed on the other fellow – the centre of his tunic to be precise. 'By Jupiter, did you eat your breakfast from a trough?' He turned to the second man. 'And you, did you polish your belt with a beggar's loincloth?'

Before either man could attempt to reply, he continued. 'Third legion, I presume. Which century? Which officer?'

Cassius took a stick of charcoal and a scrap of paper from the satchel he carried over his shoulder.

'The fifth, sir,' said the older man, 'under Centurion Matho.'

Cassius made a show of noting the name. 'And you two are . . .?'

The younger man sighed. Legionaries always hated giving their names.

'Well?' snapped Cassius. 'I am sick and tired of having to deal with soldiers who look like cave-dwelling auxiliaries from some northern backwater.'

They gave their full names, which Cassius also noted.

'I am Officer Cassius Corbulo, Imperial Security, and I need to interrogate a prisoner by the name of Tychon. Is he here?'

'He is, sir,' said the older man, who was named Albius.

'You're sure?'

'Yes, sir. There's only six of them left – lot of punishments last week.'

'Good. Tell me, is Herminius still in charge here?'

'No,' said Albius. 'It's Optio Fimbria now but he's not due in until this afternoon.'

Cassius made sure he hid his reaction. The absence of an officer would make this even easier, especially as his onslaught of criticism had already put the men on the back foot.

'Well, will one of you take me up then?'

Albius grimaced. 'Sir, we're really suppose to request permission for this type—'

'And normally I would have it but the man is to be executed tomorrow. Do you really think anyone will care about a condemned double murderer?'

'Probably not, sir.'

Cassius gestured towards the doorway. Albius headed inside. Before following, Cassius pointed at the younger man's tunic. 'Got any water down here?'

'Yes, sir.'

'I want that clean by the time I come down.'

'At once, sir.'

As they walked up the circular staircase, Cassius noted that the interior was much improved, with pale red paint covering the uneven walls and only a little dust upon the steps.

'This Tychon – has he had any visitors?'

'Only one, I think, sir,' said Albius. 'His mother.'

'Did they seem to get on?'

'I believe so. She brought him some food but that's not allowed. Her last visit was yesterday. Optio Fimbria had to almost drag her out. We get that sort of thing all the time.'

'I'm sure. And Tychon himself? What have you observed of him?'

'He's been in a few weeks. Told everyone he was innocent to start with, of course. After his court appearance and the verdict he was angry. We see that a lot too. Just didn't calm down though and eventually he tried to attack one of the other prisoners. He's been in a cell on his own since then. He's ranted and raved to the gods but I think he's accepted it now. Don't worry, sir, he's chained up; and I'll stand guard.'

'Do I look worried?' asked Cassius as they reached the last step, though he was in fact relieved to hear it.

'No, sir.'

'One more thing. The fate of three innocent young women may depend on this meeting. Go along with whatever I say – do not contradict me. Understood?'

'Yes, sir.'

The condemned man was lying close to the single window, his wrists manacled and chained to a large ball of iron. The only contents of the small, square room were a bowl of water and a slop bucket which – judging by the smell – had not been recently emptied.

As Cassius entered, Tychon sat up and placed his hands in his lap. He was barefoot and wearing a filthy, holed tunic. His face was so thin that it resembled a skull with skin stretched over it.

'Chair, sir?' asked Albius, who was leaning in the doorway and had armed himself with a wooden cudgel before unlocking the cell.

'No.'

Cassius had elected to leave his helmet outside. Though he had grown used to it over the years and enjoyed the admiring glances it sometimes attracted, the scarlet crest always seemed rather ridiculous in such situations.

'Good day to you,' he said, feeling that cordiality never hurt, unless one was dealing with subordinates.

Tychon only seemed interested in Cassius's sword; a long, bulky blade with an opulent eagle's head upon the hilt.

'I have some questions for you.'

'Really?' Tychon's voice was more refined than Cassius had expected. 'What do I get in return?'

'That also depends: on the quality of the information you provide.'

'Can you get me a stay? Or a commutation? If so, I'll tell you anything you want to know.'

'The judicial prefect has made his decision. I can do nothing to affect that.'

Tychon glanced up at the roof. 'Then there's nothing to talk about.'

'Perhaps there is. Your mother – life will be difficult for her, I imagine – what with the shame you have brought to the family. And no son to look after her in old age. I could make things easier. The army has very deep pockets.'

'How deep?'

'I imagine one hundred denarii would keep her in food and firewood for quite a while. You could even watch from the window as I hand the money over – to be sure she received it.'

'What do you want to know?'

'You are known in certain areas of Syria as Hood, correct?'

'By a few unimaginative locals, yes.'

'And you took girls from an area close to Beroea several weeks ago?'

'I haven't been charged with unlawful capture.'

'Answer the question.'

'I might have.'

'I'm interested in three in particular. Young, pretty.'

'You're going to have to be more specific,' said Tychon with a smirk.

'One was named Aikaterine. The others with her were Marte and Dinora.'

Tychon shrugged. 'Not very good with names.'

'Where are they now?'

'No idea.'

'Did you sell them on?'

Tychon did not reply.

'At this rate, your mother's not going to be getting so much as a sesterce.'

'You ask me about something else – I'll answer. Those girls, yes, they were sold on – to a man I'm not going to talk about. Anyone else, I'll tell you. But not him.'

'What do you have to lose?'

'Me? Not much. But I have friends still out there in the business. It's my mistake put me in here, not theirs. Why should I endanger them?'

'You value them above your own mother?'

'My mother's survived worse than this. Like I said, anyone else. Not *him*.'

Cassius was ready with another approach. He turned to Albius. 'You would have an address for the mother, I suppose – as next of kin?'

'We would, sir, yes.'

Cassius took his time with the next comment. 'I had a visitor this morning. Aikaterine's father. He is not an old man but his hair has turned entirely white since the girl went missing. He told me he'll be at your execution tomorrow. If you hear any shouts just before the rope goes tight, that'll be him.'

'Should have looked after her better, shouldn't he? Three little beauties like that out on their own? Asking for trouble.'

'Trouble?' Though rarely given to violence, Cassius was sorely tempted to unsheathe his sword and use the flat of his blade on this callous bastard.

'Trouble might be what your mother, and indeed the rest of

your family, will find themselves in – if I give the father that address.'

'You're a centurion. You wouldn't do that.'

'I am not a centurion. I am an officer. Imperial Security.'

It was clear from the change of expression that Tychon knew of the Service; and its reputation.

Cassius threw up a hand. 'If – however – I leave here with information I can use, I will not even ask Legionary Albius for the address.'

Tychon scratched his fingers down his cheek, leaving pale marks in his grimy skin. 'You're bluffing.'

'Maybe,' said Cassius. 'But if you think I care about the life of the godless bitch that brought *you* into the world, you have seriously misjudged both me and this situation. Now, I am rapidly running out of patience. What's it to be?'

Tychon made up his mind surprisingly quickly. 'All right, I'll tell you what I know of him.'

'Good,' said Cassius. 'And by the way, I wouldn't worry too much about reprisals from this man. I doubt he'll be walking the earth much longer than you will.'

He had arranged to meet Kabir at the Beroea Gate, part of the imposing fortifications that guarded the northern approach to Antioch. The nomads were staying with friends within one of the sprawling, semi-permanent encampments outside the city's walls. The streets were busy with morning traffic and Cassius agreed that they would get more privacy at the camp.

A Roman officer accompanied by four long-haired nomads was an unusual sight and the most bemused looks came from the soldiers on duty at the gatehouse. Even so, Cassius's uniform was enough to get them through without a word. He exchanged pleasantries with the optio in charge but his mind was elsewhere: he remembered sitting in the gatehouse with Indavara, examining documentation while on the trail of the Persian banner. They had barely known each other then and had spent much of their time arguing.

He and Simo mounted their horses and followed the Syrians away from the gate. Much of the ground north of the city was low-lying and the approach road was built upon a causeway. The first cluster of tents had been erected at the end of a track running east from the road. The autumn rains wouldn't be long coming; and Idan commented that the camp would soon be moved. Kabir himself said nothing, simply leading them along at a trot. Cassius knew he would be desperate to hear what he had discovered.

Many of the tents closest to the track were owned by traders and their customers were an eclectic bunch. Cassius saw soldiers, priests, city sergeants, even a couple of administrators in togas. The nomads were selling all manner of things but spices and trinkets seemed particularly prevalent.

Kabir hailed an older man then spoke to him in their native Aramaic. The old man swiftly moved aside and gestured to his tent. Cassius had learned that Kabir's son was named Kammath, the nephew was Yablus. They all seemed keen to take part but Cassius had no desire to face a barrage of questions.

'Perhaps just the two of us for now?' he suggested.

'Very well,' said Kabir. Before entering, he put a calming hand on Kammath's shoulder. The son's face was set in a stony glare. Cassius watched Simo moving the horses into a vacant area between the tents then followed Kabir inside.

Light was admitted through an opening at the top of the shelter. Below it were several drum-like stools arranged around a table. Cassius put his satchel on it and retrieved the half page of notes he had made while interrogating Tychon.

'Well?' enquired Kabir as they sat down.

'The girls – all three of them – were sold on only days after they were taken – at a location not far from Gindarus. According to Tychon this is common practice, to avoid them being traced and for the likes of him to make a quick profit. The buyer was a Cilician named Meliton. Tychon cannot be entirely sure but this Meliton usually sells on in Tarsus – his native city. He seemed to have already gathered a large number of slaves, which makes it more likely that he would have gone there soon after. Tarsus is approximately a hundred miles from Gindarus. We might surmise that the girls were taken there around two months ago.'

Kabir had not blinked once as Cassius had spoken. 'And Tarsus? What happens there?'

'These people have forgers who can provide documentation so they can sell using official markets. But there is also an underground trade. Lower prices; no questions asked.'

'Who does he sell to?'

'Tychon didn't know that. But apparently this Meliton has had run-ins with the law too. If he's known to the city sergeants in Tarsus, it may be possible to track him down.'

Kabir eyed Cassius's notes. 'The girls are taken for . . . to be . . .'

'I'm afraid so. Apparently this is what Meliton specialises in. According to Tychon, they are often taken north or west – to lands where their appearance is more exotic.'

Kabir scraped his fingers across his brow and paused for some time before replying.

'Tarsus it is then.'

'Here is what I can do. There will be a Service agent – a man like me – there. I will write to him via the imperial post. The letter will arrive before you; hopefully he will be able to help.'

'His name?'

'I don't know yet. But I'll find out and make sure you have everything you need before you depart.'

'We will leave at dawn.'

Kabir's white hair shone under the light from above, framing his dark face. He stared blankly past Cassius. 'If we ride hard, we can reach Tarsus in four or five days.'

'Do you have money?'

'Enough. This man will definitely help us?'

'Yes,' said Cassius, though he was far from sure. From what he had gathered, the average 'grain man' was more like Abascantius than himself.

'I must thank you,' said Kabir. 'We would not have discovered this without you.'

Cassius thought it typically magnanimous of the man not to mention that if Cassius had reacted to his letter sooner, Kabir might be well on his way to Tarsus already.

The Syrian stood. 'I'll tell the others.'

'Kabir, these girls. They will be kept – forgive me – in good condition. The money they can generate depends on it. I doubt they'll be seriously harmed.'

'Do you know why I let her go to the village unescorted? Aikaterine – Katia, we call her – is almost as good with a sword as Kammath and far better on a horse. She never left home without a blade hidden behind her belt.'

'You could not have known this would happen.'

'I could; had I bothered to find out what was going on in the area. But that's in the past; I can do nothing about it. I am sure she would have tried to defend herself but what worries me now is that she will continue to fight back against these men; and that she will be dead before I find her.'

That afternoon, Abascantius and Shostra came to the inn. The agent seemed in an ebullient mood but to Cassius it appeared rather false. Shostra was carrying a money bag containing an advance of one hundred denarii. Cassius didn't ask about the rest; it was obviously being withheld until he made up his mind. Abascantius commented that he was lucky to be getting even that as he'd wasted most of what he'd been given previously on wine.

The agent did not stay long, but did offer another reason to remain in Antioch. If Cassius accepted the post, one of the operatives he would be working closely with was Lady Antonia (an older women he had conducted a brief affair with). According to Abascantius, she was looking forward to seeing him again. Though he found the agent's tactics typically grubby, Cassius couldn't deny that he found the idea appealing.

Just before leaving, Abascantius ordered Cassius to meet him at the fortress at the eighth hour of the following day. They would attend the baths and discuss his future. The agent asked if he was close to a decision.

Cassius replied that he was; and that by the time they met he would be certain.

IV

Simo had run out of work. He had tidied the room twice, all his master's dirty clothes were washed and drying and he had packed up as much as he could. With a final adjustment to the blankets and pillows on the two beds, he looked outside. Cassius was sitting against the wall in his favoured spot. He hadn't said a thing since Abascantius had left.

Simo had little idea about what his master would do, though he had his own views on the matter. He thought it best that the young officer return to Italy and spend some time with his family. Cassius had been through an almost unending series of trials since arriving in Syria three years ago; and Simo had witnessed almost all of them. Though he'd been better over the last few days, the drinking was once again getting out of hand. Simo was in no doubt that he would benefit greatly from the support of his loved ones; that he would be renewed enough to complete his last two years of service – even if Indavara could not be found.

And yet he could not help hoping they stayed. Master Cassius had promised Simo that when his army career was over, he would become a freedman. But until that time, he had to remain with him and serve as best he could. Their return to Antioch had allowed him to spend time with his father; to return to a familiar congregation and help poor Mahalie. She at last seemed to be recovering from the trauma of losing the man who'd rescued her from a terrible life.

Like his master, Simo would have given anything to know where his friend was. He had never prayed so much for some sign or suggestion that Indavara might be found.

That sign had never come; and now he prayed for the strength to carry on. His father told him not to neglect those he *could* help; to always remember that he would see Indavara in the Kingdom. Simo had told his father that Indavara was a good man; a man who always tried to help those less fortunate. He had not told him about all the killing the ex-gladiator had done. Could such a man ever be admitted to the Kingdom? Simo could not bear the thought that he might never see him again.

'Simo.'

'Sir?'

'Come here. This decision affects you.'

Simo walked outside. The sky was grey overhead, the flower garden gloomy.

'Despite what Abascantius may think, I am no use to the Service at the moment. Nor will I be until I have exhausted every possibility of finding Indavara. I will not stay here and I will not return home.'

Cassius closed his eyes for a moment and his throat quivered.

'Sir, about going home. It has been three years. Perhaps—'

'No. Not now. I can't. I know you would prefer to stay here but there is a way to help Indavara *and* this poor missing girl. I will make Kabir an offer: in return for doing everything in my power to help him find his daughter, he will do the same.'

'How can Kabir help you, sir? Us?'

'Whoever has Indavara is powerful. We will not be able to take on him and his men alone. You've seen how effective the nomads are in action.'

'What about the army, sir? The Service?'

'Abascantius won't allow this. So I'm not going to tell him. We'll leave before he can do anything about it.'

Simo took a moment to absorb all he'd heard. The thought of leaving so quickly was not a pleasant one but he could not help admiring the clarity of thought that he'd seen so often from the young man. Most admirable of all was his utter refusal to give up on Indavara and his determination to see the abducted girls found. Simo could not begrudge him this, even though he could see two major flaws in the scheme.

'Well, what do you think?'

'Master Cassius, I think it a noble choice. And you know I will always stand beside you. But what of Master Abascantius – he has often threatened you before because of our time in Cyzicus. If you were to directly disobey him again?'

Cassius let out a long breath. 'I know . . . '

'And he has eyes and ears everywhere.'

'He knows nothing about Kabir. And he's going to know nothing. When I return, I will simply have to face whatever punishment awaits.'

'Also, sir, what if some information reaches Antioch – the basilica, and we are hundreds of miles away.'

'I'm already working on that – leave it to me. Simo, we're going to need more money. I want to take nothing more than eight saddlebags. Fit all of my precious belongings into them and as much of the clothing and other essentials as you can. The rest you will sell.'

'Yes, sir. And Indavara's belongings? There's not much but—'

'The bow and arrows take up space and will fetch a decent price. Everything else you keep. Everything, Simo.'

'Yes, sir.' Simo's head was abuzz; he could not imagine how he was going to tell his father he was leaving.

Cassius put a hand on his arm. 'I will give you time to go and see him.' He stood up. 'Come, there's only a few hours of light left. We have a lot to do.'

During the many occasions on which he had visited the basilica to check the post, Cassius had often observed the clerks at work. Vibius – the young, keen fellow – did not seem particularly popular with his colleagues. Cassius guessed he worked too hard and made the others look bad; and probably toadied to their superiors. Vibius was therefore utterly unsuited to what Cassius had in mind. But he could still be useful.

The working day was nearing its end. The eight clerks were all seated, sorting through the flurry of communiqués still arriving from all over the city and further afield. Anything urgent to go out would be dispatched by a runner; a line of willing boys occupied the space between two columns. Today, Vibius was supervising them.

The more well mannered boys stood up straight as Cassius approached. He had left his helmet at the inn but was wearing his cloak.

He greeted Vibius and ushered him behind the closest pillar, shielding him from the other clerks. 'Do you have a moment?'

'Of course, sir.' Vibius was young enough to still have an unpleasant collation of spots on his chin.

'This is an important – and rather urgent – matter.' Cassius lowered his voice. 'There is a suggestion that the integrity of the imperial post has been compromised. The leak has been traced to the basilica. Now think about this very carefully. Amongst your fellow clerks, is there anyone you think might be open to . . . manipulation?'

Vibius gulped and looked anxiously around. Many of the administrators had gone home for the day but there were still a dozen senior men in togas and several army officers.

'Do not worry,' added Cassius. 'Anything you say will remain anonymous and no action will be taken without proof. Any names?'

Vibius began chewing his cheek.

'Just the names,' said Cassius.

'There is . . . I don't think I should . . . '

'Come now. I wouldn't want to have to mention you in my report for obstructing the investigation.'

He felt a slight pang of guilt at the reaction this provoked.

'Calidius, perhaps. Or Denter.'

'Are either of them here now?'

'Calidius is.'

'Good. Thank you.'

'Sir, you won't mention my—'

'Never. I thank you on behalf of the Service.'

Vibius brightened.

Cassius strode past the boys and up to the counter, which was currently unmanned.

'Who is Calidius?'

A seated man raised his hand. 'Here, sir.'

'I have a small job for you.' Cassius beckoned him forward.

The clerk – who was a chubby fellow, perhaps a little older than Cassius – neatly negotiated the tables between them.

'Is there somewhere we can talk in private?'

Calidius looked mystified but nonetheless pointed towards the rear of the basilica. 'There, sir?'

'That's fine.'

Most of the small offices and storage rooms were locked shut but one – empty other than a stack of tables – was open.

Once inside, Cassius got straight to the point. 'You've seen me here before?'

'Yes, sir.'

'And you know about the letters I sent out about the missing man? He is my bodyguard and friend – his name's Indavara.'

'Yes, sir.'

'I am leaving Antioch tomorrow. It is possible that another man, a senior man, might send someone to collect any relevant replies, or have them sent on to him. But they will still come here first. I need you to monitor any such communication for me. If you can, open them and make a copy. If not, at least take a note of where they came from. You must keep a scrupulous, accurate record. But you must *not* let your colleagues or anyone else know what you are doing. I will of course pay you well.'

Calidius scratched his neck. 'Sir, aren't you with the Service? I wouldn't want to cross Pitface.'

'As long as you're careful, he'll never know. I need you to do this for a month, two at the most. I may also write to you here requesting the latest news, if any. Name your price.'

'Ten denarii.'

Cassius made a show of his consideration, though he would have paid twice as much.

'Very well. I suggest you keep your records and any copies at home.'

Cassius checked again that they weren't being watched, then counted out half the coins and gave them to the clerk.

'The rest when I return.'

Calidius could hardly hide his glee as he slipped his easy earnings into a pocket. 'Sir, there's been nothing about your friend so far. What if nothing more comes?'

'Then that's how it is. But if something does arrive – anything – and you miss it, then you and I will have a serious disagreement. And you can forget the rest of the money. A man's life may depend on me receiving that information. Understood?'

'Yes, sir.'

The night was several hours old when Cassius and Simo finally sat down. As well as visiting both his father and Mahalie, the Gaul had also been to a local clothier and a cobbler. He had sold two pairs of boots, one pair of felt slippers, two belts, two belt buckles, a cape, a cloak, three blankets, two pillows and one cushion. Having settled up with the innkeeper he had also swapped some supplies (including candles, olive oil and soap) for fresh food for the journey.

Simo counted up the coins he had just tipped on to the table. 'Almost sixty denarii, sir.'

'That and the advance will keep us going for a while.' Cassius glanced at the floor, where Simo had packed the saddlebags.

'Two for each of us—'

'—and four for Patch, sir, yes.'

'Are the mounts all right?'

'Yes, sir, the grey's ears have cleared up nicely. Stable fees all paid off too.'

The two horses had been with them since they'd left Bostra in the summer and had served them well.

'Let us hope their good health continues. We cannot afford replacements.'

Simo returned the coins to the bag, then stared at the flame of the oil lamp between them.

Cassius eyed the hunk of bread on his plate and realised he couldn't eat any more. It was too late.

'How were they both?'

'I took Mahalie with me to my father. Fortunately they have met several times at the church house. She did not take the news well but after a while he managed to get a few words out of her. At least she knows someone will be there if she needs anything. I left them together and assured her that I – we – will be back soon. I'm not sure she believed me.'

'She's in good hands, Simo.'

'Sir, I told my father about Kabir's daughter and the other missing girls. I hope you don't mind. I felt I had to say something.'

Cassius almost snapped at him; Abascantius knew about Simo's father – it was one method of tracking them down. But he could understand why the Gaul would want to explain. 'As long as he tells no one else.'

'He won't, sir. He will pray for us. And Indavara. And the missing girls.'

Cassius emptied his mug of wine. 'I expect Kabir and his family have prayed to their sun god for hours on end. I expect Indavara has prayed to his precious Fortuna too. Doesn't appear to have done them much good, does it?'

Simo – who had long mastered the art of sleeping lightly and waking when he was supposed to – roused Cassius well before dawn. As the innkeeper helped him take their saddlebags around to the stable, Cassius placed his crested helmet on the table in the parlour. He had instructed the innkeeper to present it to Abascantius or Shostra when one or both of them turned up, which they inevitably would. He took out the brief note he had written the night before and held it close to the nearest lamp.

Sir,

I am sorry but I must leave. Please do not try to find me. I will return as soon as I can.

Cassius Corbulo

He knew what it might mean for him. This was a direct contravention of orders. If he so desired, Abascantius could strip him of his rank and send him back to Italy in disgrace. Cassius had already shamed his family once; that was why he had been forced to join the army in the first place. There were few worse eventualities he could contemplate. Not finding Indavara was one of them.

As the sun rose, the walls and columns of Antioch were first drawn from the darkness then coloured a deep, dark orange that eventually became a pale, warm yellow. Above the Beroea Gate, the stone sculpture of Romulus and Remus stood proud, thirty feet above the ground. Lower down was the sparkling silver statue of the local goddess Tyche.

A legionary appeared beneath the portcullis, then walked out beyond the great arch and relieved himself beside the road. At the nomad encampment, fires were lit and thin trails of smoke drifted high into the cloudless sky.

Cassius and Simo were a quarter-mile from the gate, waiting beside the causeway. Though they had been there since dawn, Cassius began to fear they might have missed Kabir and his party.

But as a column of carts carrying broken tiles rolled past, he spied a group of four horsemen trot out of the camp. They bypassed the carts, then guided their mounts on to the causeway.

'Good morning.'

Kabir seemed as surprised as the others. Like them, his eyes took in the heavily loaded horses and the donkey roped to Simo's mount. The chieftain also inspected Cassius's clothing: he had dispensed even with his wide military belt and could have passed for a middling merchant or a Roman holidaying in the East. With his pale skin and brown hair, Cassius could never hope to blend in with the locals.

The nomads were travelling light, their horses burdened mainly with fodder and water skins. Cassius noted that every man was also carrying his sling and ammunition bag where they could easily be reached. Kabir's unit of auxiliaries and their deadly skills had turned the tide during the siege of Alauran. Idan in particular was uncannily accurate.

'Kabir, I would like to make you and your men an offer.'

'Go on.'

'I will accompany you to Tarsus and do everything I can to help you find the girls. If we do, in return I ask for your help with finding my friend. I cannot take on those who have captured him alone.'

Kabir glanced back at each of the others. Cassius saw no obvious reaction from any of them. They would obey his decision. The chieftain nudged his horse closer to Cassius and reached out to him. They shook hands.

The Syrian then cast a cynical look at Patch. 'Will that thing be able to keep up?'

Simo tutted.

Cassius grinned. 'That donkey has been across desert wastes, mountain passes and hundreds of miles of ocean. You needn't worry about him.'

V

Once again, Indavara had no idea where he was. The room was square and built of stone, with a dusty floor and a single wooden door. It seemed to him like an old hut or part of a farmhouse. There were two windows, which meant he got more light than in the ship or the covered cart used for the last few hours of the journey.

He did know he was on a coast; the intermittent boom of surf and the cry of gulls told him that much. Indavara didn't know a lot about geography and the few maps he'd seen had mystified him but he remembered that Rhodes was in an area with lots of islands, so he supposed he might be on one. Then again, they had travelled for eight days after leaving there – almost entirely in the ship – so it was no more than a guess.

At least they were feeding him well. He had been there for four days and had received one good meal in the morning and one in the evening (and plenty of water). Warty and Narrow Eyes usually brought it to him and there was a third, older man who had been in only once to look him over. He hadn't spoken.

Warty and Narrow Eyes had beaten him three times in the days after his attempted escape. Indavara had curled up tight, covered his head and restricted the damage to a few bruises and cuts. The worst blow had been from Warty, who had caught him low with a boot. Indavara had been sick afterwards and unable to eat for a while.

He was also able to move around a bit. They had replaced the manacles with a newer set on his first day in the hut. There was no connecting chain this time so he could at least hobble over to the latrine – a recently dug hole in one corner. It was deep; and one of his captors came in every day to drop earth on to the waste. Indavara wasn't sure what to make of the fact that they now seemed almost to be looking after him.

Despite the windows, day was little different to night. He lay on the bed (a pile of blankets) and drifted in and out of sleep. Though his spirits had never been lower than in the days immediately after Rhodes, he had eventually resumed his prayers. And now he tried to do so for at least an hour a day: simple requests for help and promises of future devotion. He asked also that Fortuna send him a sign that hope was on its way.

The gulls – a type of bird he found hard to like – were now his friends. Both the windows were small and high, so he could see almost nothing beyond them but sky. He had to look for some time but occasionally one of the birds would fly past. There were a couple of other friends too: a mouse he had glimpsed speeding along the base of a wall and a large black beetle that had appeared three times. Indavara was glad to have them there. He wasn't sure if animals had thoughts – Corbulo always seemed sure that they didn't – but it gave him a little comfort to see other creatures sharing this particular part of the world with him.

Several times he had considered shouting. But as they hadn't gagged him and he'd seen or heard nothing of anyone other than the guards, he assumed there was no one close. On the rare occasions he'd been able to snatch a glance through the door, he'd seen only pale grass and a dusty trail. He also thought that appealing for help would make him seem – and feel – weak.

As for escape, they were not taking any chances this time. He reckoned the entire room had been searched because he couldn't find a single nail or anything else that might help him pick the padlocked manacles. And whichever of Warty or Narrow Eyes was on duty would regularly look in on him, day or night. There were always two of them present at meal times.

The pair had only one thing to say when they'd delivered his meal that morning: apparently he was to receive a visitor. Though Indavara was hungry and the plate of sliced bread, salted pork and figs looked appetising, he managed only a third of it. It was the sickness of anticipation and fear; a sickness he knew well.

He felt sure that he would soon learn why he had been captured and taken what felt like halfway across the world.

He was still at the window when he heard voices outside, then the key turn in the lock. As was normal, they first pushed the door wide open to check where he was. Then Warty and Narrow Eyes – both holding cudgels – came in.

'Down,' grunted Warty. This was another routine: Indavara had to sit and remain still when they entered. He sat against the wall, the stone chilling his skin.

The third man wore a fine pair of boots, a pale blue tunic and a belt with a pricey-looking buckle. Indavara – who did not expect to be introduced – decided he would call him Slab, because his face was almost square in shape and grey in colour.

Slab came within two yards then stopped and looked him over.

'He healthy?' As usual, they spoke in Greek.

'He seems right enough, sir,' said Warty. Judging by how he and Narrow Eyes were now acting, they had great respect for their superior; were perhaps even scared of him.

'That so?'

Indavara held up his wrists, which were sore where the manacles rubbed.

'You'll have to live with that.' Slab noted the unfinished meal and spoke to the others over his shoulder. 'Make sure he eats all his food.'

He squatted down and held Indavara's stare for some time. 'I know you, young man. I know all about you, so I doubt you scare easily but I will simply make you aware of the facts. These two told me what happened in Rhodes. If you try it again, I'll take enough fingers to leave your right hand useless. You'll not be much of a fighter after that.'

'Why am I here?'

Slab spat, leaving a glob of spittle on the ground between them.

'We're going to be doing some things to you. You won't like it; and I'm sure it will hurt; but we have an expert who assures me that – if you behave yourself – there's a decent chance you'll come through it.'

'Through what?'

Slab stood, eyes still locked on him. 'I doubt it will be worse than the arena and you survived that. Just let us do what we have to and it should all be over in a few days, couple of weeks at the outside. There is a reason why we've let you know nothing about where you are: when the time comes to let you go, you'll never find us.'

Indavara did not believe for a moment that they intended to let him live. It didn't seem wise to let them know that.

'What is this? Revenge? Why—'

'See you soon,' said Slab as he turned away. 'The surgeon should arrive tomorrow or the next day.'

He walked out, leaving the other two to lock up.

When they had gone, Indavara stood and looked out at the sky. He felt sure that he would suffer greatly before he died.

VI

As both Cassius and Kabir had hoped, they reached Tarsus in five days. After following the main northerly road out of Syria, they had passed through the city of Issus then entered Cilicia and travelled west to the capital. They were now in sight of the Taurus mountains; the range that ran for hundreds of miles across four provinces.

As predicted, Patch performed well and soon earned the respect of the nomads. The party stayed in a series of low-priced inns, squeezed into dormitory rooms with some unpleasant company and a selection of equally unpleasant odours. Cassius was usually too tired to worry; he remained almost as focused as Kabir and the Syrians on reaching their destination and finding some answers.

He could not help feeling that every day counted; the sooner he found the girl, the sooner they could look for Indavara. If there was no clue when he returned to Antioch – and if he could avoid the clutches of Abascantius – he planned to return to Berytus and start again from there. With his old ally Diadromes now magistrate, he would not be short of help.

Unsurprisingly, they had attracted some curious looks from other travellers and questions from the soldiers and tax collectors they encountered at army way stations and toll gates. A few words from Cassius regarding the Service was generally enough to put them off. He knew this entailed some risk (should Abascantius be sufficiently concerned – or angry – to send someone after him) but it was a necessary measure. He also had his oft-used letters of recommendation if required. He didn't plan to employ the missive written by his superior but those from Prefect Venator of the Fourth Legion and Marshal Marcellinus, Protector of the East, remained invaluable.

An hour after dawn on the sixth day, Cassius and Simo left the latest unsavoury dormitory and met the Syrians in the inn's courtyard. On the way outside, Cassius admitted that he was beginning to tire of the accommodation, even though they were making substantial savings. Simo didn't seem to particularly enjoy such places either: he took great exception to the language and topics of conversation used by their room-mates. By contrast, the Syrians were always quiet and well mannered. Cassius had noted more than a few wary reactions but none of their fellow guests had been foolhardy enough to provoke the well-armed nomads.

Kabir and the others had already claimed the courtyard's largest table.

'Food's on its way,' said the Syrian as Idan poured Cassius and Simo some watered wine. The scarred warrior remained generally monosyllabic but polite and cooperative. Kabir's son Kammath was cordial enough but Cassius detected an underlying suspicion of him and his involvement in their cause. The chief's nephew, Yablus, was a cheery fellow, always ready with a quip or a helping hand. Both youths seemed keen to practise their Latin and enjoyed hearing Cassius describe some of his travels. They had been particularly rapt by his tale of their trip to Africa: until their arrival at Issus, neither had ever seen the sea.

'I spoke with some of the locals,' said Kabir. 'The slave market opens at the second hour. It's less than a mile from here. How do you intend to begin?'

Cassius had woken before dawn and already given the matter some thought. 'Ordinarily I would go directly to the magistrate and see what the authorities know of Meliton, or perhaps recruit some informers. But as we are pressed for time, we will simply go straight to the market and ask whomever we find. It would seem logical to start with the traders themselves. If that turns up nothing, we will have to seek out the illegal sector, which will not be easy. Another lead might be these forgers who produce the fake documents. Based on what we know of him, I would imagine this Meliton does not make himself particularly easy to find.'

The Syrians spoke amongst themselves for some time. As usual, Kammath came across as somewhat impetuous and Kabir remained his usual composed self. Idan rarely contributed to any conversation unless asked to by his chief; Yablus usually kept quiet.

During the journey, Cassius had discovered that Kabir's tribe numbered over two hundred and that Idan owed him a lifelong blood-oath of brotherhood and protection. As children, Kabir had plucked Idan from a raging river and dragged him two miles to their camp. They had seldom been separated since.

'Problem?' asked Cassius when the exchange was over.

'Kammath says his sister could be here in the city. Right now. Somewhere close.'

'He's correct,' said Cassius. 'But we must try to remain patient and calm. We are going to be encountering some unpleasant characters – I hope your son can keep control of himself.'

'He can,' interjected Kammath in Latin.

'Good.'

A maid had just arrived with a tray of food.

Cassius added, 'I suggest we eat on the way.'

He had seen several slave markets; the first occasion when he'd accompanied his father for the purchase of a gardener. He remembered Corbulo Senior's advice: always ask the seller for their licence to trade, always insist on two written references, and try to spend some time talking to the slave. Though he could be immensely strict when he thought it necessary – and occasionally deployed the odd slap – Cassius's father's treatment of his slaves had been little different to that of his children. He also contended that an unhappy slave would work poorly and that it was in the household's interest for relations to remain good.

Cassius had not, however, attended a slave market *with* a slave, and it soon became obvious that the silent Simo would rather be anywhere else. Cassius recalled the period in Bostra when they had returned from the Arabian desert and he'd almost sold the Gaul. The sense of guilt was familiar but the relief of a close escape was now more powerful. He could not even countenance a life without Indavara *and* Simo. Recently it had occurred to him that – in some ways – they too were his family now.

The slave market was less busy than most other types of market but there was plenty of business going on. It was located in a wide square between a row of high warehouses and a pleasant-looking sanctuary where a gang of workers were trimming trees and collecting leaves. Some of them seemed more interested in the goings-on next door than their work. Within the market were six circular wooden stages, two of which were currently unoccupied. The largest was positioned centrally and mounted on some sort of contraption that allowed it to revolve. Cassius guessed there would be some unfortunates inside powering a treadmill.

Checking that Kabir and the others were still close behind, he moved slowly across the square. Most of the slaves were standing with placards around their necks, declaring their province of origin, age and skills. In the first minute, Cassius spotted an elderly blacksmith's assistant from Thrace; a skinny Arabian farmhand and three Galatians described as 'general labourers'. Here and there, negotiations were going on. The traders were not hard to spot: middle-aged, dressed in expensive cloth, often overweight; and invariably accompanied by both clerk and bodyguard.

Cassius himself was dressed in a modest – but clearly superior – tunic of dark green with a band of black at the sleeves. He was also wearing his best pair of boots and a bronze belt buckle. His aim was to blend in but appear wealthy enough to be treated with respect by those he needed to extract information from. If that failed, there was always his letters, a small bribery fund and four Syrians with a singular sense of purpose.

Cassius was suddenly aware that the nomads had overtaken him and were running. They were headed for the last stage, which was situated close to a broad street. Quite a crowd had gathered there and it was not difficult to see why: this was where the female slaves were on display.

The Syrians stopped at the back of the throng, which was three or four deep. There were five female slaves on show and a very loud fellow adding detail to the information displayed on the placards. He was playing to the crowd, throwing in the odd salacious detail and aiming several japes at one of the slaves: a rather plain, middle-aged woman. She had wrapped her arms around her body and was staring down at the stage, as if trying to convince herself she was somewhere else.

The least plain of the women was named Fortunata. According to her placard she was an expert seamstress but that didn't seem to be of any interest to some of the more boisterous onlookers, who wished to see her unclothed.

'Serious buyers only!' shouted the announcer in response.

Sitting on a small, square platform beside the stage was the trader, as easily identifiable as the others. He was sheltered by a broad parasol and seemed to be negotiating with a toga-clad fellow accompanied by quite a retinue. The subject of the negotiation was a young woman. She was sitting on the edge of the stage, talking to a well-dressed lady, nodding politely and answering questions.

Kabir and Kammath were already on their way towards the trader.

'Where are you going?' said Cassius.

'To talk to him.'

'He's busy. We'll try him later.'

Cassius pointed at an empty stage nearby. Another seller was lining up his slaves and instructing a clerk what to inscribe on the placards. Amongst his charges were what looked like a family, including a father, mother and three children.

'We'll try over there first,' he said, turning round. 'And then there.'

Situated in the middle of the market was a low enclosure inside which were several tables and chairs. Stationed there were four clerks and four city sergeants.

'They might have some answers for us.'

'Sir,' said Simo. 'Look.'

Kammath had pushed his way to the stage and was calling out to the girls, his shouts audible even over the noise of the crowd. Kabir, Idan and Yablus followed but Cassius was dismayed to see that they did nothing to stop him. Before long, one of the trader's bodyguards was dispatched to intervene. Shaven-headed and a foot taller than all those he was now shoving aside, the enforcer didn't look like the type to take no for an answer.

'By the gods.'

One of the most appealing aspects of life as an officer of the Roman Army was the way most people moved respectfully aside. Without this advantage, Cassius arrived several moments after the enforcer, who was already berating Kammath.

The Syrian ignored him. 'Aikaterine. Her name is Aikaterine. She's very young, very pretty.'

The attractive seamstress seemed to be listening but was shaking her head.

'You!' barked the enforcer. 'Away!'

Idan moved between him and Kammath. A sight of the Syrian's ruined face might have put most people off but the enforcer didn't seem concerned. As he reached for the club hanging from his belt, Cassius darted forward.

'No need for that. I shall have this lot out of your way in no time.'

Kabir already had his hand on Kammath's shoulder but the youth could not be deterred and his cousin was trying to talk to the other girls. Not for the first time, Cassius was surprised by how disobedient the son was. He suspected this was down to Kabir's physical weakness. Apart from the change in his appearance, the nomad often seemed tired, his movements laboured. Simo suspected some kind of long-term condition.

Cassius gripped Kammath's other arm and spoke into his ear. 'Listen to your father and listen to me. This is not the way to go about things. Move back.'

'What if they know something?'

'Then we'll find out. But not like this.'

Kabir's patience had evaporated. He hauled his son backwards and Kammath did not resist as his father escorted him to an open space. A gesture from Idan sent the cousin after him.

'You too, handsome,' suggested the enforcer.

Idan held his gaze for a moment then followed.

'Sorry about that,' said Cassius. On his way back through the crowd, he realised the trader had observed the whole incident.

He waited for Kabir to finish admonishing his son in Aramaic before speaking. 'This simply will not work if we're pulling in different directions. We cannot afford to bring too much attention to ourselves. With the greatest respect, the magistrate's men won't need much of an excuse to arrest you. City-dwelling Romans don't have a lot of time for desert tribesmen. I don't say it's right but that's how it is. If we need to use a bit of force, be assured that I will alert you. Until then, I ask that you let me do this my way.'

'Of course,' said Kabir.

'Apologies,' offered the cousin.

'Kammath?'

The youth looked close to tears. Despite his bravado and bulky frame, the eighteen year old was acting his age. 'Yes.'

'I suggest you remain here for the moment. Simo, you know what to do. Got the money?'

'Yes, sir.'

Not for the first time, Cassius planned to use the attendant to mingle amongst the lower ranks. Simo had a remarkable way with common folk and was invariably able to make subtle enquiries without getting into trouble.

'We'll be quick,' Cassius told Kabir before hurrying over to the empty stage. While the scribe continued to write on the placards, the seller was poring over a waxed tablet.

'Good morning,' said Cassius.

The man appraised him swiftly. 'Morning, sir. Buying or selling?'

'Buying. But not slaves – information.'

The seller frowned.

'A man in your profession by the name of Meliton. Know anything of him?'

'The name, yes. A criminal, if memory serves.'

'Does he sell here?'

'I believe he did in the past, yes.'

'Have you seen him recently?'

The seller shook his head. 'No. Look, I'm afraid I'm rather busy – unless you're—'

'If you tell me something I can use, I'll make it worth your while.'

'I'll decide what's worth my while.'

He hurried away and started issuing instructions to a woman who was combing the hair of the slave family's children. The father caught Cassius's eye and spoke quietly so that the seller wouldn't hear.

'Sir, you look like a decent man. I must tell you something. We are not slaves. We should not be here. We—'

'I'm sorry,' Cassius said tersely.

'Sir.' The clerk had subtly approached while keeping an eye on his master. 'This Meliton – I have some information. Two denarii?'

'We'll see about that. Tell me.'

'He was taken in by the magistrate's men a few weeks ago. Him and some of his gang.'

'Anything else?'

'They'd been after him for a while. That's all I know.' Cassius blocked the view of the seller then plucked a denarius from his money bag and handed it over.

'Where's the other one?'

'Don't push your luck.'

As the clerk departed, Cassius walked away with the pleading father still calling out to him. His voice was surprisingly refined. Cassius continued past the Syrians, gesturing for them to follow him, just to get away from the man.

'It seems Meliton and his gang were apprehended by the magistrate's officers several weeks back.'

'Like Tychon,' said Kabir.

'Yes, though that wasn't related to slavery. Even so, I doubt it's entirely coincidental – now that the various revolts have finally been quietened, the magistrates are getting back on top of things; more sergeants on the street, cases quicker to court, harsher sentences.'

Kabir considered this for a moment. 'This is good news.'

'Yes, especially if he hadn't had time to sell the girls on. Wait here, I'll see what *he* has to say.'

Cassius had just spotted what looked like the market inspector; a civic official whose job was to ensure transactions were lawful and order was kept. A well-dressed fellow, he had just arrived at the stone enclosure with the clerks and sergeants.

On his way across the market, Cassius spied Simo, now deep in conversation with a dishevelled man who seemed happy to talk. As he negotiated the eclectic mix of buyers and curious city folk, Cassius considered how to approach the inspector. Bribery was a non-starter; the setting was too public and he could not predict how the man would react (that was without even considering his limited funds). Cassius had hoped not to disclose his true status unless he had to, but Meliton's run-in with the law left him with little choice, even though he would be leaving yet another footprint for Abascantius to follow.

The inspector was talking to one of the clerks. A couple of the sergeants eyed Cassius but said nothing as he waited beside the entrance to the enclosure. Their attention soon moved on to a voluble and very competitive auction unfolding at the nearest stage. The subject for sale was a squat, bald fellow who – according to the announcer – was one of the finest chefs in the Empire, and had cooked for senators, generals and kings.

'Excuse me,' said Cassius, when the inspector had finished his conversation.

'What is it?'

'Might I have a brief word with you, sir?'

Cassius's politeness, distinguished accent and appearance was enough to convince the official that the visitor was worth his time. They spoke over the low stone wall.

'Yes?'

'Cassius Quintius Corbulo.' He offered his forearm, which the inspector could not refuse.

'Marcus Lartius Gurges.' He was about thirty, well built apart from a prominent stomach.

'Good day.' Cassius kept his voice low and gestured to his satchel. 'I am with Imperial Security. I have my letters with me if you'd like to see them.'

'An agent, eh?'

Cassius was not sure what was coming next. It wasn't just the army who disapproved of 'grain-men'; administrators also often viewed them with suspicion.

'You're very young,' added Gurges.

'I was commissioned straight into the Service.'

Gurges shook his head. Cassius guessed this was going to be a struggle.

'You lucky . . . fellow. I would have loved to have done something like that. I tried to join the army three times.' Gurges pointed downwards. 'Flat feet. I mean, I know the Service isn't exactly loved but . . . it must be very exciting. Is it exciting?'

'At times.'

Gurges looked over his shoulder. 'And I'm stuck here with these dolts. Anyway, what are you investigating?'

'I'm interested in a slave-trader named Meliton. I believe he was arrested recently.'

'That's right. A long time coming it was too.'

'Oh?'

'I believe he'd sold legitimately here in the past but more recently he'd become a major figure in the illegal trade. We had to supply some old documents to the court, even though he hadn't shown his face round here in a while. I think he was picked up with a number of others not long ago. Wait a moment.'

Gurges walked along the wall and spoke to the sergeants before returning.

'Yes, about three weeks ago. The magistrate has been cracking down on anything that results in tax avoidance – governor's instructions, apparently.'

'Has it gone to court?'

'I'm not sure. Some have become legal cases, others not. Where the facts are beyond dispute, the judicial prefect has been handing down a lot of sentences without trial: mutilations, hard labour, that kind of thing – to send a message.'

'I see. Who would know more?'

'Well there'll be records somewhere at the basilica. And anyone under the magistrate or the judicial prefect might be familiar with the details.'

'And if I wanted to avoid official channels?'

Gurges thought for a while before answering. During this time, two of the sergeants hurried away to attend to some dispute.

'There are several good restaurants on the Via Roma, of which The Golden Arrow is the best. By the eighth hour, many of the senior legal men will have retired for lunch. You would probably be able to find someone there with the information you need.'

Aware that Simo was lurking behind him, Cassius kept his focus on Gurges. 'Excellent, thank you. Even so, I won't know who's who. It would be useful to have someone there to make a few introductions.'

Gurges – who had been leaning on the wall – stood up straight. 'I am busy now but the market will be closed by that time.'

'The Service would be extremely grateful. I'll gladly pass on a commendation to my superiors.'

'Really? Well, in that case shall we say the eighth hour outside the Arrow? It's close to the northern end of the avenue, opposite the statue of Vespasian. Can I ask, what's all this about?'

Cassius leaned in close. 'I'm afraid I can't disclose all the details but it is a matter of the utmost importance to the Empire. I thank you again.'

Gurges gave a slight grin as Cassius departed.

'Well, Simo?'

'I spoke to four people, sir. Two confirmed that Meliton was apprehended some weeks back.'

'Anything more?'

'One commented that he was glad he and his gang had been stopped – apparently they were known for intimidating the other sellers, fixing prices and so on. But even now, nobody would give any names. One man reckoned that *he* would know more.' Simo pointed back across the market to the stage where the female slaves were being sold.

'The dealer?'

'Yes, sir. He's named Hirtius; he has been in the trade here for more than a decade.'

'Excellent. Well done, Simo.'

'I'm afraid the information wasn't cheap, sir. Nine sesterces.'

'No matter. Come, let's tell the others then see if we can get some time with Hirtius.'

Achieving this turned out to be rather difficult. When Cassius asked Hirtius's clerk if he could speak with his master, he was told he could only do so when the auction was concluded. As it was still early and a new group of slaves – male *and* female – were now being introduced to the crowd, that still seemed some time away. Conscious of the impatient Syrians looking on, Cassius told the clerk that he needed only two minutes of the trader's time. He doubted that he could offer a bribe sufficient to grab the man's attention; nor could he be certain that it would be worthwhile. The clerk passed on his message but Hirtius literally waved it away and continued to nibble on food plucked from a variety of silver bowls. The clerk turned in Cassius's direction and shrugged.

'Why won't he see us?' asked Kabir.

'He's more interested in seeing how much money his slaves make for him. We shall just have to wait; it's not worth antagonising the man.'

'You want to just stand around here and do nothing?'

'Kabir, we've had a productive hour. The fact that Meliton was arrested will make things far easier for us. We should be grateful for our luck. If you wish to go and ask around about the girls, please do so.'

'I will.'

'A word of advice, however,' added Cassius, 'do not be too forward. As I said, these people will be wary of you.'

Cassius and Simo looked on as the nomads spilt into two groups: Kabir and Kammath hurried away, Idan and Yablus began questioning those nearby.

While they waited, the auction continued. Cassius watched Simo, who didn't seem to know where to look.

'You'd like to get away, I suppose.'

'I won't pretend I like it here, sir.'

'Neither do I particularly but it fulfils a need. Slaves have to be traded somewhere. Better that it happens in a lawful, organised fashion.'

'It's their faces, sir. They don't know who will take them, how they will be treated; what kind of life awaits. I can't help thinking of poor Mahalie.'

'The girl was unlucky. Her mistress was as bad as her master – cutting the girl just because she thought her husband was interested in her. Cruel bitch.'

'I believe there are as many bad masters as good, sir. I have been fortunate.'

'I don't know about that, Simo. I've dragged you around most of the eastern Empire. You've faced Palmyran rebels, corrupt centurions, Arabian warriors. All a far cry from being an accounts clerk, eh?'

'I suppose so, sir.'

'You'll never find yourself in a place like this, Simo. I pledge it. Have you ever thought what you'll do once I leave the army?'

'Perhaps settle in Antioch, sir. With two years of work I could become a teacher.'

'Which would mean?'

Simo beamed. 'That I could educate others, sir – spread the word.'

The next round of sales seemed to go well for Hirtius and his evident good spirits extended to inviting Cassius over. While his assistants readied the next batch of slaves, the trader stood up and stretched his legs. He was a large man with a large head topped by wavy, black hair. His tunic was maroon, emblazoned with gold lozenges.

'What exactly can I do for you, young man?'

Cassius – standing below the platform – was aware that the shaven-headed bodyguard had moved to within a few feet.

'Thank you for taking the time to speak with me, Master Hirtius. My name is Corbulo. I am an investigator working on behalf of those men you saw earlier. We are looking for three Syrian girls named Aikaterine, Marte and Dinora; all of whom are seventeen.'

'We've had a few Syrian girls over the years. Don't remember three together though – certainly not recently.'

'They could have been split up. Perhaps you could check your records?'

'With respect, why should I?'

'Sir, these girls were taken illegally. Their families are distraught. You clearly sell a lot of female slaves and we both know that ownership documents can be forged.'

'I do not handle illegal slaves.'

'I'm sure you don't. Knowingly.'

'You are trying my patience, young man. I suggest you take your search elsewhere.'

'One more question. Please.'

Hirtius looked at the stage. His assistants were positioning the slaves and putting the placards on them.

'One.'

'A man named Meliton was involved. He was arrested not long ago.'

'And good riddance too. He gave the whole Tarsus trade a bad name. I hope they chop his head off.'

'Do you know anything about any of his associates?'

'That's two questions.'

'Sir, please.'

'I have a daughter myself, though I hardly see her now she lives with her mother. So I shall tell you what I know. The magistrates got most of the gang and apparently their cover operation in the city was a rope merchant's down by the river. It's close to the biggest shipyard.'

'Thank you.'

'For what it's worth, I hope you find these girls. Not everyone in my business is as scrupulous and good-hearted as I am.'

VII

They learned nothing more of use at the market and – with several hours to go before the meeting with Gurges – Cassius and Kabir decided there was time to investigate the rope merchant's.

Tarsus was busy and with no knowledge of the city it took them an hour to find their way down to the Cydnus; the river which ran into the Great Green Sea only a few miles downstream. The Cilician capital was a centre of shipbuilding and they passed one large yard where the prows of two galleys poked out, one already complete with a great blue eye. Dozens of painters and craftsmen were at work, creating a cacophony of hammering and shouting.

Staying well clear, Cassius and his party strode along the top of a broad ramp that ran down into the water. As they continued along the riverside road, the Cydnus – somehow both clear and green – flowed swiftly past. On the far side was a long, low barge being pulled by a team of horses and several dozen slaves. They were struggling against the current and the cracks of an overseer's whip carried across the water. Moored and anchored close by were several high-masted galleys and numerous smaller craft. Half a dozen women were kneeling in a row upon the bank, sorting through wicker baskets of shellfish laced with weed.

Next to the shipyard was a compound packed with timber of every imaginable form and size. Beyond it was a patch of open waste ground, then an isolated stone building with double wooden doors facing the road. Hanging above the doors was a sign: a faded image of coils of ropes.

'There.'

Once they reached it, Cassius looked along the side of the

building and saw a series of high, narrow windows. The adjoining yard was empty apart from a decrepit cart and a long-abandoned stable.

'The back?' suggested Kabir.

Cassius nodded then took a brief look around to check who was watching. The only people who seemed to have noticed them was a group of locals mending a fishing net, which they had laid out beside the road.

Cassius was first into the yard. Though the cart was missing two wheels, the muddy ground bore the signs of recent movement and there was a large basket with fairly fresh-looking hay in it.

'Someone's been using this place,' observed Kabir.

'It's not that long since Meliton and his mates were taken in.'

The area at the rear of the building was a mess, containing an overflowing and malodourous pit as well as several piles of rotting rope. The narrow, arched entrance was secured by an iron gate, which required a key. The only window large enough to fit through was five yards off the ground, where the stone wall met the sloping, tiled roof.

'Hello?' shouted Cassius. 'Anyone here?'

No answer.

He examined the lock and the door. 'We're not going to get through that.'

Kabir said something in Aramaic. Yablus walked up to the wall and examined the section beneath the window. He gripped some of the knobs of stone and ran his fingers across the cracks. He turned to his uncle and shook his head.

'Simo,' said Cassius. 'Back to that yard – see about borrowing a ladder.'

'Don't think we'll need it,' said Idan, who had been pottering around beside the pit. The veteran was holding a length of rope and a small, rusty anchor.

'Ah,' said Cassius. 'Ingenious.'

Over the next few minutes, he found himself once again impressed by how the Syrians worked together. Idan and Kabir tested the rope, then Kammath tied it to the anchor. With his typical uncanny accuracy, Idan got the anchor through the window on the second attempt. It took five more throws for him to lodge it securely on the edge. Yablus – who was far leaner and more agile than his cousin – climbed up in a matter of seconds.

While Cassius was readying himself to follow, Yablus first disappeared then returned to the window to announce he could open the double doors from the inside.

'Most convenient,' said Cassius as they traipsed around to the front. Though it was impossible to avoid the attention of the locals mending the net, they slipped inside as subtly as possible.

The windows admitted slender beams of light that illuminated the interior well. At the front was an open space, then dozens of empty baskets and amphoras. Hanging from posts embedded in the walls were numerous coils of thick rope and several chains. Cassius recognised some of the tools he had seen used by the crew of the *Fortuna Redux*.

'Some of this stuff will be worth quite a bit – somebody must still own the place.'

Kabir had walked past him and was close to the rear wall. 'Look here.'

Piled up on the floor was some riding equipment and saddle-bags; all dirty but usable. Upon a table were further signs of habitation: bowls, cooking utensils and a lump of bread, which had only just begun to go mouldy. Idan bent down and picked a few short lengths of rope and pieces of cloth off the floor.

'Bindings and gags,' said Cassius.

'Blankets over here,' said Kammath, who had ventured into another corner.

'It's well positioned,' said Cassius, 'away from other buildings but close to the river and the rest of the city.'

Kabir took a deep breath and glanced around at their sordid surroundings. Cassius could imagine what he was thinking.

Simo had not left the centre of the building and once again seemed uneasy.

'Look,' said Kammath. His cousin was holding something up to one of the beams of yellow light. 'You'll have to come here to see.'

Cassius, Kabir and Idan walked over to the youngsters. Yablus stretched out a single strand of black hair more than ten inches in length. Though the nomads wore their hair long, very few men in a Roman city did.

Kammath shook his head and shut his eyes.

His father put an arm around him. 'They were here. I'm sure of it.'

They all left via the front entrance apart from Yablus, who remained behind to secure the double doors then exited through the window. Kabir thought it was important to leave no trace of their entry as he wanted to return later in the day. Cassius considered the warehouse little more than a distraction compared to what Tarsus's senior officials would know but he agreed they could leave no stone unturned.

As they passed the fisherwomen, Cassius watched a man reach the bank upon a skiff. He gave a last shunt with his pole and came alongside a rickety pontoon. Once he'd tied up, one of the women came to help him take some baskets from the boat. Cassius spied a notice with a poorly spelled Greek warning that the pontoon was private property. It seemed likely the fisherman would know the riverside area and its people well.

'Wait a moment.' As the others halted, he directed Simo towards the Cilician, who was an older man wearing a ragged cap and an equally ragged tunic.

'Ask about the rope merchant's – if he's seen anyone going in and out. Meliton and his friends, too.'

'Yes, sir.'

'Catch us up. We'll ask over here.'

Cassius led the others back to the shipyard. Once there, he looked for a foreman.

'We'll have a word with *them*,' said Kabir, pointing at a group of dark-skinned labourers who were transferring timber from the building into the yard. There didn't seem to be anyone supervising them.

'Good idea.'

Just as Cassius entered the building, a man hailed him and strode over. Unlike the workers, he was wearing shoes.

'No visitors in here, sir – the office is out the back.'

'I don't need the office. I'd like to ask you about that rope merchant's.'

They both had to shout above the noise of the work.

The man ushered Cassius outside. 'What was that?'

'About the rope merchant's.' Cassius pointed back along the road. 'Know if anyone's still using it?'

'No idea.'

'What about a man named Meliton?'

'Don't know the name. Listen, I have work to do. Stay out of here.'

Cassius almost admonished the man; it was difficult to get used to being ignored while out of uniform.

He stood at the corner of the building and watched the Syrians. Kabir was sensibly talking to the labourers alone, leaning over the wall as they stacked the timber. He didn't seem to be faring much better; the locals were shaking their heads and shrugging.

Cassius crossed the road and stood close to the ramp. A couple of lads were fishing; sitting either side of a pail and each holding a line.

'Catch anything?'

They were either too shy to answer or didn't speak Greek.

Cassius looked back at the busier area of the docks. They had passed an inn; that might be the most likely place to pick up some useful information.

He checked on Simo. While the women kept working, the old fisherman seemed happy to talk. He pointed at the rope merchant's twice. Cassius was about to join the pair when a group of men strode past.

There were six of them, each carrying a heavy-looking wooden chest on his shoulder. Though none of them were speaking, one was whistling. Their clothing told Cassius little: middling tunics, middling sandals. Judging by their physiques, the six were either soldiers or labourers.

Cassius looked back at the pontoon. When the fisherman spied the men, he instantly bowed his head. Simo kept talking to him but the Cilician retreated towards his boat. Simo glanced over his shoulder then opened his hands towards the local, as if asking a question. Cassius switched his gaze to the six men. He was not surprised when they reached the rope merchant's and turned into the yard.

Kabir and the others crossed the road. They'd been so intent on questioning the workers that they'd completely missed the new arrivals. Though they carried only daggers on their belts, Kammath had a large leather pack on his back containing their long knives and slings. Cassius had advised against this but was now glad he'd let Kabir have his way.

'Nothing,' said the Syrian. 'Useless.'

Before Cassius could disclose what he'd seen, Simo arrived. 'Sir, he told me that he only found out the slave-trader had been using the place after he and his gang were arrested. No one had been seen there for several weeks but in the last few days, some men have been coming and going. Then he just went quiet, I couldn't get anything more from him.'

'Did *you* find out anything?' asked Kabir.

Cassius said, 'Follow me.'

Whoever they were, they clearly weren't stupid. Apart from designing their appearance to blend in, the gang posted a lookout at the front of the rope merchant's.

Once Cassius passed on what he'd observed, the Syrians swiftly devised a plan to surround and enter the building. Cassius had always known this type of situation might arise. There was no question of involving the authorities; that would take far too long and lead to far too many complications.

When Kabir outlined what they intended, Cassius agreed but reminded them all to use the minimal force necessary. The last thing he needed ahead of the later meeting was for them to draw attention to themselves. Having said that, he guessed the gang might not be keen on involving the city sergeants either.

Asking only for a corner of paper from Cassius's satchel, Kabir sauntered off down the road alone towards the sentry. Cassius and Simo remained behind Idan and the others, who advanced quickly across the waste ground towards the side of the building. As Kabir neared the sentry, the five of them waited behind the scant cover offered by a cluster of leafless trees.

Kabir hailed the sentry, who was standing outside the yard, slouching against the wall. When the man came forward, Kabir showed him the piece of paper. As soon as he looked down at it, the nomad clubbed a hand into the side of his head. The sentry dropped like a stone.

Kabir dragged his prone form to the front of the building then lowered the sentry to the ground. Idan and Kammath ran across the waste ground to meet him, with Cassius and Simo not far behind. Yablus made for the rear. As they neared the doors, Kammath and Kabir retrieved their long knives.

Idan took his sling from inside his tunic. The weapon was a two-foot length of braided hemp, with a small leather cradle for the shot. At one end was a loop of cord, which Idan slipped over his little finger. With what appeared to be a single movement, he dropped a lead ball into the cradle and gripped the other end between thumb and forefinger. Despite the circumstances, Cassius was reminded of what he'd observed of the Syrians at Alauran; they were so comfortable with the slings that the weapons almost seemed like an extension of their arms.

As they gathered by the doors – which were slightly ajar – Cassius looked around once again. Other than the fisherman, nobody in that direction seemed to have noticed. The locals mending the net, however, had. When they saw Cassius watching them, they all looked away.

It had been agreed that Simo – who was even more of a liability in a fight than Cassius – would remain outside. His master had decided to leave his dagger in the sheath; it would only make him a target and he had the utmost faith in the nomads.

With a nod from Kabir, Kabbath swung one of the doors open and the pair slipped inside. Idan shifted so that the sun was behind him and raised his arm to deploy the sling if need be.

Cassius moved up beside Kabir and got his first view of the men. They were gathered in the open space, some on their knees, some standing. All were now staring at the interlopers. The lids of the chests were open. They were packed with straw to protect the religious icons and other trinkets within.

'Who in Hades are you?' grunted one of the men, a broad fellow with a greying beard. As he got to his feet, he pulled out a dagger.

Cassius glimpsed a whirl of movement to his right. The man cried out and dropped the blade. As it clanged to the floor, he gripped his hand.

'Uh! You piece of shit.'

Idan had another shot ready.

'Leave the blades where they are,' ordered Kabir.

Cassius had just realised he could see only four men when two shapes emerged from the shadows at the rear of the building. Yablus was being pushed forward by a man with a knife to his throat. The light coming from the door glinted off the blade, illuminating the Syrian's unblinking eyes.

'Never send a boy to do a man's work,' said the fifth man.

The rest of the gang looked relieved. 'Nice one,' said the injured man as his compatriots drew their blades.

Idan and Kabir spoke to each other.

'Cut that foreign chatter.' The injured man seemed to be their leader.

'All weapons on the floor.'

Cassius tried to stay calm. Apart from the fact that this had gone so wrong so quickly, he noted how these men had overcome their initial shock with some speed. The situation had turned completely; the best he could hope for now was to get himself and his allies out alive.

'I can make them to do that,' he said. 'But you'll have to take that knife from our friend's throat.'

'Why should we?' spat the leader. 'That ugly prick damn near broke my hand. And look at *him*.'

Outside, the sentry was now up on his knees but still looked in a bad way.

Idan said, 'Your hand's not broken. If I wanted to break it, I would have.'

'We just need information,' said Cassius hastily. 'It's in none of our interests for this to turn nasty.'

'You're funny,' said the leader. 'It was you lot came in here with blades drawn.'

'You ain't getting these,' said another man, pointing down at the chests.

'We don't want them,' said Cassius. 'Just infor—'

He heard the familiar whoosh of the sling, then saw the man holding Yablus stagger backwards. The youth took his opportunity and elbowed his former captor in the ribs. Already stunned by the blow to his head, the man tottered back and tripped over a chest.

The remaining four men raised their knives.

'No!' yelled Cassius, fearing this was about to turn into a bloodbath. He didn't fancy his chances of emerging unharmed from a knife fight.

Yablus joined the others and took the blade Idan offered him.

Simo appeared and ran over to join his master.

Cassius put his hands up high and positioned himself between the two groups.

'There is no need for this.' Cassius was close to the leader, no more than a sweep of a blade away. 'We don't want your stuff. You tell us what we need to do know and we're gone.'

'What?'

'You know Meliton?'

'The name, yes. If you're after him, you're too late.'

'What about illegal slaves?'

'That's not our trade.'

Cassius glanced down at the chests. 'Smugglers?'

'What we do is our concern. Who are you?'

'An interested party. Meliton traded three young Syrian girls recently. We think they may have been kept here. You know anything about them?'

'No.'

'Any of you?'

Those that were able shook their heads.

'They could be lying,' said Kabir in Latin, apparently assuming the men might only speak Greek.

'We're not,' said another man, also in Latin. 'We used this place because we knew it was empty. We've only been in here three times, the first barely a week ago. Trading girls – we wouldn't do it.'

'I would,' said the tallest of them, a beady-eyed man who also happened to possess the largest knife. 'I'll trade anything that makes a profit. But we don't know anything about these girls, and you've already hurt two of my mates. So why you don't you lot piss off before I run out of patience and stick this in one of you!'

The leader seemed displeased by the interjection.

Cassius didn't dare turn his back on the gang. 'Kabir, they've told us what they know – that good enough for you?'

During the time it took the Syrian to reply, Cassius alternated his gaze between the four men. The groans coming from the fellow struck by the second shot were not helping the situation.

'Kabir?' demanded Cassius through gritted teeth.

'Yes.'

'You leave first. I'll follow.'

When he heard the Syrians move, Cassius spoke again to the leader, who was still nursing his hand. He got the feeling he was less inclined to violence than his fearless friend.

'Some recompense for your injuries is only fair. Shall we say five denarii each?'

Cassius thought it essential to avoid the possibility of a fight outside or a later revenge attack. Before the leader could reply, the tall fellow intervened, knife now aimed at Cassius.

'Ten. I'd say ten would be fair.'

'As you wish,' said Cassius, who was relieved that Simo was still beside him. The Gaul's fingers shook as he counted out the money. Cassius took it from him and handed it to the leader.

He and Simo then turned and walked out of the building and into bright sunlight.

Yablus was several shades paler than the others. The other three were still holding their knives.

'Put those away,' said Cassius. 'And let's get out of here. Now.'

VIII

'Peace and quiet at last.'

Cassius and Simo were alone, sitting on a bench facing a pretty fountain in a sanctuary devoted to Juventas, goddess of youth.

'Another roll, sir?'

'No.'

'May I have the last one?'

'Go ahead.'

Cassius watched Simo slice off a lump of hard, yellow cheese with his pocketknife then place it inside the fresh bread roll. While the Gaul ate, Cassius picked at the little basket of dates and walnuts they had also purchased for lunch.

'Gods, I hope this afternoon is productive. I still haven't recovered myself from that face-off and we learned virtually nothing of use.'

'It was horrible, sir. Horrible. All those blades . . . to think what could have happened.'

'I shall simply have to remember that Kabir and the others are not soldiers. They can be unbiddable. And unpredictable.'

'Young Kammath went too far, sir. He was very disrespectful.'

'Mmm.'

The intervening hours had not gone well. Once safely away from the rope merchant's, Cassius had asked Yablus what went wrong. It appeared that the youth had completely missed the man stationed at the rear, who had sprung out of the shadows and disarmed him. Hearing this, Kabir lambasted his nephew, who appeared on the verge of tears by the end of it. Kammath took his cousin's side and got into an argument with his father and Idan.

Kabir's son had then turned his ire on Cassius, questioning why he hadn't even drawn his blade. Cassius countered that it was fortunate for them that he hadn't; and that they'd been lucky to extricate themselves at all. The youth seemed to think they should have fought the smugglers anyway; that they undoubtedly knew more than they were letting on. At this point, Kabir and Idan – who did not concur – shouted him down.

Even so, Cassius had given much thought to Kammath's words. He imagined the Syrians would be talking about him. Kabir and Idan had known Cassius when he was even less able with a sword. They knew he didn't have the stomach or the skill for a fight against a practised foe. What they didn't know was that Cassius had killed a man in Arabia, though he hadn't meant to. All he had done was strike him with the hilt of a dagger: that had been enough.

He looked down at the blade on his belt. Thanks to Indavara, he now felt comfortable wielding a sword but he'd always rather hated daggers, though he'd carried one ever since joining the army. Nasty, common little weapons.

'You all right, sir?' asked Simo as he finished his roll.

Cassius was watching a family who had occupied a nearby bench. Two young boys – twins by the looks of them – were both holding toy chariots. They dropped to the ground instantly and placed the little vehicles side by side, ready for a race.

'Simo, while I'm in the Golden Arrow, you can go and find a long bag – it will need to be hardy and easily carried.'

'Sir?'

'It's for a sword.'

Gurges was at a table by himself and just finishing off a bowl of stew when Cassius arrived.

'Please,' said the market inspector, gesturing to the empty seat opposite him.

Just as Cassius sat down, a maid whisked away the bowl.

'Two sesterces for that?' said Gurges. 'My mother makes better and could do a whole pot for half the price.'

'I'm happy to reimburse you, of course,' said Cassius. 'This is much appreciated.'

Gurges waved at another maid. 'A glass for my friend.'

Cassius looked around. The Golden Arrow was indeed exceptionally well appointed for a city eatery, with marble upon the floor, mosaics and hanging tapestries; and silver cutlery for the diners. Close by was a large table occupied by eight important-looking fellows all clad in spotless togas protected by eating bibs.

'Any likely candidates?' asked Cassius.

Gurges was trying to get his tunic to hang correctly. Cassius guessed he was trying to disguise his paunch, which rather spoiled an otherwise impressive physique.

'Yes, I would think so. You know, I thought your name sounded familiar. Then I recalled the tale of the young Service officer who raised his spearhead amongst a tribe of rampaging Arabians and brought them to heel. Was that you?'

As he had already given his name, Cassius saw little point in denying it. Improving his currency with Gurges and whoever else he dealt with here was important.

'It was rather more complicated than that but . . . yes.'

Gurges leaned on the table and poured wine from a jug into the glass a maid had just delivered. 'And it's true – about shining the light into the leader's eyes? The crystals from The Black Stone of Emesa?'

'It's true. The leader had used trickery to convince his followers that the sun god's light was shining upon them.'

Though the restaurant was warm, Cassius felt a chill wash over him as he thought of the scene in the valley that day.

'And you brought it back dragged on a litter by camels, with the Arabians pursuing all the way?'

'Er, no. It was returned in a cart. Word of mouth tends to lead to exaggerations and untruths.'

'And the German giant who worked for the leader?'

'Oh, he's real enough.'

'You defeated him?'

'I suppose . . . Listen, can we get down to business?'

'Yes, of course, just one more question. Didn't the Emperor want the stone for himself? Have you met him?'

'No, though I did receive a personal message of thanks.'

Gurges's eyes widened and he offered his glass for a toast. 'By the gods, what a job you have.'

Cassius clinked his glass. 'There are more disadvantages than benefits, believe me. Now, who is here that can help us?'

'Right, well, when I came in I spotted Gaius Scribonius Costa; he's a tribune with responsibility for the city prison. He would probably know what happened to most of the men that have been through there. He just left.'

'What?'

Gurges held up an appeasing hand. 'Fear not. Sitting behind you, quite close to the door is Numerius Sentius Merenda. The small fellow, sitting with another small fellow.'

Cassius did not turn around. 'How long have they been in here?'

'Not sure. I only noticed him just before my stew came.'

'What's his position?'

'First assistant archivist to the deputy judicial prefect. I've spoken to him a few times. If he doesn't know every sentence handed down since the summer, I'll be very surprised.'

The maid returned to the table, offering to recite the menu.

'No thank you,' said Cassius, 'just wine for me.'

He turned his chair to retie his bootlaces and glanced towards the door.

'Facing us,' whispered Gurges, who seemed to be enjoying himself. 'With the big ears.'

Cassius turned around. 'They've finished eating. We'll wait then talk to him outside. Do you think he'll tell me about Meliton?'

Gurges's head bobbed from side to side. 'Probably. The prefect runs a tight ship but it's a matter of public record. Plus you have that letter from the marshal.'

While Cassius considered other methods of twisting Merenda's arm, Gurges pledged to keep on eye on the archivist. He could not, however, resist pestering Cassius about the black stone and his other assignments. Cassius remained vague; much of the rest he wasn't supposed to discuss.

After about ten minutes, Merenda and his dining companion left. Gurges had already paid the bill (Cassius contributed half) and they intercepted the pair outside.

'Master Merenda?'

The diminutive archivist was already hurrying away along the street.

'It's Marcus Arius Gurges, senior inspector of markets.'

When they turned around, neither Merenda nor his companion showed any sign of recognition.

'Might I introduce Officer Corbulo; he's with Imperial Security.'

'Good day to you both,' said Cassius. 'I have a simple enquiry but I need the information urgently. My credentials.'

Simo had backed both letters on to leather so that they didn't get damaged. One was from Prefect Venator, who commanded the Fourth Scythican Legion and belonged to one of the most important families in Rome. The other was from Marshal Marcellinus, arguably the second most powerful man in the Empire. Both letters recommended Cassius as an officer of good character and requested that the reader offer him help. Cassius had lost count of the amount of times these two pieces of paper had made a crucial difference while on assignment.

Merenda seemed suitably impressed. 'Perhaps we should adjourn somewhere—'

'As I said, it's rather urgent. My enquiry concerns a slave trader by the name of Meliton who was apprehended recently. Gurges here thinks it possible that he has already been sentenced. I need to speak with him.'

Merenda took a while to reply. 'Well, normally I would suggest that you go through the normal channels but' – he gestured at the letters as Cassius replaced them in his satchel – 'Meliton was part of a group convicted of serious offences in the last few weeks. I believe the entire gang was apprehended.'

'And the slaves they had with them?'

'From what I recall, no.'

Cassius only just stopped himself cursing out loud.

Merenda continued: 'Certainly none were used as witnesses. It's possible they had been sold on. There was more than enough evidence from previous cases against Meliton. I believe it was suggested that he knew the sergeants were closing in. That may be why he moved the slaves on quickly.'

Cassius grimaced. He was not looking forward to telling Kabir and the others that Aikaterine could still be hundreds of miles away.

'Not that it did him any good in the end,' added Merenda. 'Over a hundred aurei were taken off him and the rest of the gang. All in the provincial coffers now.'

'How many others were there?'

'Three, I think. Perhaps four. All long-time accomplices.'

'What about the court records? There might be information I can use.'

'Such as?'

'Anything relating to female Syrian slaves or known associates of Meliton. Could you get me copies of the documents?'

'For that you *would* have to go through the proper channels.'

'Master Merenda, I am helping someone who has been of great service to the Empire. His daughter and two other girls are missing. He and the family are in a terrible state.'

Cassius took some comfort from the fact that only part of what he'd said was exaggeration.

'I could look through the documents for you, I suppose.'

'By the end of today?'

'I don't see why not. There won't be too much – the court session lasted less than an hour. This Meliton was a wanted man; and the judicial prefect is known for quick decisions and strong sanctions.'

'If I gave you the address of the inn where I'm staying could you let me know of anything relevant?'

Merenda looked at Gurges, then back at Cassius. 'Very well. I shall contact you by the twelfth hour, whether I have found anything or not.'

'My thanks. Now, what about the sentences?'

'Hard labour for all of them. I expect a military escort has taken them north already.'

'To discourage appeals,' said the other man with a knowing grin.

Merenda didn't seem to appreciate the interruption.

'North?' said Cassius. 'To where?'

'I couldn't tell you for certain but in all likelihood the Galatian salt mines. Tuz, probably.'

Cassius knew the name; nothing more.

'The Galatians always need more labour, especially now.'

'Tuz,' said Gurges. 'About one hundred and fifty miles. You don't know when they left?'

'No. But these escort parties depart from the fortress, organised by Chief Centurion Terentius. He should be able to give you the details.'

'Right,' said Cassius. 'Thank you. Sorry, you said "especially now". Why?'

'Some of the areas close to the salt mines were struck by plague over the summer. They say there are whole villages and towns that have been deserted. The soldiers in the escorts are paid double – danger money for passing through. If you're headed that way, best be careful. Very careful.'

They returned to the inn before the Syrians and waited in the courtyard. While the innkeeper and his lads unloaded firewood from a handcart, Cassius examined the bag which Simo had laid out for him to inspect.

'Looks good. Bit ragged but the leather's still thick.'

'It needs a bit of stitching, sir, but I got a good price.'

'You don't see many sword-bags around. Where did you find it?'

'A military supplier, sir.'

'Good work.'

Cassius observed a large jug of wine being delivered to a nearby table by a maid. 'There is at least one advantage of our parlous condition – it stops me spending too much on drink.'

'If I may say so, sir, I am glad to see you cutting down.'

'Don't mention that business about my shaking fingers again, Simo. That was entirely a product of your imagination.'

The attendant did not reply.

'Though I must confess, my mind is rather clearer now.' Cassius glanced towards the gate, then up at the sky. 'Must be close to the eleventh hour. Gods, I hope they won't be much longer. We probably shouldn't have split up – there are innumerable ways that lot could get into trouble.'

'Sir, what this man told you about the plague. I thought the worst of it had passed?'

'The worst, yes, but it never really goes away. You're lucky to have been in Syria, Simo – the East didn't suffer like the central provinces. The first deaths came in the year of my birth and by the time I was ten, my father had moved all his affairs out of Rome. They say two thousand people were dying *every day*. I lost two uncles, an aunt and three cousins. There was an outbreak in Ravenna when I was about thirteen or fourteen. My mother would hardly let us leave the house but my friends and I heard about a cove where the plague-ridden went to die – many of them driven there by the authorities. Being young and stupid, we had to see the place. We climbed down from the cliffs. We saw a few tents, some piles of belongings. And bodies – out in the open, unburied. The children – I can still see them as clear as day. Poor little sods with every last portion of their skin blistered. Lying on the sand, writhing around, some of them coughing up blood. On our way out, we met some soldiers whose job was to keep the diseased in the cove. They had been to fetch bows. They were going to put the children out of their misery.'

As he observed Simo's reaction, Cassius realised he had suppressed the full horror of that memory for a long time.

'I thought not everyone died from it, sir.'

'That was the bleeding type of plague – the most lethal. Even those spared death are often terribly scarred, or blinded, or crippled.'

Simo touched his cross, which – at Cassius's insistence – was hidden under his tunic.

'Many blamed your people, of course. Punishment from our gods because some had turned to a new power.'

'I am not sure that it is gods who cause disease, sir.'

'Are you referring to Columella? His contention that they derive from unhealthy areas; stagnant water and such like?'

'I think there might be some truth to that, sir, yes, but I was thinking of the works of Varro. He agrees with Columella about the dangers of unhealthy areas but believes disease can be spread by small creatures.'

'Like flies – yes, I've heard of this. They do gather upon corpses and waste. It makes sense, I suppose.'

'Varro also argued that there are even smaller creatures – ones we cannot see, that float in the air and enter our bodies through the nose and mouth and corrupt the four humours.'

'Also possible – there are some little insects that are barely visible at all so there might well be some even more minute. But you know there were whole areas that almost avoided the plague entirely. The people in such places considered themselves blessed.'

'Sir.' Simo pointed at the gate.

Kabir and the other three had at last returned.

IX

The twelfth hour passed and there was still no letter from Merenda.

The Syrians were restless. They had discovered nothing of use themselves and – once over the initial shock of hearing that Aikaterine had probably been sold on – were keen to head north. Cassius told them they had to wait; the information from Merenda could be crucial. But by dusk, it seemed likely that nothing would come.

Realising he could delay no longer, he went to speak to them outside the inn's stable. All four had already packed and saddled their horses.

'Here is what I propose. I know you're keen to get on the road but I must first try and talk to the chief centurion; find out all we can about exactly where Meliton is being taken.'

'Now?' asked Kabir. 'It's late.'

'We should just be able to reach the fortress before sundown. I will have to go in alone, of course. Simo can remain here, in case a message does arrive. He will meet us at the north gate.'

'The innkeeper says that the road is safe at night as far as Podandus. We have the torches and your lantern. These prisoners would be taken on foot, yes?'

'Yes.'

'If this place Tuz is one hundred and fifty miles away, might we may be able to catch them before they reach it?'

'Possibly. You there.' Cassius pointed at the stable lad, who had been helping the Syrians. 'Bring out my mount. Did you clean her as I asked?'

'I did, sir.'

Simo had just emerged from the inn, with Cassius's saddlebags over each shoulder. As he lowered them on to the nearest table, Cassius took his money bag from his belt and handed it to the Gaul. 'I'll leave you to settle up. Wait for half an hour after sunset. If no message comes, ride straight to the north gate. Understood?'

'Yes, sir.'

'We'll see you there.'

'Do you remember the directions to the fortress, sir?'

'Of course.' He hurried back across the courtyard to find Kabir and the others had already mounted up. The groom had just led his horse out of the stable. Cassius gripped his saddle and launched himself upwards.

An hour later, he marched into the headquarters building, situated at the exact centre of Tarsus's fortress. He had sent Kabir and the others on to the gate, having advised them to stay away from legionaries and watchmen if possible. The sight of the four nomads on the city streets at night would undoubtedly draw attention; they would struggle to deflect it without Cassius present.

The pair of soldiers on duty at the gatehouse had seemed rather confused about exactly what the Imperial Security Service was but mention of Marcellinus had been enough to persuade them to summon the guard officer on duty. He in turn had been sufficiently alarmed by talk of the marshal to take Cassius straight to the headquarters. Apparently, the chief centurion maintained a residence there and was currently present.

Cassius gave a brief nod of thanks to the gods as he passed from chill darkness into the well-lit warmth of the building. Glowing braziers lined the central corridor and there was a strong smell of roasted meat in the air. The legionaries on duty all cast curious glares at the young 'civilian' in their midst and Cassius attracted more interest from a tribune standing by a map mounted on the wall.

The guard officer led him almost to the end of the corridor.

As the soldier knocked on a hefty door, Cassius noticed that two of the legionaries had followed them. One was an optio, with two red rings upon his tunic sleeve.

A gruff voice sounded from beyond the chief centurion's door, which the guard officer then opened.

'The Service agent, sir.'

Chief Centurion Terentius walked up to the doorway. Like almost all men of his rank, he was a veteran in advanced middle age. His grey hair was very thick but none grew in the pink, furrow-like scar that ran across the top of his head. Cassius dragged his eyes downward; not quickly enough.

'Good evening, sir. Thank you for agreeing to see me at such notice.'

'*You* are with the Service?'

'Yes, sir.'

'By all the gods, I must be getting old.' He turned to the guard officer. 'Dismissed.'

Terentius – who wore only a modest red tunic and a plain belt – pointed at the optio and the second man. 'These nice fellows will have to accompany us. Official policy for visitors – some provincial fanatic tried to stab the prefect last month. You'll also have to give them your dagger. Hope you don't mind.'

'No, sir.' Cassius took the sheath off his belt and handed it to the optio, a grim-looking individual with a tattoo of a bird on his neck. Cassius followed Terentius inside. The chief centurion went to sit behind his desk and gestured to the chair facing him. The office was a large room made smaller by walls packed with shelves containing waxed tablets and scrolls. Lying in front of the hearth was a bearskin. Mounted above it was an exotic-looking curved blade.

Cassius sat down, conscious of the two guards directly behind him.

'Well?' said Terentius, leaning back into a voluminous cushion. 'You told my men the matter was both urgent and important. I am of course always happy to help Imperial Security.'

Cassius felt sure that the opposite was true. He also felt as if he was being toyed with. Then he realised.

'Ah,' said the chief centurion, reading his expression. 'Yes – you have made a big mistake.'

Cassius could not believe he hadn't considered it. He'd been so busy trying to assuage Kabir that he'd missed the obvious conclusion to be drawn from Merenda's failure to make contact.

'You received a communication from Antioch?'

'Just this afternoon.'

'I suppose a copy might also have reached the governor; and the basilica staff?'

'Indeed. The note sent out by the prefect's clerk mentioned a young agent named Corbulo – currently absent without leave. Any information regarding his movements or activities is to be sent to Antioch. If possible, he is to be arrested and held until further notice. The order was signed by one Aulus Celatus Abascantius.'

Cassius just sat there, numbed by a full appreciation of his own stupidity. They had already been in Tarsus for more than a day; of course the imperial post could have caught up with him. Why had he not been more careful? Perhaps deep down he'd thought the agent might just let him go.

'Not very bright, young man.'

Cassius glanced over his shoulder. Neither soldier looked at him. The optio was still holding his dagger.

As if it made any difference; what was he going to do – fight his way out of here?

Kabir and the others? They would go on without him but what chance did they have now? Even worse, he would have to wait here under guard, unable even to work on finding Indavara.

You stupid, ignorant prick.

'I must admit I'm intrigued,' continued Terentius. 'The Service are adept at controlling people, especially their own. Why have you disobeyed Pitface, Corbulo? What brought you here?'

Cassius couldn't see much harm in telling him; perhaps the chief centurion might take pity on Kabir's plight.

After he had described everything from the capture of the girls to that day's developments, Terentius rapped his fingers on the table, then dismissed the men. The optio protested briefly but his superior insisted.

The sheathed dagger tapped against Cassius's shoulder. He took it and replaced it on his belt as the pair left.

A little hope returned; surely this was encouraging.

The chief centurion scratched his scar. 'Why are you so keen to help these nomads?'

Cassius saw a further opportunity to persuade him that his mission was a noble one. There seemed little point in clouding the issue by mentioning Indavara.

'Have you heard of Alauran, sir?'

'I have not.'

'It is a small fort in the Syrian desert. My first – my only – field command. We held out against a force of Palmyran rebels. This man Kabir led the auxiliaries – without them we would have lost. I owe him a debt.'

'Loyalty. I admire that. It is not often to be found in the younger generation.'

Cassius thought it best to stay quiet.

'You'll not be surprised to hear that I don't have a lot of time for the Service. I have encountered the odd decent agent – who actually helps the army instead of getting in its way – but a lot of your kind become . . . inebriated with the power they are given. And Pitface is one of the worst.'

Cassius was definitely not about to interrupt now. From the large door that seemed to have closed in front of him, a chink of light.

Terentius adjusted the left sleeve of his tunic. 'My cohort fought with the Emperor at the Battle of Emesa. Instead of six centuries I had only four. Why? Because Abascantius pulled them out of the line the day before – as extra protection for the Emperor. There was some administrative foul-up and they never even got near Aurelian. They sat out the first hours of the battle twiddling their thumbs while my cohort got pummelled by the Palmyran cavalry. We lost two hundred and forty-one men that day.'

Cassius had seen the aftermath of the battle: the skeletons of countless horses, half-buried in the sands of the Syrian desert. Despite significant losses, the victory had contributed much to Aurelian's triumph over Queen Zenobia.

'I could go on,' said Terentius. 'But the fact is I am simply not inclined to do Abascantius a favour, especially not at the expense of a young man who seems to be engaged in a worthwhile cause. My men and I will forget we saw you. Nobody – your superior included – will know you came here.'

'Sir, I cannot thank you enough, I—'

'Yes, yes. Enough of that. Let's see what we can do to help you find this bloody criminal.'

Terentius disclosed all he knew about the column heading north, including the name of the man in charge, an Optio Chariton. And when Cassius reluctantly admitted that in fact he was in need of directions to the gate, the guard officer was assigned to escort him.

As they trotted through the streets, Cassius commented that the chief centurion seemed like an exceptionally considerate officer. His companion – who'd said little up to that point – regaled him with a series of anecdotes that highlighted both the centurion's exceptional military record and his habitual concern for those serving under him. Apparently the men referred to him as the 'Father of the Legion'. He was due to retire in two years and none of the other centurions seemed keen to step into his shoes. Cassius made a mental note to thank the gods for putting this man in his path.

The guard officer hailed the legionaries on duty at the gate; an imposing arch of large limestone blocks. While he instructed them to let the 'civilian' through without question, Cassius heard hooves on stone. From a side street, five men leading horses emerged: Kabir, Kammath, Idan, Yablus and Simo.

'We were starting to worry, sir,' said the Gaul as they entered the glow of the torches mounted at the gate.

Cassius dismounted. 'Not as much as I was, believe me. Nothing from Merenda, I presume?'

'No, sir.'

The guard officer turned his horse around and surveyed the unlikely looking party. 'You know about the Tyana road?'

'Yes,' said Cassius.

'And the Podandus approach?'

'Yes.'

'If you're intent on continuing on through the night, the inn at Sidassa remains open at all hours. It's about twelve miles from here – to the right, surrounded by trees.'

'Thank you.'

'Farewell.' The guard officer waved at the sentries and trotted away back down the street.

Cassius turned to Kabir. 'Shall we get moving? I can tell you on the way.'

With the sentries looking on, he led the others under the arch and on to the open road. A little colour remained in the sky. Far away to the north, streaks of white and grey cloud lay low over the dark peaks of the Taurus mountains.

X

Two days after his first visit, Slab returned. He was not alone. As well as Warty and Narrow Eyes – who entered first with daggers drawn – there was an older man. He was quite old in fact; stooped and white-haired, with a heavily wrinkled brow and a mouth that seemed to have collapsed in on itself. He was carrying a cloth bag.

Indavara was standing by the window. Though he could hear their cries, he hadn't caught a single glimpse of the gulls for a long time. The beetle and the mouse hadn't reappeared either.

'This is the surgeon,' said Slab. 'You will let him examine you.'

Indavara had decided to continue to appear compliant in the hope that his captors would eventually grow relaxed and make an error.

The old man put his bag on the bed, then walked over to the prisoner and examined his face. 'Tongue.'

Indavara stuck it out.

Surgeon looked at it, then took Indavara's hand and placed his fingers on the veins at his wrist and closed his eyes. The other three watched. Indavara spied sunlit grass between Warty and Narrow Eyes. Surgeon then placed his hand over Indavara's heart and closed his eyes once again. After about a minute, he retreated and asked him to walk to the corner and back. Doing so was difficult.

'Are the irons necessary?' croaked the old man.

'Entirely,' said Slab.

Surgeon inspected the manacles. Indavara tried to move them – and himself – as often as he could but the sores were getting worse.

'What about loosening them?'

Slab shook his head.

'He needs to move around more,' said Surgeon. 'His condition will deteriorate. I take it you're feeding him properly?'

'Big meal, twice a day,' said Slab, his large face stern.

Surgeon returned to Indavara and held up his arm, the right one this time. He peered down at the skin then ran his fingers over the numerous scars and prominent veins.

'We shall need some more light for the procedure.'

'We can do it over here. By the door.'

Surgeon lowered Indavara's arm, then returned to his bag and extracted a length of string with knots tied at regular intervals.

'I shall need some help to measure him.'

Slab waved the other two forward. 'Either side.'

As they took up position, daggers at the ready, Slab sheathed his weapon and went to help the old man.

'Shoulder to shoulder first.'

Slab held one end while Surgeon stretched the string across Indavara's chest.

'Now shoulder to wrist.'

Though the three guards were watching him intently for any move, Indavara's mind was far away. He had been injured several times during his time in the arena, and often been treated by his owner's surgeon. He could not work out what these people intended to do with him.

Having also measured his height and the length of his legs, Surgeon shook his head. 'It would be useful to know his weight but unfortunately we don't have the equipment. Make sure he eats and drinks well today. If you wish to start tomorrow, he may not be able to take on much sustenance after that.'

'But is he strong?' asked Slab. 'Healthy?'

'Exceptionally, I should say.'

Indavara now realised that there might not be another chance. He examined his options. His wrists were manacled together but he could still use a dagger if he got hold of one. The chances of getting to the three of them were slim but he had to try something before it was too late.

Surgeon had already retreated. Slab did the same, careful not to turn away from the captive. Warty followed, also careful to keep a good distance between them. Narrow Eyes passed close. Close enough.

Indavara made a grab for the knife. His fingers closed over Narrow Eyes's hand and the hilt. He jerked it forward, out of the smaller man's grip.

Just as he was about to slice at his throat, something smashed into his chest. He found himself pinned back against the wall, Slab's hand on his wrist.

'Take it. Hurry up, you useless prick!'

Narrow Eyes had recovered himself sufficiently to retrieve his blade.

Slab's face was an inch from Indavara's. 'No, no, no, boy. It's not going to happen. You need to accept that.'

Indavara would have tried to knee him in the balls had he been able. Slab – who was stronger than he looked – had turned side on to protect his groin. He held Indavara's arms down by the manacles and slipped his dagger out.

'And now I'm going to have to take off those fingers so this doesn't happen again.' He glanced back at Surgeon. 'Lucky we've got you here – you can patch him up afterwards.' Slab pointed at Narrow Eyes. 'You two get him on the floor – think you can manage that?'

'No,' said Surgeon.

'What?'

'You can't cut him. Or hurt him. Not now. Why do you think I came to check on his condition? The better health he is in, the more likely our chance of success. I made that perfectly clear to . . . to our employer.'

Slab looked genuinely disappointed. He moved backwards, the tip of his dagger still aimed at Indavara's throat.

'And afterwards?'

Surgeon shrugged. 'By the way, we're also going to need a bed. Something with a proper frame.'

Slab gave a reluctant nod. 'Out.'

As the others complied, Slab glared at Narrow Eyes, who mumbled an apology as he passed him. He turned back to

Indavara. 'Lucky boy. But it's going to run out tomorrow. See you then.'

Slab withdrew, shutting the door behind him. As the key turned in the lock, Indavara slumped back against the wall.

He remained there for some time and eventually decided to pray to Fortuna once again. There was no more he could do himself; he needed help.

He only noticed he was crying when he saw the tears splashing on to his arms. He almost let out a cry of rage but he didn't want to give his captors the satisfaction.

After some time, he began to think about methods. He was giving serious thought to killing himself.

XI

The six men sat on a patch of grass below the aqueduct, enjoying the shade. In front of them was a broad corral – empty of horses for the moment – and beyond that the stable itself. Two grooms were struggling to pull a large black horse from its stall, causing much amusement to a nearby trio of lads who were supposed to be mucking out.

'Where *are* they?' moaned Kammath, who generally spoke in Greek when he had a complaint to make.

'Rest awhile,' said his father, who was leaning back against the roughly hewn blocks of one of the aqueduct's piers. Beside him, Idan continued a repair to his sling that seemed to have been going on for days. The aqueduct ran straight into the heart of Tyana, which they had reached in exceptionally good time, stopping only at night and to rest their horses. The Podanus approach – where the road passed through the famed Cilician Gates – was notorious for bandits but there had been not a single incident. Cassius had been this way before, when summoned from Cilicia for his second assignment in Syria. He had pointed out the ancient fortifications and regaled the nomads with tales of Alexander and the Army of the Ten Thousand. Simo described the journeys of the Christian Paul of Tarsus, which Kabir and the others seemed even less interested in.

Their progress had slowed as they neared Tyana due to road repairs and the morning traffic. And with two of the horses requiring attention, Cassius had suggested they stop at the first stable they saw, which was on the edge of the city. They had already been waiting an hour.

'Perhaps you could see how they're doing?' said Cassius to Simo.

Kammath's mount had turned a hoof on the road while Simo's had some sort of skin infection that was clearly causing it great discomfort.

'Sir.'

The attendant got to his feet and hurried down a short bank towards the corral. The restless Kammath and Yablus took their slings from their packs and went to practise, which they and Idan did on a regular basis. Though he had seen them in action before, Cassius was always impressed by their accuracy. The nomads had found some apples the previous day and placed them in a row upon a log. Even from a range of fifty feet, they would hit them more times than they missed. For such an apparently rudimentary weapon, the slings – in the right hands – were remarkably effective.

'You have heard of the Emperor's vision?' asked Cassius.

Kabir frowned. Idan ignored him.

'His forces besieged this city just last year while putting down the Palmyran rebellion. One night he had a vision of Apollonius, a famous philosopher who hailed from Tyana. Apollonius begged him to be merciful, to spare his city. The Emperor did precisely that.'

'You Romans do love your philosophers – what was he known for?'

'Several things – he wrote about science and nature and was said to have raised a senator's daughter from the dead. I believe he also concurred with Ptolemy that the sun revolves around the Earth.'

'With that, I might agree. The Glorious Fire moves constantly to give its heat and protection to all.'

'An interesting interpretation. He was also a vegetarian.'

'What's that?'

'Someone who refuses to eat meat.'

The chief frowned again. Idan snorted.

'So what now?' asked Kabir.

Cassius stood up and stretched his aching legs. 'We find the nearest army way station. I doubt they'll still be here but we know we're not far behind.'

By making enquiries as they went, they had charted the progress of the column. Cassius knew from Terentius that Chariton's group was made up of around fifty prisoners and an escort of two squads of legionaries. They were – as Merenda had suggested – bound for the Tuz salt mines. Terentius had also explained that these mines were not underground, but salt flats around Lake Tuz, where workers extracted the valuable mineral for transport around the Empire. Due to the outbreak of plague in the area, there was a shortage of workers. An arrangement with a private businessman named Draco provided a secure destination for the condemned men and a flow of much-needed revenue into Tarsus.

'About a hundred miles, then,' said Kabir. 'From here to the mine?'

'About that. I shall also ask about the route.'

The main road, which cut north-east through the centre of Galatia, had always been considered secure but the arrival of the plague had left way stations unmanned and whole sections unguarded. According to Terentius, Chariton had used it on his previous trips but had occasionally encountered groups of bandits and plague-ridden locals. The legionaries kept both at a distance with arrows.

Kabir stood up too, which seemed like quite an effort for him; whatever his affliction, the relentless riding had clearly taken a toll. 'These diseased people Terentius spoke of – how is it that they are still alive?'

'There is the bleeding plague, from which most victims expire; and then different non-fatal varieties. Those who catch it are covered with the pox and usually suffer other symptoms. They must try to live on but of course others do not want them near. They often retreat to caves or forests and other remote areas; scratch out a living as best they can.'

'Or turn to banditry?'

'It always worsens in an area where disease strikes. Trade slows; wealth declines – people turn to crime.'

'The Empire seems to have criminals everywhere.'

Cassius wasn't about to argue with him about that. 'And amongst *your* people?'

'Occasionally – very occasionally – someone acts against the tribe. But not often. We are all related by blood or marriage. We would not hurt our own.'

'It seems a fine way to live.' Cassius gestured towards the high buildings visible in the distance. 'But we build cities. Dark, dirty places – where crime can flourish.'

'I hate cities,' said Idan suddenly, his first contribution. He spoke again without looking up from his repairs. 'And I hate Rome.'

They left the stable two hours later. Simo's horse had been treated and he had been given a poultice to apply over the next few days. Kammath's mount, however, could hardly walk. The stable owner offered an exchange and the ensuing negotiations went on for some time. The Syrians felt that he and his employees were exaggerating the condition for gain and Cassius ended up playing peacemaker. In the end, Kammath left with a fine-looking horse but the Syrians were now a dozen denarii poorer. Kabir confided that their funds were running low; they couldn't afford to lose another mount. Cassius didn't admit that he was in the same position; he had resolved to solve the problem by the time they left Tyana.

The first way station they came to was virtually deserted but they were directed to one closer to the centre. Unusually, the city's fortress – which housed the garrison – was three miles away, built upon the site of another ancient fortification.

Upon reaching the second way station, Cassius discovered that the ranking officer was an optio, who the legionary on duty sent for. While they waited, he asked about the prisoner column. The soldier confirmed that they had passed through Tyana three days ago; due to Chariton's previous trips, his face was well known. As they spoke, a courier arrived with a delivery of post from the south. Cassius eyed the package, concerned there might be something from Abascantius.

The optio entered the office with an older man in civilian

dress. After they'd exchanged greetings, he made straight for the pile of post. 'Excuse me, I must just check these. I'm waiting for something from Tarsus – my men haven't been paid in months.'

As he began checking through the recently arrived scrolls, Cassius interrupted. 'Sorry, but this is urgent – I need information on the situation to the north.'

'Who are you with?'

'Imperial Security.'

The optio looked up. 'Well, then this is your lucky day.' He pointed to the older man, who was leaning languidly against the wall. 'You can talk to Tarchon – he's a grain man too.'

Cassius had spent very little time with other agents of the Imperial Security Service. There were many things he would have liked to discuss but – given the danger of facing arrest once more – he told Tarchon that time was short. As it turned out, the agent was also in a hurry. He had only dropped in at the way station to pick up a map and was heading east into Cappadocia. He didn't say why.

As the two of them exited the way station, Cassius realised he hadn't formally introduced himself. Deciding whether to do so seemed a rather taxing issue. As it happened, he didn't have to decide.

'Are you Corbulo?' asked Tarchon as they both shaded their eyes from the sun. He was an imposing character; almost as tall as Cassius and solidly built. His cropped, spiky hair showed the early signs of grey and his face was handsome but rather weathered. Cassius guessed him to be not far off forty. He didn't plan to lie to him any more than was necessary.

'Yes.'

'I thought so. Abascantius doesn't have any others of your age. I've heard a few tales about you.'

'Ah.'

Tarchon was now looking at the four Syrians towing horses who had hurried over to meet them. He cast a sideways glance at Cassius, who smiled.

'They're with me.'

The agent showed them where to tie up their mounts beside the station then led them to a rickety table sheltered by a tree. Not far away, a squad of legionaries were conducting a sword drill. Cassius couldn't stop thinking about the contents of the imperial post but he relaxed when the optio arrived bearing a wooden sword to join in the drill. With only a cursory glance at the two agents, he announced to the men that pay would be arriving in a week. The news was greeted with a cheer.

There was only space for Cassius, Tarchon, Kabir and Idan at the table. The two youths stood behind the older men while Simo went off to look after Patch. Before Cassius could speak, Tarchon addressed Kabir in what sounded like perfect Aramaic. Cassius watched the Syrian's reaction. After a few terse comments, he nodded cordially.

The agent turned to Cassius. He had a presence about him that went beyond his stature. Even the bold Syrians seemed wary of him. He reminded Cassius slightly of Indavara.

'So why has the old man sent you here?'

'Actually he hasn't.' Cassius had decided to stay as close to the truth as possible. 'I'm on leave. These men are old allies and friends. Kabir's daughter and two other girls from his tribe were captured by slave-traders in northern Syria. They were sold on in Tarsus – we don't know who to – by a man named Meliton. He was recently sentenced to a period of slave labour and was with a column that passed through here three days ago. We need to catch up with them.'

'They're headed to the salt mines, I presume?'

'Indeed. Do you know the most likely route?'

'The situation is fluid up there, what with the banditry and the last outbreak, but the fastest route is to follow the main road until you reach a town called Zynnada. From there is a passable trail that runs about twenty miles north-west to Tuz. There are other ways in and out but that will take you straight to Draco's mine.' Tarchon grimaced. 'Not sure you'll catch them before they get there though; that Chariton keeps the men going at quite a lick. Nobody wants to hang around in that area for too long these days.'

'It's that bad?'

'The area south of Tuz is the worst; half the population lost, much of the rest stricken. I rode down from Nazianus last month. They hear a horse on the road, you see bands of them coming out of the trees. Some begging, some with weapons. Some of them just groups of children. I took three horses. Barely stopped from sunrise to sunset.

'And at the mine? Will this Draco character cooperate?'

'I've not met him but he has a reputation for being his own man.'

'As reptilian as his name suggests?'

'I've never been sure if that's his actual name or a moniker he has acquired. He's certainly an opportunist; many of the more respectable concerns left the area when the plague struck. He has a virtual monopoly now and several sources of cheap labour. I imagine profits are good.'

'Nobody ever lost money selling salt.'

'True.'

Cassius summoned the courage for a rather impertinent request. 'I feel . . . awkward mentioning this but well . . . we're running rather low on funds. I don't suppose you'd be able to help?'

Tarchon's brow furrowed for a moment but then a grin appeared. 'I'm sure you're good for it. How much do you need?'

'A hundred denarii.'

'Not a problem. I have a banker friend just round the corner; we do each other favours from time to time. I shall have to ask a question though – to check you are who you say you are.'

Cassius tried to look relaxed. 'Right.'
'What's the old man's horse called?'
Now Cassius grinned. 'Antheon.'

XII

They parted less than an hour later. Tarchon emerged from the banker's well-guarded townhouse with a bag of money and handed it over with no further query. He wished the group well; speaking to the Syrians in Aramaic once more and reminding Cassius to get in and out of the Tuz area as quickly as possible. As the pair shook forearms, Tarchon also asked him to pass on his greetings to Abascantius, in case he saw him first.

Having replenished their supplies, they left Tyana and – in the three hours of daylight left – covered a respectable ten miles. Much of the terrain was flat, arable land though they passed close to a smaller range of mountains to the east. As dusk neared, they reached a hamlet and asked a local about accommodation, discovering that there was only one inn. Following his directions, they rode along a dusty trail and came to a large but rather decrepit building. The substantial hole in the roof seemed to have been plugged with sticks and straw.

Cassius had given up worrying about their lodgings; he just hoped for a decent bed and palatable food. There was at least a young lad on duty, who hurried out of the adjoining yard.

'Staying the night, sirs?'

'We are,' said Cassius. 'What rooms do you have?'

Instead of replying, the lad turned towards the inn and shouted something in Aramaic.

Cassius slid down off his saddle and cursed as his first steps revealed the true extent of the soreness across his backside and thighs. Simo seemed similarly weary – Kabir too – but the others looked remarkably fresh. Cassius could never understand how; the nomads rode without a saddle – just a folded blanket and sometimes not even that.

The lad was already at work, detaching Patch's rope from Simo's saddle. When he pulled the donkey into the yard, the tired animal lost its footing in a hollow and stumbled. Cursing in his own language, the lad jerked the donkey forward and cuffed its ear. Unused to such treatment, Patch brayed his disapproval.

The lad received admonishing shouts from two of the Syrians but the loudest came from Simo.

'Leave him alone!' The Gaul snatched the rope and shoved the youngster towards his horse.

By now, a woman had emerged from the inn. Wiping her hands on a greasy apron, she counted the visitors. 'Six, is it? All staying?'

'Indeed,' said Cassius.

'We've just the one room left,' said the woman. 'There's space for you all but only the one bed.'

They had encountered such situations before. The nomads carried their own bedding and seemed happy to sleep anywhere. Simo was well used to the floor.

'That's fine,' said Cassius.

'That'll be seven denarii, two sesterces for the night, meal included. Three more for the mounts.'

'A little high. I hope dinner will make up for it.'

'I've enough lamb for you all, sir.'

'Mmm,' said Cassius. He did not particularly like lamb.

'We have been lucky, sir,' said Simo as he rolled his master's blankets on to the bed.

'Really? It seems a long time since I last felt lucky.'

'Sir, I know there have been many obstacles but we have received help too: the centurion and that man Tarchon in Tyana.'

'A fair point, I suppose. Interesting character, wasn't he? Wonder what he's up to in Cappadocia.'

'Do you think Abacantius will send someone after you, sir?'

'I doubt it. If he so desires, he'll certainly pick up enough of our trail to know I've headed north. But I can't see him wasting manpower actually following me; and definitely not where we're headed. Simo, where's my facecloth, I can't find—'

Cassius had noted that there might be a more pressing situation unfolding outside. The room was on the first floor and the window overlooked the yard. As was their habit, the Syrians had gone outside to complete their daily ritual while the sun set. Once they had knelt, one man would lead a chant and then they would bow as low as possible, faces touching the ground. The whole thing lasted about five minutes and was repeated at sunrise. Worship of solar deities was not uncommon, but the sight of such an overt display by the strange-looking foursome had attracted some interest along the way. Now it had attracted some more.

'Balls,' said Cassius. A group of six workers – some of whom were carrying vicious-looking scythes – were walking along the track towards the main road and one had just spotted the Syrians through the gate. He waved the others over and they looked on.

Kabir and the others realised they were being watched but continued with their chant. Cassius had expected the labourers to perhaps laugh and mock them but instead they seemed angry. One man rattled the gate, which disturbed the horses more than the nomads.

Cassius leaned against the window ledge, looking on. He knew the Syrians would not halt the ritual. Another of the locals shouted something that sounded offensive but then two moved off and before long they had all drifted away. Kabir and the others finished and got to their feet.

'Something happening, sir?' said Simo as he continued searching for Cassius's facecloth.

'Thankfully, no.'

To be fair to the innkeeper's wife, the lamb stew was better – if only slightly – than Cassius had expected. He and the others ate from bowls, squeezed around the largest table in the parlour. It was a low, dark room that reeked of smoke and stale sweat. The other guests – four seedy-looking merchants – were clearly well known to the owners; they ate their dinner at the counter and conversed in a mix of Greek and Aramaic.

'Bread, sir?' said Simo, offering a wooden platter with a few slices left.

'One bit was enough – I'd prefer to keep my teeth if you don't mind.'

Cassius watched his companions, who had each taken a large helping of stew. Though all – Idan and Yablus included – could speak enough Latin for a conversation, they rarely said much. Cassius could understand their grim mood, but he preferred to try and distract himself from wider concerns from time to time, especially after a hard day's ride.

'So what's an average meal for you fellows back home?'

He didn't expect a reply from Idan. The chief and his son were busy chewing on the lamb.

'We like goat,' said Yablus.

'Ah, requires a lot of cooking, doesn't it?'

Yablus gestured at his bowl. 'Still better than this. Northerners can't cook.'

'Well if you consider these folk northerners, what does that make us?'

Yablus shrugged.

Cassius imagined his grasp of geography was fairly rudimentary. 'I come from Italy and Simo here is of Gaulish stock. And I'm afraid your contention doesn't stand up to scrutiny. Simo is an excellent cook.'

'Where is Gaul?'

'Far to the north and west. Thousands of miles.'

Yablus's eyes widened.

'To get there from here you would have to cross the Great Green Sea, then traverse almost the whole of Italy before you even got close.'

'Why would he ever want to do that?' said Idan.

'Never had any interest in seeing the world?' asked Cassius. 'You were an auxiliary – you must have travelled around a bit?'

'We never left Syria,' replied Kabir, having finally ingested the lamb. 'We were recruited by a centurion who told us that the Palmyrans would enslave us. We knew it for a lie but the fighting had disrupted trade and we needed the money. We only fought in two engagements other than Alauran: one at a bridge on the Euphrates, one supporting two centuries sent to attack a Palmyran supply column. We spent most of our time walking from one fort to another or awaiting new orders. As you know, we never received the full amount we were owed.'

'I suppose I shouldn't blame you for disliking the Empire.'

'*Disliking*?' said Idan.

Cassius was beginning to wish he'd never started this conversation.

'We always liked *you* though,' said Kabir. 'Well, I did at least. Isn't that right, Idan?'

The disfigured warrior gave an almost imperceptible nod.

Kabir continued, 'When you arrived at the fort and the Palmyrans came, we had a wager. Idan thought Alauran would fall at the first attack. I doubt if he was the only one who underestimated you.' He turned to his old friend. 'Actually, did you ever pay me for that?'

'Yes,' said Idan indignantly, drawing a chuckle from Yablus.

Kammath had finished eating but was staring down at the table, lost in thought.

The lad came in from the rear door, wiping dirt off his hands.

'How are those mounts?' asked Simo.

'Well, sir. All fed and watered. Your donkey too. I gave him some roots – I think he likes me now.'

'Good boy,' said Cassius.

Simo took out a coin for him.

'Come and get it while it's hot,' said the innkeeper's wife. The lad ducked under the counter and grabbed himself a stool.

Yablus got up and walked across the parlour and through a

door to the latrine. Cassius was not looking forward to his next visit; as with most provincials, basic plumbing and hygiene was a mystery to these people. Hearing voices outside, he looked out of the window but saw nothing other than shapes dimming the lantern until the door latch went up. In came a rough-looking fellow, followed by another, then another. By the time the door finally shut, there were no less than eight of them gathered by the counter. Greetings were exchanged and the innkeeper instantly set about filling some engraved mugs that clearly belonged to the new arrivals. As some of them strayed near to another light, Cassius recognised one of those who had earlier watched the Syrians. He chose to say nothing but noted a few sly looks and comments when the locals realised who they were sharing the parlour with.

'Katia is a terrible cook,' said Kammath suddenly. 'Mother tried with her, the aunts too – but she's just no good at it. She almost poisoned us once – remember those mushrooms, Father?'

'She probably did it on purpose,' said Kabir. 'So she'd have more time outside with you and the other boys.'

The chieftain's faint smile soon faded.

Cassius made an attempt to distract him. 'You remember Strabo, the guard officer at Alauran?'

'Of course.'

'Quite a character. I think of him often.'

Idan said something in Aramaic.

Kabir spoke for him. 'Idan was even less fond of the man than I was. A gambler and a drinker. He did not seem to us like a professional soldier. But I must confess that, when it counted, he did very well. We have a word for such a man but it is not easy to translate: someone others look to; someone they will follow into battle. Stand beside. Die for.'

'I understand. Yes, he had that. Like you.'

Kabir shook his head ruefully. 'I've said it before, I'll say it again – you are not a typical Roman officer.'

'I wish I had an aureus for every time I'd heard that.'

Yablus returned. There wasn't much space to get past the locals, who predictably didn't make it easy for him. He was almost through when one of them flicked the Syrian's long hair and made some comment that his friends found amusing. Yablus shot back a glare but wisely continued on to the table.

He had just sat down when one of the locals walked over, mug in hand. He stared at Idan and took a sip of his wine before speaking.

'Where you from?'

'Syria,' said Cassius. 'Moving on tomorrow.'

'Good.' He was a short man but quite wide, with a double chin and a fleshy mouth. Hanging from a string around his neck was a large bronze pendant. Cassius couldn't quite make out the inscription but the design was familiar: it showed Jupiter, greatest of all Roman gods.

Kabir and the others looked up as two more came to join him.

Cassius turned away and whispered to Simo. 'Fetch my bag – you know the one.'

Simo slipped off the bench and out of the parlour.

'We don't want any trouble,' Cassius said. 'Allow me to buy a drink for you and your friends.'

'Very kind, sir. You seem a proper gentleman. But it's your mates here. You see, we don't want any trouble either. We're good Roman folk and the gods have looked after us. You'll find none of the diseased here.'

The innkeeper spoke up but was rapidly quietened by another of his patrons. The other five stalked over to join the leader, who clearly liked to talk.

'Then we see this lot on their knees praying to the sun. There's no surer way to make the great gods – the true gods – angry.'

'If I were you,' said Kabir, 'I would avoid mentioning the sun again.'

'And if I were travelling through, I'd be more respectful to the people who live here.'

A big, bearded man came forward and stood only a couple of inches from Idan, who was staring up at the loudmouth.

Another of the locals spoke up: 'You best stop staring at my mate like that or your face is going to end up even uglier than it is now.'

Idan and Kabir calmly exchanged comments in Aramaic.

Cassius saw Kammath's hand drifting towards his dagger.

'We have finished our meal,' said Cassius. 'We shall leave the parlour to you. All right?'

The loudmouth wasn't finished. 'I expect this lot will be out there again at sunrise.'

'We're not having it,' said the bearded man. 'Not here.' Cassius wasn't sure if they were simply bored brutes looking for a scrap or genuinely in fear of offending the gods; possibly a mixture of the two.

Even though the Syrians didn't appear to be in the mood for a tactical retreat, Cassius caught Kabir's eye and held up an appeasing hand. Simo reappeared, now carrying the long bag.

When the bearded man passed his mug to a friend and smacked a fist into a palm, Idan and Kabir sprang to their feet, closely followed by Kammath and Yablus.

Cassius stood, snatched the bag from Simo, and threw it on to the table, smashing several pieces of crockery. The Syrians and the locals all stared down at it.

'My name is Corbulo. Yours?'

The loudmouth looked around at his cohorts, who seemed just as taken aback as him. 'Aniketos.'

'A pleasure to meet you, Aniketos. I assume you are a farm-hand of some kind?'

'Er . . . yes.'

'Perhaps you would like to open that bag. It will give you a clue as to *my* profession.

'Enough games,' spat the bearded man.

'No game,' said Cassius. 'If you still want to fight with us you can – but I would suggest checking that bag first.'

Aniketos undid the ropes at one end and pulled out Cassius's sword. Eagle-head hilts were synonymous with soldiers: officers, in particular.

'I am a centurion, travelling incognito. These men are auxiliaries. If you harm so much as a single hair on one of their heads, I'll make it my business to ensure you are all flayed unconscious in whatever passes for a square in this shithole you call home. Now, I suggest you piss off back over there and keep quiet.'

'You could have got that sword anywhere,' said a voice from the back.

'True,' said Cassius. 'So let's fight. In the unlikely event that you win, you'll probably want to get something for your efforts. When you go through my bags you'll turn up a letter from Marshal Marcellinus, on whose orders I'm in this province. Name ring any bells? Surely even a mob like you have heard of him.'

In truth, the fight had already gone out of them long before a red-faced Aniketos and the bearded man followed the others back to the counter.

Cassius finished his wine. 'Simo – grab the sword, would you? And tell the innkeeper to add the breakages to our bill.' He then addressed the Syrians. 'Might I suggest we retire upstairs?'

XIII

Indavara knew he must truly be without hope when he realised there wasn't even an easy way to die. With no blade or so much as a sharpened nail, he could not open up his wrists or his neck. There were alternatives: he could try to block his throat or hang himself though neither method was reliable. He could also fight his captors but – whatever Surgeon said – Indavara was sure Slab would follow through on his threat to remove his fingers.

He thought of his friends: Simo and Cassius. He tried to see them in his mind: where they were, what they were doing. He imagined them upon a ship, sailing towards wherever he was. Corbulo did not like being outwitted and he was as intelligent a man as Indavara had known; surely there was a chance they might find him. He held on to that flicker of hope but wondered if it was enough to keep him alive.

More powerful was the force that had sustained him his whole life, which to him was the eight years he could remember: rage. There was no better reason to stay alive than to defy his tormentors.

He could not understand why it was that once again his fate was to be the plaything of others: even now that he was a freedman; even though he had fought and killed for years to escape the arena.

This was another fight. If he could survive it, he would avenge himself upon every last one of his captors. He was already looking forward to it.

They came not long after dawn.

Indavara – who had been unable to eat the previous day – felt a gnawing pain in his stomach as the door opened and he got to his feet. Slab entered first, dagger already drawn. Then came Warty, Narrow Eyes (who was carrying a wooden chest) and Surgeon.

A new bed had arrived the previous day. It was wide, high and very well made, with an iron pole attached to each side. Indavara had slept on the floor, where he had heard the mouse moving around close by. It had given him a little comfort, as had the gulls wheeling and crying outside. He had always loved the open spaces of the world and to see the animals that dwelt there. They were not always safe but they were at least free; free of the endless evils invented by men.

Slab had clearly oiled and polished the blade of his dagger, which he now aimed at the bed. 'On there.'

Indavara was still staring at the wooden chest, which Narrow Eyes had placed on the floor at Surgeon's feet.

The old man tutted. 'I can smell that latrine. I told you we need to keep this place clean.'

Slab nodded at Narrow Eyes, who walked outside.

'I'm not going to tell you again. On the bed.'

'Come,' said Surgeon. 'It won't be all that bad.'

Indavara hobbled over to the bed and sat upon it. He was suddenly struck by the feeling that if he gave into them now his life was already over.

Slab seemed to see it in his eyes. He moved close and held the dagger against his neck. 'Now lie down. Like he said, it's not going to be that bad.'

'Did you eat anything today?' asked Surgeon.

Indavara shook his head.

'Lie back,' said Slab.

Indavara looked at Surgeon, who had opened the chest and taken out several wooden bowls. 'What are you going to do to me?'

'Try not to worry. It's actually often prescribed as a cure.'

Narrow Eyes came in with a pail full of earth to deposit in the latrine.

'What?' said Indavara.

'Enough,' snapped Slab, grabbing the collar of his tunic and pushing him back. He held Indavara there, the cold blade against his skin. 'Undo the iron.'

Warty took out the key to the wrist manacles.

'Don't you move an inch,' hissed Slab.

Warty undid the manacles and took them off Indavara's wrists. Surgeon gripped his left arm and tutted again as he inspected the sores. He then retrieved four short leather straps from the chest and held one of them up. 'We will need to tie your—'

Slab yelled, 'You don't have to explain, just do it!'

Indavara wondered if he could get his hands up quickly enough to take the knife off Slab. But Warty and Narrow Eyes were now looking on and his legs were still manacled. Slab was so close he could feel his breath on his face. There was no chance.

Surgeon placed his left arm on the outside of the metal pole and strapped it on just above the elbow. The second strap was affixed above the wrist. He repeated the process with the right arm, during which time Slab pressed the dagger blade hard enough into Indavara's neck for him to feel it pierce the skin.

'By the gods, man,' said Surgeon when he saw the blood. 'He can't do anything now.'

Indavara felt even more vulnerable than when he'd been manacled. As Slab moved away, he felt his stomach begin to spasm. He was going to be sick.

Noting this, Surgeon quickly located a water flask and put a calming hand on Indavara's shoulder. Though he tasted the bitterness in his mouth, Indavara somehow didn't throw up. Surgeon held the flask to his mouth but he didn't open it.

'It's just water, young man. I'll give you some wine in a moment too. That will help.'

Indavara drank. This water was cold and pure; far better than what he was normally given.

'Spread these around the bed,' instructed Surgeon, tipping what looked like dried flower petals into four bowls. Warty took them and did so. Before long, a pleasant smell filled the room.

Slab, meanwhile, had taken a length of rope from outside, thrown it to Narrow Eyes and told him to tie Indavara's feet to the bottom of the bed. Only when this was done did he sheath his dagger.

Surgeon had poured some of the water into a bowl. He dunked a cloth into it, then began to clean Indavara's upturned forearm. 'Now listen carefully, young man, and I shall tell you what's going to happen.'

Slab grunted.

Surgeon turned. 'It's better that he knows – then it will be less of a shock to him. Would you fetch my stool, please?'

With a shake of his head, Slab went outside and returned with a stool, which he placed beside the bed.

Surgeon sat on it and finished cleaning the arm. He then took several items out of the chest and shut it. He laid a white square of cloth over the lid and placed the items there: two small leather cases and a bronze dish with an opening on one side. Next to the chest were two empty glass flasks and a third of wine.

Surgeon removed the stopper and held the wine flask to Indavara's mouth. 'I'll give you more in a moment. I know you must be very frightened; believe me when I tell you that this is your best defence against fear and pain.'

Indavara did believe him and he glugged down the wine quickly.

'Not too much, I also need you to stay awake as long as possible.'

Surgeon put the wine down, then opened up the leather cases. Indavara couldn't quite see over the side of the bed but he glimpsed a set of bronze scalpels.

Surgeon held his arm as he spoke. 'We are going to take your blood. A little at first, then more. There will be some pain when I make the incision but after that it should decrease. You may feel cold but do not worry, we have blankets for you. You will see your own blood – a lot of it – but judging by the amount of scars you have, I doubt that will scare you. You will also be a man who knows just how much blood there is in a body and therefore that you will have plenty left. As long as there aren't any . . . complications, we should be done in a quarter-hour.'

Surgeon plucked one of the scalpels from the case.

Narrow Eyes had gone rather pale. As he shakily turned away, Warty and Slab laughed.

'Why?' said Indavara. 'Why me?'

Surgeon did not answer. He glanced back at the others.

'Because of who you are, Indavara,' said Slab, the first time he had used his name. '*What* you are. We know all about you – the arena, the victories, the kills. My master saw you fight and he never forgot you. He is very ill. He needs the blood and the life force of a gladiator like you. He calls you a god among men. He believes you will save him.'

XIV

The rain came just after they left the inn and barely stopped for the next three days. With a blanket of thick grey cloud overhead and regular bursts of blustery wind, the spirits of the group sank ever lower. The Syrians saw the disappearance of their beloved Glorious Fire as a bad omen and it was obvious to Cassius that only the older pair were wise enough to realise he had rescued the situation with the labourers. Kabir had even gone so far as to apologise, though he made it clear to Cassius that his people would not tolerate insults to their deity.

What they saw from the road did little to encourage them. The villages they passed through were bleak, sombre places, where the locals also seemed wary of the Syrians. The second night was spent in an inn barely deserving of the name, the third in a stinking outhouse that they were still charged too much for. Cassius drew strength from the knowledge that they were at least making good progress and that their mounts remained healthy. The indefatigable Simo did as well as he could with limited ingredients and provided his companions with a fine meal in their lowly surroundings. After dinner on that third night he recited the only song he knew in Aramaic. Even the stubborn Kammath couldn't resist this gesture and the nomads sang a song of their own. Cassius defied their imprecations to join in and the Syrians seemed unimpressed by his offer of a poem. After Kabir explained that the song was about the Sea of Sand, they shared tales of the haboob – the blasting sandstorms that they had experienced in Arabia.

Halfway through the following morning, the clouds finally cleared. Simo draped the wettest of their clothes across Patch's back and Cassius was finally able to rid himself of his soaking and malodorous woollen cloak.

They had learned enough in the villages to know they would soon reach the last army way station before Lake Tuz. The locals seemed certain that it was still occupied and that these men would have seen Chariton and the column. Cassius and the Syrians reckoned they were now only two days behind them, having spoken to a farmer whose land they'd used.

By noon, they had reached a section of the road that ran through woodland close to the Eskaril mountains; an isolated cluster of crags south of Lake Tuz. They encountered two men on a cart coming the other way who spoke only some local dialect but Simo and the Syrians managed to discern that the pair had been turned back at the way station. This didn't concern Cassius; he still had his letters and it seemed clear that Chariton had been allowed through.

Around the ninth hour, they passed a trail running north towards the mountains. Just a few hundred yards beyond the junction was a grand arch that seemed rather incongruous. Beside it was the way station: a low, squat building with a stable and corral at the rear. Two carts had been left in the middle of the road as a barrier.

As the six riders neared the station, a shout went up from a man riding a horse around the corral. Within moments, two-dozen soldiers had trotted out and lined up. One of them put on a crested helmet and walked into the middle of the road.

Cassius halted the party thirty feet away and went forward on foot alone. The legionaries seemed a well-drilled bunch. They all stood still but kept their eyes on him and their hands on their sword hilts.

The centurion was clad in a fine – if rather dull – brown cloak and a well-polished pair of boots. His main belt looked expensive, as did his sword belt, which was decorated with bronze discs. He was comparatively young for a man of his rank – perhaps about thirty – a tall, muscular fellow with a stern expression upon his face.

'Identify yourself.'

'Officer Cassius Quintius Corbulo.' The reply drew some quizzical looks from the legionaries, who had no reason to think the stranger was any more than a merchant with a strange choice of travelling companions. 'Might I ask your name?'

'Centurion Decimus Modius Regulus of the Fifteenth Legion. Your business here?'

Cassius approved of his accent. Regulus was clearly a man of considerable breeding. He would not present any difficulty.

'I am following a column of prisoners headed for the salt mines of Lake Tuz. I believe the main road leads north-east from this one.'

'It does. But I'm afraid you cannot pass this point.'

Cassius took a breath. 'I am an officer of the Imperial Security Service and I hold letters of authorisation from both Prefect Venator of the Fourth Legion and Marshal Marcellinus himself.'

'With respect, my orders are less than a week old and come from the governor of this province. He will not allow these fresh outbreaks of plague to infect the rest of Galatia. No one can pass in either direction until I hear otherwise.'

'What about Optio Chariton? You spoke to him?'

'Yes; and I told him the same thing.'

Cassius glanced at the watching legionaries – most of whom seemed determined to glare at him – then looked back at Kabir and the others.

'Perhaps we could talk inside.'

Regulus assented with a gracious nod.

Despite the disagreement, the centurion soon confirmed Cassius's earlier impression. He tasked a guard officer with giving the visitors a meal and a place to dry their clothes as well as use of the stable. The legionaries seemed suspicious of the nomads but it was clear that Regulus ran a tight ship: his every order was obeyed swiftly.

Assuring Kabir that this was best handled between the two of them, Cassius joined Regulus in his office. On his desk was a framed map of the province. Once the centurion had put his cloak and helmet on a hook beside the door, he pointed to several lines drawn in red ink.

'These were distributed only a couple of weeks ago. The governor is determined not to fall back into the chaos that has afflicted the region in recent times.'

Regulus moved his finger north-east, to a point Cassius estimated to be about eighty miles away. 'At Pessinus they are doing the same and at other points around the worst afflicted area. I was left in no doubt about the seriousness of my orders. Sorry.'

Regulus sat down and gestured for Cassius to do the same.

As he did so, Cassius looked at the satchel on his lap. He'd intended to show the centurion Marcellinus's letter anyway, thinking that the sight of the marshal's hand might sway him. That now seemed unlikely. Regulus also had the men to enforce his orders; there were quite a number housed at the station.

'You have a half-century with you here?'

'I did. Down to thirty-eight now.'

'Plague?'

'We think they caught it while on a provision run. Both handled it remarkably well, even though one had a wife up in Cyzicus. They took themselves off into the forest, stayed on the other side of a stream. I tried to go up every few days. Fullo didn't last long. We've heard nothing from Macer. I imagine he's gone too.'

'Gods.'

'Oh that's nothing,' said Regulus, pointing at a collection of scrolls on a table in the corner. 'Logs of the last officer posted here. He lost a third of his men. We replaced them last autumn.'

'Surely you must have problems with desertion?'

'Any man who made that choice would forgo his bonuses.'

'Ah.'

'Double pay, men and officers. Pox money, the lads call it.'

'So what about Chariton?'

'He tried his luck but, as I told him, I follow the orders of the governor of Galatia, not Cilicia. He had to take the Eskaril road – the trail you passed just before reaching here. The salt carts don't use it because it's too narrow but it's actually a quicker route to Draco's mine.'

'I sense a qualification.'

Regulus grimaced. 'The trail takes you through the village of Eskaril itself. Many there died or abandoned the place. Most of those still present are diseased. Then there are those who have elected to stay with the afflicted: family members and so on. There's no work, no trade, little food. We have to keep an eye out. Half a dozen times I've had to use my archers on them to send them back into the woods. It's a shame – the settlements in the passes of the mountains are known for their beauty. It is a place unlike any other.'

'You think Chariton would have got through?'

'With that amount of men and armament, yes; and I know he wasn't planning to hang around. But I would guess that will be the last prisoner column for a while. They'll probably return today; then you'll know more. Who's in this column anyway?'

'Bit of a long story.'

Regulus got to his feet. 'Then I best pour us some wine.'

Despite the knowledge of what the next few days might hold, Cassius enjoyed a pleasant two hours with his fellow officer. The centurion requested some lunch and they ate on a bench next to the corral, looking on with the Syrians as the legionaries put their eight horses through their paces. Regulus confided that he needed treble that number of mounts to do his job properly.

It turned out that he had family in Ravenna and the pair exchanged a few observations about Cassius's home city. At twenty-eight, Regulus was five years older and had been stationed in several different provinces. He had fought in engagements against the Persians, the Goths and numerous varieties of brigand. His only regret seemed to be missing the Battle of Emesa. Both officers chuckled when he revealed the cause of his absence: an ingrowing toenail that had left him unable to walk.

The conversation took on a more serious tone when Cassius questioned him about Draco's mine. The centurion shared Tarchon's view that he was very much his own man. Draco had fought hard to keep his profitable operation open and had employed blackmail and bribery to do so. To compensate for the upheaval and the new travel restrictions, he had forged relationships with buyers as far afield as Armenia and Mesopotamia.

'He's also made sure that no one asks too many questions about how he runs things up there,' said Regulus. 'As I understand it, the officials who should keep a check on things have been . . . persuaded not to bother.'

'A bribe might work then?'

'If you have enough.'

Cassius doubted he did. 'I also have my letters – not everyone is as confident as you in ignoring the mark of the Emperor's deputy.'

Regulus took this in the spirit it had been intended. 'You must understand I've never met Draco. All I know is his reputation. Perhaps when he hears of the girls' plight he'll hand this slave trader over for questioning.'

'The gods rarely make my life that easy.'

'Join the crowd.' The centurion hunched forward, elbows on his knees, hands together. He was watching the Syrians, who were cleaning their horses using pails of water and brushes.

'Interesting travelling companions. I wouldn't pick a fight with the scarred one.'

'I first met them three years ago – a fort in the Syrian desert we had to hold against the Palmyrans. Without them, we would have lost. Idan – the disfigured fellow - shot a bird out of the sky. It was at least a hundred feet up, moving fast. I've never seen anything like it.'

'And your man there?'

'Simo? He's been with me ever since I first travelled to the East.'

'Your own attendant? Wish I could afford—'

'Sir!'

They turned round. A man Cassius hadn't previously noticed was sitting on the ridge of the way station's roof, pointing east.

'What is it?' yelled Regulus.

'Riders on the Eskaril road – looks like Chariton's lot.'

They intercepted them where the two roads met, though the route to Eskaril barely deserved the name, being narrow and unpaved. The first thing Cassius noted was the state of the horses. Their heads were hanging low and the snouts were flecked with spittle. The legionaries didn't look much better; they were all breathing hard, skin wet with sweat. Cassius couldn't tell which one was Chariton until Regulus hailed him. The centurion had accompanied Cassius and the Syrians as they ran to meet the man whose column they had pursued for a hundred and fifty miles.

When he dismounted and dropped to the ground, Chariton almost overbalanced. Regulus put out a hand to help the optio: a squat, barrel-chested man with a dense, black beard.

'Sorry,' he said. 'Long ride.'

As the others slid off their horses, several muttered a prayer or raised their eyes to the sky.

'Men, tether your horses and sit.' Chariton pointed at a pile of timber lying in grass close to the road. Cassius and Kabir exchanged a glance as they followed them; they needed information urgently but it was clear the legionaries might take a while to recover.

They seemed low on water and drank greedily from the canteens and gourds offered to them by the centurion and the Syrians. Simo had remained at the way station, already preparing to leave.

Because of the long return journey they faced, the legionaries' horses were well laden and unsuited to a fast ride. It became evident that several bags had been lost. One man had also sustained an injury to his arm.

'Well?' said Regulus when Chariton had composed himself. Cassius and the Syrians gathered closer to hear what he had to say. The optio frowned. 'Who are these?'

'We'll get to that. What happened?'

'Trip in wasn't so bad. Saw a few with the pox lurking in the forest but there's more than a few at Eskaril. The bows were enough to keep them at bay but they followed us through the pass. Then some bloody prisoner turned his ankle on the slopes. I was even considering unchaining them but the others helped the injured man – they wanted to get out of there as much as we did. On the way back, the scabby rats were waiting for us. Wasn't until a couple caught arrows that we fought our way through. Even then they were trying to grab at us. Horrible – worst I've known it by some distance.' He took a gourd from one of his men and drank.

'Women and children,' added a legionary. 'All with the pox. Every one. Skin like lizards.'

'Like one of them crocodiles,' said another man. 'And all dark.'

'Just had to keep moving,' said Chariton. 'In the forest they're different. They're not all diseased – just desperate.'

'And they have spears,' said the injured man. He was holding up his tunic sleeve while a compatriot sloshed water over the wound.

'It's getting worse,' said Regulus.

'You think?' retorted Chariton.

Regulus let the comment go, instead gesturing to Cassius. 'This is Officer Corbulo, Imperial Security. He's been on your tail since Tarsus – needs to speak to you about a prisoner named—'

'Meliton.' Cassius and Kabir spoke simultaneously.

Chariton shrugged. 'Can't say I bothered to get to know all their names.'

'He was there,' said the man treating the wound. 'With some others. Slavers.'

'That's him,' said Cassius. 'He's at the mine now?'

'We didn't lose one of them,' said Chariton. 'Handed them over to the guards and went to see Draco for the money.'

'He lives there?' asked Cassius.

'Comes and goes. He's got a mansion looking out over the flats – from where he can survey his kingdom.'

'Do you think he'll let me speak to the prisoner?'

Chariton pointed along the trail. 'You want to go in *there?*'

'Just answer, would you?'

'As long as you can pay him what he wants, probably. Bastard even made us cough up for sleeping in some bloody outhouse next to the guard barracks. Then again, I suppose you Service men have your ways and means.'

'How long?' asked Kabir. 'To reach the mine?'

'Depends. It's about eight miles to Eskaril, then two miles through the pass. Maybe another six of marsh, then you reach the flats. The route's clear enough.'

Cassius moved away and turned towards the trail, which was almost entirely shaded by the surrounding trees. A couple of the legionaries holding their horses were still looking that way. The state of the men told their own story but what concerned him as much was the possibility of infection. Passing through such an area, close to groups of diseased people, posed quite a risk.

'What about bypassing the trail?'

Regulus said, 'Through the forest? It would take twice as long and you need to go through Eskaril for the pass anyway.'

'I mean right around.' Cassius gestured at the mountains.

'Three days.'

Kammath and Idan were already looking back towards the way station, ready to leave.

Kabir moved close to Cassius and spoke quietly. 'Depending on what Meliton tells us, we may only have to go through once.' He glanced back at the legionaries. '*They* made it.'

'Some people believe the plague lives in the air. This place will be thick with it.

'We will move quickly.'

Cassius could see no other choice. 'Let's go and fetch Simo and the horses. We will try to reach the pass before nightfall.'

XV

The forest seemed to consist exclusively of silver birch and the striated bark of the slender trees at least gave a little colour to the apparently endless depths on either side of the road. The rain had turned the ground to mud and created numerous brown puddles.

For the first mile or so, the six men repeatedly looked back. Cassius knew the dutiful Regulus would have provided more assistance if he could but he had his orders and the main road to guard. Cassius didn't blame him at all; this was not a mission for the Empire.

The beleaguered Chariton had elected to remain at the way station overnight and set off for Tarsus in the morning. Several legionaries were heard to say they hoped this would be their last trip to Tuz and the optio did nothing to contradict them. Two of his men actually approached Cassius and the Syrians as they prepared to depart and warned them not to continue. Kabir thanked them for their concern but replied that they had no alternative.

Before leaving, Cassius had asked Simo to prepare some flowers to keep the air clean around their mouths and noses. Though it wasn't the season, the resourceful Gaul did what he could, combining hardy and sweet-smelling blooms from a nearby meadow with some herbs from his collection. These were placed in small, open-topped bags that each man wore on a string around his neck. In truth, Cassius had no idea if it would make any difference. He was, however, certain that it would make him and the others feel better.

'Caesar's balls.'

For the tenth time since they'd set off, his mount lost its

footing on the uneven ground. He tried to be patient and gave the beast only a nudge; it soon moved off again. Cassius had been riding alongside Simo and had to trot past Patch to catch up. As usual, the donkey seemed to have absorbed the prevailing mood and was trudging along with its head down, occasionally slipping and sliding. Even though Simo had tried once again to rationalise their luggage, there was a limit to what they could discard.

'Why do you say that?'

Idan was bringing up the rear behind them, which at least gave Cassius a little reassurance.

He was surprised to hear the warrior initiate a conversation. 'Sorry?'

'"Caesar's balls" – you use it is a curse. Don't you Romans view him as a god? Isn't it—'

'Disrespectful? I suppose it is, a bit, yes. I learned it from the soldiers at Alauran and unfortunately now seem unable to "unlearn" it. I really should try harder.'

Ahead of him and Simo was Kabir. Kammath and Yablus rode together at the front, a position they seemed to relish. Like the other two, they had their knives and slings at the ready. Cassius did not enjoy riding with his heavy blade hanging from his shoulder but he wanted to keep it within reach. He was also wearing his expensive copper-alloy mail shirt. Simo had been told that he was to use Indavara's fighting stave if necessary. For Cassius, this was a satisfactory compromise; the attendant could protect both himself and his master without causing another serious harm (which would be considered 'a sin').

He glanced up at the sky. The cloud was at least light grey instead of dark but he could see nothing of the sun. His hour-glass was packed somewhere but was close to useless when on the move.

'Eighth, Simo?'

'About that, I should say, sir.'

After years of such journeys, he made a point of regular consultations. Simo was as able a judge as he and they were seldom out by much more than half an hour. It was a skill

Indavara was yet to master. Cassius wondered if – wherever he was – the bodyguard could see the sky.

Kabir held out a hand and pointed down at the ground. Cassius saw the tracks instantly; a group on foot had crossed the trail at right angles, fairly recently.

A half-mile further on they reached a stream. The timber bridge was about ten feet long and roughly made, with almost as many holes as solid sections. The wood was slick with moisture and weed and – though the water below was not deep – they passed across carefully, one at a time. On the other side was a small inlet, ideal for the horses to drink from. As Simo and Yablus led them over, the others gathered beside the trail.

Kabir and Kammath were already engaged in an urgent conversation in Aramaic.

'What is it?' asked Cassius.

'He thinks he saw something in the forest,' answered the chief. 'Possibly men on the move.'

'Where?'

'To the right. Some distance away,' said Kammath.

'Did *you* see anything?'

Kabir shook his head.

'You?'

'No,' said Idan. 'But Kammath has the best eyes.'

'If we could trot they wouldn't be able to keep up and stay hidden,' said Kabir, 'but there's not a chance in this mud.'

'Higher ground will be better,' said Cassius.

'We *must* reach it before night,' said Kabir. 'We cannot defend ourselves here.'

'Agreed. Simo, Yablus – hurry up.'

At what he estimated to be the tenth hour, the trees began to thin out. Then the trail dropped steeply downward, taking them into a bowl-like valley unlike anything Cassius had ever seen. The sight of it was enough to halt them all.

Ahead, the trail divided into a number of narrow, crisscrossing paths that traversed dusty ground broken up by patches of grass and the odd spindly tree. But what drew the eye of every man was the bizarre rock towers that dominated the valley, some hundred feet high. They resembled a variety of candles, some narrow and tall, others short and fat, all composed of the same pale rock that became almost black at the angular peaks.

'Like spears,' said Simo.

Kabir said something in Aramaic, then turned to Cassius. 'A god must have placed these here. As a warning?'

From what Cassius had gathered, the Syrians accepted the existence of other gods in foreign parts of the world but contended that the God of the Glorious Fire pre-dated them all and would always remain the most powerful. Cassius wasn't particularly concerned with which gods were watching over them, as long as they got through unharmed. Chariton had disclosed that these towers occupied about a mile of the approach before the village of Eskaril itself. Beyond that lay the pass. There were at least three choices of path ahead, all with space only for a single horse.

'We may as well continue on foot.' As they dismounted, Cassius decided to take advantage of the remaining daylight to ensure everyone knew where they were headed. He pointed at the two highest peaks. 'It will be dark soon but we should be able to see those even then. The pass runs between. I suggest you all mark them.'

Kammath asked, 'What if we do see these diseased people?'

'As long as they stay at a distance – nothing. Any suggestion that they're getting too close – perhaps a shot or two to dissuade them.'

'Sir, allow me.' Simo came forward to take Cassius's reins. After so many months, the horses were happy to be roped together. 'Poor old Patch, I don't think he likes being at the back.'

'I don't blame him.'

Idan had given his horse to Yablus while Kammath had given his to his father. The men at the front and rear of their little column would therefore be free to move unencumbered. As the temperature was dropping as quickly as the sun, Cassius put on a cloak. He then took a long drink from his flask, which was half water, half wine. He made sure that Simo had the fighting stave within reach and moved up so that he would be behind Kammath.

'Ready?' asked the stocky Syrian.

Cassius gestured forward and they advanced into the valley.

It was impossible to find anything like a direct route. The paths meandered around the rock towers, regularly crossed each other and occasionally petered out. The Syrians performed an abbreviated version of their ceremony and soon the sun had disappeared, leaving only a few coloured rays above. Every little noise seemed magnified by the huge slabs of rock. Cassius saw ashes where small fires had been lit and some painted markings – mostly crude pictures of animals and hunters. The party also startled carrion feeding on the remains of a pony. Cassius covered his mouth and nose with a handkerchief and felt even worse when he saw the writhing maggots and insects feasting on the gore.

He already felt exhausted. The nature of the landscape made it impossible to know what they might find around the next corner and he could not forget the looks on the faces of the harried legionaries who had passed this way. Kammath kept up a good pace, however, and seldom looked back. Occasionally one of the Syrians would say a word and they would halt and examine their surroundings before moving on. Cassius didn't imagine they had ever been anywhere quite like this either.

As the last traces of sunlight vanished, he considered halting the party to prepare torches. But the combination of a half-moon, the pale sand of the paths and the height of the mountains ahead left Kammath able to still navigate his way. Lighting torches would take time and might draw unnecessary attention.

They had just passed between two of the wider towers when Kammath stopped once again.

Cassius walked forward. 'What is it?'

'I heard something.'

A whistle. Then another two notes from a different source. Someone was communicating.

'Keep going,' said Cassius.

They rounded a bend but soon halted again. Ahead was a group of larger towers with doorways and windows hewn out of the rock. Within, fires were alight. More whistles pierced the darkness.

'The village?' said Kammath.

'Not sure,' replied Cassius. If it was, he had seldom seen a settlement more unusual.

Kabir came forward. 'We can't stumble through here in the dark. They know we're here – isn't it best to show we're just passing through? Light torches?'

'You're right. Tell Simo too.'

While Kabir gave out the instructions, Cassius and Kammath watched the towers. Some of the doorways looked to be ten or twenty feet off the ground. More figures had appeared, several holding torches of their own and now moving down steps cut below the doorways. The whistles had been replaced by shouts.

Cassius watched one torch – and one man – in particular. He was the closest to them, about thirty yards away, and had stopped halfway down the steps. He was now standing still, waiting.

Cassius heard the familiar sound of a fire-striker hitting flint. If he was lucky, Simo could have a flame going within a couple of minutes. The Syrians were equally adept.

Kammath turned suddenly to his right.

'What is it?'

'I think there are people out there. Not many. But they're watching us too.'

'Probably after the horses. Or food.'

'Warning shot?'

'Not yet.'

Hearing the crackle of oil and goatskin, Cassius turned to find

Kabir approaching with a torch. Two more were alight behind him. Kammath took one.

'Quickly,' said Kabir. 'Let's show them our intent – that they've nothing to fear.'

Kammath held his torch out in front of him and continued onwards.

Soon they were approaching the tower where the man stood, still watching them. A boy was now beside him, holding the torch. The man didn't appear to be carrying a weapon.

As they passed beneath the tower, Kammath raised a hand in greeting.

Cassius spoke in Greek, trying to sound friendly. 'We mean no harm. We're heading for the pass.'

From inside the tower came a female voice. The man answered in what sounded like Aramaic.

Kammath spoke to him in the language but the man simply turned away and pointed at the doorway. He and the boy made their way up the steps and inside without turning round.

There were six more visibly occupied towers in front of them.

Cassius said, 'Keep moving.'

As they did so, he avoided looking at Kammath's torch, which would leave him almost blind. He spied glimpses of movement within the occupied towers and heard snatches of conversation.

When they passed the last of them and Kammath stopped, Kabir said, 'I've a feeling they have a very good reason for staying up high.'

'I'm sure,' replied Cassius. 'The people Chariton described would not have had enough wood to keep fires burning and torches lit. At least we can still see the peaks. The pass can't be more than two miles now.'

He didn't air the obvious thought that the worst was undoubtedly still ahead.

'Strange smell,' said Kabir.

Cassius hadn't noticed it but he pushed the flowers up towards his face and drew in a long breath through his nose.

'All right at the back?'

'They're fine,' replied Kabir, 'though Simo says the donkey is shivering.'

'I'm not surprised. Kammath, lead on.'

After another half an hour spent traversing the valley, aching eyes boring into the darkness, they reached what seemed to be the outskirts of Eskaril itself. The trail widened out. Walls and low dwellings appeared, built in the spaces between the rock formations.

Cassius had seen no trace of a light nor any movement but there were definitely people watching them from the dwellings. He could feel it.

Kammath suddenly moved to the right side of the path and approached a wall. He lifted the torch.

A lone man was standing on the other side, hand raised against the light. Slowly, he lowered it. Every inch of skin on his face was covered with blister-like pustules. They hung from his eyelids, nose and lips, as if part of his body. His ragged tunic hung from a skeletal frame. He opened his hand and muttered something.

'Keep going,' hissed Cassius.

He dragged Kammath away. Checking that the others were close behind, the two of them marched on through the village.

The sounds of movement increased. Shuffling feet. Whispers.

They stayed in the middle of the trail, unable to see more than five or six feet into the darkness. Cassius kept his hand on his sword hilt. As the route began to slope upwards, they passed another group of dwellings. He heard a woman wailing.

Idan shouted something from the back.

'Some are following,' said Kabir. 'He's asking whether to shoot at them or not.'

'Just at the ground,' said Cassius, 'just a warning.'

Ten paces later, he and Kammath had to stop.

A group of five or six villagers were on the road. Cassius was glad to see they were all women and all unarmed. Only one was not covered with the pox. She opened her hand and spoke in Greek.

'Food. Please. Food.'

The others repeated it; almost like a chant.

'Food. Please. Food.' They moved forward.

Cassius and Kammath retreated until they reached Kabir and the others. Covering his mouth with his hand, Cassius spoke over his shoulder. 'Simo, bring me something to give them.'

He had seen poor people before but the villagers were clearly starving. The women's breasts had withered along with their faces. They were hunched, bony, wretched creatures.

Simo had retrieved a loaf of bread and some cuts of meat. The eyes of the women widened.

'Put it there,' said Cassius, pointing to a wall.

Once the Gaul had done so, the women moved with remarkable speed. In moments they were fighting over the food.

'Quickly,' said Cassius.

They continued on, hearing cries and shouts from the darkness behind them. Cassius kept close to Kammath. The torchlight illuminated the beads of sweat upon the youth's face.

Jupiter, god of gods, I am a noble son of Rome. Please protect me.

Cassius could not help thinking of the starving women and the man's pox-ridden face. What of the little plague creatures Simo had spoken of? Surely the valley was alive with them? Surely they were besieging his body at this very moment?

But the next danger they faced was far more tangible. Faces and figures emerged out of the gloom ahead. The men were no less malnourished than the women but they spread out to blockade the road with purpose and organisation. Most were barefoot and clad in filthy tunics and robes. But each man had a long spear with an iron head. Cassius counted eight. Not one was covered with the pox.

A broad-shouldered man with a lank head of hair aimed the point of his spear at the interlopers. 'Food – what you have?'

Cassius glanced back; the others had arrived with the horses. All except Idan.

'You want to give them something?' asked Kabir quietly.

'Yes.'

'You think they'll leave it at that?'

'What do you suggest? There are eight of them.'

'More, actually.'

A second group of warriors had appeared behind the first, two holding torches. The leader was tapping the base of his spear upon the road.

Kabir relented and took a sack from one of the horse's saddles. He threw it at the feet of the leader, who picked it up and looked inside.

Now Cassius was even more concerned. It was clear there would be no in-fighting here. Though some of the others looked longingly at the bag, not one of them moved. This man was clearly in charge. He took out a handful of raisins and stuffed them in his mouth, then handed the bag to the man beside him.

'You look rich,' he said, pointing at Cassius. 'Pay silver. Tax here now.'

'No. This is a public road.'

'Was. Things different now.'

The horses were puffing and snorting.

'I can give you—'

'No.' Kabir put his hand on Cassius's arm. 'We need the money. I'm not giving it away for nothing.'

'Just tell me who you want me to drop,' said Kammath, hand hovering near his sling.

'This won't end well,' said Cassius.

'Not for them.' Kabir turned and spoke in some language Cassius had not heard; it certainly wasn't Aramaic. Idan's reply was brief. Kammath exchanged nods with his father.

'Kabir, what are you doing?' asked Cassius.

'Take the horses and run – to the right, there'll be a path.'

The leader jutted his spear at Kabir. 'You – what you say? Where silver?'

Just after he heard a familiar whirring sound from behind him, Cassius saw one of the warriors topple, his spear clattering to the ground beside him. Idan's sling whirred again. Another man staggered backwards, put a hand to his head then collapsed to his knees.

The locals descended into panic; some scattering, some shouting.

'Go now!' yelled Kabir. He and Kammath drew their long knives and charged at the remaining warriors.

'Simo, with me!'

Cassius snatched up the reins of one of the horses and made for the right side of the road, his path clear. He grabbed a torch dropped by one of the warriors and charged away up the slope.

XVI

With the noise of the horses pounding along, Cassius had no idea what was going on behind him. The road curved round a wall of rock and then began to descend. After about fifty paces he stopped, narrowly avoiding being knocked over by the first mount. There were four of them roped together and – unsurprisingly – they wanted to run on. Cassius tugged hard twice on the reins and brought the first one under control but the other three continued to range around, one whinnying as if in pain. While trying to calm them, he dropped the torch.

'Shit. Simo? Simo, are you there?'

He recovered the torch just before it went out. A few well-placed breaths rejuvenated the flames. Relieved, he gazed back along the road.

'Simo? Kabir? Stop pulling, damn you.'

He heard muttering close by then realised someone else had hold of the horses. He walked around the first mount and spied two youthful-looking figures hauling on the reins of the second. With both hands full, all he could do was wave the torch at them. Two more boys clambered over the wall and began to strip bags from the Syrians' saddles. Suddenly the second mount began to buck. The first animal veered away, ripping the reins out of Cassius's hands. Leaving the youths burrowing into the saddlebags, he walked back along the road.

'Simo? Simo?'

'Sir?'

The attendant sounded some distance away.

Cassius was about to break into a run when something hit his legs from the side. He fell, dropping the torch as he threw his arms out to protect himself.

Scrabbling fingers clawed at his left leg. He tried to crawl away but then a blow struck his flank. Judging by the chink of metal on metal it had been a blade; and his armour had saved him. Trying to ignore the jabbing pain caused by the blow, he kicked out with his left boot and connected, hearing his unseen foe grunt.

Cassius scrambled to his feet, backed across the road and drew his sword. The torch was picked up by a startlingly thin figure. The man wore only a loincloth. His skin was riddled with the pox.

By the gods. Jupiter, please spare me this fate.

In the man's other hand was a roughly made knife of wood and iron. As he advanced, similar figures appeared behind him. Two, four, five of them. One was holding a rock in his hand.

Cassius touched the low wall at the edge of the road. As they came closer, the diseased men caught sight of his sword. Without his money bag, it was the most valuable thing he had – enough to buy food for a year. Aside from the armour, it was the last thing he would give up.

Keeping the sword pointed at them, Cassius got his backside on to the wall, then twisted over it. His feet came down on a slope. As the ground gave way beneath him, he threw the sword down first for fear of cutting himself. He slid seven or eight yards on his rear before toppling forward and rolling to a halt at the bottom.

Other than the continuing ache from the first attack, he was not hurt. Still on his hands and knees, he looked up. Lit orange by the torchlight, the cadaverous faces peered over the wall then disappeared. Knowing he didn't have long, Cassius scrabbled around, fingers searching for the blade. They ran across dust, shale and pebbles; but not metal.

Until – 'Uh! Shit, just what I need.'

He'd cut his finger on the blade. Wiping it on the back of his tunic, he realised he could hear the men on the move. It seemed they had followed the road down to an easier descent and were closing in. Not far away was a very large shape, a boulder or some other formation. Cassius hurried towards it, hoping to hide.

The villagers appeared from his left, the skinny bastard holding the torch and jabbering to the others. Cassius halted and remained absolutely still. They passed within ten feet of him, not stopping until they reached the foot of the slope where he'd landed.

As they continued the search, Cassius retreated until he could feel the cold rock at his back. Still facing the men, he put one hand out behind him and felt his way into a fissure.

The villagers had gathered in one place and several were now examining the ground. They had found his tracks. The man with the torch led the way.

The fissure narrowed to a dead end after ten feet. Cassius put himself flat against the rock and held the blade behind him to obscure the reflective surface.

Gods, help me. They're coming.

This is exactly what he had feared: finding himself alone. Indavara would have seen these bloody peasants off with a single punch or sweep of his blade.

They reached the fissure. Cassius was grateful that they would at least only be able to attack one at a time. Perhaps if he took out the first man and extinguished the light, they might give up? He was better armed.

I can do this. Me or them. Me or them.

When he moved his feet back, Cassius realised the fissure did not end but continued low down. He turned and knelt and saw the lighter shade of open ground beyond. With the torchlight almost upon him, he set off. The gap was about a foot and a half high but with a leopard crawl he could move quickly enough.

Hearing shouting from behind him, he increased the pace, which was not easy with the heavy sword. The space lessened but just as he feared he would be trapped, he reached the other side of the formation and pulled himself clear.

Sheathing the sword, he looked up and to his right. The road seemed some distance above, the slope still too steep to climb. As the shouts of the villagers got closer, the light reappeared from around the giant rock. He ran, desperate to get away and rejoin the others.

The moonlight allowed him to see only dim silhouettes and

shapes. He met another low wall built at right angles to the road. Keeping a hand on it, he followed the structure to his left until he reached a path leading northwards, parallel to the road. He'd just started along it when he heard a cry from behind him.

Spinning round, he saw the torch on the move, no more than thirty feet away. He quickened his pace and came to a gap in the wall to the right. He entered what seemed to be a small compound with a building to the rear. He ducked down low behind the wall.

The villagers approached; their voices low and urgent, the torch crackling. Cassius watched and listened as some of them moved into the compound opposite. The man with a torch came towards him.

Still facing him but hunched over, Cassius backed away once more. As he neared the building, the man called another over to help him and they each advanced along one wall, unwittingly cornering their prey. Cassius retreated as far as the murky doorway of the building. He didn't want to trap himself but there was nowhere else to go.

He slid along the wall of uneven rock then ducked inside. The smell hit him immediately. And the air was very warm, as if –

His foot landed on something soft. Whatever it was wriggled away and screamed.

The man with the torch shouted and ran at him. Cassius tripped on a moving body and fell. In seconds, the dwelling was alive with fast-moving and hysterical children. Some ran for the doorway, where they met the warrior trying to come in. Others ran into Cassius or past him. They were screaming and yelling and sobbing.

Spotting a pale square behind him, Cassius forced his way through, knocking small bodies aside. The window was at a good height and just about wide enough – but there was a wooden grille blocking his way.

Trying to ignore the tumult behind him, Cassius drew his sword and drove the iron hilt into the grille. It buckled on the third blow and the fifth knocked it clean through.

The warrior was bellowing at the children.

With not even a glance backwards, Cassius chucked the sword out and clambered through the window until he was hanging from it. Levering his long frame out, he landed on his side. Just as he located and lifted his sword, he heard a panting pursuer come around the corner of the dwelling.

'Stay there! Stay back!'

The faceless figure did not.

Driven by fear of the disease as much as fear of injury, Cassius set his footing and swung the sword at his assailant. He must have hit a hand or an arm because a shriek went up.

Cassius climbed over the rear wall of the compound and sprinted away. To his right was the road but the slope was still too steep to climb. He could not risk trapping himself again.

'Cassius!'

'Master Cassius, where are you?'

'Cassius!'

They were close but he dared not shout out.

Cassius used the wall to guide him until he reached a sloping path that ran up to the road. He spied Simo and the Syrians, all on horseback. Two of them were clutching torches as they galloped north. Behind them was a noisy mass of villagers.

He had just opened his mouth to shout to his friends when he saw two men dead ahead, silhouetted against the sky. They were standing where the path met the road. They were holding narrow weapons, which they drew back as the interlopers came near. Spears.

You or them. Us or them.

Though his calves were burning, Cassius ran up the slope.

They heard him at the last moment but by then the heavy sword was already arcing through the air. The blade sunk deep into the first man's shoulder. Strangely, he did not make a sound and somehow stayed on his feet. While Cassius tried to pull the blade free, the second man twisted around and brought his spear to bear.

Cassius threw himself backwards, hauling the blade free.

Hearing the warrior's grunt as he drove with the spear, Cassius crouched low and swept up as Indavara had taught him, knowing that gave him the best chance of hitting the shaft. The steel sliced through the wood with ease.

Stunned that this had actually worked, he wasn't ready for the swing of the broken shaft that caught his arm above the elbow. The armour absorbed the worst of the blow but he staggered down the slope.

He glimpsed Simo and the others reining in.

'I'm here!'

Keeping his sword up in front of him, Cassius somehow parried the next sweep. 'Here! Help!'

He didn't really follow exactly what happened next. One or more of the Syrians dismounted at speed. A blade flashed in the moonlight then the villager was on the ground, choking.

'Quickly,' ordered Kabir, who was still on his horse. Cassius realised it was Idan who had saved him. The veteran sprang back up on to his mount.

'Here, sir.' Simo was just behind them, towing Cassius's horse.

'Quick!' yelled Kammath.

As Cassius sheathed his sword – not easy with trembling fingers – Kammath twisted around and plucked his sling from his belt. A single whirl of the weapon sent a shot into the pursuing villagers.

Cassius hauled himself up on to his saddle and grabbed the reins that Simo threw to him. 'I'm on. Go!'

With Yablus and Kammath covering them, Cassius and Simo urged their horses away. Ahead, Kabir and Idan rode side by side, keeping the mounts at a canter even though they could see little ahead. Normally tetchy when riding into darkness, the horses were in fact more concerned about the mob chasing them and Cassius had to stop his breaking into a gallop. Kabir gave a cry and pointed to the side of the road. Riding without his hands, Idan whipped another shot away, sending pale figures diving for cover. Kabir continued his shouts and Cassius and the others joined in, hoping that the loud charge would dissuade anyone else from blocking their path.

The road began to steepen as it left the valley and neared the pass. It also narrowed, twisting and turning around outcrops of rock. The glimpses of buildings and villagers lessened and by the time Kabir halted, Cassius guessed they were at least a mile from where he had rejoined the others, several hundred feet above Eskaril.

As the riders slumped upon their mounts, the horses snorted and whinnied. Cassius looked down at the valley. He could just make out the line of the road and some of the rock towers to the south.

'Sir, are you all right?'

In normal circumstances, Cassius would have been thinking about one of his few forays into combat. It had been more successful than most.

'All right? I got stuck in the middle of that cesspit – almost trapped in some hovel. Gods, I was amongst them. I can feel the plague upon me.'

'Are you injured?' asked Kabir.

'No,' said Cassius. 'Not by a weapon at least. What happened? You were supposed to be with me, Simo!'

'My apologies, sir,' replied the Gaul breathlessly. 'My path was blocked.'

'I hadn't thought there could be so many,' said Kabir. 'We almost didn't get through.'

'By the gods, I feel as if I have seen Hades. Those creatures down there are like something from a nightmare.'

'Yablus?' Kammath dismounted and walked over to his cousin, who gave up his torch and seemed barely able to stay in the saddle. Kammath moved the light so that he could he see Yablus's arm. Just below the elbow was a bloody cut.

'It's not bad,' said the youth. 'At least we got all the horses out.'

'And Patch,' breathed Simo.

Kabir spoke to his son and Kammath hurried over to him. When the chief bent over, they could all see he'd been injured too – struck in the side of the head. Idan went to inspect the wound.

'I can stitch that,' said Simo.

'I think it was the back end of a spear,' said Kabir. 'We were lucky.'

'Speak for yourself.'

Cassius slid to the ground and gave his reins to Simo. As he passed Patch, he put a hand on the donkey's neck. The beast shied away at first but, as usual, relented when his ears were stroked. Cassius continued a few yards down the slope but could neither see nor hear any sign they were being pursued.

He closed his eyes, clasped his hands together and looked to the skies.

To all the great and honoured gods, protect me from this pestilence. In return I offer a life of devotion and worship. Please protect me. I beg you, please protect me.

They continued on foot. After about a mile the path levelled out and entered the pass, which was at no point wider than a hundred feet. There was little vegetation here and the only trace of any wildlife was the occasional distant howl of a wolf. This did little for the state of the unsettled horses, who were already struggling on the uneven, unforgiving ground. With Kabir and Yablus's wounds still bleeding, they stopped at what Cassius estimated to be the fifth hour of night. According to what they had been told by Regulus and Chariton, they would still have enough time to reach the salt mine the following day.

Gathered in a hollow that would provide some protection should it rain, each of the four Syrians did their bit. Once the horses were unloaded, Kammath and Yablus tethered them and took out water and feed. Idan began work on a fire while Kabir – though clearly exhausted – retrieved blankets and food from their packs.

Simo was instantly commandeered by his master. Despite the cold, Cassius stripped off completely and told the Gaul to wash him. Cassius did not consider it a waste of water and he instructed the Gaul to use plenty of soap and scrub his skin and hair well. At the same time, he drank as much strong wine as he could stomach. He paid little attention to the cut on his hand nor the bruising and laceration where the blade's blow had sunk the mail into his skin.

While Simo dried him off, Kammath returned from dealing with the horses. 'None of that will make any difference. Your god will spare you the pestilence if you have led a pious life.'

'Then I should be fine,' replied Cassius, sloshing down more wine.

'Sir, are you sure you should be drinking all that?' said Simo as he rubbed his master's hair.

'I intend to make myself sick – so I can purge myself of the corruption. Good idea, isn't it?'

'Perhaps, sir. Though you might also make yourself weak.'

'I was *amongst* them, Simo. In a dwelling. Gods, I've got no chance.'

'But some of them didn't have it,' said Kabir as he settled down in front of the fire. 'You'll be all right.'

'Three days,' said Cassius. 'If I'm still healthy after three days, I'm clear.'

'I shall pray for you, sir.'

'Simo, for once I shall accept your offer.'

With not a single care for what any of the others thought, Cassius continued to drink – the strongest wine they had, which Simo kept for medicinal purposes. He kept up the rate with such commitment that within half an hour he was standing alone in the dark, spewing into the rock face. He was not unused to throwing up after drinking and he found the empty feeling almost reassuring. He felt he had done what he could to save himself, though there was one more measure to employ.

With Idan standing guard (a hundred yards away to give them adequate warning), Simo was now stitching Kabir's head. Kammath was holding a lantern close by.

'Where are those flowers?' asked Cassius.

'In my medical box, sir.'

Cassius found the box but not the flowers. 'Where?'

'In the little leather bag, sir.'

'There are *several* little leather bags.'

'He's busy,' snapped Kammath.

'Calm yourself, young man,' replied Cassius. 'He can stitch with his eyes closed. Simo, you can find the flowers for me later.'

'Is there any of that wine left?' asked Kammath. 'These two need some.'

'Of course. I saved a bit.' Having located the right bag, Cassius passed the skin to Yablus, who thanked him. He then pulled a cloak over his shoulders and moved himself and his blankets closer to the fire.

Kammath pointed at Cassius's sword, which was lying next to the sheath and belt. 'You actually bloodied it.'

In any other circumstance, Cassius would have been thinking of little else. 'Indeed.'

'I struck down three of the enemy,' added the youth.

His father said something stern in Aramaic.

'If you wish for a contest it will be very short-lived,' said Cassius. 'You are without doubt the superior warrior. Congratulations on your victory.'

'I meant no offence,' said Kammath. 'But I am curious about how a man can become a centurion without being . . . a warrior.'

Kabir barked a reprimand at his son.

Simo tutted. 'Excuse me, I am trying to stitch your head back together.'

'Sorry.'

'Don't worry, Kabir,' said Cassius, 'I like to see curiosity in the young. As it happens, I was directly commissioned as an officer, which is unusual other than in times of great need – such as in the first year of the Emperor's reign. As to how I've retained my rank, I suppose it's because I have been able to solve certain problems.'

Kammath nodded.

Cassius looked down at the sword: the blood had dried in black trickles. He shivered as he thought of those moments facing the villagers. He was glad he'd at least remembered some of what Indavara had taught him. He was also relieved that the guilt was yet to strike; perhaps because the men had been about to attack his friends.

Suddenly hungry, he turned and rummaged through a saddlebag until he found a hunk of bread.

Once finished with his stitching, Simo cleaned up Kabir's head, though much of the silvery hair remained discoloured. The Syrian refused the offer of a bandage and held the lantern while Simo cleaned his needle and threaded a new length of catgut.

Cassius washed down his bread with more wine (watered this time). 'Tell me, Kammath, how is *your* problem-solving?'

'What do you mean?'

'Well, what about mathematics – eleven times twelve?'

Kammath paused.

Cassius said, 'I'd offer you an abacus but we don't appear to have one handy.' He noted Kabir's grin.

'One hundred and thirty two.'

'Well done. You got there in the end.'

'All my children know their numbers,' said Kabir.

'And eight multiplied by six multiplied by six?'

Kammath shut his eyes to concentrate.

'It was never his strength, however,' added Kabir.

'Two hundred and eighty-eight,' replied Yablus, happily looking on as Simo put the first stitch into his arm.

'Correct.'

Kammath shot his cousin a glare then turned back to Cassius. 'And what about you? What's six times three times seven times . . . nine?'

'Er . . . one thousand, one hundred and thirty-four.'

The youth snorted. 'That can't be . . . how can you . . . '

Cassius feigned a yawn. 'I think I might retire to bed – hopefully you'll have worked out if it's correct by morning.'

'Is it right?' asked Yablus.

'Inevitably,' said Simo. 'There's no point trying to confound Master Cassius with matters mathematical. I've tried enough times, believe me.'

In fact, it was usually Cassius that pressed Simo to present him with a challenging calculation.

Kabir was the first to break the silence that ensued. 'It is right. Very impressive, Cassius.'

'If you wish, we could move on to rhetoric, or history, or geography. Tell me, Kammath – do you know the five biggest cities in the world?'

'Do you know how to find water in the desert?' countered Kammath. 'How to string a bow? How to pull a newborn out of a mare?'

'The bow – yes. The others – I must confess I do not. It would probably be best if we consider the contest a draw. Agreed?'

Kammath's stony expression finally softened. 'Agreed.'

Cassius put down the wine and moved his hands closer to the fire; he'd got cold while being washed and still hadn't warmed up. No one spoke for some time and it seemed to him that thoughts of what they'd been through and what they might yet face occupied every man. The previous exchange already seemed ridiculous.

'I feel sorry for them,' said Yablus.

'I too,' said Simo, without taking his eyes off his work.

'You said there were children?' asked Yablus.

'Yes,' said Cassius. 'Well, at least we gave them food – that's more than most would have done. Not that it did us any good.'

'They are desperate,' said Simo.

'You did well.' Kabir had spoken to the Gaul but then turned to Cassius. 'Gave a few of them a crack with that stave. Helped us get through.'

'Is that right?'

'Just enough to . . . dissuade them,' said the attendant quietly. 'I don't think I really hurt anyone.'

'Simo's people believe that violence is a sin,' explained Cassius, knowing the young Syrians had only a passing knowledge of Christianity. 'He will pray for forgiveness now.'

'Your Christ always advocated peace,' said Kabir.

Simo had paused his work, the needle still in his hand. 'Yes.'

'A noble idea,' said Kabir, 'and a lofty goal. But man will always do harm to man. Man will always fight.'

Yablus and Kammath clearly agreed.

'We can strive to lead a good life,' said Simo. 'But we are all imperfect. Sometimes we will fail.'

'You did not fail,' said Kabir. 'You did what you had to. We wish to help our girls, you wish to help your friend. Our god knows that. And so must yours.'

XVII

It was a different kind of fear. Cassius knew the symptoms of the plague well: vomiting, headache, chills, pain in the stomach and back. Though the first one was self-inflicted, he reckoned he had them all. And having hardly slept, he did nothing to help as they packed up and got under way.

Once upon the flank of the mountain, the northerly trail twisted down through barren slopes of boulders and scree. Below they could see the area of marshland, beyond that a remarkable sight: the Tuz salt flats stretched away into the distance, an expanse of white nothingness resembling a vast field covered by snow. The Syrians stopped when they reached a convenient viewpoint.

'See there, sir?' said Simo, who was facing west.

Cassius – the only one on his horse – followed the line of the attendant's arm and spied a cluster of buildings close to the edge of the flats. At that range, it was difficult to estimate their size.

'That must be Draco's mine,' he said. 'Regalus said the others are much further north.'

'Strange to think of a mine that doesn't go underground,' remarked Simo.

The Syrians continued down the trail.

'I'm very cold. Unusually cold.'

'Another layer, sir?'

'No.' Cassius was already wearing an undershirt, a tunic and his warmest cloak, not to mention his thickest pair of socks.

'It is very early, sir. And the air is damp.'

'But my stomach.'

'You ate hardly anything at breakfast, sir.'

'And my back?'

'There is bruising. Probably from when you fell down that slope.'

'Possibly. As soon as we stop later, you will take out the box.'

'Yes, sir.'

Within were Cassius's twelve figurines of the great gods. He had never felt such a desperate urge to pray.

By the middle of the morning they were in the middle of the marsh. Half the ground was made up of low, circular mounds of turf; the rest was bog. Though muddy and wet, the trail remained clear to see and had bent around to the east some time ago.

Cassius would have continued along it but the Syrians had spotted very fresh tracks clearly belonging to a group of some size. No one had passed them so it seemed unlikely they were from the village. The swiftly reached consensus was that they didn't wish to risk another fight, having been lucky to escape the last. There was no definitive evidence of danger but about a mile ahead the trail moved into a wooded area from which birds had suddenly flown up twice. The Syrians seemed sure there were people in there and had identified an alternative route; they could head straight for the salt flats.

'I concur. The edge is only – what – three miles?' Cassius still had a headache but felt a little better for some dried pork and a mug of wine. 'No danger of ambush and the ground's not too bad.'

'It's not too bad *here*,' said Kammath. 'Might get worse.'

'Let's try it,' said Cassius after another wary glance at the woodland. 'We can always turn back.'

'Agreed,' said Kabir.

Knowing his horse could do without the extra weight, Cassius dismounted and followed the nomads. Idan led the way and did a good job of using the grassy mounds where possible and avoiding the worst of the mud. On several occasions, large flocks of long, leggy birds flew overhead. No one was sure of the species.

Moving directly north became more difficult as they encountered increasingly wide bogs. These were shallow but the mud was so clinging and thick that the horses' hooves often got stuck. Idan continued to find ways round them but their path became so circuitous that after an hour they were perhaps only a third of the way to the flats.

As they stopped yet again, Cassius slapped at an insect that had just landed on his arm. 'A night in a village of the diseased and now stuck in a marsh – I'll be lucky to survive the week.'

Kammath turned round. 'You're lucky we're letting you stay so close. If you are diseased, you might pass it on.'

Cassius might have snapped back at him were it not for the fact that he was feeling better. Concentrating on negotiating the marsh had distracted him from his symptoms, which he had begun to suspect were at least partly imaginary.

'If I do, I'll make sure I give it to you first.'

'Is that a house?'

Cassius turned. Simo was staring at an angular shape about a half-mile to the east, close to one of the few trees.

'I believe it is. Funny old place to live.'

Ahead of him, the Syrians were on the move again.

Cassius looked down at his boots and socks, every inch of which was now slick with grey mud.

Soon the party were doing little other than taking increasingly slow steps and emitting a steady stream of curses in a variety of languages. Every man had fallen at least once, Patch had twice required rescuing, and they didn't appear to be more than halfway towards their goal. The Syrians had been arguing in Aramaic but had now given up even that.

They were so intent on finding the next half-solid piece of ground that they didn't notice the interloper until she was close. Cassius first caught sight of her when Yablus suddenly stopped and looked towards the house. Walking in their direction at some speed was a girl of about ten. As she approached, Cassius realised she had devices strapped to her feet to help her traverse the marsh. The 'shoes' turned out to be flat rectangles of wicker about eight inches wide and twice as long.

'Stay there,' said Cassius, holding up a hand when she was twenty feet away.

'She's probably got more to fear from you,' muttered Kammath.

The girl was quite well dressed, wearing a clean tunic and wrappings to protect her legs. Her face was pretty and untouched by the pox. She said a few words in something that sounded like Aramaic.

Yet Kabir and the others didn't seem to understand.

The girl pointed towards the salt flats.

'Is she offering to help?' asked Cassius.

'I think so,' said Kabir, before trying once again to communicate. It soon became clear that the girl's help was not unconditional.

Cassius had Simo take out a denarius and throw it to her. The girl could barely contain her glee. She walked past them, heading parallel to the edge of the flats and waved for them to follow.

Cassius looked at Simo. 'This is turning into a very strange day.'

Their diminutive guide led them westward for some time before turning north. She clearly knew the area exceptionally well and, though it was impossible to avoid all the bogs, they reached the flats in under an hour. The girl promptly sat down, removed her strange footwear, then sprinted away barefoot across the flats towards her home.

As the others began to remove their boots for cleaning, Cassius examined his new surroundings. The glazed surface of the flats was actually a very pale grey and striped by narrow channels. About a hundred yards away was another flock of the slender birds. They seemed pink in colour and had extremely long necks. Their legs were so thin that they appeared to be floating in the air.

'Are those flamingos?'

'Perhaps, sir,' replied Simo, who had located a brush and was now removing mud from the horses' legs and hooves.

'We call them something else,' said Kabir as he took off his sandals. 'But yes.'

'They are considered a delicacy,' said Cassius. 'Especially the tongues.'

'Want one for lunch? Yablus tapped his sling.

Cassius smiled and realised he really was feeling better. Doubt swiftly followed and he warned himself against over-confidence. He helped Simo by cleaning the worst of the mud off Patch with a stick.

'Your boots, sir?'

'Don't worry – most of it will fall off when it's dry. Kabir, how far would you say?'

The buildings were not difficult to see; they were dark against the flats and the green of the marsh.

'Five or six miles.' Having watered their horses, the indefatigable nomads set off.

Though he would have preferred to ride, Cassius could see his horse was exhausted. He waited for Simo to hang the water bowl from his saddle and give a carrot to each mount. Master and servant walked along side by side.

Before reaching the buildings, they passed three men armed with bows; each on his own and facing south. Cassius addressed them, identifying himself as an army officer in his most distinguished tones. The sentries cast some suspicious looks at the Syrians but one disclosed that their task was solely to deter the diseased villagers.

The salt miners at work on the flats appeared almost as wretched as the inhabitants of Eskaril. Some were clad only in loincloths, others in thin, filthy tunics. All were barefoot, their skin leathery and parched from exposure. Many had sores upon their flesh and most looked only a meal or two from starvation.

Watched by overseers armed with whips, the first group they encountered were labouring inside a large rectangle marked out with twine. Many were simply walking across the brittle surface of the flats, apparently to break it up. The next step seemed to be the collection of the salt using chisels and elongated rakes. It was then collated in piles that were scooped into wooden pans and loaded on to carts. The only time one of the overseers spoke to them was when they passed close to the third gang of workers. He felt they were causing a distraction and told them in no uncertain terms to move along.

By the time they approached the largest of the buildings – an immense timber warehouse – they had seen no less than five gangs, each with at least a hundred labourers. There were more groups at work in the distance too, leading Cassius to estimate that Draco had acquired at least one thousand prisoners. There were at least a hundred guards.

An older man watched the strangers from the warehouse for a time then strode towards them. He had the look of an ex-soldier: sturdy legs and a broad body running to fat. Like his compatriots, he was armed with a dagger and a whip.

'Good day,' said Cassius cordially.

'Do you have permission to be on this property?'

'Who would I obtain that from?'

'Me. Or Master Draco.'

'Well then, I request permission. My name is Corbulo; I am an officer of the Imperial Army.'

'You've come from the south? Through the pass?'

'Yes but we moved quickly. We are all in good health.'

'You'd better be.'

Cassius showed the man the Marcellinus letter, though he wasn't entirely sure the thug could read. This suspicion was confirmed by the change in the guard's expression when Cassius added, 'Protector of the East. The Emperor's deputy. I'm here on a matter of the utmost importance. There is a prisoner I need to speak to.'

The man looked past him at the Syrians.

'Might I ask your name?' said Cassius.

'Caepio. Chief of Guards.'

'You served in the army?'

'I did. What's a grain man doing with this lot for company?'

'They are why I'm here. The Service – and the Empire – owe them a debt. I'm here to ensure it's fulfilled.'

'You'll have to see Master Draco. Can't do nothing without his say so.'

Cassius looked to his left. Beyond two smaller warehouses and a stable was a wide trail that ran up a slope to a house overlooking the flats. The villa was the most expensive-looking building he had seen for weeks.

'I take it that's his residence?'

'It is. But he's not in. Went out hunting a couple of hours ago.'

'Any idea when he'll be back?'

'Depends if he bags anything. It'll be before dark.'

Cassius guessed it was at least the eighth hour.

Kabir came forward. 'We can talk to the prisoner now. His name's Meliton—'

Caepio kept his gaze on Cassius. 'Who am I talking to – you or him?'

'Me. We'll wait. But I have two requests. Firstly, will you tell Master Draco we're here as soon as he returns? Secondly, can you at least check if the man in question is present? Meliton arrived with the last column from Tarsus a couple of days ago.'

Caepio nodded and looked past him again. 'You can water your horses at the stable. Stay there – Master Draco don't like people going where they're not supposed to.' With that, the chief guard sniffed noisily and stalked away.

Cassius was not surprised by the expressions that greeted him when he turned round. Even Kabir and Yablus looked annoyed.

'So – what?' demanded Kammath. 'We just sit around?' He pointed at a gang transporting full pans of salt from a cart into the warehouse. 'He could be one of them. We could get what we need and be gone.'

'To where?' said Cassius. 'We don't even know the best route out of this place and the horses are exhausted.' He lowered his voice. 'This is Draco's domain and we are entirely dependent on his cooperation. So we will do it *his* way. Now, let's get a couple of hours' rest so that if we do get under way again we're not all dead on our feet.'

Not waiting for their assent, Cassius grabbed his horse's reins and led it towards the stable.

Once he and Simo had unburdened the horses, the attendant took them for watering. Cassius found a bit of shade below an overhanging roof and sat on a barrel close to the stable entrance. The setting was as bleak as his thoughts. There were operations such as this across the Empire (in fact the Service ran some of them) but it seemed to him a place of utter misery.

Though he knew that most of the men he could see would be murderers, rapists and thieves, it was never anything less than pitiful to see people without hope. And – just like the villagers on the other side of the mountains – these men surely didn't have much. From the looks of it, they were given barely enough sustenance to survive and the overseers were as relentless as they were cruel. In the time he sat there, Cassius saw several men stumble or drop their load, only to be struck with a whip. The prisoners didn't seem to even raise their heads or communicate. Every one of them seemed broken by the grinding effort.

Cassius did not want to endure the wait with the Syrians. Their sense of anticipation and frustration had reached its peak; they were desperate to discover the fate of Aikaterine and – assuming they had the right man – that moment was close. But what if he didn't know where the buyer had taken her? What if *this* was the end?'

The thought of it sent a chill down Cassius's spine. He reassured himself with the same notion he'd explained to Kabir: the girls were valuable only if they were kept in good condition. And surely the gods – any gods – could not leave three such innocents to this fate?

Drawing lines with his fingers in the pale dust, Cassius scoffed at his own naive optimism.

The good and the worthy suffered and died every day. He had seen it more times than he could count.

XVIII

When Caepio came to confirm that Meliton was indeed present and that his employer had returned, Cassius had a difficult job of convincing Kabir that he should speak to Draco alone. The Syrian eventually relented but – as he walked up the trail to the villa with the chief guard – Cassius knew it would be even harder to keep Kabir and the others away from Meliton.

Caepio was quite full of himself. He seemed proud of his position and – judging by the way he avoided further mention of his army career – Cassius guessed he might have been prematurely dismissed. The chief guard also seemed to like numbers. He merrily informed Cassius that the area of the salt pans owned by Draco ran to a hundred square miles and produced at least four thousand carts' worth a year. Despite the difficulties caused by the plague outbreak, profits were only down ten per cent. They currently had nine hundred and thirty labourers employed on the site, each of whom worked solidly for eleven hours a day. With the autumn now upon them, the race was on to extract as much salt as possible before heavy rain ruined the yield. Apparently, Draco planned to divert much of the labour to improving his villa during the quieter winter months.

When Cassius asked him about the villagers and the brigands, Caepio boasted about an attack he had led after raids upon their food store and the valuable salt. They had captured three local men and chopped their heads off, leaving them nailed to trees to deter any further attacks. The measure had worked well.

As they neared the villa, Cassius saw more evidence of such methods. Upon a plateau of rock, which would be visible to the workers, was a cross. Nailed to it were the decaying remains of a man. Two crows where nipping what they could from the many hollows in the ruined body.

'Can't remember the name,' said Caepio. 'He tried running off across the flats one night. Ignorant bastard thought he was going to reach the other side. We found him about six miles away – feet cut to ribbons.'

'Presumably that wasn't punishment enough?'

'We haven't had any runaways since.'

Though indeed very large, the villa was rather less impressive up close. Despite the colossal columns, bronze door and marble flooring, much of the building seemed unfinished. As he and Caepio waited in the atrium, Cassius observed four artisans: two were plotting out a mosaic on one wall, two on high ladders were making adjustments to a glassed skylight. On the way in, Cassius had passed what was obviously supposed to be a garden, but the plants seemed neglected and even the turf was patchy. Caepio explained that it was due to the dusty soil; his master was planning to bring in some experts the following year.

'There she is,' said Caepio seedily as a tall woman entered the atrium. She was wearing a flowing, pink stola and a fine pair of velvet shoes. Her hair was decorated with a headdress of pearls, which Cassius adjudged excessive for a woman in middle age but he had to concede that the overall effect was pleasing. She, however, seemed displeased by the presence of Caepio, and perplexed by the presence of a guest.

'Korinna,' said the chief guard. 'She runs Master Draco's household.'

'And who is this?' Korinna countered sharply.

'Officer Cassius Corbulo, Imperial Army. I need to see your master as soon as possible.'

'Master Draco is bathing. I shall, however, tell him you are here.' She clapped her hands together twice.

After a few moments, a woman of about twenty trotted out from the same doorway. She was clad similarly to Korinna, though her stola was pale green. Cassius felt sure he could see a family resemblance.

'Roxana will escort you to a waiting room.'

The new arrival gave a slight bow. 'Please follow me.'

As they traversed the atrium, Cassius looked back at Korinna and Caepio, who watched him and spoke quietly to one another. Turning his attention to his guide, Cassius's eyes dropped to the contours of her bottom moving beneath the smooth material. It seemed a long time since he'd been so close to an attractive woman.

Roxana led him along a corridor with unpainted walls to a room that seemed in a better state than most of the others. Three plush couches had been arranged around a glass-topped table. Roxana hurried over to the long, low window and opened the shutters.

'Please take a seat, sir. Can I fetch you any refreshments?'

'Just wine, please.'

'Of course.' Though her eyebrows needed some work, the girl was really quite pretty. Despite the reason for his presence, Cassius couldn't entirely curtail his normal instincts.

'Is Korinna your mother?'

'Yes, sir.'

'Must be a bit lonely for you – working here.'

'I have two sisters here also. We ensure Master Draco is well taken care of. And his guests, of course.'

'I'm sure you do.'

'I won't be a moment.' With another neat bow, Roxana went on her way.

Cassius walked over to the window. As an afterthought, he took his money bag from his belt and concealed it inside his tunic. He didn't want his purpose to be too obvious and he would first endeavour to win Draco's cooperation without recourse to bribery. What he had observed so far was informative but without some measure of the man, he was not yet sure how to proceed.

Thankfully, he couldn't see the crucified worker from the window. He could, however, see most of the buildings below;

the carts on the move and the men at work. From this high position, he could also just make out the higher ground at the edge of the salt flats to the east. To the north, however, the featureless expanse of white seemed to go on forever.

Draco kept him waiting. Roxana returned to refill his silver goblet but wouldn't be drawn beyond pleasantries and left as soon as she could. Cassius paced around and eventually settled on one of the felt-lined couches. He looked at the collection of well-polished vases on the table; most were silver and of Greek extraction. In each corner of the room was a different kind of lamp-holder. One in particular caught his eye: it was five feet high, constructed of pink marble carved into excellent renderings of swans, goats' heads and griffins.

Alone with his thoughts once again, Cassius thanked the gods that none of the plague symptoms had reappeared.

He heard Draco before he saw him. Issuing orders in Greek to both his staff and the artisans, the mine owner entered the lounge at pace. Cassius had expected a degree of vulgarity but he found it difficult to hide his reaction at the sight of his host.

Draco was barefoot and clad only in a yellow silken tunic that left little to the imagination around the groin area. His thick, shoulder-length hair had been streaked with some sort of blond dye. His face was that of a peasant: heavy brow, broad nose and fleshy lips. Cassius detested him instantly.

He offered his hand. 'Master Draco, good day to you. I thank you for welcoming me into your home.'

'You will excuse me if I don't shake hands – sure you understand given the present circumstances. And you are?'

'Officer Corbulo.'

'That's it. You will have to excuse all the work going on. It is endless! Let's sit.'

'How was your hunt?' said Cassius, taking a seat opposite his host.

'Not bad. A couple of small deer. There's not much of any size around here – bloody locals have had most of it. I sometimes think I should start hunting *them* – do everyone a favour.'

Cassius couldn't think of a reply to that.

'"Officer",' said Draco thoughtfully. 'Like a centurion.'

'My rank is considered equal.' Cassius had left his satchel on the couch. He took out Marcellinus's letter, rounded the table and handed it to Draco.

'My credentials. This is from the marshal himself.'

Draco glanced at it briefly then handed it back. 'Very nice.'

Somewhat perplexed by this response, Cassius returned the letter to the satchel and sat again.

'You have wine?' asked Draco.

'I do.' Cassius gestured to his goblet.

'So which legion are you with?'

'I'm not. Imperial Security is a separate organisation within the army.'

'I think I've heard of it.'

'We deal with all manner of issues. In this case, I am operating on behalf of my travelling companions, who are valued allies of Rome. May I explain why I am here?'

Draco bellowed to Roxana to hurry up with his wine then smiled. 'Please.'

Cassius briefly detailed the abduction and ensuing events. Draco seemed to listen without being particularly interested. While Cassius iterated the distress of the missing girls' relatives, Draco nodded earnestly. As Roxana handed him his wine, he pinched her thigh. The leer remained on his face even after the girl had left. He tried to look interested again as Cassius concluded.

'I see. So you wish to . . . ?'

'Question him – Meliton.'

'You can have him.'

'You wouldn't object to that?'

'Not at all. I know the army pays its due. I'm not in the habit of selling workers but each is worth about six hundred denarii. As I'm in a good mood, let's say five.'

'I can't do that,' said Cassius. 'Apart from the fact that I don't have the money, Meliton was sent here by an imperial court.'

Draco grinned, showing a mouth stained red with wine. It was un-watered and had left Cassius feeling slightly groggy.

'You think they care? You think they'll send someone to check on him? My labourers are here to be worked to death. Surely a man with a marshal as a patron can afford a measly five hundred. Tell you what, let's call it four and a half.'

'We have been travelling for weeks to track this man down. We don't actually need him; just what he knows.'

'Ah. Well, I'm sure we can accommodate you. You wouldn't need very long?'

'Hopefully not. Assuming he can give us what we need, we will aim to leave immediately.'

'You mentioned that others you have encountered were not keen on giving up information. What makes you think he will be?'

'As a condemned man, he has little to lose.'

Cassius knew from experience that this might not be true; he just wanted Draco to let him carry out the interrogation.

'Perhaps.'

After a pause in the conversation, Draco reached down into his tunic and pulled out an amulet on a gold chain. It was shaped like a drop of water and appeared to be made of carnelian. It was hollow and half full of something.

'Do you like it?'

'Very . . . unusual.'

'I had it made. That's salt inside – to remind me to what I owe my fortune. Without those little white granules I would still be a poor man.'

Not to mention the endless, back-breaking labour carried out by your slaves.

'Ah.'

Draco glanced down at the amulet, then looked out of the window. 'You disapprove of me.'

Startled, Cassius straightened and instantly shook his head. 'Not at all. What made you—'

'It is difficult for men of your class to hide your contempt. I would guess from your accent and bearing that your family have been at the top of the tree for many centuries.'

'Master Draco, if I have—'

'Am I right?'

'Well, my family are not . . . exceptional. We come from Ravenna. My father was a military man. Now he has several business interests.'

'But in the *right* businesses, I expect. Not a filthy trade like this.'

'Sir, I know for a fact that the courts of Tarsus are grateful for what you are doing here. And I am grateful for your cooperation. I mean that.'

Draco rubbed a finger across his thick lower lip. 'You seem to me more like a tribune than a centurion. I have had my fair share of dealings with tribunes and prefects and governors. I grew very tired of the looks on their faces when they spoke to me. I think perhaps that might be why I stay out here. I'd wager I'm worth a good deal more than your father though.'

Cassius stood. 'If I have offended you, I am sorry.'

'I'll give you half an hour with this man. My guards will ensure no harm comes to him. He is of no use to me if he cannot work.' With that, Draco picked up his goblet and drank. He then stood and walked towards the window. 'I'm sure you can find your own way out.'

XIX

Once back at the stable, Cassius took Kabir aside. He'd admonished himself for the slip that had soured the meeting but saw no reason to tell the Syrian. 'We're getting only half an hour. The guards will be there to make sure we don't hurt Meliton.'

'What if he won't give us the information?'

'Then we grab him. Either now or later, perhaps when it's dark.'

'Come back, find him and escape? At night?'

'I know. So now it is – but only if we've no choice.'

'Where is he?'

'Not sure. A messenger came past me on the way down so I expect Caepio's getting his orders and he'll take me to wherever Meliton's working. Judging by his employer's attitude, you won't be allowed to accompany me. If Meliton doesn't cooperate I'll give a signal. We'll have to hit hard and fast.'

'Not a problem,' said Kabir.

'And if they follow?'

'Leave it to us. Ah, looks likes you were right.'

Cassius turned around.

Caepio – accompanied by four guards – was marching towards the stable.

The quartet had clearly been selected with intimidation in mind and boasted an impressive selection of scars. Like Caepio, each man had a dagger and whip upon his belt.

As they walked north to where Meliton was working, Cassius forced himself not to look at the scrubland to his left. Idan and

Yablus had succeeded in not being seen but he hoped they had also kept up. Kabir and Simo, meanwhile, had gathered the horses and were ready to move. Kammath was in place to disrupt any mounted pursuit.

When they reached the gang, the overseer in charge bellowed at his charges to keep their eyes down and keep working. Caepio spoke to him briefly, then approached a man who was shovelling salt on to a pan. The labourer blew out his cheeks as he straightened up then glanced warily at the strangers. Caepio took him by the arm and escorted him past the other workers, leading his men and Cassius some distance away.

Due to his recent arrival, Meliton appeared rather better nourished than the others. Cassius was struck by how ordinary he seemed; a man of average height and build with a face that was neither handsome nor unattractive. His greying hair formed a 'V' upon his head, much of which had already reddened and blistered from exposure. His hands were in a similarly poor state.

'Be quick,' said Caepio, placing his hand on the thick handle of his whip.

Electing not to remind him that his master had stated 'half an hour', Cassius stepped forward. 'I have come a long way to find you. I am here with the father of a Syrian girl you purchased along with two others from a slave trader named Tychon. I want to know where they are.'

Meliton examined his bloodied fingers for a moment then shrugged. 'How would I know?'

'There's no point lying. You sold all the slaves in your possession before you were arrested in Tarsus. Who has the girls?'

Meliton frowned. 'Who are you?'

'An officer of the Imperial Army.' Cassius wished he had a sword on him but Caepio had insisted he not bring a single weapon. 'Who I am isn't important. All that matters is where those girls are. Who did you sell them to?'

Meliton looked back at his fellow prisoners, who had all obeyed their overseers' instructions to keep working. 'What are you going to do to me if I don't cooperate? Take me in for questioning? Put me back in prison? Please, I'd welcome it.'

'What do you have to lose?' demanded Cassius. 'You're stuck here either way. Just give me what I need to find these girls.' Even as he spoke, Cassius realised how ridiculous it was to appeal to the better nature of the man.

'Maybe I have something to *gain*,' said Meliton. 'You're in the army – what can you do to help me? Can you get me out of here?'

Caepio chuckled. 'What do you think, you cretin?'

Cassius had had about enough of this unfeeling bastard and others of his ilk. 'I'm not leaving here without the information I need.'

'I want something in return,' said Meliton, who seemed to be growing more confident by the minute.

'You admit you bought them and sold them on?'

'Which one was the daughter?' said Meliton slyly. 'Dinora, Marte or Aikaterine?'

Cassius felt his whole body tense.

'Steady there, officer,' said Caepio.

'Give me the name.'

'Give me a reason to. Get me out of this shithole.'

Cassius let out a long breath, then looked over his left shoulder and crouched down on one knee.

'What are you doing?' asked Caepio.

'Ducking.'

A moment later the first of the lead balls fizzed past. The second hit Caepio.

Face wracked with pain, the chief guard fell to one knee and cried out.

'You really want to get out of here?' said Cassius.

Meliton overcame his initial confusion with creditable speed. 'Yes.'

'Then follow me.' Cassius stood up and loped away across the flats, heading north.

'Hey!' One of the guards gave chase.

The shot caught him in the leg. He dropped like a stone, shrieking as he gripped his calf.

Having checked that Meliton was with him, Cassius looked to the east. Yablus and Idan had broken cover and already reached the flats. Simo and Kabir were riding away from the warehouse, the other horses in tow.

The panicked guards had scattered, some fleeing towards safety. They didn't seem to have noticed the Syrians. The prisoners simply stood there, watching their captors run.

Meliton tripped and came down hard on his front. Cassius helped him up and led him towards the edge of the flats where they were soon intercepted by Idan and Yablus. Idan reached into the bag of ammunition hanging from his belt and continued to fire at any of the guards that showed any sign of intervening. Yablus unsheathed his long knife and brandished it.

'Not going to give us any trouble, are you?'

Meliton shook his head.

When Kabir and Simo arrived, Cassius told the slave-trader to get on to Patch, then mounted up with the others.

'You go,' said Idan, turning his horse around using only his feet; sling ready for the next shot.

'Come,' said Kabir. 'He'll cover us.'

Before turning to the north, Cassius covered his eyes and looked at the stable. Dozens of horses were stampeding away. Only one had a rider on it.

After a couple of miles, Cassius stopped and wheeled around. Kammath was now alongside Idan and the pair were galloping across the flats, their mounts' hooves kicking up clods of salt. Earlier, Cassius had seen them turn backwards while riding and unleash shots at two guards who had staged a belated pursuit on foot. They had given up the chase some time ago.

Cassius took in the rather bizarre sight of Meliton sitting upon Patch. Even though Simo had spared the donkey the additional burden of saddlebags, the beast was unused to being ridden and was making quite a noise. Simo clearly wasn't happy about the situation either. Meliton was eyeing Kabir.

'What do you think?' said the Syrian, moving close to Cassius so that their captive couldn't hear. 'Will Draco send more after us?'

'If he looks at the situation sensibly – in terms of profit and loss – no. It's not worth risking his guards and disrupting work. If he takes it personally . . . '

Kabir commended the other three as they reined in.

'Those loose horses will keep them busy for a while,' said Kammath with a grin. 'I think I saw a couple of prisoners making a run for it too.'

Kabir pointed at a stand of trees twenty yards from the edge of the salt pan. 'Over there?'

Cassius directed Meliton. The slave-trader had little choice but to obey.

Once there, Cassius was first to dismount. The ground was relatively hard underfoot, with deposits of salt visible in the standing water. Cassius looped his reins around a branch and came up behind Meliton as he slid wearily off the donkey.

Cassius threw an arm round his neck, pulled him backwards then let go. Meliton tripped over a bush and landed on his back in a puddle.

As he tried to get up, Cassius drew his sword. When Meliton spied the gleaming tip of the long blade only a foot from his throat he stayed where he was.

The Syrians gathered around.

Cassius had acted swiftly for two reasons: firstly, to take some of the fire out of their anger; secondly, to control the interrogation.

'Give me that name.'

'Or what? You'll kill me?'

'No. I'll turn you over to these fellows. It will hurt a lot more than dying.'

'If I tell you, you'll let me go?'

'Yes. But you better be quick. We won't be leaving you the donkey.'

'All right. I've sold a few girls to him over the years. Only the prettiest. He pays well.'

'Name.'

'He never uses names – and he never shows his face. He'd send me a note when he was in Tarsus and we'd always meet up in a different place. He'd stay at the back – in the shadows. The girls would get undressed, talk a bit and he'd choose who he liked. He took all three of them.'

'When?'

'Like you said – just before I got arrested. I knew it wasn't safe to stay in Tarsus but I suppose I got greedy – wanted one last pay out.' Meliton moved his backside out of the puddle. 'Cost me everything.'

'That's it?' said Kabir.

'What else do you know?' hissed Kammath. 'We need more.'

'I don't know any more.'

Kammath stormed forward, wrenching his knife from the sheath.

Cassius made no attempt to stop him. He needed their anger now, to ensure the criminal really gave up all he knew.

Meliton threw up his hands just as the Syrian reached him. 'Wait! Listen, I know this other trader; he'd sold to this man before. He knew a little about him. No name but that he belonged to this group up in Byzantium – they own some villa where rich men can get the most beautiful girls from all over the Empire and do whatever they like to them.'

'Byzantium?' said Cassius. 'What else?'

'They have this nickname – because they do what they want and take what they want. They call themselves The Earthly Gods. I swear on my life that is all I know. That is everything.'

'Think carefully,' said Cassius. 'You never saw the man's face or heard a name or any other information?'

'He made sure of it. That's all I know, I swear.'

Cassius lowered the sword and turned away. He placed a hand on Kammath's shoulder. 'Watch him.'

The youth gave a grim nod.

'Byzantium?' said Kabir, rubbing his brow. 'Will this ever end?'

'At least we know.'

'How far?' asked Idan.

'No further than we've come.'

'How far?' demanded the nomad.

'About two hundred miles.'

Kabir rushed past him and stood over Meliton. 'What do they do to the girls? What do they do?'

Meliton retreated back into the puddle. 'Hey, officer – can I go now?'

Cassius turned round. 'You knowingly bought illegal slaves and sold them on. I don't know what my friends think but I reckon your present punishment just about fits your crime.'

'You said I could—'

Meliton dragged himself to his feet. He had taken only two steps when Kammath swept a crunching kick into his ankle, sending him on to his back once more.

Cassius said, 'I suppose we should make sure our friend here lacks the means to get away from the guards.'

Kabir glanced back at him as Cassius continued. 'Some damage to his legs, perhaps?'

The chief spat in the captive's face. Kammath put his foot on Meliton's chest. His father took out his blade and reversed the hilt, then knelt over the squirming figure. He hammered the hilt down on to his knee.

Meliton screamed.

Cassius told himself that he hadn't really allowed it – because he could not have stopped the Syrians. At least this way they wouldn't kill him; and they could take out their frustrations on a deserving target. Leaving Meliton behind might also dampen Draco's ire.

While Yablus and Idan looked on, Cassius walked over to Simo, who had taken Patch around to the other side of the trees.

'Don't look at me like that,' he said. 'I'd gladly do it myself if I had to.'

The ship crashes through the waves. Spray strikes the cabin. Annia's hand is warm in his. The lantern swings from side to side. He glimpses her face, her smile.

He and Mahalie walk along the street together, happy. The men seem to come out of nowhere. Suddenly, he's surrounded. He shouts at her to run.

His cheer of triumph is drowned out by the crowd. Around him lie his fallen foes, bloody and broken. He walks towards the gate. Nothing else matters but reaching the light.

It took Indavara a while to realise what he was looking at. Then the outline of the doorway appeared; and a familiar face and voice.

'Wakey wakey,' said Slab. Warty and Narrow Eyes were with him.

Slab slapped him on the arm. 'How you doing then? Recovered yourself? I think you've got a bit more colour about you today. What do you reckon, lads?'

'Better,' agreed Warty. 'White as a sheet yesterday.'

Indavara rubbed his eyes. He could not recall ever feeling so weak. The only thing he could compare it to was when he and all the other fighters had picked up some sort of illness. It left the victims completely devoid of energy, barely able to lift a limb or eat. Eventually a third of the fighters had succumbed.

Then he remembered.

Blood spurting out of his vein, hosing the bowl as Surgeon collected it. The old man had filled two more before Indavara lost consciousness. Waking half a day later, he had found his arm bound tight with bandages. At least the straps had been removed.

Surgeon had returned yesterday, or was it two days ago?

'How much?' Indavara hardly recognised his own voice; it sounded thin and faint. 'How much did he take?'

'Three bowls both times,' said Slab. Only then did Indavara realise he was holding his knife.

'Couldn't believe how much came out,' said Narrow Eyes.

'You're doing well, considering,' added Warty.

Slab loomed over him, the morning light picking out his weathered features. 'Surgeon says we've got to move you around a bit. Can you get up?'

Regardless of what these evil bastards wanted, Indavara knew he had to do it if he could. He gripped the side of the bed and tried to push himself up but it was a struggle.

Narrow Eyes came forward.

'Leave me.'

Indavara turned to his right, then lowered his legs to the floor and eventually hauled himself into a sitting position. He was astonished to find that he felt out of breath.

'He's a fighter, this lad,' said Slab, knife still in hand. 'Don't worry – old fellow says you can make *new* blood.'

'Still don't believe it,' replied Warty.

'You can make shit and piss,' said Slab. 'Why not?'

'A man loses a few pints, he goes to sleep and never wakes.'

'Old fellow knows what he's doing. Help him up.'

Narrow Eyes did so.

Indavara felt another wave of light-headedness as he got to his feet for the first time in more than a week.

'We've got some food for you too,' said Slab. 'Let's try a few steps first – across the room and back.'

Even though he would have liked to fling Narrow Eyes into the wall and disembowel Slab with his own blade, Indavara had to devote all his energies to moving. He needed help to traverse the room but then continued on his own, at which point Narrow Eyes moved clear and Warty slipped his cudgel from his belt.

'Scared?' said Indavara as he walked gingerly past the end of the bed.

'Of you? Yes. Don't mind admitting it.'

'I told them about your performance in the arena,' said Slab.

'Your master knew of me?' said Indavara, halting for a moment to get his breath back.

'He watched you fight. He said you were the closest thing to a god walking the earth.'

Indavara almost laughed at this. 'And he thinks my blood will save him?'

'He does.'

'Do you?' Indavara set off again. Warty kept his eyes on him and his cudgel at the ready.

'Not my place to say.'

'What does he do – drink it?' Indavara stopped at the wall and turned himself around.

Slab nodded. 'Mixed with wine. A little at a time. Says he's already feeling better.'

Indavara reckoned this might be his only hope. He had no doubt whatsoever that Slab would happily dispatch him as soon as he was no longer useful. But if his master really did believe all these things about him, perhaps he would let him live.

'He doesn't want to come and see me?'

'Maybe if he improves.'

'What's wrong with him?'

'Enough questions. Few more minutes' exercise then you can eat.'

'When I'm ready.'

Slab scowled. 'Need to use the latrine?'

'Yes. Actually, tell you what – your master drinks my blood, maybe you want to eat my shit?'

Warty's chuckle did not last long. The flicker of amusement on Slab's face disappeared even quicker. He gestured with the knife for his captive to keep moving.

'No?' said Indavara. 'Up to you.'

Back straight, chin up, he continued walking.

XXI

The horse died quietly. Startled by something in the undergrowth beside the road, it had reared then tripped and come down on the metal stake used for the tethers. Once they had moved the other mounts away and seen the severity of the wound, the outcome was obvious. The gash was upon the haunch of its rear right leg. The beast had already lost a lot of blood and there seemed to be considerable damage within.

Idan held the horse's head for a time to calm it, then opened its throat with his dagger. Having dragged it a little further from the road, Yablus and Kammath were now butchering the carcass: the meat would save them some money.

Cassius looked over his shoulder to the south. Some way behind them lay the rocky spurs they had traversed over the last four days. Progress had been painfully slow since they'd reached the northern end of Lake Tuz, even though they'd taken the shortest possible path across the high ground to the Ancyra road. The Galatian capital – recently reclaimed by Aurelian after Zenobia's adventures and Goth advances – lay some twenty miles to the north-east. Cassius looked ahead along the road. Bordered by woodland, it ran as straight as an arrow.

He sighed. They had covered a pitifully small section of the overall journey and now would be slowed even further. Yablus could take turns riding with the others but midday was not far off and there was only a slim chance of reaching the capital by nightfall. Even if they did, they had barely enough money for another mount and at least another hundred and twenty miles between them and the coast.

As ever, their collective determination had driven them on but the weeks of travelling and uncertainty were taking their toll.

Kabir was not the only one looking weary and Cassius's rump and thighs were in dire need of a rest from riding. He watched Simo petting Patch. The sturdy donkey had coped with the relentless pace better than any other man or beast.

Yablus continued his work, carving pink handfuls of flesh from the animal that had served him so well. Cassius couldn't imagine himself or many other Romans of his class doing so. Though the Syrians valued their steeds greatly, they were far more pragmatic.

'He'll be quick,' said Kabir, noting his interest.

'But will we?' Cassius drank from his water flask.

'At least we're clear of the mountains now.'

Cassius – who could now be completely sure that he had avoided the plague – was also relieved that they had left the area of the outbreak. On the previous day, they had encountered a half-century of legionaries at a well. The soldiers were heading south to man the barricades at Pessinus; all part of the governor's policy to prevent the spread of the disease.

Kabir looked to the north. 'It could happen again, I suppose. We find these men then discover they've sold the girls on.'

'I'm not sure. It sounded to me like this might be the end of the chain.'

Cassius had given a good deal of thought to these 'Earthly Gods'. Though they evidently took great precautions to protect themselves, the name suggested an arrogance he hoped to exploit. It seemed obvious to him that this was essentially a high-class brothel for rich men, of which there would be plenty in Byzantium.

'The name gives us something to work with. Don't lose hope.'

'Never.'

'What did the signs tell you?'

On the previous evening, Cassius had watched the Syrian plant sticks in the ground then examine the length and pattern of the shadows.

'I cannot be sure. None of us here are holy men.'

'Something, though?'

Kabir seemed to be about to say more but Yablus interjected.

'Done,' he said as he placed the full sack of meat inside another.

'Shall we walk to start with?' suggested Cassius.

As the Syrians got under way, he took the reins of his horse from Simo.

'Would you like to keep your cloak on, sir? We'll be warmer when we walk.'

'For now. There's still a chill in the air from that rain.'

As they set off, Simo looped the reins to his belt. As with people, animals generally remained calm around the gentle attendant; his mount and Patch followed obediently.

Simo took a leather pack from his shoulder and retrieved a little cloth bag. He always kept some snacks on hand and this one contained Cassius's favourite: chopped dates and mixed nuts. He held out his hand and Simo dropped some on to his palm. Cassius ate his way through them then found himself looking down at his boots. He told himself that every step took them closer to salvation for both the Syrian girls and Indavara.

'I'm so glad to have you with me, Simo.'

Unused to such sentiment, the Gaul took a while to respond. 'I am glad to be here with you, sir.'

Once beyond the woodland, the road crossed an area of gently rolling hills and isolated farms. There seemed to be few large estates here, just small properties with their own fields, olive groves and orchards. The lush green pastures were well suited to grazing and they saw countless sheep and goats. It was clear that the vagaries of fate had spared this land from the plague.

Just after a milestone that denoted there were only ten miles to Ancyra, they reached the peak of a hill. About a mile ahead of them, the road crossed a river via a large, single-arched bridge. The river was broad and a similar green hue to the Cydnus. The waters were calm.

'The Sakarya,' said Cassius. He and Simo had journeyed this way before with General Navio's convoy; long before he had been recalled to Syria by Abascantius.

As they guided the horses down the sloping road, Cassius

found himself behind Yablus, who was now the only one on foot. The youth dropped back.

'These bridges – how do you Romans make them?'

'Well, it is not only us,' replied Cassius. 'And to be honest that is not the most impressive example you'll ever see.'

'But *how*?' Yablus had expressed similar amazement at the aqueducts, towers, arches and other structures they had passed.

'Well – one step at a time, I suppose. It's not really my area but I believe the piers go in first.'

'Piers?'

'Yes, the towers of brick or concrete that support a wide bridge.'

'But the arches – how can they build them so they meet without them collapsing?'

'Er . . . ' Struggling to pick details out of his memory, Cassius was saved by an unusual sight below.

'Look,' said Kabir. 'I wonder who they are.'

Distracted by the river and the bridge, Cassius hadn't noticed the thirty or so travellers sitting at the bottom of the slope. They were close to a farmhouse and some seemed to be purchasing produce. They had only a few pack animals with them, which were munching their way through the grass beside the road.

'Make a stop?' suggested Kabir.

'Yes,' replied Cassius, who was desperate to get out of the saddle. Considering their predicament, they had made good time and would reach Ancyra not long after dusk. He planned to find the nearest army way station and use his letters to borrow more money. With a new horse for Yablus and perhaps a spare, they could be heading west for the coast the following morning.

They dismounted on the opposite side of the road from the farmhouse. Though there was no time to unburden the mounts, they could at least graze for a while and Simo and Kammath had soon filled enough containers for them all to drink.

Cassius accompanied Kabir and Idan as they crossed the road to inspect the farmer's offerings. He and his wife were standing behind a broad wooden table. Upon it were jugs of wine and milk, plates of cheese and dried meat, as well as collations of fruit served in leaves.

'No bread?' asked Cassius.

'Sorry, all gone,' said the farmer. Cassius glanced over at the travellers. He noticed two things: first, that there was an unusual number of women in the party; second, that several of the group had wooden crosses around their necks.

Simo had also seen the Christians. After a moment's hesitation, he crossed the road and hailed one of them.

'Anything for you then, sir?' asked the farmer. His wife was already doling out meat to the Syrians.

'What's that cheese? Goat? Give me a taste.'

Cassius plucked the sample from the end of the farmer's knife and ate it. 'Not bad. My man will come and get some.'

As he turned away, Idan and Kabir supped from the mugs supplied to them and grimaced.

'Never buy wine from a farmer,' advised Cassius quietly.

He didn't see the little boy until he came out from under the table. The wife called to him but the boy was interested in the new arrivals. When he spied Idan's maimed face, however, the youngster's expression turned to horror. He ran back under the table and gripped his mother's leg, pressing his face into her apron.

Idan coughed and continued drinking his wine.

Cassius felt great sympathy for the quiet warrior. 'How did it happen? If you don't mind me asking.'

'I don't mind. Just wish it was a better story.'

Kabir gave a slight grin then drained his mug, returned it to the table and walked back across the road.

'It was a knife fight. Over a woman.'

Even now, Cassius always had to force himself to look only at the Syrian's eyes. The tangle of flesh and bone where his nose should have been contorted when he spoke and ruined an otherwise distinguished face.

'She had been pledged to a man from a neighbouring village. When he heard we were together, he challenged me. The two of us fought in the market square with a crowd looking on. I caught him twice but neither was a telling blow. I slipped and he stuck the blade into me as I fell.'

'Gods. You did well to survive it.'

'At the time, I wished I hadn't.'

'That's understandable, I suppose.'

'I was as vain as any young man, present company excepted.'

Cassius smiled. 'I don't know what you mean.'

'At the first sight of a woman, your hand goes to your hair, then to check the shape of your tunic.'

'There doesn't seem much sense in denying it. What about now? Back home? You have a woman?'

'Yes.'

'It's good to have someone.'

'Face like a camel's arse, to be honest but . . . ' Idan shrugged and gestured at himself.

Cassius laughed so loudly that everyone present turned towards him. He couldn't believe how much the taciturn Syrian had disclosed. Then again, he hadn't really tried to talk to him before.

'It made me what I am, in many ways,' added Idan. 'I vowed I would never be outfought again.'

Cassius had by now recovered himself. 'Kabir is lucky to have you by his side. Tell me something, how do you do it? With the sling? I know you practise incessantly but—'

'It's not just practice. My uncle explained it to me well when I first started. A hunter might follow his prey for hours, days even. He might only get one chance. If he misses, his family starves. It's the same in battle – you learn how to make that chance count. Every time, or as close to it as you can get.'

'But battle is so chaotic.'

'It is if you let your enemies get close.' Idan tapped the sling. 'We prefer to fight from a distance.'

'Perhaps you could show me how to use one if we get a spare moment. I was quite useful with a catapult in my youth.'

'I think Kabir would prefer it if you concentrate on finding the girls. What happens after that you can leave to us.'

Idan glanced across the road and saw that the others were already preparing to leave. With a brief nod to Cassius, he went to join them.

'Sir.'

Cassius turned to find Simo standing behind him.

'Ah, there you are. Get a wheel of that goat's cheese, would you? It's really not bad.'

'Yes, sir, I will, but I think we might have an alternative to continuing the journey on foot.'

'Oh?'

'These people travelled by river. They say there are many trading boats and that it's possible to reach the coast in only three or four days. If there's space, the captains will allow passengers aboard.'

'The Sakarya meets the Chalcedon road not too far east of Nicomedia. From there it's only a couple of days to Byzantium. We could save a day or two at least, not to mention a bit of money. Well done, Simo. Kabir!'

Cassius walked along the road towards the Christians. 'Who did you talk to, Simo?'

'This gentleman, sir. His name is Elder Nahir.'

The man – who was considerably younger than the other Christian leaders Cassius had encountered – stood.

'Good day to you.'

'Good day,' said Cassius just as Kabir arrived.

'Some interesting information.' He turned to Nahir. 'Simo tells me it's possible to get passage downriver.'

'Yes. And for a reasonable sum. There is not much shelter aboard but with a good captain it's quick. The river is busy with trade this time of year – the last seagoing ships will be sailing from the ports before the worst of the winter weather sets in.'

'Where are the nearest docks?'

'About two miles downstream – a town called Karolea. Excuse me a moment.' Nahir called over another man, who also spoke Greek and seemed to know the place well.

'It's not very big but there'll be half a dozen or so boats tied up there for the night. I'd be surprised if you can't get on one of them.'

'Well, Kabir? The horses are tired and it'll take time to find another for Yablus.'

'A river? Couldn't we be held up there too?'

'Where are you headed?' asked Nahir.

'Byzantium.'

'You'd save two days at least,' came the confident reply.

'It would give us a rest, too,' said Cassius. 'We've been on the move for so long.'

'If you think it's best,' said Kabir.

'I do. A chance to gather our energies. Make sure we're at full strength when we need to be.'

'Very well. I'll tell the others.' The Syrian crossed the road.

'Thank you,' said Cassius to Nahir. He then looked at the Christian men and women. 'You're heading south?'

'Yes.'

'Why?'

'To aid those afflicted by the pestilence.'

'You're not serious?'

'Entirely,' said Nahir. 'I had a vision. The Almighty summoned me; told me that my fellow man was in need.'

'There's nothing you can do there. If you have food, they'll rob you. All that will happen is that you will all be struck down too. Simo, did you tell him what we saw?'

'I did, sir.'

Cassius ushered Nahir away from the others. 'Listen to me. It is utterly pointless. All you will do is cause more suffering – to your own people.'

He would have preferred it if the man had argued. But there was a peacefulness about him of the type that only came from total conviction.

'Sir, if some of us fall, it merely means we will enter the Kingdom sooner.'

Cassius could do nothing but shake his head. He didn't see much fear in the Christians, just the usual blind optimism he had observed amongst these people before. He had seen the impermeable intransigence too; and he wasn't about to waste time trying to change their minds.

'Then I shall simply say farewell.'

Nahir shook the hand offered to him. 'Farewell.'

Considering the small size of the town, the riverside area of Karolea was surprisingly well developed. Cassius imagined this was due to its position, nestled between the Sakarya and a wide tributary that ran south. They reached the water just before dusk, and tied the horses up at a sprawling stable built only a stone's throw from the nearest wooden pontoons. Despite the dim light, Cassius counted more than a dozen masts; he hoped they would be able to find passage for the morning.

Two lads came out to greet them with a well-practised and polite welcome. Before they could lead the new arrivals inside, Cassius spoke. 'Hold there. We're here to sell – fetch your master.'

The lads exchanged a few comments in the local dialect then one sprinted towards a low building opposite the stalls.

It had already been agreed that the Syrians would sell the mounts while Cassius went to make enquiries. The more they'd discussed this new alternative, the more it made sense. The horses had been pushed too hard; it was only a matter of time before another one was injured.

Cassius noticed that Kabir was already unloading. 'Don't bother. The mounts can carry the gear down to the ship – the buyer can take them from there. And make sure you get every coin you can out of him.'

'Sir, shall I come with you?' asked Simo. He had already untethered Patch and was holding his reins. 'They will sometimes take pack animals aboard, won't they?'

Cassius had been too preoccupied with other thoughts to consider what to do with the donkey. 'Ah. Well, sometimes. Let's see.'

Simo sighed. 'Yes, sir.'

'Anyone care to accompany me?' asked Cassius, who knew how rough any locale dominated by sailors might be.

'I will,' said Yablus. He passed his reins to Kammath then walked with Cassius along the riverside path. Here, a few stall-holders and fishermen were packing up for the night. Beyond the shorter pontoons and the smaller boats – mainly punts and skiffs – were the larger galleys, some up to sixty feet long. A few were high-masted vessels much like seagoing ships. Those of the oar-driven variety tended to be more low-lying and squat. There was also a barge, identifiable by the towing post situated towards the bow.

Though a few crewmen were still completing jobs in the fading light, most of the activity was centred around the half dozen inns facing the river. One was particularly busy, with the strains of a song projecting from within and a group of men clustered around a pair of tables.

Cassius knew the likeliest source of information was the local harbour master or equivalent. The first man they spoke to understood neither Greek nor Latin. The second was far more helpful, which Cassius felt was at least in part due to the amount of wine he'd imbibed. Escorting the pair through the packed inn just as the song finished, he tugged on the sleeve of a man behind the counter.

'This here is Chares, he knows more about the boats and the captains that come through here than any man alive. He'll help you out.'

'Thank you,' said Cassius.

As the sailor belched and stumbled his way back towards the door, Chares finished serving a customer then leaned over the counter. He had almost to shout to be heard.

'Where you headed, sir?'

'Downstream as far as the Chalcedon road. I need a fast vessel that will take six passengers.'

Before Chares could answer, a mug thudded down on the counter and a man barged into Cassius. The innkeeper glared at the fellow but it was Yablus's intervention that did the trick. The stocky nomad tapped the interloper on the shoulder and gestured for him to move away. He didn't need to be told twice.

'Sorry, sir,' said Chares, who – like any half-decent innkeeper – seemed to know a gentleman when he saw one. 'Your best bet is probably Tolmai. He has a galley with space on deck and he charges a flat silver a day per man. I saw him come in this afternoon. He's been on this river his whole life and there's no one will get you there quicker.'

'Excellent. Is he here?'

'Not a chance. He likes the quiet life, does Tolmai. You'll find him on-board – last pontoon. Word of advice though – if he does take you.'

'Yes?'

'Don't get in his way – and don't go anywhere near his daughters.'

There was in fact no sign of any females when they reached the galley: just a bearded fellow re-tying the warps that connected his vessel to the pontoon. Cassius introduced himself and found that he was talking to the captain himself. Tolmai continued working as they spoke and maintained a gruff tone throughout, questioning him about exactly who his travelling companions were and how much luggage they had. When the discussion was concluded, Cassius shook his strong, calloused hand. Tolmai informed him that they were free to sleep on deck: there would be plenty of space now that his other passengers had departed.

When the captain went below, Cassius heard several voices, one quite high-pitched. Tolmai returned with a lantern, which he hung from a pole above a square marked on the deck just ahead of the mast. The area was no more than ten foot by eight.

'At night, you can spread out. By day, you stay inside the lines – that clear?'

'Perfectly. How many days to the Chalcedon road, do you think?'

'Depends.'

'Five?'

'Depends on what the gods have for us.'

'But five is possible?'

'Bring your own food,' said Tolmai, turning away. 'And make sure your bedding and luggage is tied up and secure before we get underway. We'll leave three hours before dawn to catch the current.'

Cassius knew the answer to his question before he asked but he felt he owed it to Simo to at least try. 'I don't suppose you have any space in your hold for a donkey? He's actually done a sea trip before and came through it rather well.'

Tolmai started chuckling and was still doing so when his new passengers reached the end of the pontoon.

Back at the stable, Cassius was relieved to find the Syrians had secured a decent price for the horses. The owner and his two young employees accompanied them on their way to the ship, during which time Cassius struck upon an idea that might spare Simo from a painful separation. He also admitted to himself that he didn't like the idea of never seeing Patch again; he still looked forward to seeing the beast reunited with Indavara.

'Now listen,' he said, dropping back to speak to the owner as they neared the ship. 'About the donkey. What do you consider a fair price?'

'Eighty denarii.'

'Right. We will entrust it to your care. You may use it but you must not sell it for a period of one year. If we return in that time, I will pay a hundred and twenty – but only if he is in good condition. If we do not return, he is yours. How does that sound?'

'Fine with me, sir. I've got a water delivery contract – I'll put him to work there.'

'Carrying barrels?' interjected Simo anxiously.

'Skins mostly.'

'That's fine,' said Cassius, 'but do not overwork him.'

When they reached the ship and the others began unloading, Simo was more concerned with listing Patch's existing ailments and dietary preferences. Unfortunately, the stable owner was more interested in taking charge of his valuable new horses.

Cassius helped his attendant remove their bags, then their saddles, which would also travel with them.

'He'll be all right, Simo.'

The Gaul did not reply; a highly unusual occurrence. Leaving Patch's tack attached, he retrieved a sack of vegetable cuts he kept as treats and handed it to one of the lads.

While the Syrians hauled their bags down to the ship, the stable owner wished them a good trip and set off with his new acquisitions.

'Wait a moment, would you?' said Simo to the lad leading Patch. Simo put his face against the donkey's and rubbed his neck. 'There's a good Patch. We'll be back for you soon and Indavara will be with us. We'll be back.'

Despite himself, Cassius came over and rubbed Patch's ears one last time. 'He'll be fine. Don't worry.'

Obedient to the last, the animal did not resist as the lad led him away into the darkness.

XXII

The galley glided down the river. The wind was from the east, filling the single huge sail and making the going easier. The captain and crew seemed relaxed, apart from the occasions when a change in the channel's course demanded modifications to the rig or the breeze grew fluky in those areas where cliffs overlooked the water. The Sakarya was a pretty river, edged for the most part by forest that had not yet yellowed with the onset of autumn. In some areas, a blanket of water lilies stretched from one bank to the other. Though rarely less than forty yards across, the channel narrowed sharply at various points, sometimes taking the *Adva* close to treacherous outcrops of rock.

Many other boats were also heading downstream but none seemed to be travelling faster. As midday approached, they had still not passed a settlement as large as Karolea, though there were countless buildings and hamlets built close to the water.

Lying on his back, head against his saddle, Cassius felt sure he had made a sound decision. The days of endless riding had drained them; now they had a hope of arriving in Byzantium refreshed and renewed. He had little doubt that seeking out the mysterious group known as 'The Earthly Gods' would be exceptionally difficult, especially as he would again have to sacrifice subtlety for speed. But he had resolved to not think of it this day; or Indavara – if he could.

The Syrians also seemed keen to rest. Barely a word had been said since they'd been woken by the sudden outburst of activity from Tolmai and his crew. Watching curiously, they had stayed within the confines of their perimeter as the sailors cast off, used their oars for an hour or two then raised the sail. From what Cassius could gather, there were at least eight men aboard, all of whom worked expertly and quietly, with only Tolmai ever raising his voice. They had completely ignored the guests, as had the captain's daughters. Though he'd done his best to appear disinterested, Cassius had watched the girls as they handed out wine and bread to the crew around the fourth hour. One looked to be seventeen or eighteen, the other closer to his age. The crew were notably polite and respectful towards them and Cassius could see why their father might often have cause to ward off suitors. Though she wore only a plain tunic, the older girl in particular was attractive: tall and slender, with a fine head of sleek, black hair. Like the sailors, she and her sister went about the vessel barefoot.

Cassius sat up and glanced towards the stern. Other than the four men holding guide ropes for the yard, he could see only Tolmai. The captain was holding the ship's tiller, eyes fixed on the river ahead.

'Hungry, sir?' asked Simo.

Yablus groaned. Despite the calm water, he had been complaining about sickness since the first hour of the journey. Though Kabir and Idan appeared unperturbed, Kammath also seemed disturbed by their new environment. Cassius was not surprised to discover that Kabir's people didn't swim. Most Romans did not, so it was hardly to be expected of nomads who never neared the coast. Cassius's father had always maintained an attitude born of familial service in both the army and navy: swimming was an essential skill almost as important as riding. During training, Cassius had seen many men struggle; it was very difficult to learn once one had reached adulthood. Similarly limited in this capacity, poor Indavara possessed a mortal fear of the water. Simo, however, had also been taught by his father, who hailed from a long line of fishermen.

'I am a bit,' Cassius told the attendant, who had done an excellent job of assembling all their gear into a single pile. 'What do we have?'

Simo retrieved a sack from under his saddle. As he delved inside, a shift in the wind caused the sail to flap above them. While the sailors made adjustments, Cassius and the others all looked warily up at the yard. If it fell, they stood a good chance of being crushed.

'Sir, we have dried apple, a few nuts, a roll – rather stale – and two of those sausages. I expect you'd like the fruit and the nuts.'

'I would. And the roll. You'd prefer the sausages, I imagine?'

Simo had bought a dozen several days earlier and cooked them up. They were well spiced and tasty but Cassius suspected they were responsible for the rather liquid state of his bowels. The fruit wouldn't exactly help but there was nothing else. He was hoping a proper meal would be available wherever they stopped for the evening.

While Simo poured two mugs of well-watered wine, the galley passed a cove where several lads were fishing with rods. They waved to the passengers. Yablus waved back.

By the middle of the afternoon, grey cloud had all but covered the sky and the wind had picked up, drawing a chop from the water. As the course of the river meandered, Tolmai elected to drop the sail and put his crew to the oars. From what Cassius could see, the men used a long, economical stroke that pushed them along well. In anticipation of rain, the captain had also sent two men forward to rig a cover for the passengers and their gear.

When the need to visit the vessel's latrine became overpowering, Cassius walked carefully back along the deck. With the crew all below rowing, Tolmai was accompanied only by his family. His wife and the girls were sitting together, doing something to a sail with large iron needles and thick twine. All three were now wearing woollen shawls.

'I'm just going down to . . . er . . . '

'Yes, yes,' said Tolmai. He had explained that the only time the passengers were permitted below was to make use of the latrine. Now long accustomed to people relieving themselves over the side, Cassius imagined this accommodation was made to spare the ladies.

He had almost reached the steps when the wife spoke up. Like her husband, she used Greek.

'Good afternoon, sir.'

'My apologies,' Cassius replied, halting. 'Good afternoon.'

'I am the captain's wife, Marit. You will have to forgive his lack of manners. These are my daughters, Talitha and Talya.'

Cassius bowed. 'Delighted, I'm sure. Cassius Quintius Corbulo.'

The younger girl giggled. Her sister slapped her knee and glanced coyly up at him before looking away.

Tolmai tutted as his wife continued. 'My husband tells me you are a Roman army officer.'

'Indeed.' Cassius felt this would at least assure them that he was a trustworthy fellow to have aboard.

'And your companions?'

Cassius had established a basic story with Kabir. 'My bodyguards. We are on a special assignment and need to reach Byzantium urgently. I was told that your husband would convey us safely and quickly. Clearly, I was not misinformed.'

Tolmai nodded reluctantly but soon had cause to appear disapproving once more. Marit – who had a lined but pleasant face – gestured towards the bow.

'You are comfortable?'

'We are.'

'And have sufficient provisions?'

'Yes, thank you. For the moment. Any idea where we'll be stopping tonight?'

'Depends,' said Tolmai.

'Roughly?'

'Depends. Depends on—'

'—what the gods have for us? Of course.' Cassius pointed up at the sky. 'Bit miserable now, eh?'

'It's the season,' said the captain. He then shouted an order at his oarsmen and moved the tiller, which was a two-handed job.

'Our last trip this year,' said Marit. 'I shall be glad to be still for a while.'

'I think my friends are looking forward to that already. They have not travelled by water before.'

'If they are sick, tell them to look at the land. It helps.'

'I shall pass that on.'

Tolmai coughed impatiently.

'Well, if you'll excuse me.' Cassius headed below.

Though a light rain fell for much of the afternoon, the skies began to clear before dusk. Despite the weather, captain and crew made full use of the daylight and Tolmai seemed satisfied with the miles gained. The orange sun was already sinking below the high ground to the west when the *Adva* tied up against a stone quay at which three vessels were already moored. The settlement adjoining it seemed to be little more than a combination of inn and supply depot. The proprietor was clearly well known to Tolmai but wasted no time in hurrying out to claim payment for the night's stay. There was no rest for the crewmen, who instantly set about placing extra fenders between the vessel and the quay and spreading out the damp sail for drying.

The passengers were more than happy to get out of their way. Cassius grinned as the four Syrians paused upon the quay – readjusting to dry land. Kabir in particular looked so unsteady that he needed a hand from Kammath.

'It'll pass,' said Cassius. 'And tomorrow you'll be better.'

Kammath shot him an unduly harsh glare, which Cassius ignored.

'Wine all round?' he asked, striding towards the inn, which was dwarfed by the stone-built warehouse beside it.

'Not for me,' murmured Kabir. Only then did Cassius realise how pale he was.

'Come, have a seat,' said Simo, directing them towards some tables.

Kabir simply shook his head and said something to his son. Instead of stopping with the others outside, the youth escorted his father inside.

A large, bald head appeared in a small window. 'Evening, sirs. What can I get you?'

'Half and half – a jug and six mugs,' instructed Cassius.

'Right you are.' With a salute, the man disappeared.

Cassius sat down with Yablus and Idan. One of the other tables was occupied by a trio of men staring into a cage that contained some sort of squeaking rodent.

'He *will* feel better tomorrow,' Cassius told the Syrians.

'I'm not sure it's the seasickness, sir,' replied Simo.

'It isn't,' said Idan. 'You've seen how often he has to void his water.'

Cassius had only noticed the fatigue.

'He gets dizzy too,' said Yablus, prompting Cassius to remember the occasion when the chief had almost fallen from his saddle.

'And he cannot see well,' added Idan quietly. 'There has been something wrong for many months. He does not want to admit it; neither does Kammath.'

'Any ideas, Simo?'

'With those symptoms, sir, it could be a number of afflictions. The dizziness and vision problems suggest something within the head, the bladder problem something else. It is difficult to be sure.'

'You can't do anything?' asked Yablus.

'Not without a proper diagnosis. If I could get more information from Master Kabir, I might make some progress.'

'He wouldn't like that,' said Idan.

'He'd prefer it if we just say nothing,' added Yablus.

'Then I suggest we do so,' said Cassius. 'The sooner we get to Byzantium and find Aikaterine, the sooner you can head home. His condition might improve. It may be that all the worry is causing these symptoms. Like my headaches, Simo.'

'That's possible, sir.'

Nobody spoke for a while. The four of them watched the sailors continue their work, then another group unloading large amphoras from their vessel. It was Yablus who broke the silence.

'What chance do we have, Cassius? In Byzantium?'

Cassius had made no complaint when Kabir used his first

name, and he now found that he couldn't summon much displeasure at the cheerful youth, who suddenly looked very young and very uncertain. Though he could be sure of nothing yet, Cassius knew he had to keep the party's spirits up. 'I'll tell you this, Yablus – if they're there, I'll find them.'

Though the wine at the inn was passable, the food was some of the worst Cassius had ever encountered. Simo offered to prepare him something but he was still not feeling well and the sight of the local offerings did nothing to improve his stomach. Thankfully, Kabir appeared to have recovered and ate alongside the others. Neither Tolmai nor any of the crew ventured into the inn; they dined together with the family in the *Adva*'s cockpit. Having completed a few jobs, all seemed to have now disappeared below, even though it was no later than the third hour of night.

'Hope it doesn't rain,' said Kammath as they left the inn and walked towards the quay.

'They left out the cover in any case,' said Cassius.

'It's chilly, sir,' said Simo, rubbing his hands together. 'I shall take out the thick blankets.'

'Please do.' Cassius paused.

'Sir?'

Cassius glanced down at the narrow sandy beach to the left of the quay. 'I shall take a short walk in an effort to settle my gut.'

'Would you like me to get some hot water, sir? An infusion might help.'

'No, I'll be all right. Just sort out the beds. Two blankets on the bottom for me – those timbers are as hard as stone.'

'Yes, sir.'

He watched the others as they approached the ship; Tolmai had hung lanterns on the stays to help them find their way. Cassius tucked his thumbs into his belt, retraced his steps and then ambled down a short grassy slope on to the beach. He hadn't been there long when a shift in the cloud spilled moonlight on to the water, illuminating a strip of the river, which was once again calm.

Other than the odd shout or bark of laughter from the inn, all was quiet. Cassius walked along the beach, the sand soft under his boots. As often happened at night, he could not help thinking of Indavara. His imagination summoned an image of the ex-gladiator trapped somewhere – in a small, bare room.

Did he still pray to his Fortuna? Had he tried to escape? Though Indavara was without doubt a born survivor, a return to captivity would erode his spirit quicker than anything else. During their last mission, Cassius had seen the look on his face when he'd been forced to spend a night behind bars. Like Yablus – like everyone – he would need hope to sustain him. But where would it come from? Perhaps Indavara had more anger than hope. Would that be enough? There was only so much a man could take. Even him.

Cassius looked up at the grey crescent moon. Like the weather, like the river, it was constantly changing. From what he had seen, fortune was much the same: unpredictable, unknowable. The gods knew few men could have experienced such trials as Indavara. They owed him a favour.

Cassius thought of all the letters he had sent out, wondered if anything had turned up in Antioch and if that shifty clerk Calidius had done his job. He just needed something – anything – that might put him on the right trail.

The clouds converged again, leaving the sky and the river dark.

If you are listening, my friend, we will find you. I tell you, we will find you.

He walked on until he reached the end of the beach, then turned back. As he neared the quay, he saw a figure descending the slope. Though he had no reason to be fearful, his hand moved instinctively to his dagger.

Then the moon reappeared, allowing him to see that the figure had stopped and was looking at him.

'Hello, sir.'

The older of Tolmai's daughters.

'Hello,' said Cassius warily. 'I daresay you're supposed to be on the ship.'

'I couldn't sleep. I noticed you didn't come back with the others.'

She walked across the sand until she was close. Even with the moonlight, Cassius could see little of her face.

'Are you Talya or—'

'Talitha. And you are Officer Cassius Corbulo.'

'Well remembered.'

'I like that name. It suits you.'

Cassius told himself to keep walking. He suspected the girl's unexpectedly forward approach was precisely the reason why he had been warned. Perhaps she had done this before; perhaps that was why her father guarded his daughters so closely.

And yet it was rather pleasant to be standing there alone with her in the darkness. It seemed an age since he had spent time with a woman, especially a pretty one.

'What do you mean – "it suits me"?'

'It sounds . . . fine.'

He wondered if she meant rich.

'You look fine,' she added. 'And your clothes are fine.'

'Very kind. Listen, Talitha, normally it would be my pleasure to take a walk with you, or give you flowers, or otherwise initiate an acquaintance but I do not wish to upset your father. I am dependent on his help.'

'He won't know. He doesn't know anything about me.'

'I doubt that's true.'

She came another step closer. When her hand touched his, he moved it away.

'Come now, sir. Where's the harm?'

'You want to talk, we can talk. Nothing more.'

'Don't you like me? Don't you want to kiss me? Most men do.'

'I don't doubt it.'

'Is it because you're a gentleman?'

Cassius smothered a smirk. Were it not for the circumstances he would have already had her in his arms by now.

'Perhaps.'

'Where do you live?' asked Talitha.

'I suppose I don't really have a home at the moment. Originally, I'm from Ravenna.'

'Where's that?'

'Italy. Do you have a home – other than the ship?'

'Only the *Adva*. I was born on it.'

The inn door slammed. Several talkative sailors ambled to the quay, oblivious to the two people only yards away.

Talitha added, 'Sometimes I think I'll die on it. Did you say you're going to Byzantium?'

'That's right.'

'A man from Byzantium once asked my father for my hand in marriage. He was only a little older than me, very successful. But my father refused. He and mother want me to marry a captain – to stay on the river.'

'Do they have someone in mind?'

'There have been a few. But my father doesn't have much for a dowry. I'm twenty-two next month.'

'You could do a lot worse than a captain.'

'I like soldiers. Why don't you wear Roman red?'

Cassius was used to exploiting his role in the Service and the army to sound either impressive, mysterious or a combination of both. Not this time.

'I'm basically an administrator. Quite boring really.'

'That's why you're with those long-haired southerners? Don't lie.'

'You're a bright one, Talitha, I'll give you that.'

'What else will you give me? A kiss?'

She leaned in close, hair brushing his face as her lips neared his.

Gods, grant me strength.

If he hadn't stepped backward, Cassius would have weakened. He could not allow it; there was simply too much at stake.

'Talitha, I'm sorry. You are a very attractive girl. But this is not going to happen. Excuse me.'

As he walked past, she grabbed his arm – with some force. 'Why? I'm not good enough? If I was your wife I would do everything you wanted. *Everything*.'

Cassius could hardly believe this. The girl had barely exchanged a word with him before now; known him for one day! It was clear she really did feel trapped aboard the *Adva*.

Then again, was such behaviour really so strange? He himself had occasionally made intimations of marriage to get his way.

'Goodnight.' Cassius removed her hand. He had taken only a few steps when she spoke again.

'I'll tell him. Come kiss me now or I'll tell him you forced yourself upon me.'

This was said with such calmness and conviction that Cassius felt sure she had done such a thing before. He considered countering threat with threat; he reckoned he could scare her enough to keep her quiet.

But he did not want to do that. Beneath the bravado, this girl seemed very unhappy.

'If you do, I will tell him the truth. We shall see who is believed.'

'You pig.'

'By Jupiter, girl, I just came here to take a walk. I do not have the time or patience for your silly games. Grow up.'

As he headed for the quay, she started to cry.

XXIII

It seemed to Cassius that perhaps the gods were smiling on his party and their dual missions once again, though he suspected the skill of Tolmai might be a more decisive factor. Only a little more rain came and the captain used the currents, the wind and his tireless oarsmen to good effect. After three days, he made a rare foray forward to announce that they stood an excellent chance of reaching the Chalcedon road before nightfall on the fifth day. Cassius and the Syrians expressed their gratitude; and Tolmai seemed appreciative that his passengers had kept themselves to themselves.

Cassius had done his utmost to steer clear of Talitha, and was sure she had said nothing of the encounter. Despite the limited confines of the vessel, he had passed her only three times. Twice she had given a fierce stare, the second occasion causing such a stirring in Cassius's loins that he'd had to cover his tunic with his sun hat. On the third occasion – when they had met on the quay of a small village – her expression had softened to the point where Cassius risked a polite smile. Watching her walk away, his attention was drawn once more to her shapely brown legs and lustrous hair. He could do nothing but shake his head and try not to let his imagination get the better of him.

The river wove its way through lowlands covered with trees. The channel grew wider and they passed dozens of islets, sandbanks and beaches. In the middle of the afternoon on the fourth day – as the *Adva* rounded a tight bend – Tolmai gave a shout. Cassius, who had been dozing under his hat, sat up.

At another order from Tolmai, the rowers backed their oars. As the galley slowed, the captain hurried past the passengers to the bow. After a third shout, the crewmen shipped their oars; and with the *Adva* drifting along the centre of the channel, Cassius and the others stood up to see what was going on.

Ahead – close to the middle of the stream – was a narrow island surrounded by banks of reeds. At the near end, a cluster of rocks broke the surface. Jammed sideways against one of them was a rowing boat no more than ten feet long. Inside it was a woman, hands gripping the sides as the little craft juddered.

Cassius walked up to the bow and saw a child on the island, standing where the sand met the reeds, perhaps forty feet from the boat. He couldn't tell if it was a boy or a girl.

Tolmai walked back to the cockpit.

As the *Adva* drifted on, Cassius saw a man emerge from the reeds carrying another child, which he placed next to the first. Without a moment's hesitation, he turned back to fetch the woman. But after only a few steps, he staggered and fell.

'He's exhausted.'

Cassius heard the captain give another order but was bemused to see the galley continuing on its course, staying well clear of the rocks and the fast-moving water where the current divided around the island. Dropping the blanket he'd had over his shoulders, he pushed his way past the Syrians and ran back along the side deck. Even though the oarsmen weren't working, the tide had already taken the vessel level with the children. Tolmai was staring straight ahead, both hands on the tiller.

'What are you doing?'

'I'll not risk the ship near those rocks.'

'What about the woman? I doubt that little boat will hold together much longer and the man's had it.'

Cassius looked back at the island. The man had plunged into the water but seemed to be making no progress.

'They are helping.' Tolmai pointed at the shore, where a group had assembled. Two men with a line were entering the water upstream but they had half the river to cross.

'We're closer.'

'I'll not risk the ship – or my clients' cargo.'

Cassius pointed over the stern. 'Your tender then?'

'You need four oarsmen for that.'

Cassius kicked a pail out of his way and rushed over to where the captain stood. 'Then give me them!'

'There's no wind. I need my crew.'

Below, the sailors were jabbering to one another. Marit came up the steps, closely followed by Talitha.

'Tolmai,' said the wife.

'Please, father,' added his daughter.

Cassius said, 'Just drop me upstream, I'll do the rest.'

After a long sigh, the captain ordered the oarsmen to pull and shifted the tiller.

'I'll need a line,' added Cassius.

Talitha opened a locker and took out a long coil of rope. Cassius placed it over his head and put his arm through so it wouldn't impede him. He trotted back along the side deck.

'Simo.'

The attendant had already removed his sandals and belt. Cassius was barefoot but also took off his belt, leaving him clad only in a light tunic. As the *Adva* spun around, they climbed over the yard – which was resting on the deck – and hurried along the left side of the galley until they were behind the rearward oar.

'Sir, look.'

The man was flailing around in the water, trying to grab the closest rock.

'Gods.'

Now that the ship was traversing the river, Cassius could see the true strength of the current. For every twenty feet forward, the vessel shifted ten to the side. Even though Tolmai had kept his precious craft well upstream, the island – and the rocks – were getting closer very quickly.

'Now!' shouted the captain.

'Don't waste your strength swimming,' Cassius told Simo. 'The current will take us down. Ready?'

Simo nodded. The pair stepped up on to the side rail and jumped into the water.

Though he was used to the rigours of icy baths, Cassius was

surprised by how cold the water was. Considering he had been dozing only a few moments earlier, he certainly felt awake by the time he surfaced.

Looking around, he glimpsed the *Adva* veering away and spied Simo only a few yards to his right. Pushing away a clump of weed and branches, he turned his attention downriver.

With a splintering crack, the little boat split in two. The woman's arms flew up as she was tossed into the water. The front half of the boat ended up on its side, hull facing upstream as the water pressed it against the rock.

'Can you see her?'

'No, sir.'

'We're drifting.'

Forced in two directions by the land, the current was even more powerful here. Both men put in a dozen powerful strokes to get themselves in the right position.

'Uh!' Cassius's ankle struck a submerged rock.

'You all right, sir?'

'Just a knock. Watch your legs.'

They were bearing down on the boat, now no more than twenty feet away.

'I see the man,' said Simo, who had been pulled further to Cassius's right. 'He . . . he's struggling.'

'You go after him. I'll—'

Simo said something but Cassius never heard it. He thrashed to his left to avoid striking the boat, then had to frantically readjust to reach the rock. Once close enough, he pushed his hand into a crevice and pulled himself in. The bow of the boat was right in front of him, the sides almost flat against the rock.

'Are you there?'

He heard a whimper. Two fingers appeared.

'All right. I'll try and get it off.'

Locking his left foot into a hollow, Cassius got his arm between the rock and the boat, then moved around, trying to prise the wreckage away. But the forces at work were strong. Only once he'd re-positioned both feet could he push the bow off the woman.

At last he could see her. Deathly pale, her face was framed

by sodden hair and a headscarf. She tried to say something but her chattering teeth rendered it incomprehensible. Back to the rock, she was still holding on to the side of the boat.

'You're free. Turn and hold the rock.'

She just looked at him, eyes wide with panic.

Cassius grabbed her arm.

She resisted and shrieked at him.

Cassius reckoned his knees were about to buckle. 'I can't hold it forever. Turn around. Hold the rock!'

He gripped her wrist and pulled it off the boat. Though she continued to thrash around, when he placed her hand firmly on the rock she at last understood and turned. Fingers white, face flat against the outcrop, she hung on.

Cassius moved towards her to get a better angle. Wincing as his bare toes scraped the rock, he moved his feet up and was able to lever the boat another six inches further away. Once all the weight was on his back, he moved left.

Suddenly water rushed into the remains of the hull and dragged the boat away. Only a despairing grab at the crevice stopped him going with it.

By the gods.

He clung on there until he'd caught his breath, then crabbed his away around until he was beside the woman. 'Right, let's get to shore.'

Whether it was a language difficulty or fear, she showed no sign of having understood.

'We are going!'

The clearest path between the rocks was on her side. Cassius clambered over her and held her arm as gently as the circumstances allowed.

'Come on, I'll help you.'

She shook her head, teeth still chattering.

Gods, these bloody ignorant peasants.

'Come on.'

Cassius prised her hand off the rock and pulled her away. He had expected instinct to take over and that she would be able to at least stay afloat.

Instinct did take over. Fear.

The woman threw herself at him, dragging them both under. Cassius had time only to grab half a breath. Pushing her away, then gripping one hand, he kicked out with both legs and came up again. Though she was still beneath the surface, he managed to get a hold on the nearest rock and pull her up. Coughing and spluttering, she threw herself at him again. This time a hand caught him on the nose. When he'd recovered, Cassius found her coming at him once more.

He slapped her. Hard.

While she was still stunned, he turned her towards the rock, where she hung, limpet-like, once more.

'Simo! You there?'

No reply.

Hearing a tapping sound, Cassius saw that another section of the boat had become entangled in a mass of weed and branches between two rocks. He swam over and found an even better prize nearby – a large paddle.

He returned, showed the woman the paddle and demonstrated what he wanted her to do. Whether it was the slap or some sense of reason at last returning, she took hold, realising it would keep her afloat.

'I'll be with you. Come on.'

Treading water, Cassius encouraged her away from the rock then coaxed her towards the island. Once she got going and realised how close they were, she began kicking like a thing possessed, soon overtaking Cassius and showering him with water.

He almost laughed; and before long felt the immense relief of his feet touching the bottom. His charge didn't seem to realise she could stand until he walked up to her and took her hand. Once through a bank of high reeds, they came across Simo and the man. The poor fellow was lying on his front, coughing and retching. Simo was on his knees, water dripping from his hair, broad chest heaving up and down.

When they saw their mother, the children ran to her. She collapsed to the ground and they threw their arms around her neck, tears streaming down their faces.

Only now did Cassius feel the knocks and scrapes he had sustained. His arms and feet were bleeding in several places. Simo had taken a similar amount of damage.

Bent over, sucking in breath, the attendant looked up at his master. 'You all right, sir?'

'Fine.' Cassius slapped him on the back. 'Nothing like a nice, bracing afternoon dip, eh?'

Once able to speak, the father of the family had offered profuse thanks, embracing Cassius three times and Simo four. When Cassius saw the family reunited and considered what might have been, he felt a lump in his throat.

While they waited for the *Adva*'s tender, another boat arrived to take the family ashore. They were able to salvage not only the paddle but also several bags lodged in the reeds. From them, the father retrieved some coins, which Cassius of course refused. They parted without a single exchange other than 'farewell' understood by both sides; wherever the family were from, they had no grasp at all of Latin or Greek.

Four silent crewmen returned the tender to the *Adva*'s stern and Cassius and Simo disembarked first. The stony-faced Tolmai was already telling his men to hurry up.

Though he knew he needed to keep him on side, Cassius could not recall many displays of such heartlessness. It was true that he had warned the Syrians about the perils of dangerous distractions but this had been a measured risk and they had saved one, possibly two lives – in half an hour.

'My apologies, captain, for the *inconvenience*.'

Tolmai ignored this, instead bellowing at his remaining oarsmen to get the galley underway again.

Cassius added, 'I hope your gods see fit to spare you and *your* family such a fate.'

'Such a fate would not befall me. I would not act so stupidly.'

'Perhaps he had no choice.'

Tolmai tapped the shoulder of his wife, who had been holding the ship's tiller. He jumped down beside her and took over. 'I will not be lectured to aboard my own ship. Return to your place. Sir.' The last word was laced with contempt.

On any other occasion, Cassius would have castigated the man. For once in his life, he longed for the days where he wore his scarlet cloak and carried his great sword and nine out of ten people did precisely what he told them to.

He felt a hand on his arm: Simo, who was as wet and bedraggled as Cassius. The attendant was not in the habit of giving his master unsolicited advice. But the message in his eyes was clear.

Cassius took a long breath. 'Come, Simo – the breeze will dry us.'

The two daughters were standing on the side deck, from where they had apparently watched the incident unfold. The younger girl smiled admiringly but swiftly looked away.

Talitha whispered something.

Cassius did not hear it, nor did he dare look at her.

'Well done,' said Kabir as they approached. Yablus had dug out a couple of towels for them.

'Very good,' said Idan stiffly, which to Cassius meant a great deal.

'I tell you, it is a curse upon the world that the lower classes fear the water so.'

'Fortunate for those people that you do not,' said Kabir.

The galley lurched away as the oarsmen set to work. The others sat down while Cassius and Simo continued drying themselves. Glancing over at the island, Cassius could see the family in the boat approaching the shore. He experienced a surge of euphoria unlike anything he had felt in a while. On such occasions he felt tempted to scoff at the gods (which he had done many times in his youth): an able, courageous man could often be of far more use to someone in peril.

'And what about Simo?' he said proudly.

The Gaul patted his stomach. Despite the lost weight, he had the type of build that would always be regarded as 'well covered'.

'Extra buoyancy perhaps?' he said sheepishly.

The Syrians laughed.

'Nonsense,' exclaimed Cassius. He dropped the towel and squeezed the attendant's shoulders. 'Strength. And courage. Well done, Simo. Now tell me – where's the wine?'

They drank two full flasks that afternoon. Even Simo imbibed more than his usual one-mug limit and the Syrians had their share too. Feeling better than he had in some time, Cassius lay on the deck for the remainder of the day, watching the world go by. He saw herders with their sheep and goats, gathering their flocks by the river to drink. He saw a broad lagoon where some enterprising folk collected decaying boats and reused the timber and metal. He saw a group from some religious sect bearing colourful banners and clothes; watching from the road as the *Adva* passed under a high, arched bridge. Though taking down the mast cost them an hour, Tolmai and his crew continued to force the pace.

An incident later in the day darkened the mood among the passengers. Kammath and Yablus had been speaking in their own tongue for some time when Kabir snapped at them and both became quiet and sullen. Later, when the chieftain went below, Idan explained that Kabir could simply not bear to hear too much talk about his missing daughter.

As they bedded down that night, Simo discovered that they would indeed reach their destination on the following day. The captain made it clear that he would not converse with Cassius, so it was Simo who paid what they hoped would be their last fee the next morning.

Other than a thunderstorm that slowed their departure, the *Adva* once again progressed well and they arrived at the point closest to the Chalcedon road with an hour of daylight to spare. The village was quite large, built upon partially terraced slopes above the Sakarya. Cassius expected the ship to remain there for the night but as the passengers disembarked, Tolmai bade them farewell. Those crew on deck also said a word or two as the Syrians jumped from the side of the vessel to the timber quay and Tolmai explained that they were stopping only for half an hour – not long enough to bother with the gangplank.

The captain shook the hand Cassius offered him without looking him in the eye. His wife and youngest daughter were coiling ropes and politely wished him well. Of Talitha there was no sign.

Once ashore, the party met a local who confirmed they had enough light to reach an inn upon the Chalcedon road. He also divulged that they could hire mounts from the stable owned by the same man.

The path to the road led up through the terraced slopes. The largest building beside it was a surprisingly respectable villa, with a colonnaded doorway and a garden full of exotic plants. As the six men made their way upwards, a gate clanged open and a rotund, middle-aged woman waddled out. She was wearing an apron over her tunic and holding a piece of paper.

'Are you Master Corbulo?'

'I am,' said Cassius once he'd recovered from this unexpected development.

'This is for you. The name and details of my master, who is a former centurion and tax collector. We receive post here, so if you want to send a letter, we will keep it.'

'A letter?'

'Yes.' The woman turned and pointed down the slope. 'For her.'

In the fading light, Cassius could just make out the slender frame and dark locks of Talitha. She was standing at the corner of a wall, looking up.

'She can read and write Greek quite well. The *Adva* passes through at least three or four times a year. I would make sure that anything from you reached her. She was very insistent that I tell you so.'

'I see.'

At a word from Kabir, the Syrians continued up the slope.

Cassius took the paper, and made sure Talitha saw him do so. The likelihood of him ever coming here again was slim. And the truth was – even without his current preoccupations – the pair of them were simply too different in background. Cassius wished it were not so; he often preferred the company of common girls to those of his class. But without any chance of marriage, he would simply be leading her on.

And yet he could not bring himself to tell the woman that, though he knew it would be kinder. If he had learned anything in the last few years, it was that life could take the most unlikely of turns.

Her efforts were probably no more than desperation or infatuation but there was something deeply touching about the lengths Talitha had gone to. Like him, she needed hope. There was always a chance.

'Thank you.'

The woman smiled politely and returned inside.

Cassius put the note inside his money bag, then raised his hand.

Talitha waved back and blew him a kiss.

For the briefest moment, he was tempted to charge straight back down that path and run away with her. But the fantasy was merely that.

'Sir, are you all right?'

'Yes. Walk on.'

Cassius blew Talitha a kiss then turned away so that she would not see him wipe his eyes.

XXIV

Sleeping and dreaming gave him respite. When he was awake, he was either examining his failing body or waiting for the next visit from Surgeon. He wasn't sure how many times they had bled him but he knew it was more than ten. They tried to make him keep eating but the solid ball of pain in his chest had quelled any remaining appetite. He was thirsty all the time, however, and his captors made sure the mugs by his bedside were always full.

Twice Indavara had heard Surgeon complain that his 'patient' needed a rest. Once, when they'd thought he was asleep, he'd heard Slab insisting that the treatment was working; that his master needed more blood. Indavara found himself praying to Fortuna once again: not to directly help him – it seemed she was unwilling or unable to do so – but to help this man. If the mad bastard improved, they would leave Indavara alone. He had seen fighters lose a lot of blood and survive; and he reckoned it was true that the body could make more. But every day he felt worse.

His skin was so pale now; paler even than Corbulo's. It felt cool too; and wet. And though he was lying down and had not risen for days, he felt dizzy; a little like he'd drunk too many mugs of wine. The pain in his chest seemed to suck the rest of his body inwards, slowly sapping every last ounce of strength.

Indavara wasn't sure how much more he could take. Unable now to stay awake for more than an hour or two, he feared that he might soon drift off forever.

And then there were the dreams.

Forests shrouded by fog. Frozen lakes. Houses made of timber.

One house in particular he saw again and again: a conical roof of thatch; a high, fenced yard beside it. The door was dark. He never saw inside. He never saw anyone.

On this day, Indavara had managed to stay awake longer than usual. The gulls were shrieking loudly, reminding him that there was a world outside. The thought formed slowly. Might these not be dreams? Might they be memories?

Of all the cruel tricks played upon him, this might prove to be the worst of all. Now as he faced death, was he at last beginning to remember where he came from? Who he was?

When he next awoke, they were there.

Arms crossed, Slab looked down at him with his usual cold curiosity. Warty and Narrow Eyes were there too, behind him. Indavara couldn't remember the last time they had bothered to unsheathe their blades. He could barely summon the energy to lift a mug to his mouth.

'How are you feeling today?' Surgeon stepped into view and peered at him, his tongue poking out as it always did when he carried out his examinations.

Indavara didn't answer. He had stopped speaking several days before because nothing he said made any difference. What he did notice was that Surgeon didn't have his wooden chest with him, which gave him a little hope.

'A visitor for you,' said Slab, gesturing towards the door.

It was bright outside and the stranger had to come close before Indavara could see him. He was walking with a stick, and beside him was a servant who put a chair down so his master could sit.

He was old, but not as old as Surgeon. His hair was quite dark, his beard almost white. Though he was fat, his limbs seemed weak and withered. His eyes were very bloodshot, and he dabbed at them with a handkerchief before speaking.

'I am so glad that I have the strength to come at last, Indavara. It is you who has given me that strength.'

His voice was gentle, reasonable.

'They told me there were no other alternatives, no treatments left to try. But I remembered you – I believe it was your eighth fight. The two Africans and the barbarian with the axe. By all the gods, three times I thought they had you. I have seen men with such power, and men with such agility, and men with such quickness of thought. But together? Truly, you are one of a kind. When they at last found you in Arabia, I knew there was hope.'

He placed his hand on Indavara's, which was again strapped to the pole.

'I can never apologise enough. And were I to do so, it would be meaningless because of what I have done to you. Believe me, I would never have even entertained the idea if I'd had any other choice. All I can do now it try to re-balance the scales. I am improving all the time. We will not need too much more . . . help from you. We can give you time to recover between each session now. And soon it will stop. We will wait until you are able to travel then take you to the mainland.'

Indavara noted a roll of the eyes from Slab. So he was on an island. Again, he wondered how far from Rhodes it was.

'And you will be paid,' said the old man. 'Not just well, but well enough to ensure that you never have to work again. That is the least I can do – the very least.'

Indavara heard himself speak before he even realised he wanted to break his self-imposed silence. 'Let me go. I beg you.'

'Soon. Very soon.'

'Why do you think I am worth less than you? I was free. I had a life. You have taken it from me.'

The old man removed his hand. He dabbed at his eyes.

'Perhaps you should go, sir.'

The man let Slab help him to his feet. The attendant handed him his stick.

'We will do all we can for you, Indavara, I promise you.' He turned to Surgeon. 'Not today. Nor tomorrow. I don't need it.'

He walked out, his form lost quickly to the light.

'You hungry?' asked Slab.

Indavara turned away and closed his eyes. He wanted to sleep and he wanted to dream. He wanted to see the house with the conical roof and the darkened door. He was beginning to think it was his home.

XXV

'I'm glad to see you're feeling better.'

'It may only be because we are close to the city now,' said Kabir. 'The illness, whatever it is, seems to fade when I am required to take action.'

He and Cassius were standing outside a stable, waiting for the owner to assemble the coins he was exchanging for the horses. The six mounts had been of decidedly average quality but had conveyed them to Chalcedon within two and a half days; a reasonable time. Simo and the Syrians were re-packing their gear, ready to cross the mile of water that separated Chalcedon from Byzantium. Cassius didn't anticipate any difficulty; one of the stable lads had disclosed that dozens of vessels – large and small – made the trip from dawn to dusk. He and Simo had also sold their saddles, bringing in much-needed funds. If necessary, he could hire a mount by the day.

The pair watched a squad of legionaries approaching, each man armed with pilum and shield. The locals gathered on the street made sure they were well out of the way by the time the soldiers marched past.

Kabir turned to the west, and the gently sloping street that ran down to the harbour. It was a bright day and sunlight glittered upon the calm water. Beyond the channel lay the walls and towers of Byzantium.

'You have been there before?'

'No,' said Cassius. 'Though I've always wanted to. It is an important city for us, strategically speaking. Apart from its position upon the peninsula, there is a large and easily defended estuary to the north – the locals refer to it as "the horn".'

'A rich city, is it not?'

'It is – mostly as a result of trade and the taxation of vessels passing through the straits.'

Kabir shielded his eyes. 'It looks very large.'

'Not as large as Antioch. And most of it is concentrated on the peninsula.'

'You said you would tell me what you intend to do. That was two days ago.'

'I have had to give it a good deal of thought.'

The street was noisy. Cassius guided Kabir into an unoccupied alley that ran between the stable and dwelling next door. Three brown rats scurried away, tail to tail.

'Clearly these people take considerable precautions to protect their identity. However, we can make some educated guesses about their clients. They will be rich men: risk-takers with exotic tastes—'

'—who are not concerned about associating with criminals.'

'They may not even know that they are. All the clients will care about is the girls. Meliton mentioned that there was a great . . . variety on offer. That alone may set this place apart. There are different types of brothels; different levels. I wouldn't be surprised if this place is rather "exclusive" – possibly invitation only, probably in some secret or remote location.'

'You have used such places?'

Cassius reckoned Kabir thought he might be ashamed. But he was not.

'On occasion. It is practically mandatory for soldiers; men *and* officers. But only decent, well-run places, you understand. They are generally regulated by the magistrates – like any other business.'

'If they use illegally bought slaves, might the authorities know of them?'

'They might. Unfortunately, I must assume that word of my unsanctioned absence has also reached here. I cannot risk approaching the army or even giving out my name. Not only for my own benefit, I might add – I will be no use to you locked up in a cell.'

'Then what we can do?'

'The fact that this operation is able to keep going despite some highly unsavoury connections might in itself be instructive. The best way to protect any such organisation is to have well-placed contacts among the authorities – especially as some of them might well be clients. If they have been going long enough to earn themselves a nickname, then they may well have some powerful patrons.'

Kabir did not look encouraged by what he had heard. 'But what can we do?'

'Apart from the need for haste, I'm not convinced that conventional enquiries will get us anywhere, especially as we have limited funds to grease the wheels. However, I imagine that these men – whoever they are – secretly enjoy the notoriety of this nickname. But they have made a mistake in allowing it to spread so far. I intend to make sure they regret it.'

'How?'

'As there is little chance of me finding them, I must ensure that *they* find me.'

It was a calculated risk; of the type Cassius had taken several times in the last few years. If these 'Earthly Gods' took their security as seriously as the evidence suggested, he reckoned they would show themselves either on this day or the one after. He certainly hoped so, because his other options were limited.

'Last trip!' came a particularly loud cry from outside. 'Last crossing of the day!'

'Gods, shut your hole, man.'

Having dispatched the others to the city on a crucial errand, Cassius was alone in the room they had rented. The inn was a decidedly unpleasant place; musty and damp, being next to the water. But it was cheap and utterly anonymous amongst the similar establishments that lined the northern end of the harbour. With sailors and passengers coming and going at every hour, they would be lost in the crowd.

Cassius had asked Simo to take out his hardwood box before he left. He now opened the lid of a smaller box, placing it on the room's only table. Standing there in two rows were the great gods of Rome, each two inches tall and carved from well-oiled mahogany. It always struck Cassius as vaguely ironic that Simo took such good care of them; symbols of a pantheon that meant nothing to him. Typical of the man.

'Last trip of the day! Any takers? Last trip!'

Cassius tutted, then stood up and closed the shutters of the window. Though the noise from outside would be reduced, the room's odour – sweat? urine? fish? – would grow stronger. Leaving the gods for a moment, he grabbed a cloth and finished cleaning his dagger. He would not be able to take the sword with him, so the wide blade would be his only defence. Once it was sheathed, he walked over to the selection of tunics Simo had hung from a hook. After some thought, he selected a pale green outfit with dark blue lozenges at the collar and wrist. He also retrieved an opulent silver belt and some similarly vulgar rings he kept for his merchant alter ego.

He would put it all on later, just before they left. For now, he was clad only in his loincloth.

'Ugh.' The air soon became intolerably stuffy without ventilation. He pulled back the shutters and leaned over the sill. The room was at the back of the inn, overhanging the water. Several well-packed skiffs and boats were taking passengers across the straits as the sun set. They would have to be careful. A dozen large galleys were powering north and south under oars; there was barely enough wind to fill a sail.

For the thousandth time, Cassius considered where Indavara might be. So many weeks had passed now; his captors could have reached just about every province of the Empire; every corner of the world. Cassius realised he had almost stopped speculating about why they had taken him.

If he could find the girls, he and the others could find a ship heading south. The sailing season was coming to an end but there would be someone prepared to take them. With a fair wind, they might be back in Antioch within two weeks. He could also head straight for Berytus to resume the search but both cities held the danger of discovery. He winced at the thought of coming face to face with Abascantius.

Cassius turned his mind to more immediate concerns. He knelt in front of the figurines and bowed his head.

'Jupiter, god of gods, I speak to you now as your loyal and dutiful servant. I know I have asked you many times for help but I am in greater need than ever. There are four people lost to us; innocents in great danger. We must find them. Father Jupiter, I beg for your help.'

Having evaded the party of noisy Arabian sailors at the inn and the porters bearing baskets of fish along the side of the harbour, Cassius and his four companions halted beside a round stone mooring post, to which several thick ropes were tied.

He had earlier sent Simo and the Syrians to buy some more typical Roman clothing and the warriors were now clad in plain, low-quality tunics. He had, however, allowed them to keep their durable leather shoes: they might well have to run. Other than Idan (who was to fulfil the role of bodyguard), they appeared unarmed. In fact, Kammath was carrying their long knives and slings in Cassius's sword bag.

'Now,' he said, when he had the nomads' attention, 'according to the innkeeper, the main street of taverns and brothels is close. There are two more areas nearer to the city but we will start here. I – we – will be going to lots of different places so it's essential that you keep track of us. Don't get too far away. If a city sergeant or a soldier asks what you are doing, reply that you are attendants waiting for your master. You remember the name?'

'Cyrillus,' said Kabir. 'Cloth merchant.'

'Good,' said Cassius, who had decided he could not even risk using his usual cover identity. 'It is unlikely that anything will happen early on. We might attract interest later tonight but it may well be tomorrow. Now, if you do see a confrontation unfolding, get as close as you can but do not intervene unless I call for you. Clear?'

'Yes,' said Kabir.

Cassius addressed Kammath. 'You will see girls on the street. You will see men with those girls. But unless you spy your sister or one of the others, you will do nothing. Is that clear?'

'Yes.'

Cassius turned to Idan, who seemed uncomfortable in his new clothes and his new role. He was undoubtedly the best choice. Apart from his quick reactions and steely presence, he was less impetuous than Kammath, less raw than Yablus and less personally involved than Kabir.

'Your job is simple. Stay close. If I need you, you'll know it – but don't go out of your way to provoke. And no blade unless you absolutely have to.'

Idan nodded.

'Never thought I'd say this – but you make my usual bodyguard seem talkative.'

The street in question was the Via Bithnyia. At first it seemed rather quiet but upon closer inspection Cassius could see that most of the taverns were quite full and that for every three taverns there was a brothel. Some were clearly denoted by a phallic symbol above the door and Cassius identified five establishments on his first pass along the street. One in particular looked promising. It boasted no less than four doormen, glassed windows on the ground floor and a fine fresco of intertwined naked figures. Cassius had, however, decided to try the taverns first; he could pick up information there more easily.

One of the more respectable-looking places was occupied mainly by merchants, rich youths and officers of both the army and navy. Cassius ordered a mug of cheap wine for himself and took a seat at a small table with Idan. The Syrian attracted quite a few looks. His distinctive appearance would mark them out, which Cassius considered an advantage for what he had in mind.

The patrons' apparent devotion to their peers was not helpful; there were few opportunities for Cassius to isolate an individual. He waited for a likely-looking fellow to approach the counter, then joined him. Cassius had settled on the man – who was a civilian – because of his drunken state, merry demeanour and the golden rings upon both hands: a decadent fellow who liked to spend.

'Decent place this,' said Cassius. 'Some decent girls, too.'

'Not bad.' The patron was tall and rather noble-looking, with a strong nose and wavy, black hair.

'A tad mundane perhaps,' added Cassius, 'do you know of anywhere that a man might have more choice?'

'Plenty of choice here on the Bithnyia; the old quarter too.'

His drink had arrived.

'Mmm,' said Cassius. 'I've heard of one outfit who offer a most eclectic variety – The Earthly Gods. Mean anything to you?'

'No. Hope you find what you're looking for.'

With that, he took his drink and returned to his friends, seemingly saying nothing of the encounter. Cassius had no clue if he had told the truth; he seemed like a man who might be quite adept at lying.

A minute later, Cassius asked the same questions of a serving-girl. Her face was more readable but she seemed to have no idea what he was talking about.

The pair visited three more taverns on the Via Bithnyia. Cassius spoke to ten patrons and five workers and was met with nothing but blank faces. The only response of more interest came from a young, very well dressed fellow who could barely stand up.

He gave a dramatic shake of his head, then pointed at Cassius. 'Naughty. Very naughty. You shouldn't—'

At that moment, his similarly young and similarly drunk friends grabbed him as they exited the inn. But as it was the only grain of hope to be drawn from the night's enquiries, Cassius felt rather encouraged.

From the Via Bithnyia they moved on to the old quarter, then a third area close to an impressive statue of Julius Caesar. Kabir,

Kammath and Yablus did a good job of tracking them and avoided any encounters with the city watchmen, of whom there were many.

By what he guessed to be around the fourth hour of night, Cassius had spoken to at least thirty men, without improving on what he had gleaned from the young drunk. But from at least two of those he questioned later on, he'd detected an underlying fearfulness at the very mention of 'The Earthly Gods'. When he and Idan met with the other three at the statue of Caesar, he had already established where their limited funds would be best spent.

'It's called Dianthe's Den – I spotted it earlier on the Via Bithnyia. Sounds cheap but apparently there are some exotic girls.'

'They could be in there?' asked Kabir.

'Possibly. But from what I've heard, it's a big, well-established place. Very well known. It's unlikely they would risk using illegal slaves. Then again, they may not know who is illegal and who is not – they might pay off whichever inspector is supposed to check on such things. In any case, there's still a good chance that someone might know something. Let's get back there. Even brothels don't stay open until dawn.'

If Idan was uncomfortable with the night so far, it was about to get far worse for him. Having each paid the two denarii entrance fee, the pair gave up their weapons to the quartet of burly enforcers at the door. They were then shown through to a subtly lit reception room staffed by a middle-aged woman and a maid who reappeared swiftly from an anteroom with a complimentary glass of wine. Neither she nor the madam seemed at all concerned by Idan's appearance.

'Are you Dianthe?' asked Cassius.

'Her granddaughter.'

'Ah. So this place really has been going for a long time.'

'It has, sir – since the time of Gordian. Now what can we do for you?'

'Actually it's not for me. Something of a gift for my bodyguard here. You wouldn't think it but he's a picky sod. Perhaps we could see what's on offer.'

Though he felt like he knew the girl, Cassius had never seen Aikaterine – or Dinora or Marte. He would need Idan with him to make an identification.

'Your price range, sir?'

'Oh anything.' Cassius gestured at Idan, who was standing bolt upright, looking apprehensive. 'Saved my life, he did.'

The woman adjusted her necklace; an expensive-looking collation of amber. 'Really? Well, of course many of the girls are occupied. But we can show you the others. They'll be outside their rooms. Any specific interests or tastes? I might be able to help you.'

Idan shrugged.

'I'm afraid if he doesn't make a selection we'll have to charge another denarius – our viewing fee.'

'Fair enough,' said Cassius, 'I may indulge myself.'

'As you wish, sir. Ioanna here will take you through, and she'll also inform me of any transactions. Most of the girls charge by the hour. You'll see more of our men in the corridor but don't worry about them – they'll stay out of your way as long as the girls are treated well. Would you like to take your drinks with you?'

'Yes.'

'Best of luck.' The madam reached out and patted Idan's arm. 'And don't you worry, sweetheart – we get all sorts in here. The girls will treat you as well as a handsome prince.'

Ioanna pulled aside a heavy curtain. It seemed obvious to Cassius why she was tasked with such duties; some affliction had left one of her eyes half-closed. The corridor beyond the curtain ran a surprisingly long way back. It was illuminated by lanterns and provided access to rooms on either side. An enforcer was stationed at both ends of the corridor. The one they passed nodded cordially to Cassius but glared at Idan.

The doorways were covered with thinner curtains. The first two were pulled across. From one came the sounds of amorous activity, from the other male and female laughter. Under the lantern outside each door was a square of slate in a wooden frame. Written upon these two in chalk was a single word: *busy*.

The next two prostitutes were not busy and each stood in a doorway. Both wore diaphanous gowns and lots of jewellery. According to the slates they were Aoide and Photine. Both charged five denarii per hour.

'Good evening, sirs,' they said, almost simultaneously.

'Evening,' said Cassius, trying to look like a normal customer. 'We're just browsing for the moment. Might see you later.'

As they continued on, Cassius turned to Idan. 'See anything you like?'

'I don't like anything about this.'

About half the girls were not engaged and they had encountered five more by the time they reached the end of the corridor and turned right. The second enforcer – who was mining his mouth with a toothpick – waved them onwards.

'More on the other side.'

They passed what looked like an office, where a portly man was counting coins and an elderly woman was operating an abacus at impressive speed. Then came a spacious lounge, where a group of well-dressed men were playing dice. Musical accompaniment was supplied by two female flautists in revealing outfits.

There was no enforcer at the next corner but they saw a third at the far end of the corridor. Six more girls came out to offer themselves, some more enthusiastic than others.

'Nothing take your fancy?' asked Cassius loudly as they neared the man, who was standing with his back to the wall, one boot up against it.

Idan shook his head.

Just as the enforcer reached for the curtain, Cassius held up a hand. 'A question. Which of the girls is the newest? I prefer them . . . fresh.'

The enforcer – a bear of a man with a stench that radiated outwards – just looked at him.

'Ah.' Cassius reached into his money bag and handed over a sesterce, ensuring the girls behind him did not see. 'And a lively one, perhaps. Can't stand it when they just lie there.'

'Like a sack of onions,' grunted the enforcer.

'Exactly.'

'Zosime will see you right. Seems to enjoy her work and she's only been here a couple of weeks. They change them all the time.'

'I'm sure. Thank you.'

'Round the other side,' added the man.

Once past prying eyes and open ears, Idan stopped at the corner. 'What was all that about?'

'I need to talk to one of the girls. Obviously a new arrival suits our purposes, as does one who likes to talk.'

'You're not going to—'

'Gods, of course not. I'll be as quick as I can. I suggest you wait outside. If anyone asks, just say nothing appealed to you but I am partaking. Don't divulge any more than . . . well, I'm sure you won't.'

The prostitutes were clearly not surprised by clients who took their time but there were some unpleasant looks when Cassius approached Zosime and Idan returned to the reception room.

While the girl turned her slate over and pulled the curtain across, Cassius examined the room. With the small bed and only a table for furniture, it was similar to others he'd seen. The fresco on the wall beside the bed was so faded that only a tree and the head of a woman could be discerned. Considering its apparent popularity, Dianthe's Den seemed to Cassius rather downmarket.

'What's your name, sir?' asked Zosime.

'Cassius.' Like most Roman first names, it was so common that he was not concerned about using it.

'Would you like more wine?' She gestured to the flask on the table. 'I can have some fetched if the house blend isn't to your liking.'

'No thank you.'

Noting that the sheets upon the bed at least appeared clean, Cassius placed five denarii in Zosime's hand and sat down.

'As I am paying for your time, do you object to me using it however I see fit?'

The girl was already removing the green belt of cloth around her waist. She stopped. 'Sir?'

'Come. Sit. Leave that on.'

Zosime possessed a curvy figure and a round face. Her make-up was little short of disastrous but her soft, even features compensated. She sat down.

'I'm going to be completely honest with you, Zosime. I have been hired by a man whose daughter and two friends were illegally taken as slaves. We believe they are working somewhere in Byzantium – in your profession. They are Syrians, from nomadic stock: their names are Aikaterine, Dinora and Marte. All are seventeen. Do you know anything of them?'

Zosime looked at the wall opposite and gave this some thought. 'I don't think so. I've been here since the Festival of Vesta and five – no, six – girls have started here since then.'

'The names don't ring a bell?'

'No – but a lot of girls don't use their real names. One was young enough – she didn't say she was Syrian though. Don't remember the name.'

'Is she still working here?'

'No. She only did a couple of days. Don't know what happened.'

'I have another question.'

Cassius watched a man's feet walk past the door. He waited ten seconds then got up and peered though the gap between curtain and doorway. The man – a small fellow carrying a cloak over one arm – spoke with a girl further down the corridor then followed her into her room.

Cassius returned to the bed. 'Have you heard of another brothel – an expensive place with girls from all over?'

'There are some other places in the city. I think they all have lots of different girls.'

'I mean from *very* far afield – Britain and Germania perhaps, even Africa or Arabia.'

When she shrugged Cassius realised he had not been particularly clever after all. A long-serving girl might have known more.

'And this name: "The Earthly Gods" – does it mean anything to you?'

'No, sir.'

'Right. Now, listen. I don't want to get you into trouble, but if you could find out what happened to that girl and listen out for anything about any of the three I mentioned, I would be very grateful. The names are Aikaterine, Marte and Dinora.'

He made her repeat them twice.

'All from Syria,' she added. 'All seventeen.'

'That's it. I'll come back in a few days and pay you the same again. If you know girls from other places, ask them too.'

'And about these earthy gods?'

'*Earthly*. No. Don't mention that.' He didn't want to expose her to the risk of directly attracting their attention. 'Right, we'll leave it a few minutes then I'll get going.'

Zosime squeezed up close, her right breast against Cassius's arm. 'Sure you don't want to?'

'Yes. Not that I wouldn't enjoy it, of course.'

In fact, Cassius wasn't sure that he was ever going to use the services offered by such a place ever again.

Though he thought it wise to keep a clear head, he downed another mug of wine before leaving Zosime. Afterwards, he was never sure how much it affected the decision he made once back in the reception room. Idan was loitering by the door because the rest of the space with packed with at least a dozen men.

'Can we go now?' asked the nomad, who was as usual attracting quite a bit of attention from the patrons.

Cassius appraised them: well off and of varying ages, possibly the members of a guild or simply a large group of friends. Frustrated by the results of his night's work, he decided on another calculated risk.

'Greetings, gentlemen,' he declared loudly. 'This is a fine establishment but my man and I are seeking more exotic fare. Tell me, have any of you heard of "The Earthly Gods"?'

The madam turned and stared at him, along with every single one of the men.

'No? None of you? I'll say it again – "The Earthly Gods" – I was told they are well known in Byzantium. Was I misinformed?'

'You should leave.' A man at the back appeared from behind another. He was about fifty, his face grim.

'You should leave *now*,' said a second man. He was younger but with a similarly resolute expression.

'I think perhaps you should, sir,' said the madam.

The enforcer pushed his way through the curtain and another appeared on the far side of the room.

'Very well,' said Cassius.

He and Idan crossed the silent room. By the time they left it, he was sure: some – if not all – of the men knew precisely what he was talking about.

'And now?'

Cassius and the four Syrians were sitting on the low wall of a darkened sanctuary with a fair view of the Via Bithnyia.

'Now we wait,' he told Kabir. 'To see if word of the big-mouthed idiot at Dianthe's reaches the right people.'

'Nothing from the girl?' asked Idan.

'No, but I asked her to keep an ear out. If this proves fruitless, we'll do the same thing tomorrow and I'll return to her in a few days – if they let me in.'

'The girls in there are legal slaves?' asked Kammath.

'Probably. I mean probably slaves. Some might be doing it temporarily – for the money.'

'I don't see how it works – surely many of them will be with child if they—'

'How do your women avoid that?' asked Cassius.

'They don't. Before marriage, we do not . . . we do not do that.'

'Ah, I see. Well, it does happen, of course. But there are ways – medical ways, that is. Vinegar, for example.'

'These women,' said Kammath. 'How—'

His father silenced him.

Idan muttered something in Aramaic, which Kabir seemed to agree with.

'How long must we wait?' asked the chieftain.

'In an hour, I will walk along the street once more, mentioning our secretive friends to whomever I encounter. In another hour I will return again.'

Cassius gestured to the strip of grass in front of them. 'Rest if you wish. We have had little sleep and I might need you alert and ready later on.'

He did precisely as he'd said he would. Before visiting the street for the third time, he expanded on his instructions to Kabir, Kammath and Yablus.

'So remember – if we're approached, leave it to us unless I give the signal. I can't believe it will be any more than a warning, though just how fierce a warning remains to be seen. There are three of you. I'll be surprised if there aren't at least three of them. Follow as best you can. If *they* split up, *you* split up. If they go into buildings, mark the areas. I know it won't be easy. Just do your best.'

It was by now the sixth hour of night and even the Via Bithnyia was virtually deserted. As Cassius and Idan walked along it, they saw only a few enforcers and some drunken patrons lurching out of the inns with a late-night licence. Cassius took his time and slowed down as he neared Dianthe's Den. One of the doormen had seen him half a dozen times.

'Ain't you got a home to go to?'

Cassius ignored him and continued on his way, noting a few workers cleaning up inside the hostelries. The pair were two-thirds of the way along the Via Bithnyia, approaching a side street.

It was Idan who turned first. Cassius heard the rasp of the Syrian's dagger being drawn as he spun around.

Two figures had stepped out of a shadowy alley ten feet behind them. They had chosen the place well; barely a trace of light from the surrounding buildings reached them. All Cassius could make out was the outline of two tall, well-built men, and the hoods with which they covered their faces.

'Good evening, young man.' The man to the left spoke in Greek, with no obvious accent.

Knowing he had to try and draw them closer to a light, Cassius grabbed Idan's wrist and backed away. But the Syrian stopped after three steps.

'Behind us,' he breathed.

Cassius looked over his shoulder. Two more men had appeared from the side street. He could see almost nothing of them either.

'Stay exactly where you are. You are only in danger if you move.'

Behind the first pair, a man was walking unsteadily along, whistling a tune. The leader's compatriot turned, grabbed hold of him and with a few hissed words in his ear, sent him back the other way.

'Sheathe that knife.'

'Go ahead,' Cassius told Idan. The Syrian obeyed.

'I'm told you've been talking a lot tonight,' said the faceless stranger. 'Loudly.'

'I'm just curious. I was told about these "Earthly Gods" and this paradise of girls from all over. But nobody seems to know a damn thing.'

'Who told you that name?'

'Some drunk. It sounded like he'd had the time of his life. I don't suppose you could get me into the place?'

'The name you speak of belongs to a gang of criminals once based here in the city. They were of the worst kind – pederasts and rapists. Nobody wants to hear that name in Byzantium. Understand?'

'I'm sorry but I had no idea. Might I ask what your interest is in all of this?'

'You will not come to this street again and you will not mention that name again. Understand?'

Cassius didn't have to feign anxiousness for his answer. There was something utterly chilling about the calm way in which the man spoke.

'I shall do as you say. I pledge it.'

'Good. Because if you do not, we shall tear out your tongue. You'll note I didn't say *cut* – I said *tear*. By the root. We have done it before. We use workman's pliers. There will be a lot of blood and an indescribable amount of pain.'

With that, he and his compatriot walked away – to their right, into the middle of the street so that the gloom would hide them.

Neither Cassius nor Idan moved until they were sure all four of the interlopers had gone. They remained there for a while but saw no sign of the other Syrians either.

The next two hours passed painfully slowly. Once back at the inn, Idan busied himself sorting through the nomads' collection of sling ammunition, while Simo prepared his master a strong mug of wine. Cassius sat by the window, unable to avoid mulling over the scenarios that might play out with the Syrians trying to follow the mysterious quartet. Few of them were good, and as two hours became three, he began to think this had been a calculated risk taken without proper calculation.

Yablus returned first. Breathing loudly, he sank to the floor and gratefully sloshed down the water Simo gave him.

'They split up about a half a mile away, further into the city. We were with a pair but then they separated so I had to follow one. He kept taking strange turns and I thought he knew I was there. Then I lost him completely.' Yablus put a hand to his head. 'Then I got lost myself. Sorry.'

'You did what you could,' said Cassius. 'Where you lost him – would you be able to find it again?'

The young nomad grimaced. 'Maybe . . . probably not.'

A quarter-hour later, Kammath turned up. Cassius had harboured fears of him pouncing on one of the men in an effort to get information. But although Kabir's son had restrained himself, his news was little better than his cousin's.

'It was almost impossible. Twice I was nearly seen by city sergeants. The second time I ended up so far behind, I lost him.'

'You followed the other man from the same pair as Yablus?'

'Yes.'

'Where were you when you lost him?'

'I checked the area. The only marker was an arch. I could find it again.'

'That's something,' said Yablus.

'They could have been setting a false trail,' said Cassius. 'You're both sure they didn't see you?'

'I am,' said Kammath. Yablus admitted he could not be certain.

When Kabir returned, it took him a moment to compose himself. He was so tired and soaked with sweat that he instantly began to shiver. Kammath put a blanket over his father's shoulders.

Cassius squatted in front of him. 'Well?'

'They split up. I stuck with one – I think it was the leader, who spoke to you. He kept taking turns and doubling back. I stayed with him as long as I could but I lost him in an area of narrow streets and alleys. It was like a maze. I tried to mark the location. The only place of note was a high wall and when I had a closer look I realised there were legionaries guarding a gate. It was a fort. While I was watching it, he arrived. He must have taken another detour. The guards saluted when they let him in.'

'Well done, Kabir. Could you find it again?'

'Yes. Yes, I think I could.'

XXVI

The sense that not a moment could be wasted was inescapable. Cassius somehow slept for an hour or two then lay awake, looking up through the window at a sky packed with white-blue stars.

They had come so far – and might now be so close that he could think of nothing else. The Syrians lying on the floor seemed restless too. Cassius decided that they had to act immediately. Rousing Kabir (who was the only one sleeping soundly) he asked the chief to take him back to the fortress. They would need to be there when the sun rose.

Cassius strode up to the main entrance of what they now knew to be one of three fortresses within Byzantium's walls. The local store owner they'd consulted had also disclosed that it housed two centuries of the local garrison, which was charged with the defence of the city and the Thracian peninsula.

Nipping ahead of a pair of cavalrymen, Cassius hailed the two night-time sentries just as they walked away from the gate towards the parade ground. Their replacements were already in place, having arrived with the dawn.

'Yes?'

'My name is Cyrillus. I'd like to talk to you.'

'We've just finished the night shift, sir.'

He was glad to hear the soldier address him so. He had dressed in his best tunic and adorned himself with most of the jewellery.

'It won't take long; and I promise to make it worth your while.'

Despite their obvious weariness, the soldiers asked their compatriots to open the gate.

'Excellent. Thank you,' said Cassius. 'There's a quiet spot just down there.' The helpful store owner was more than happy to earn a denarius for the hire of his courtyard.

As they crossed the street, the second man spoke up. 'Sir, what's all this about?'

'You shall find out presently.'

The owner – who seemed to specialise in household utensils – guided the four of them through a packed storeroom and then into the courtyard, which was dank, chilly and dark. Simo was armed with one of the Syrian's swords. As instructed by Cassius, he was to stand at his shoulder and try to look like a bodyguard.

'Allow me to explain – I am in Byzantium investigating a criminal matter for a private client. As I said, my name is Cyrillus. And yours?'

'Legionary Apius Mucius, third century under Centurion Octavius.'

Mucius was the younger of the two.

'Legionary Gaius Helva, third under Octavius also.' Helva seemed less impressed by Cassius; and more suspicious.

'All I need from you is some information. And if I get what I ask for, you will be very well rewarded.'

Though both made some effort to conceal their enthusiasm, neither was successful. Cassius knew just how avaricious the average soldier was; pay was usually doled out quarterly and they were always on the lookout for money-making opportunities.

'I happen to know that one of your officers returned to the fortress late last night. His name?'

'This reward you speak of,' said Helva. 'Let's see it.'

Cassius held up his hand, which was adorned with two identical rings; both silver, both worth at least forty denarii.

'I don't like carrying a lot of coins. Will these do?'

'Let's have a proper look,' said Helva.

Cassius held up his hand as the legionary inspected the metal.

'Not bad.'

'The name, then?'

'Optio Barba,' said Mucius.

Cassius turned to Helva. 'That right?'

'Yes.'

Somewhere in the buildings around them, a woman was shrieking at her children to get up.

'And when did he return?'

'Just after the seventh hour,' said Mucius.

'I do not want you to feel that you are going against your own. There is currently no evidence of wrongdoing by this man. It is a case of eliminating him – and many others – from my enquiries. To which century does he belong? Yours?'

Cassius had purposefully addressed Helva, to force him to contribute.

'No. The fourth.'

'His reputation?'

Mucius shrugged.

'Good,' said Helva. 'Tough but fair.'

'How long has he been stationed in the city?'

'Longer than me,' said Mucius, 'and that's six years. The third and the fourth centuries almost never leave the city.'

'Likes to gamble, does he? Drink?'

'No more than anyone else,' said Helva. Cassius got the impression he was offering up the minimal amount of information possible, which was entirely understandable.

'Gets on well with his centurion? Other officers?'

'Wouldn't really know, sir,' said Mucius.

It was Helva's turn to shrug.

'Women? Is he married?'

Mucius nodded. 'Wife lives out in the sticks somewhere, I think.'

'Hearth girl?'

'Think so,' said Mucius. 'Can't remember the name but she hangs out at Natta's a lot.'

'Which is?'

'Eatery. Not far away.'

'I really need the name.'

Mucius scratched his face. 'Er . . . might start with a "C" . . . '

Helva was looking down at the ground.

Cassius fingered one of the rings. 'It would be unfortunate if I couldn't give you one of these each but – as it stands – the contribution has hardly been equal, has it?'

'I don't mind, sir,' said Mucius.

'I do,' said Cassius.

'All right,' said Helva, 'I get the point. Her name's Sousanna.'

Natta's was three streets away. Cassius spent a few coins and had her address within ten minutes. Aware that every such step he took risked exposure and the attention of his foes, he pressed on regardless. He would not stop until he found The Earthly Gods, and he reckoned he could do so before nightfall.

Having reunited with the Syrians, he led them into the three-storey apartment block where Sousanna lived. It was a comparatively spacious but grimy place; malodourous and noisy. A pair of boys directed him to the woman's door. Instructing the Syrians to stay back, he knocked.

She opened the door only an inch.

Cassius deployed his most respectable voice. 'Hello. You are Sousanna, a . . . friend of Optio Barba?'

'Who's asking?'

'May I come in? I'm afraid I have some bad news.'

Her hand went to her mouth and she backed away. Cassius pushed the door open and he and Simo entered.

'What is it? What's happened?'

Cassius gestured to one of the stools beside a circular table and waited for her to sit down.

'Kabir.'

The four Syrians rushed in and shut the door behind them.

Sousanna – a statuesque woman of about thirty wearing a pale red tunic and huge earrings – looked at them then back at Cassius. 'What—'

'You needn't be alarmed,' he said. 'I'm afraid I don't actually know where Barba is but I need to see him immediately. Rest assured that if you cooperate, neither you nor he will get hurt. Now, Sousanna, can you write?'

'A little.'

'Do you ever send him messages?'

'Sometimes.'

'Excellent.'

It took the optio an hour to arrive, and when he did he was not happy. They had left the door slightly ajar and he burst in, already berating Sousanna.

'What are you playing at, woman? This better be a matter of life or death! What could—'

Idan – who was stationed behind the door – cracked him between the shoulder blades with his elbow. Barba went down on his knees. As Yablus shut and locked the door, Kabir and Kammath flanked the Roman, both with their long knives against his throat.

Cassius – who had been behind the door with the others – walked over and sat beside Sousanna. He had warned her what would happen; and how much worse it would be if she screamed. There was only one window in the apartment: it had no curtain so they had covered it with a blanket. She had assured them that she was not expecting any visitors.

Barba shook his head and sucked in some deep breaths. He was a muscular man, barrel-chested and thick-necked. His hairless head was oval, the jaw covered by a light beard. He looked up at Cassius, eyes raging. This would not be an easy man to break.

'You – from last night.'

'Yes.'

'You picked the wrong man to mess with.'

'Actually *you* did. I need to know everything you do about The Earthly Gods.'

'I told you what I know last night. That's all anyone knows. '

Cassius reached across and held Sousanna's clammy, trembling hand.

'Seems a nice girl.' Cassius pointed at Kammath and Kabir. 'Those two are the father and brother of another nice girl who was purchased by your friends. We have come a long way to get her back and we will wait no longer. Either you tell me what you know or I'll give Sousanna to them in return. Perhaps they'll take her back to the desert.'

'I'm not a slave,' said the woman.

'Neither was she,' replied Cassius.

Barba grinned. 'Take her. I have three – and she's bottom of the pile.'

'You son of a bitch,' cried Sousanna.

Cassius held the optio's stare for a moment, then stood up, dragging Sousanna with him. He walked her to the door and unlocked it.

'Simo, Yablus.' He turned to Sousanna. 'These two are going to take you for a walk. Don't give them any trouble. When you come back we'll be gone.' He told the men: 'One hour.'

Yablus hesitated. Cassius felt he was the obvious choice to accompany Simo. There wasn't so much at stake for him; he might not act with the zeal Cassius required.

'Go on,' said Kabir, one hand on Barba's shoulder, the other still holding the knife to his neck.

'Somewhere quiet,' Cassius added.

Once the trio had left, he locked the door again. He looked down at Barba's bald head. He made himself think of the three girls; taken and exploited without a thought for them or their families. By the men this bastard worked for.

Still, he was a soldier: a low-ranking officer, in fact. Attacking him was dangerous.

'One last chance, optio. We can still do this the easy way. Who are The Earthly Gods and where can I find them?'

'I told you, lad. They don't exist any more. Someone's playing games with you.'

Cassius lashed his boot into the base of his back.

As Barba's head shot up, he swung his right fist into his ear, sending him sprawling on to the ground.

'Uhhhh.' The grunt came from between gritted teeth. 'You skinny little shit! I'll tear you apart.'

Cassius booted him in the back again. As with the men he had hurt in the village, there was simply nothing in his mind to stop him. Two years ago – perhaps only one – he could not and would not have done this. He had changed. He did not consider that an entirely bad thing.

If this thug wanted to stay faithful to his employers, he would pay for it.

'Where are they?' demanded Cassius. 'We don't have workman's pliers but we can still do plenty of damage.'

Barba was on his back now, face twisted by pain. 'There ain't no Earthly Gods.'

Kabir and Kammath looked down at him, knives at the ready. Cassius spoke to Kammath, whose face was set in a resolute stare. 'This man knows where your sister is. Let's try it without the knives first.'

The youth needed no encouragement. He kicked out, striking the captive on his legs and backside and sending the optio crawling into a corner. Barba held his hands up to his head but Kammath simply walked around him and carefully selected the location for the next blow. After one sharp kick to the groin, Cassius almost had to look away. But he could not. He had started this; he made himself watch it.

Kabir said something to his son then darted forward, grabbed Barba's tunic and dragged him backwards until he was propped up against the wall. The optio was struggling to breathe.

'Tell us. Who are they?'

Barba spat in his face.

Kabir wiped it off then back-handed him across the jaw. Now it was his turn to rain kicks down on the man. Barba continued to vainly try and defend himself but then Kammath joined in again.

Idan said something under his breath. Cassius got the impression that he did not approve of his methods.

When Kammath caught Barba on the nose, he rolled on to

his back. As he put his hand up to check his face, Kabir thudded a boot into his side. A rib cracked.

Now Cassius did turn away. He wasn't sure how much of the nausea he felt was down to what he was witnessing or the fact that he had caused it.

Then Idan joined in. Cassius wondered if it was simply out of loyalty; because he felt he had to be complicit in his friend's actions. But he soon realised it was because the warrior was intent on bringing the attack to a swift close.

Idan dropped to the floor, one knee on Barba's throat.

He spoke to Kabir and Kammath, who each held down one of the optio's hands.

Idan pushed his knee downwards. Despite the damage he had taken, Barba struggled on; and his big frame caused them some difficulty until Kabir and Kammath pinned his arms close to the shoulder. Idan took the weight off.

'Speak quickly – the truth. Or your life will end here and now.'

When the optio did nothing but grind his teeth and glare at Cassius, Idan put the weight on, the knee pressing down on Barba's windpipe.

Cassius felt almost paralysed, as if he could not affect what was happening.

Barba's eyes were bulging and bloodshot. His mouth trembled.

Idan took the weight off. Barba's head dropped back. The Syrian slapped him.

'Who are they?' hissed Kabir, his silvery hair covering his face.

Barba managed to hold up a hand. 'House of Screams.'

'What?'

'House of Screams. South of the city. You'll find them there.'

'Who are they?' asked Cassius, now standing over him. 'Who are The Earthly Gods?'

'Just men. Rich men.'

'Names,' said Cassius.

'I've told you all I know. I've never even been there.'

'Who's your contact? Who sent you to find me last night?'

Idan spoke into his ear. 'Tell him everything.'

'You bloody barbarian. I'll have you all for this. Every one of you.'

'Names!' repeated Cassius.

'You . . . you can't tell them it was me. They'll have me out of the army in a week.'

'Why would we? Just tell us and this is over.'

'There are three: Centurion Octavius, Tribune Phaedrus and a deputy magistrate – Nereus. They run it.'

Octavius – the centurion of the other unit based at the fortress.

'Very good.'

The three Syrians moved away.

Barba lay still for a moment, face contorting with every breath.

Cassius tried to help him up but the optio waved him away.

'You snapped a rib. I can feel the bloody bone sticking in.'

Cassius tried not to think about that. 'I suggest you remain here. Assuming she's the forgiving sort, Sousanna might help you. If anyone asks, you were attacked by robbers in the street. Understand?'

Barba wiped blood off his nose.

'They keep the women there?' asked Cassius.

The optio nodded.

'All the time?'

'Yes.' Barba spat a wad of pink spittle on to the floor.

'Have you seen three Syrian girls? Young?'

'They don't invite the likes of me! I just do as I'm told – to keep people away. It was just for a bit of extra money.'

Cassius had what he needed. He unlocked the door and gestured outside. As the Syrians walked into the corridor, a door opposite opened to reveal a middle-aged couple.

'Close it,' instructed Cassius.

The couple did so immediately.

As he reached the door, Barba spoke up again. 'You won't tell them?'

Cassius turned round. 'You should have cooperated when you had the chance. But I give you my word. We won't tell them.'

'How do we know he won't go straight to his superiors?' asked Kammath as they hurried down the last set of steps and out of the apartment building.

'We don't,' conceded Cassius. 'But you shouldn't underestimate what the possibility of being dismissed from the army means to a career soldier.'

'We should have killed him,' said Idan.

'Logically, yes,' said Cassius as they continued along a dank, arched corridor towards the street. 'But I did not want that and I don't believe you do either. Clearly an unpleasant man but it's his employers we're interested in.'

'But to just leave him?' said Kammath.

'What else could we have done? Post two of our number to guard him for the next few days? Where? How? No, we just have to do as we've been doing all along: move quickly and hit hard before our enemies have a chance to react. Let's find the others, then find out what we can about this House of Screams.'

XXVII

Running through the forest in the middle of the pack, spear heavy in his hand. They reach the edge of the trees, close to the precipice. Below, the river snakes across the valley. The village lies within one of the bends. Smoke drifts up from the houses.

Open ground. The red target is mounted on a tree. He fires all his arrows, collects them then starts again. He stops for a while, sits upon a log and chews through a hunk of bread. A few birds return. He picks up the bow and continues. He fires until his fingers bleed.

The town is noisy. They stop the cart and unload the timber, placing it in neat piles between the dwellings. Next stop is the merchant's by the well. He watches the girls come and go with their pails. Long hair; slim, graceful bodies. Laughter.

Indavara was surprised to still be dreaming of what he now knew to be the place where he had grown up and worked and lived. Before Abascantius and Corbulo and Simo. Before the arena. Before everything.

Surgeon hadn't come again and they hadn't taken blood from him for three days. He'd been convinced that the letting was connected to the dreams, as if somehow the loss of blood released the memories. But still they came. The town – the girls – that was new. He had not seen the house again for some time but each fresh vision amazed him.

Many times in the past few years he had experienced what he believed to be memories only to realise they were imaginings based on what he'd lived through since leaving the arena. But there was something inescapably solid about these dreams. He could almost make out the sounds, the smells of these places. He had no doubt that he had visited them many times, spent much of his early life there. Even so, he still had no idea where they were.

Sitting up in the bed, he was astonished to find himself smiling. More than ever he wanted Simo and Corbulo there – just to tell them. He had even begun to hope that he might actually get out of this alive. He had eaten three meals and his body felt warmer. His skin had coloured a little. Surely every day that Surgeon didn't come, his chances improved. If the old man did recover, might he be true to his word?

They arrived around the second hour. As soon as he saw their faces, Indavara knew something was wrong. Warty and Narrow Eyes had seemed almost relieved not to have to assist with the bloodletting over the last few days. They had even spoken to him, made a couple of jokes. But not today.

Indavara watched Surgeon walk through the door.

'No.'

'Sorry,' said Slab without even pretending to mean it. 'He's taken a turn for the worse.'

'Might only be temporary,' said Narrow Eyes, earning himself glares from the others.

'Let me go.' Hands bunched into fists, Indavara could feel his entire body shaking. 'Let me go!' Before he knew it, tears were pouring down his face. Unable to wipe them away, he could soon see almost nothing.

'Now, young man, try to stay calm or it will be worse for you.' Surgeon leaned over him and ran a cloth across his face. 'You've done it before. You can do it again.'

XXVIII

A fierce northerly wind was blowing down the straits, whipping up waves and providing plenty of work for the sailors. Those vessels on the move were doing so at some speed, the crewmen constantly adjusting sails and lines and yards. The mariners on land, meanwhile, had to secure their craft against the pressure of wind and water. Cassius looked on as a procession of small boat owners walked along the wooden pontoon where he was standing to check their vessels.

After the events of the morning and the increasingly tight knots that had formed in his stomach, he hadn't been able to eat anything and was now waiting for the others to finish lunch. There would be no time for anything later. He had spent his time making enquiries with the locals, dispensing coins when necessary. It had been difficult to discover the precise history of The House of Screams but an elderly fisherman had finally been able to tell him the whole tale.

Cassius closed his eyes, enjoying the refreshing breeze on his face. He could not help reflecting on the irony of his situation. Having disobeyed and rejected Abascantius, he now found himself employing exactly the type of direct, underhand tactics the agent favoured. If his superiors ever found out what he had done, his career would be over. The army would not be interested in the cause of a Syrian nomad; only in the harm done to one of their own by another (while absent without leave). And now it seemed he would have to take on two fellow officers; and whoever else they were associated with.

Simo came out first, carrying a cloak for his master. Cassius refused it but took a long slug of wine.

Kabir arrived slightly ahead of the others. He looked out at the straits for a time before speaking. 'You are risking much for us.'

'Let's put it this way,' said Cassius. 'I don't plan on returning to Byzantium anytime soon.'

'I am grateful.'

'I know.'

Another galley sped past: sails full; lines taut.

'I consulted the signs again yesterday.' The nomad paused, running his fingers across his forehead. 'They say that one of the girls is already dead. I do not know which.'

'And you believe that to be true?'

'Ever since Katia was taken, the signs have told me the truth. They told me that you would help, that we would have to travel far, and that our enemies would be powerful men.'

'With respect, those notions are rather vague. I can see no reason why the girls shouldn't still be alive. But I warn you that they will have been affected by what has happened. You should prepare yourself for that.'

'And that they might not even be there.'

'It's a possibility.'

When the others appeared, Cassius gathered them close. 'Our enemies are clearly not stupid. The House of Screams is an old villa close to the coast on the southern side of Byzantium. It was built about three decades ago by some rich merchant who bought the land cheaply. It was cheap because local legend holds that when Darius of Persia levelled the city eight hundred years ago, a force of defenders was wiped out on that site. It's said that the cries of man and beast can be heard and apparitions seen. This merchant paid no attention to the stories but lasted only two years there. Apparently, he and his wife were sent mad. None of the locals will go near the place. All of which makes it an ideal location for The Earthly Gods – that and the fact that there's only one gate and a very high wall.'

'You know how to get there?' asked Kabir.

'I do. We shall move as close as we can before nightfall, then try to get inside. Even if Barba has a change of heart, we have a decent chance of finding the girls; or at least finding out more.

Yablus, you are clearly quite a climber. I suggest the purchase of grappling hooks and a rope ladder. Judging by the look on Simo's face, he will be glad to hear I have another task for him. We will use our remaining funds to hire a boat for the night and a man who won't ask too many questions.'

'A boat?' said Kammath.

'If we find the girls, we must leave Byzantium tonight. I also found out a little about the three men named by Barba. The deputy magistrate, Nereus, is known as a heavy drinker and man who makes outrageous demands of those who require his cooperation. No particular surprise there – I could say the same of half those in his position. As for the tribune, Phaedrus, he is young, well connected and thought by some in the city to be rather lazy. He has had numerous affairs and has only been saved from scandal by his contacts. The centurion – Octavius – is the man I believe we must be most concerned by. He is around fifty, a veteran of numerous campaigns against the Persians and the Goths. In his youth he was a champion athlete and – if the locals are to be believed – he is still the best swordhand in Byzantium, despite the fact that he has only one eye. If at all possible, we shall avoid him.'

Simo had to ask the way several times and eventually found himself on a wide road that led down to the water. He sighed with relief when he spied the pale stone of the curved moles that protected Byzantium's Great Harbour. According to his master's instructions, he would have to hire a boat of at least fifteen feet. They would head west, half a mile along the coast to an area known as Philo's Point. Close by was the small quay where he would wait for Cassius and the Syrians.

Though glad not to be accompanying them, Simo could not remain entirely focused on his task. Thoughts of the harm he had seen his master and the nomads inflict on the men they had caught were never far away. Simo realised that they would do anything in their power to find the girls, but he was disturbed by how easily his master now turned to violence, where previously he would have used almost any other means. Simo could not imagine what would happen now, with the Syrians facing the men who had kept the girls captive. Blood would be spilled, of that much he was sure.

He was worried for Cassius. The young man seemed to have given up some part of himself; as if he had decided the only way to defeat evil-doers was to emulate them. Simo understood the logic of this – and that neither they nor the Syrians had time to waste – but he was alarmed by the speed and scale of the change. Master Cassius had put on his armour and sword alone and in silence. Little of the usual fear could be seen in his eyes; only resolve.

Simo had to be careful with the heavily laden handcart as he descended the slope. Packed upon it were the belongings of his master and the Syrians. He stopped halfway down for a rest and looked out at the expanse of black water. Assuming he could hire someone and get to this place, how long would they have to wait? And how many would come? He shook his head to dispel the notion that if his master did not return, he would be a free man.

He was so ashamed by the thought that he braced the cart against a wall and knelt down. He clasped his hands and begged for the Lord's forgiveness.

Cassius knew that three broad avenues led in from the western city walls towards Byzantium's centre and that they had to follow the southernmost. He did not wish to enquire about The House of Screams when close to it, so stopped at a water-seller's to make enquiries. The man was closing up but was able to give precise directions in return for a denarius. In Cassius's experience, few tradesmen had better knowledge of urban geography.

But once they turned off the avenue and followed a dark, winding road past luxurious townhouses, they hardly seemed to be in the city at all. Some of the villas had sentries on the gates but the only noise came from the occasional guard dog. Cassius had a story ready but they were questioned by no one.

With all weapons other than their daggers hidden in their bags, he and the four Syrians pressed silently onwards, twice stopping when the meandering road reached a point where they could make out the sea below. The bright moon would help, giving enough light to see their way without exposing them.

At the second stop, Cassius was relieved to find the steep but well-established trail that led down to Philo's Point. He could see the headland itself but not the quay. He estimated it to be about half a mile away.

They had not gone much further when they spied lights up ahead.

'Any idea?' asked Kabir as they approached.

'There is a temple around here somewhere – remember, the water-seller mentioned it? – but I wouldn't have expected it to be occupied after dark.'

The road ran along the side of the temple, which was surprisingly large, with broad columns and high steps running around the entire perimeter. Even more surprising were the dozens of blazing torches mounted on slender iron stands. At the front was a group of six priests clad in white robes. Two younger men in capes seemed to be responsible for keeping all the torches alight, which was quite a job. The priests and the helpers were so preoccupied that they didn't notice the five men pass by.

Cassius observed the figure upon a plinth behind the priests: a naked male with a torch in one hand. Rendered in pale marble, it was twice the size of the men below.

'Apollo.'

'A god of hunting,' said Kabir.

'And of light – in some areas of Greece. I believe there is an annual occasion on which they honour him and his dwelling place for ten days and nights – hence the torches.'

Beyond the temple, the state of the road worsened notably. The paving stones were so loose and unsteady that it would have been impossible for a cart and unpleasant for a mount.

'Can it really be here?' asked Yablus. 'These rich men?'

'If they want privacy, yes,' said Cassius. 'One can leave the avenue and get this far without being spotted at all.'

He reckoned that the fourth hour of night was close. Not wanting to run into anyone visiting The House of Screams, he had purposefully left it late.

'The water-seller seemed to think it was no more than a mile past the temple. We will stay quiet and advance slowly.'

It seemed that the man who had built the villa on cheap ground had put the money saved into the walls. They were more suited to a fortification than a residence and were at least fifteen feet high. The gate was a similarly monstrous affair set into an arch.

Twenty yards from it, crouching with the others to the right of the road, Cassius looked for any sign of life.

'This can't be the right place,' said Kammath. 'There aren't even any guards.'

'Not that you can see,' replied Cassius. 'Idan – the trees run up almost to the wall. Can you get close – listen for me?'

Without a word, the veteran rose and padded away into the gloom.

'What next?' asked Kabir.

'Let's see what Idan finds out but if we go over, the hooks will make quite a noise on the stone. We'll have to move a good distance away.'

While they waited, Cassius looked up at the swaying branches above. The forest was mostly oak; ancient trees with wide trunks and thick, sprawling limbs. In many places, the lower branches reached almost to the ground. As cover, they were excellent and – judging by the view over the wall – also surrounded the villa.

At a suggestion from Kabir, they took out their weapons. While the Syrians equipped themselves with long knives and slings, Cassius hung his sword belt from his right shoulder. He was wearing his mail shirt and cloak; the nomads their black outfits.

He only spotted Idan when the warrior was a few feet away.

'You're right. They're there but some distance back from the gate. I heard them talking, saw the glow from a shuttered lantern.'

'Could you see anything of the house?'

'Nothing.'

'By the gods, no wonder they've been able to keep this place quiet for so long.'

'To the north or south?' asked Kabir.

'South,' said Cassius, reasoning that they were less liable to run into anyone in the seaward direction. With Idan in the lead, they hunched low and crossed the road well back from the gate, then cut through the forest, following the circular wall. Other than the low-hanging branches, the chief danger was the acorns that littered the ground: they popped loudly when crushed underfoot. The first time this happened, Idan veered further away from the wall.

Once they were at least a quarter-mile from the gate, Cassius was no longer concerned about being heard. The wind blowing in from the sea was growing stronger and he had been struck several times by falling twigs and leaves. The surges of noise from the swaying branches undulated like waves upon a beach and the timbers emitted low, forbidding groans.

Each of the two sturdy grappling hooks was attached to thirty feet of rope. Idan and Kammath took charge but it was the young man who got the first solid hold. He and the veteran both tested it before agreeing it was safe to climb.

Cassius stood out of the way with Kabir. Since reaching the wall, the chief had said nothing. Cassius thought of the premonition from 'the signs' – had Kabir shared them with his compatriots?

Though determined to focus on the here and now, he was also preoccupied by two thoughts of his own. The first was that this was an inordinate and perilous waste of time if the girls weren't here. The second was that – again – he had been forced to move far faster than he would have liked. He felt that they had been lucky so far, despite some reckless, careless tactics. That luck would run out sooner or later.

Yablus of course went up first, with a rope ladder over his

shoulder. Once into a rhythm, he ascended with impressive speed. Cassius looked on as the black shape climbed on to the top of the wall. He could not have cared less about the talk of apparitions and ghostly cries but wondered if the superstitious Indavara would even have gone anywhere near the House of Screams. He was glad that the Syrians devotion to their deity precluded them from being concerned with any such matter unconnected to 'The Glorious Fire'.

The rope ladder – which was equipped with hooks at both ends – was lowered a moment later. Kabir went up first, then his son, then it was Cassius's turn. Though the wind tugged at his hair and his cloak, the climb was simple enough. They left the ladder in place and descended using the second one.

By the time Idan was down, Yablus had already scouted out the immediate area and concluded that there were no guards close by. Kabir was bent over, suffering from another attack of dizziness, but soon recovered himself. Cassius could see no trace whatsoever of buildings, paths or any other development. It was as if they had simply crossed a wall built in the middle of nowhere.

Before they set off, Cassius ensured his pack was secure. Inside was some watered wine, a little food, a candle and Simo's fire-starting gear. It had taken him some time to decide not to bring his letters. If he was badly wounded or killed and they fell into the wrong hands, the truth of his actions would become known. The information might reach Abascantius and – ultimately – his family. On the other hand, his connection to Marcellinus might just give him some protection. But Cassius did not think he would be killed or caught – not with the determined, capable Syrians alongside him. If he was fortunate, no one would ever know what he had done in this city in the name of his friends.

Ideally, he would have used another sword – the eagle-head hilt was something of a giveaway. But he had been caught without a proper weapon and armour too many times. The precious copper-alloy mail shirt was on over the padded shirt and his tunic. It gave him a little confidence, as did the heavy blade. With his hand on the hilt, he followed the others through the forest.

Simo's mission was not going well. He had spoken to five sailors in the Great Harbour but none of them knew of anyone with a boat of the right size who was available for hire at such short notice. In desperation, he left the handcart outside a noisy tavern and went inside. The barman couldn't think of a name either but directed him to a bearded fellow playing a board game. Annoyed by the interruption, the man nonetheless pointed him in the direction of a curly haired fellow who was drinking with another curly haired fellow. Simo only realised they were twins when he got close. Suntanned and muscular, they frowned at him until they realised a financial opportunity was available.

The men finished their drinks, then took him outside to negotiate.

'What's that you said?' asked one. 'A boat with space for six?'

'Yes, though it may be as many as nine. And this gear.' Simo pulled out the handcart, which he had secreted in the shadows. The trio were illuminated by the grainy glow of the lantern hanging beside the tavern door.

'From where to where?' said the same twin, as his brother eyed Simo.

'First to Philo's Point. We will wait there for the others – it may be some time. Then we would like to cross to Chalcedon.'

Both twins let out a long breath. 'Wind's got right up and that's five miles all told, most of it with a full boat. This is a night's work.'

'Can you do it?'

'We can do it.'

'The question is, can you afford it?' said the second twin.

'Name your price.'

'Twelve denarii.' It seemed the second brother took the lead when it came to money.

Simo didn't have the full amount with him. 'I can give you eight now, the remainder when we reach Chalcedon.'

Simo suddenly realised that his cross was showing after he had bent down to move the cart. He pulled up his tunic.

'You are fortunate,' said the first twin. 'Not all Byzantines would deal with one of your people.'

'Some of our people included,' said the other. 'We are Jews. But fortunately for you, we do not let such matters interfere with business.'

'Good,' said Simo. 'Do we have a deal?'

'We do.'

As was customary, he shook hands with them and counted out the coins, which the financially-minded twin pocketed.

'My name is Simo. We will be collecting my master and his friends.'

'Bion the Younger.'

'Bion the Elder,' said the man with the money.

'Ah.'

'Only by an hour,' said his brother.

XXIX

The House of Screams was an unremarkable building and seemed at first sight to be deserted. It was a large villa of the type found in every corner of the Empire; a sprawling one-storey structure divided into several blocks, each with a sloping, tiled roof. There were no colonnades to mark the front door, which faced a dormant fountain and the long drive that led to the gate. Not a single light nor guard was visible there. But while skirting the treeline – which ran within forty feet of the villa – they observed a pair of sentries walking the building's perimeter, one equipped with a lantern.

And as they approached the rear, all doubts vanished. They saw lights and heard the voices of men and women. But only when they were directly behind the villa did they realise the true extent of the activity. There were at least six occupied rooms; all well lit, some with shutters open. Inside, people were moving around: drinking, talking, and occasionally laughing. There was also a terrace illuminated by braziers where two well-dressed men holding goblets were deep in conversation.

Shrouded by the trees, Cassius and the Syrians continued moving until they were close to a small outhouse.

'We'll get a better view from there,' he said to Kabir. 'Just the two of us for now.'

Waiting until they were sure the patrolling guards hadn't reappeared, Cassius and Kabir darted forward into the safety of the outhouse's shadows. They moved up to the right-hand corner, now only ten feet from the edge of the terrace. One of the men was talking, gesticulating theatrically. The other was listening. But Cassius did not watch this scene for long. Just yards from the men was a well-lit room with open shutters. A cheer had just gone up.

Inside was a bed, upon it a young, blonde woman on all fours. She was naked other than the metal collar around her neck, which was attached to a chain. Behind her, hands on her waist and thrusting into her with considerable force was a powerfully built African man. He too had a collar around his neck.

Suddenly, another man came into view. He was tall, fair and wearing an opulent cloak striped with red. Standing at the side of the bed, he cradled the woman's face in his hand then took her chain and gave it to the African man. Smirking, the tall man ran his hand along the woman's back and between her buttocks. Others – three men and a woman– closed in around the bed, all watching intently, all with drinks in their hands.

Cassius looked at the second room along to the right. He could see movement but the shutters had been left only slightly ajar. In the third room were three young women standing with a very large bearded man. The women were wearing silken robes and the metal collars. One was very pale with red hair, the other two were dark.

'That's Marte,' whispered Kabir. 'I think that's Marte.'

Cassius gripped his arm. 'You think? Or you know?'

While Kabir peered into the darkness, another cheer went up from the first room. One of the women was caressing the African while the tall man laughed, encouraging the others forward. He applauded when one of his compatriots lifted up his tunic and offered his cock to the girl. She obediently took it in her mouth.

Kabir was still looking at the other room. 'It's her,' he said, his voice wavering. 'It's her.'

'Come on, let's check the other side.'

As they moved left along the rear of the outhouse, Cassius glanced at the trees. He could not see a sign of the other three. Not long after he and Kabir reached the corner, the two guards reappeared. Showing a remarkable lack of interest in the goings-on inside, the men continued past the terrace and on with their patrol.

Of the three rooms to the left of the rear door, only the second was illuminated. A woman had been manacled to the rear wall. Gleaming chains adorned her body, running between her legs and around her breasts. She was dark-skinned, very lithe and muscular. Cassius thought there was no one else present there until a man sauntered past the window. Silhouetted against the light within, he was clearly naked and clearly fat.

Kabir dragged Cassius back into the shadows. 'How do we do this? There must be more guards inside and that's a lot of people to control.'

Cassius was thinking about the three men known as The Earthly Gods. There was no guarantee that they were all here but he reckoned he might have at least identified Tribune Phaedrus.

'It is. But we only need one.'

The wait seemed interminable; and it was all Cassius could do to hold the Syrians back. Kammath had confirmed that the girl was indeed Marte and when the large man grabbed her and put his hands between her legs, Kabir's son had to be physically restrained by his father.

His allies were not Cassius's only concern. He knew that more people might arrive, that Barba might change his mind and raise the alarm. But if he and the Syrians simply charged in, the least appalling outcome would be a situation he could not hope to control; the most would be a bloodbath.

It was quite clear that The Earthly Gods and their acolytes went far beyond a few decadent sex games. They saw the fat man whip the girl hard enough to tear her skin before detaching her from the wall and dragging her down out of view. A male dwarf – who was serving drinks – appeared there briefly before being bellowed at to leave. And once the larger group had seen enough of the blonde woman and the African, they were entertained by the sight of two more girls – these two alarmingly young – who were passed between their tormentors. The men and women did precisely as they pleased with them. At one point, some sort of contraption was brought out – a headpiece with a phallus attached. The tall young man with the striped cloak seemed to relish strapping the device to one of the girls and instructing her how to use it on the other.

To Cassius, the most disturbing element was the lack of resistance from the slaves, who barely made a sound. He stood in the darkness with the Syrians, who would occasionally move to see the latest horror unfold. Unsurprisingly, most of the guests sought the fresh air of the terrace at some point. Cassius was waiting for one in particular to do so.

Kabir's face emerged from the darkness. 'They have a snake in the room where Marte is. They put its tail inside one of the other girls. What is wrong with these people?'

'We will end it. Soon.'

'I have not seen my daughter.'

'Neither have we seen Dinora. That does not mean they are not here.'

The two guards completed another circuit. Then several of the guests came out on to the terrace.

Cassius whispered to the others to gather round. 'Now listen carefully. You must do exactly as I tell you.'

One minute later, he, Kabir and Kammath walked out of the shadows and straight on to the terrace. Cassius had his sword in his hand, the Syrians their long knives.

One of the three men standing there had been talking. He stopped, struck dumb by the sight of the advancing trio. The others ran for the door but were blocked by Yablus, who had crept around from the left, under the windows. Idan also did his job well, sneaking in from the right before grabbing the tall young man around the neck and holding the blade under his chin.

'You the tribune?' asked Cassius, his voice slightly muffled by the handkerchief he had tied around the lower half of his face. 'Phaedrus?'

After a momentary hesitation, 'Yes.'

Cassius guessed he was only a year or two older than him.

Kabir and Kammath pushed the other two down on to their knees.

'Call to your guests and the guards. I want every last one of them out on this terrace.'

Phaedrus stayed creditably calm. 'Who are you? Let us talk rationally.'

Cassius walked up to his fellow officer, who was barefoot. He tapped his sword against the tiles between his feet. 'Ever tried walking without toes? Call them out. Just the guests and guards for now.'

Phaedrus did so.

The guests emerged in small groups, at first confused, then stunned when they saw what was unfolding. Cassius directed them all on to the ground and before long there were a dozen sitting there, along with two more guards from inside.

'Sir,' said Yablus, who had been instructed to use the term. He pointed along the wall, to where the lantern of the sentries had appeared.

'Them too,' said Cassius.

Phaedrus was given an added incentive by Idan, who tightened his grip around his neck. The guards obeyed his orders and – like their compatriots and those others with daggers – unsheathed their blades. Kammath swiftly collected them.

'You four,' said Cassius to the guards, 'on your front, hands behind your back.'

Once they'd complied, he turned to Phaedrus. 'Is that all of them?'

'Not quite.' The voice came from the last man out of the villa. Though he was now clothed, his large gut made him easily identifiable as the fellow who liked to employ the whip. His brow and cheeks were clammy, his double chin and flabby neck too. Sweat was already coming through the tunic he had just put on.

'You are clearly a tenacious and resourceful man. I shall therefore be generous. Fifty gold coins.' He offered Cassius a heavy-looking money bag. 'It's all we have here.'

'Assistant Magistrate Nereus, I take it?'

The man did not answer but his eyes betrayed him.

Aiming his sword at Nereus, Cassius took the bag and wedged it behind his belt. 'Most generous. Now, you're going to go with my friend here and bring out your slaves. Every one.'

'What concern are they of yours? You have *fifty* aureii in your hands.'

'Slaves are valuable too. And I also want all the collars and chains removed. Go.'

As had been arranged, Kabir came forward to control the assistant magistrate. He lifted the long knife and tapped the blade against his broad chest. 'Now.'

Nereus glanced briefly at Phaedrus then turned round and led the way back into the villa.

Another man spoke up, clearly an individual of considerable breeding. 'You are foolish to even try this. These people will—'

'Shut your mouth.' Cassius aimed the sword at him. 'You get on your front too.'

'I certainly shall not.'

Cassius swung the sword. The tip passed within a couple of inches of the man's nose. He flung himself down.

The slaves began to appear from the house: first the girls, then the big African and finally the stocky dwarf. The men were clad only in loincloths. The women had all found some clothing, though the poor girl who'd been whipped was whimpering, holding a cloth against her wounds.

'Over there,' said Cassius, pointing at the patch of grass between the terrace and the outhouse.

From inside came a shout. It sounded like Kabir. Kammath pushed past two of the slave girls and ran inside.

Cassius scanned the prisoners. 'Any of you men move and my friend will kill the tribune. You'll be next.'

He grabbed two swords from the pile and handed them to the African and the dwarf. 'We're here to help. Watch these men.'

Cassius sheathed his sword, then ran past the last of the slave girls and into the house. Following the noise of shouting and crying, he soon located Kabir, Kammath and Nereus. They were standing in front of the girl Marte, who was pressed back against the wall, trembling. Kabir was holding her by the shoulders, shaking her. The girl's mouth was moving but no words were coming.

'She cannot speak,' said Kammath, who had one hand on Nereus and his knife held against the Roman's back.

Marte managed to point along the corridor.

Kabir spun around to face the assistant magistrate. 'Where are the other girls?'

'I do not know. I only—'

Kammath dug his blade in – through the tunic and an inch into Nereus's back.

'Tell us!'

Nereus tried to pull away but now Kabir grabbed him too and placed his blade between two rolls of his fat neck. 'Where?'

Nereus was groaning with pain. 'All right, all right.' He reached into his tunic and brought out a ring of keys. He held one and handed it to Kabir, then pointed in the same direction as Marte. 'There. The cellar. But—'

Leaving him and the girl, Kabir and Kammath raced along the corridor, unlocked the door and disappeared down some steps.

'Outside,' said Cassius to the girl. 'Outside with the others.'

Covering her face, she slid down the wall to the ground.

Cassius pushed Nereus's heavy frame along the corridor. 'The cellar – go.'

'Please, mercy, the pain.'

'Move yourself!'

A prod with the sword was enough to change his mind and Cassius kept at it as they reached the stairs then descended some unsteady steps into a musty cellar, lit only by a single candle.

Kabir was calling his daughter's name. Kammath grabbed the candle and followed his father to a corner. Hanging from a pair of manacles was a woman in a grimy tunic.

She was too light-skinned to be Syrian.

Kabir moved along the wall. The weak glow of the candle fell across another captive. She was in a worse state, barely able to lift her head. She murmured as Kabir held her chin and tipped it up. She opened her eyes.

'Help me, please.'

'Dinora,' said Kammath.

Both men fired questions at her in their own language. Cassius pushed Nereus down on to his knees and took the keys from Kabir. Once he'd unlocked the manacles, Dinora fell into her chief's arms. She managed a few words.

Cassius freed the other girl then lowered her to the floor.

'Help me.'

'We will,' said Cassius. 'I promise.' He looked over at the others.

Dinora was shaking her head. Then she spoke again.

Kabir's eyes closed. Kammath slumped against the wall.

'What did she say?' asked Cassius.

Nereus stood then turned and ran up the stairs. After a strange pause, Kabir sprang after him.

By the time Cassius and Kammath caught up, they were halfway along the corridor. Kabir leaped on to the magistrate's back, knocking him to the floor. Once down, he somehow turned the weighty Nereus over. Pinning him with knees on his chest, he raised the knife.

'No! Mercy! It wasn't me. It was Phaedrus. *He* killed her. It wasn't me. It wasn't—'

The knife went in under his chin. The blade disappeared into the pale, quivering flesh then came out glistening red. As the Roman's head cracked against the tiles, blood gushed from the wound, colouring his tunic.

Kabir stood and marched out towards the terrace, Kammath close behind. Cassius knew he could not stop them and he had little desire to do so; but as he passed Nereus's lifeless body somewhere at the back of his mind a voice spoke.

You are party to the murder of a magistrate. And they are not finished yet.

Before he could reach the terrace, Kabir and Kammath dragged the terrified Phaedrus back inside.

Idan called after them in Aramaic.

'Just stay there,' said Cassius.

The two Syrians pushed Phaedrus into the nearest room.

Kabir tripped him and the tribune came down hard on his back. Kabir put his knees down on one arm, his son the other.

Phaedrus's horrified gaze moved between them, then on to Cassius. 'You. You must stop them.'

'You killed my daughter,' said Kabir.

'No,' said the tribune as if outraged by the accusation. 'No.'

'Nereus told them,' said Cassius.

Kabir held the Roman by the throat and ran his knife down his forehead, carving into the skin. He only stopped when he reached the right eye, holding the blade an inch above it.

'I will have the truth.'

Phaedrus's cries soon gave way to tears.

'Tell the truth or I will take out your eyes. This one first.'

'I – I – was with her. She – she—'

'She fought you.'

'She did . . . I mean sh – sh – she had at first . . . but not that night. She was on a chain. I suppose I – I – pulled too hard. I . . . saw she wasn't moving. I told the others.'

Kammath covered his face with his hands.

Kabir's head dropped. 'When?'

'I – I don't know. Four weeks. Maybe five.'

'What did you do with her?'

'We . . . N – N – Nereus and Octavius and I . . . we . . . Octavius decided we should wrap her up and put her in the sea. I'm sorry. Truly.'

This time Kabir put the knife in between the eyes. He drove down with such force that the blade snapped, leaving half of the length of metal embedded in the tribune's skull. Phaedrus's head continued to tremble, one eye flickering open and shut before eventually becoming still.

Kammath stood, then helped his father up.

Despite all that was going on around him, Cassius felt as if he was looking on from above, separate somehow. But he was not. *You are party to the murder of a magistrate and a tribune.*

Not only could he not stop them, he would not have. Kabir would never get his daughter back, but he did have vengeance.

The Syrian pushed his son away and walked towards the nearest wall. Suddenly his hands flew up and he unleashed a bestial cry of pure agony. Then he drove his head into the wall. The crack dragged Cassius out of his stupor. By the time he and Kammath reached Kabir, he had already hit his head again.

The chief's blood splattered Cassius's hands as he and Kammath turned him away from the wall. Kabir clutched Cassius's collar. He pulled so tightly that the material cut into the skin. Spitting what sounded like curses in Aramaic, Kabir shook Cassius, who responded by gripping the nomad's arms.

'Kabir, I know. I know and the gods know. I'm sorry but we have to get ourselves and these girls out of here.'

The Syrian froze and the mask of grief-stricken rage slipped. His face seemed to collapse as he let go of Cassius and turned to his son. Kammath wiped his eyes and spoke gently to his father.

Leaving them there, Cassius spied the girl Marte still on the floor. He hurried over and grabbed her under the arms. 'It's all right. You'll be all right.'

She did not reply but at least let him take her out to the terrace. The men all looked up as he appeared. One of the female guests was sobbing.

'We will lock them all in downstairs.'

'What happened?' asked Idan.

'She's gone. They killed her. Dinora and another girl are still alive – in the cellar.'

'Men first. All of you on your feet. Hands on your heads.'

Once they were up, Cassius asked the two male slaves to watch the women while he took the men into the house with Yablus and Idan. Summoning Kammath, he sent him down into the cellar first to fetch Dinora and the other captive. While the Syrian brought them up, Cassius grabbed a lantern from the kitchen. He gave the light to one of the captured guards and sent him down the steps. Using shouts and prods with his sword, he then urged the rest of them into the cellar. As Idan and Yablus shepherded the last men down the steps, Cassius returned to the terrace. Kabir staggered out of the room in which Phaedrus had been killed. Cassius decided he would leave him be for the moment.

'Sir, please,' said one of the women when he got outside. 'We are just servants. We are also slaves.' She gestured to a woman beside her. Cassius hadn't noted that their clothing was rather different to the other three females.

'You want to be free?'

'I – I belong to Centurion Octavius. He brought me here several months ago.'

'Yes or no?'

'I should stay. I want to stay.'

'You?'

The second woman held up her hands and got to her feet. 'Please – let me come with you.'

'Very well.' He turned to the African. 'Put these three . . . guests in the cellar with the others. Understand?'

With a nod, the freed slave raised his blade and guided his charges inside.

'What about me?' asked the woman who had elected to stay.

'We can't leave you all locked up underground,' said Cassius, who did not want another dozen deaths on his hands. 'Once we leave, you can go for help.'

Still holding his sword, Cassius looked over at Kammath, who was speaking to Dinora in Aramaic. The slave girls were standing huddled together, seemingly unable to believe what was happening.

Realising that he now had some time for Kabir, Cassius hurried back inside once again. As he neared the room, he saw a light appear ahead, in the corridor that led to the centre of the villa.

'What's going on in—'

'Cilo?' The second guard was close behind.

The men from the gate. He'd completely forgotten them.

Seeing Cassius's masked face, Cilo dropped the lantern, drew his sword and charged through the doorway.

Cassius got both hands on his blade and swung. The sword struck only the door frame, slicing out a sliver of wood. Aware that the guard was already coming in low, Cassius threw himself backwards. A third blade appeared, slicing through the air and up into Cilo's wrist. The shrieking guard dropped his sword as another swing cut across his stomach.

As he fell, Cassius saw his saviour. The dwarf – a fair, curly haired fellow – watched his victim crash to the floor. As the second guard came out of the shadows, a dark shape launched itself along the adjacent corridor.

The African's shoulder-charge struck the guard in the shoulder, propelling him into the wall. As he bounced off it, the dwarf stabbed him in the side. The guard's cry ended quickly as the African swung a sword-hilt into his face, catapulting him back from whence he came.

The whole incident had lasted less than ten seconds but Cassius found himself breathless. 'By the gods, thank you.'

The African replied in as sonorous a voice as Cassius had heard. 'I have been waiting a long time to do that.'

'Best find some clothes. Some cloaks for you and the women. We are leaving.'

Yablus and Idan came marching down the corridor, then looked down at the mortally wounded guards.

'Got the cellar key?' asked Cassius.

Yablus held it up.

'Search these two – we also need a key for the front gate. Kammath!'

Once the youth came in with the women, Cassius told the loyal slave to go and stand beside the cellar door.

'Idan, Yablus, get them all outside. I'll meet you out front.'

The African and the dwarf reappeared, now wearing cloaks and carrying others, which they handed out to the women as they departed, stepping over the dying guards.

Cassius looked back at Kabir, who was once again staring down at Phaedrus, oblivious to what was going on.

'Dinora, do you mind staying with me for a moment?'

The girl seemed more in possession of herself than Marte, though she was holding tightly on to Kammath. She looked from him to Kabir, then nodded.

'Go on,' Cassius told Kammath.

Supporting Marte and the second girl from the cellar, the youth followed the others.

'Thank you,' Cassius said to Dinora. He led her to the doorway. 'Kabir.'

The nomad turned round. Some of his white hair had stuck to his forehead, which was covered with blood.

'Dinora needs you. We have to get out. Can you help her?'

The girl stepped forward and held out her hand and spoke to her chief in Aramaic. He came forward, took her hand and gently embraced her. His bloodied head at rest on her shoulder, he gazed blankly at the floor.

Cassius had to turn away to compose himself. When he looked back, Dinora had coaxed Kabir into the corridor. Cassius followed, sword in hand, and was last to leave The House of Screams.

With only two lanterns between them, they gathered just beyond the rusting iron gates, the trees swaying around them. Cassius had learned that the African slave was named Merbal, the dwarf was Ruga. The female slaves had at last quietened down, now realising that they had a genuine chance of freedom.

Cassius opened the bag of gold coins Nereus had given him and handed two each to the slaves, of which there were twelve. He gave three each to Merbal and Ruga.

'It is best for us all that we separate, especially as these men's allies will be looking for us. The going will not be easy but I suggest you head north through the forest. Keep the lantern shuttered when you can. You must get rid of those fine cloaks as soon as possible – do not sell them openly because you might be reported for theft. At first light, buy some ordinary clothes, then get out of Byzantium as quickly as you can.'

Some of the sobbing renewed, but many of the women came forward to thank him and the Syrians. One actually kissed him on the cheek above the handkerchief, whispering that she had expected to die in The House of Screams.

Merbal – who now looked quite regal in a thick, patterned

cloak – took the time to shake the hand of all of his rescuers, Cassius last of all. 'I know there's no point asking again for your name but I thank you once more.'

'You will see them all to safety?'

'On my oath.'

Cassius also shook hands with Ruga, who was already telling the women to form a line to negotiate the forest. He looked on as Merbal led the way, following a route at forty-five degrees to the wall and road. Ruga waited for all the women to pass him then gave a final wave. In moments, his small figure was lost to the darkness.

XXX

Though aware that such a thing might be frowned upon by some of his fellow believers, Simo thanked the Almighty that he had happened upon the Jewish brothers. Bion the Elder and Bion the Younger were clearly exceptionally capable mariners. They had not spoken for at least twenty minutes and – while rowing, at least – seemed not to need verbal communication.

The blustery wind was blowing the boat onshore and the waves seem to grow larger with every minute. Every now and again, one of the brothers would turn round to check their position and make some compensatory movement with his oar, which the other matched. They had managed to consistently stay at a distance of about a hundred feet from the rocky shoreline. Once beyond the moles of the Great Harbour, they had passed many villas with dim lights within.

Sitting on the deck close to the stern, water lapping around his backside, Simo now saw the value of the lashings the sailors had insisted on before leaving. They had divided up the gear and stowed it evenly across the boat, which Simo estimated to be around eight foot wide and twenty long. The burly brothers used oars that looked extraordinarily large to Simo's untrained eye but they wielded them with ease.

As they cleared a headland, the siblings stopped rowing for a moment and drew in long breaths.

'That's Philo's Point,' said Bion the Younger. 'A quarter-hour and we'll be in.'

'Very good,' replied Simo. He failed to close his mouth in time and was struck by spray. Spitting out the salty water, he wiped his chin and looked on as the younger brother turned the boat with two sharp movements. The pair made the next stroke together and launched the vessel forward once more.

—8—

Cassius sat in the ditch beside Kammath, hand covering his eyes. It was Idan who had heard the riders and sent the party scurrying off the road.

They came around the bend at a trot, half of them bearing lanterns. Though there was not a patch of red upon them, Cassius knew them for soldiers from their riding style and their arrangement in pairs. There were ten, including a tall man at the front. All Cassius saw of him was that his hair was cropped short and that he had a patch covering one eye. Beside him – just identifiable in the glow of the tall man's lantern – was Barba.

The riders were quickly past and nearing The House of Screams, less than half a mile away.

'What?' said Cassius, who hadn't heard what Kammath had passed on from the girls.

'That's Octavius with the patch.'

'Yes. Evidently our friend Barba did change his mind.'

The nomads were already clambering out of the ditch and helping Marte and Dinora up on to the road. Cassius followed them and looked to his left. Though he could no longer see the riders, he could still hear their horses. He guessed it would take them no more than ten minutes to reach the villa, discover what had happened and catch up.

As he jogged after the others, Cassius appraised the situation. With the girls slowing them down, he and the Syrians had no chance of reaching the turn down to the coastal path in time. Even if they did, the soldiers could dismount and follow them.

Now that he knew the full extent of Octavius's ruthlessness, Cassius had no doubt that the man would settle for nothing less than killing every one of them. Apart from the fact that The Earthly Gods' nightmarish creation had been dismantled and his co-conspirators executed, Octavius was now exposed to scandal and disgrace. He also had the support of a vengeful optio and eight men whose loyalty was clearly not in question.

The Syrians just kept going. Cassius wasn't sure if his companions understood their predicament and chose forge ahead regardless or were simply too upset to think clearly. He didn't expect much from Kabir: the chief had not said a word and was alone at the back of the group, leaving Kammath and Yablus to help the girls. Though Marte was just about keeping pace, Dinora was struggling to put one foot in front of the other.

They ran on. When not looking back over his shoulder, Cassius was considering alternatives. He had neither seen nor heard any trace of them but could not help imagining Octavius and his men charging straight back down the drive and through the gate to give chase.

Idan dropped back. 'Should we get off the road? Split up?'

'Maybe. But they have plenty of torches and they know this area. If we try and get down to the coast by blundering south, we'll be lucky not to get trapped somewhere or fall to our deaths. We have to reach that trail.'

'It's still more than a mile away.'

Cassius said nothing more. As they came over a slight crest, he saw the glow of the Temple of Apollo up ahead. They still had one advantage; and they needed light to use it.

'Look,' said Idan.

'I see it.'

'No. There.' The Syrian had stopped.

Behind and below them, the road was a pale line between the mass of trees. The high wall was also visible too. The torches were moving quickly away from it.

Simo was rather perturbed to find that he had been recruited as a mariner. While the elder twin stayed at the oars, the younger had moved to the bow. Simo held the rear line in his hand and was focusing on the quay. The oarsman had turned the boat into the wind to help him control the vessel; there was only a narrow section to aim for, between two larger ships already tied up.

'You'll have to stand,' said Old Bion as he manoeuvred them closer. 'The post is high up.'

Simo hesitantly lifted his rear off the floor, got to his knees, then stood. With one hand holding the rope, it was difficult to keep his balance. He was so concerned with staying upright that he was surprised when the contours of the quay loomed out of the darkness.

'We're close,' said Old Bion as he shipped his oars. 'Reach up. The post's there.'

Simo got his hand over the edge then spied the post to his right. Steadying himself, he threw the line and looped it over the post. Once it was tight, he held the boat against the quay.

'Nicely done,' said Old Bion. He took the line and clambered up a ladder Simo hadn't even seen.

Once both lines were secure, Young Bion told Simo he could go up. Careful with both hands and feet, the attendant soon found himself on a bleak, empty platform of stone that ran out thirty feet from the shore in the shadow of the headland. There was no sign of life from either the big ships or the cluster of buildings at the other end of the quay.

'This is definitely it?' he asked Old Bion. 'There are no other quays close to the point?'

'This is it,' said the sailor, still breathing hard. 'What now?'

'We wait,' said Simo, who had been in such situations more times than he cared to remember.

And pray.

The priests came out of the temple together, robes flowing as they descended the steps. The men responsible for the torches fell in with them as they strode across the rectangular, low-walled courtyard at the front of the great structure. Like the rest of the temple, it was very well lit.

When Kabir drew his sword, Cassius rushed in front of him,

meeting the priests at the courtyard entrance. 'Go inside. There will be fighting here.'

The priests were of varying ages. The oldest of them possessed a snowy white beard that reached down to his chest. 'You cannot violate the sanctity of this place.'

'We shall not enter,' said Cassius. 'But you must remain inside.'

'What is going on?' asked another man.

'I don't have time to explain.'

'What of the girls?' asked the elderly priest.

'They stay with us.' Cassius would have preferred to get them to safety but he needed them for what he intended. 'Go inside. Now.'

The holy men turned round and hurried back towards the steps. The two attendants gazed curiously at the strangers then followed.

'What are you doing?' said Kammath, grabbing Cassius's arm. 'We can't remain here.'

'Actually we must. It's our only chance.'

'He's right,' said Idan. Beside him, Kabir was staring back along the road.

Cassius ushered the others away from the torches that lined the courtyard, bathing the marble floor in misty yellow light.

'They catch us on the road – it's over. If we hide, some of us might make it out alive, but I doubt it.'

'Then what?' said Kabir, his first words since leaving the house.

'They don't know you have the slings; or what you can do with them. Remember Alauran – the killing area? We can do it again.'

Cassius stood in darkness, just off the road, a hundred feet from the courtyard. Beside him were Kabir (who was looking after Marte) and Kammath (who was looking after Dinora). Cassius reached inside his cloak and checked the straps of his armour. Despite the sweat upon the rings that had leaked through his tunic, all was secure.

'Here they come,' said Kammath.

'Follow me.' Cassius set off at a jog. He knew the crest was around three hundred feet away and that the riders would not be too close when they saw him and the others for the first time.

Resisting the urge to look back, he concentrated on his footing and the lights ahead. He heard a shout from the Romans as the rumble of hooves grew louder. When he was within twenty feet of the courtyard the noise changed; the riders were reining in.

As he reached the narrow entrance, he took his first look back. Three of the torches were still on the road. The others were in the hands of men already cutting across the grass towards them.

'Go!' yelled Kabir.

Cassius sprinted across the courtyard, dodging around the altar in the centre. Once beyond it at the base of the steps, he turned and drew his sword. He lifted the handkerchief to hide his lower face once more.

Kabir, Kammath and the girls were not far behind. As instructed, Dinora and Marte climbed the steps and took refuge behind one of the four great columns of the temple. Kabir and Kammath drew their long knives. Their slings were hidden, tucked into the back of their belts.

Thank the gods.

Nine of the ten soldiers crossing the courtyard were not wearing any army equipment other than swords. What Cassius feared above all else were bows but few legionaries even owned one and he saw nothing that could hurt them from a distance. Barba, however, had clearly come from some duty, as he was clad in his striped tunic and carrying a helmet. Centurion Octavius wore a plain, sleeveless tunic that showed off his impressive physique. He had his hand on the pommel of his sword but did not draw it, even as he rounded the altar and came to a stop. His craggy face was set in a grim sneer.

'This will not save you. *Nothing* will save you.'

Cassius could see no point in speaking.

'Where are the others?' asked Barba.

A moment after Octavius turned towards the optio, Barba's

face was torn open by the first shot. As his hand came up to the wound, a second man was hit in the head. He fell; the torch in his hand spitting sparks as it struck the marble.

'Down!' Octavius was quicker than the rest of his men.

Another shot pinged off the stone. A legionary gave a cry and hobbled sideways before diving down.

Even though the men were all now below the level of the wall, they were not safe from Yablus and Idan, who were firing from separate corners of the temple. The Syrians were aiming downwards, at well-lit targets they could pick out with ease.

The speed of the soldiers' recovery was impressive. At a shouted order from Octavius, those still able to move dived at the nearest stands and knocked them over, putting out the torches. Once concealed by gloom, the soldiers could be heard moving forward. Idan and Yablus continued to pepper them with shot. A legionary scrabbling towards the exit fell as he was struck low. His head hit the marble with a thudding slap.

Two more stands crashed to the ground, leaving the courtyard in darkness.

Cassius could hear Octavius hissing orders.

'How many down?' asked Kammath.

'Three, maybe four,' said Cassius.

'Spread out,' said Kabir.

'What?'

Too late, Cassius realised that they were blocking Idan and Yablus's shots if the legionaries got close.

Octavius already had his men on the move again. Two legionaries bolted out of the darkened courtyard, swords high as they powered up the steps. The head of one snapped sideways as the shot hit. His legs went from under him and he landed on his side before rolling all the way back down.

Aware that at least two more were coming, Cassius watched the next man spring up the steps, oblivious to the fate of his compatriot. He ran at Kammath, who was one step lower than Kabir and Cassius.

The young warrior swept his long knife at the legionary's head but a flick of the Roman's short sword deflected the blow.

Before the soldier could strike, Kabir joined the fray. The nomad's bloodied blade went in under the legionary's armpit, crunching through tissue and bone. As he retracted it, blood splattered the white stone.

Though the first two men had been accounted for, Kabir had exposed his flank and the quickest of the next group were already on him. Kammath was stuck on the wrong side.

Cassius leaped down and stretched out his arm, trying to protect the chief. The legionary's short sword crashed into his blade – reducing the impact – but the tip caught the Syrian low, sinking through his black tunic. Grunting in pain, Kabir toppled backwards between Cassius and the legionary, a stout man whose open mouth revealed jagged, broken teeth.

The other soldier darted at Kammath, who blocked with his knife but was forced to retreat. Cassius knew the slingers could do them no good now; the enemy were too close. He hoped Idan and Yablus were on their way.

Both standing over Kabir, Cassius and the legionary raised their blades. The soldier turned side on, then jabbed at him. A panicked swipe with the longer blade knocked the sword aside but the legionary launched himself over Kabir and swung again.

Cassius saw the feint for what it was and kept the sword high. The blade came back the other way, sparking as it struck his.

Vaguely aware of fast-moving figures and clashes close by, Cassius realised he had given up the initiative for too long.

Use your reach. Use those long arms and that long blade.

Cassius dropped down a step and pivoted. As the heavier weapon clanged against the short sword, the impact unsettled the soldier. One foot slipped down off a step. A glinting blade sliced across his heel. Blood sprayed the stone and Kabir rolled aside as the shrieking legionary collapsed. Holding the Roman by the hair, the nomad chief sunk the blade deep into his chest.

Cassius registered Yablus hauling a Roman off Kammath before another figure charged up the steps.

Octavius had put Barba's helmet on.

He took careful aim and kicked Kabir in the side of the head.

Cassius heard himself cry out as the Syrian's skull smacked against the stone.

Octavius didn't miss a step.

Cassius only realised his handkerchief had fallen down when the centurion's single eye glittered with amusement.

'Gods, you're not much more than a boy. What are you doing with—'

'Cassius – down!'

As he dropped to his haunches, a shot cracked the cheek-guard of the helmet. Blinking and shaking his head, Octavius put out his arms to steady himself. But by the time a shape flew past Cassius to his left, the centurion had recovered.

Idan's long hair flew in an arc as he launched a scything sweep at the Roman's stomach. Octavius batted the blade away with his sword, then brought his left fist around, catching the Syrian on his brow.

Idan staggered and barely had time to get up the knife as Octavius heaved down at him. The narrow blade shattered under the sword's weight and Idan fell back against the steps.

Octavius raised his sword again. 'Darkie, you are one ugly son of a—'

Cassius's blade sliced across the centurion's shoulder.

'Aaagh!'

Before Cassius could strike again, Octavius had turned and hacked at him. The blade scraped along the mail at Cassius's forearm then across his palm.

Pain lanced into his hand. He dropped his sword.

As Octavius pressed forward, Idan leaped up at him, gripping his wrists and trying to prise the weapon from his grasp. But for all his wiry strength, the Syrian was no match for the heavily built centurion.

Octavius wrestled himself free and swung an elbow, catching Idan on the chin. The nomad tottered, then lurched away before finally crashing on to the steps.

Palm warm with blood, Cassius recovered his sword with his left hand. Hearing shouts below, he retreated up the steps towards the temple doors.

Octavius sprang after him. His eyepatch had ridden up, revealing only a dark, gaping hole.

Cassius's foot landed on the base of his cloak and slid off a step. He fell on to his backside.

Grinning manically, Octavius drew back his blade.

Cassius covered his face as best he could. Only the mail shirt could save him now.

The flames came from his right.

The torch hit the centurion's face, showering him with sparks. He shrieked as he flailed around, pawing at his eye.

Dinora was standing there, torch still in her hand.

Octavius wiped his eye again, then he saw her. 'I'll run you through, whore.'

By the time the enraged centurion saw Cassius, the younger man was up on his feet.

Gripping his sword as hard he could, Cassius drove the tip into the side of his foe's neck. The blade made a wide, deep wound and stuck there. As Cassius let go, Octavius seemed to freeze. His single, bulging eye turned to his murderer. The eyelid flickered then closed. He slumped sideways, his frame coming straight down on to Cassius, who collapsed beneath him.

With the hot, stinking weight of the big centurion pinning him, Cassius felt warm blood streaming on to his neck. Octavius's body was shaking, even though the head was still. Cassius tried to push him off but he didn't have the strength.

'Oh gods. Get it off, please . . . '

Suddenly the body was pulled away and dumped on the steps.

A dazed-looking Idan bent over and offered his hand.

Cassius stood there, his entire chest covered in blood, the smell of it still thick in his nostrils. He had not moved; and lying just below him was Octavius's body.

You killed a centurion. You killed a fellow officer of the Imperial Army.

He watched Idan help Kabir to his feet. Kammath, meanwhile,

was cutting off the bottom of the nearest fallen legionary's tunic. He then went over to Yablus, who was sitting on a step, and wrapped what looked like a deep cut on the youth's arm.

'Are you all right?'

Feeling a touch on his shoulder, Cassius turned to see Dinora standing there.

'I think so.'

'The priests are coming. We should go.'

Cassius turned. The doors were open, the holy men looking out. He reached down to pull up his handkerchief but it was sodden with blood. Gripped by nausea he tried to wrench it off but he'd purposefully tied it tight.

Bile filled his mouth as he descended the steps. Somehow he didn't throw up.

'Sir?' Dinora – now accompanied by Marte – had followed him. She handed him his sword. The other girl was holding a torch.

Cassius sheathed his blade. 'Can he move?'

'I can move,' said Yablus before Kammath could answer for him. Kabir's son helped his cousin up. Dinora and Marte went to the injured youth.

Kabir looked like he could faint at any moment.

Though Idan had also taken a prodigious blow, he was at least able to help his chief across the steps. 'You coming?'

Cassius nodded but remained where he was. The throbbing in his sliced hand was growing stronger with every moment. Blood was still oozing from it but he knew the damage wasn't that bad; he could still move his fingers. As the others set off for the road, Kammath quickly examined the soldiers lying on the temple steps. 'All dead.' He turned to the courtyard. 'But some there are still alive. I can hear them. You want me to do it?'

Cassius surprised himself by barely hesitating. 'Yes. You must. And keep count. There were ten in all.'

As Kammath marched away, Cassius finally managed to untie the handkerchief, which he then used to soak up his own blood. He looked around. The only long knife he could see was Kabir's, which he retrieved. There was nothing he could do about all the shot that would be lying around. If anyone investigated properly, they would know that slingers had been involved. There were also the guests at the house and now the priests too, who had seen the four nomads, especially Kabir with his distinctive hair and Idan's scarred face.

They had left many traces of themselves. Cassius knew that the events of this night might dictate the course of the rest of his life. He could hardly believe what he – what they – had done. They had to get out of Byzantium immediately and put as many miles between them and this terrible scene as possible.

His grisly work done, Kammath returned to the light, shaking blood from his long knife. 'Ten.'

Cassius looked up at the temple doors. The priests had not dared to move beyond them.

He grabbed a torch from a stand, he and Kammath ran after the others.

Simo was standing alone, upon the dusty patch of ground between the quay and the road that ran north into the city. According to the brothers, the well-lit building on higher ground was the Temple of Apollo. Other than that, he could make out the angular silhouettes of a few isolated buildings but only the odd speck of light. He stared into the inky gloom until his eyes ached then returned to the quay to sit on a pile of timber.

The wind seemed to have lessened, though he could still hear the movement of the trees some distance back from the coast. As he sat there, he considered what he would do if none of them appeared. It was without doubt a possibility.

Another glance at the road revealed nothing. He turned, hearing shoes on the concrete of the quay.

'You said they will approach from the road?'

Simo had no idea which Bion was addressing him. 'I assume so.'

'So that can't be them?'

'What?'

'Look there.'

Simo saw the lights – two of them, quite close, approaching from the north-west.

'I believe there is a trail there that leads up to a larger road.'

Simo hurried across the quay then over some rough ground. Once closer, he could see there was an opening in a high hedge. He waited there, and within five minutes the first figure appeared. It was Master Cassius.

'Sir!'

'Simo?'

'Here, sir.'

'Thank the gods.'

His chest and much of his neck was sticky with blood. He was wielding a torch with one hand, holding the other gingerly by his side.

'Sir, what happened to you?'

'Later. Do you have the boat?'

'Yes, sir – just a hundred yards away.'

'And it will take all of us?'

'Yes.' Simo looked at the others. The chief, Kabir, was standing with his head bowed, swaying. The two young men were each accompanying a girl.

'Is that—'

'I'll tell you everything later. Just take us to the boat.'

'At once, sir.'

Cassius sat at the stern, looking up at the sky. The wind had dropped to a light breeze. He could hear the deep breaths of the two oarsmen as they propelled the boat along the coast, the mountings squeaking with every stroke.

Simo was beside him. He had already cleaned out the wound and was now bandaging it as best he could. Cassius held the lantern close to help him. Though the pulsing pain of the split flesh had not abated, Simo seemed certain that nothing important had been damaged, though he would need stitches.

With a little time at last, Cassius's mind had been so assailed by terrible thoughts that it now seemed to have closed itself off. For several minutes he just sat there, as quiet as the others.

With them at the stern were the two girls. Simo had found a blanket for them and they held each other close to stay warm. Kammath and Yablus were lying in the bow. Idan and Kabir were sitting in the middle of the boat, just behind the brothers. Kabir had recovered enough to speak to Idan and sit up. Cassius could not think of anything to say to him.

Half an hour later, the oarsmen took a brief rest and exchanged a few anxious comments in their own language. When they had seen the condition of their clients, Cassius had paid them the rest of their fee plus another two aurei to not reveal anything about their night's work. He could never know if they would honour the agreement.

Once underway again, the brothers guided the boat through some moored galleys with lanterns hanging in the rigging. As they started across the strait, Cassius and Simo watched Kabir crawl to the stern of the boat. He lay between the girls, put his arms around them and began to sob.

XXXI

They came ashore at a remote pontoon where there was not a single light or vessel. A mooring post broke off when one of the twins tied a rope around it but the dilapidated structure held firm as the six men and two women climbed out. While the others took the bags and trooped towards the shore, Cassius spoke to the brothers, who clearly needed to rest again before starting back across the straits.

'Any idea where we are?'

'It looks quiet but you're only a mile or so from the edge of Chalcedon. Just follow the beach then cut inland when you come to the sea wall. The highest building is the Temple of Jupiter – head for that and you'll end up close to the centre.'

'Thank you. Listen, I know we've paid you but there is another reason why I'd like you to not speak of this.'

'Go on.'

Cassius knew the brothers would hear about the events at the Temple of Apollo; it would probably be around the entire city by the following day.

'The girls. They were held captive, suffered greatly. We got them out. Regardless of what you may hear, it was done for the right reasons.'

'I'm starting to think we might have under-charged,' said one of the twins. 'Clearly some bloody business. So it is hardly in our interest that anyone know of our involvement. No one saw us leave the harbour, no one saw us at Philo's Point. I suggest you get moving.'

Cassius did so and found the others at the rear of a tiny cove beyond the pontoon, gathered around a stone bench facing the sea. Only Idan amongst the Syrians looked anything short of exhausted. Simo was holding the lantern and shaking his head as he surveyed the pile of bags.

'One last effort,' said Cassius. 'We must clean ourselves up before going anywhere in case we run into watchmen. I suggest the same inn that we used before. It's late but they know our faces and that we pay our bills – they'll let us in. We can rest there awhile but we must leave at dawn.'

They took the last two rooms left, leaving the smaller one for the girls. Cassius insisted on letting Kabir and Yablus have the two beds and slept on blankets beside Simo. Sheer exhaustion gave him three hours of rest but once he awoke, the pain in his hand stopped him returning to sleep. Simo had applied some kind of treatment to staunch the bleeding and numb the pain but the latter effect had clearly worn off.

Cassius lay there, running over the horrific events of the night. Only his experience of similar trials enabled him to grasp that it had all been real, that he had actually seen and survived such things.

He imagined the scene at the Temple of Apollo. The magistrate's men might be there already. It was possible the governor had been informed; senior military officers too. A tribune, a centurion, an optio and eight legionaries dead.

Cassius's head grew warm. He brought his good hand up and held it against his brow.

He'd barely thought twice while pursuing the girls but he had to wonder now; had it been worth it? Poor Aikaterine was dead. The others had been rescued, 'The Earthly Gods' consigned to a fate they deserved but what about him? The events of the previous night could ruin his life, bring infamy and shame to his family. Like the fear of those who had hunted he and Indavara during their last assignment, he would now have to live with this threat hanging over him.

There were some causes for hope. Whether dead or alive, all those involved with The Earthly Gods would be tainted by criminality and shame. When the chief magistrate investigated, the truth would come out. But – as with most things – it depended on the men at the top. If the governor, the magistrate and the military discovered exactly what The Earthly Gods had been doing, would they distance themselves or order a pursuit of the killers?

The killers.

Would they even allow the truth of what their fellow leaders had been involved in to become public knowledge? Whether they did or not, the friends and family of Octavius, Nereus and Phaedrus might never know what *they* had done; only what had been done to them.

Too many questions. Only time would provide the answers; and Cassius intended to discover them from a great distance. He was relieved to be on the other side of the straits but that was nothing like far enough.

'Sir,' whispered Simo. 'Are you all right?'

Cassius bent his head back and looked up at a window. He could see light through the shutters and hear movement upon the streets.

'Let's get up, Simo. That stable isn't far away, I'll get over there now to find us some horses.'

'I don't think there is enough money, sir.'

'Actually there is.'

Far from making him feel better, Cassius's trip outside only amplified his anxiety. Glancing from face to face as he returned from the stable, he was at least glad to have arranged the horses. He had used the aureii to buy eight mounts and two spares, which the stable owner would deliver within an hour.

Glad to be back inside the inn, he greeted the innkeeper's wife in the parlour and passed a group of guests taking breakfast. He realised he was in desperate need of the latrine. It was his habit to go early, when there was some chance of the place being vaguely clean. He found it empty and was just reaching down to lift his tunic when the door opened.

The man who came in immediately shut it behind him.

'I thought you were supposed to be bright.'

'Tarchon.'

'Coming back to the same inn? Frankly, I'm surprised Abascantius rates you so highly.'

For a moment, Cassius felt sure the agent knew everything. He told himself to betray nothing, stay calm, think logically. 'How did you . . . I thought you were headed to Cappadocia.'

'I was. Then a messenger caught up with me. Poor bastard had ridden all the way from Antioch. I thought our paths might cross at Ankyra but I didn't pick up your trail until Nicomedia. I arrived here yesterday and spent my day touring the inns.' He gestured at the latrine. 'Be quick. I'll meet you outside.'

'You're here to take me back? Is that it?'

'Possibly. Afterwards.'

'After what?'

'After we see what happened to your bodyguard friend. Abascantius thinks he's found him.'

Tarchon allowed Cassius to fetch Simo and they met the agent out in the courtyard. He was leaning against a shady wall, beside a wooden trellis covered with ivy. When the innkeeper's wife came out asking if they needed any breakfast, Tarchon dismissed her with a word. The woman smiled cordially; she seemed to know him.

'Only two girls with you,' he said as Cassius and Simo joined him. 'What about the third?'

Part of the reason Cassius had asked if he could fetch Simo was so they could decide how much to disclose. As before, he was under no illusions about the difficulty of deceiving the veteran.

'Dead. Killed by the slave traders for resisting them. Our friend's daughter. At least we got the others.'

Tarchon ran a finger across one thick, black eyebrow. 'What happened to your hand?'

'There was a fight when we got them out. Please, we have waited months for news.'

'The message did not come from any of our contacts but from an optio on the island of Rhodes named Clemens.'

'Clemens?'

'I believed you worked with him while investigating the Memor case?'

'Yes.'

'Clearly he remembers you too. A few weeks back he had a visit from a concerned young lady. She had seen a man trying to escape from a ship. Before his captors silenced him he shouted the optio's name twice. Her husband ordered her not to get involved but a few days later she walked into the way station and told Clemens himself. He remembered Indavara's name and when he heard the description felt sure it was him. He made some enquiries and discovered that the ship is a privately owned galley called the *Leontophoros*. Clemens kept digging and got the owner's name: a man named Cornelius. Apparently he's a retired shipping magnate who lives on the island of Chios. That's all we know. Clemens contacted Memor's daughter, Annia, who said you'd left Antioch basilica as an address for any post.'

Cassius stood there in silence, trying to take it in. All the letters sent across the Empire and this was how they found him. As suspected, Abascantius had monitored the post.

'Where is Chios?' asked Simo.

Cassius had a rough idea but could still not summon any words.

'South-west,' said Tarchon. 'Off the coast between Pergamum and Ephesus. About two hundred and fifty miles. By sea we might do it in three or four days.'

'By sea?'

'I have the necessary documentation to secure funds and passage. If it comes to it, we can approach the Fleet.'

'Abascantius gave you that order?'

'It seems he values you and that bodyguard of yours rather more highly than you think.'

'By all the great and honoured gods. Clemens? Annia? We were lucky.'

'Wasn't just luck,' said Tarchon. 'You would never have heard a thing if your man hadn't tried to escape.'

Cassius gripped Simo's shoulder. 'At last.'

Simo gave a grim smile.

'I'm sure you have some packing to do,' Tarchon told the attendant.

'Yes, of course.'

'I'll see you up there,' said Cassius.

As Simo departed, Tarchon stepped away from the wall. 'I'll get down to the docks – I know a few likely candidates.'

'Good.'

'This business with the girls. I know you came back in the middle of the night and I've seen the state of you and the Syrians. You may be absent without leave but you're still a Service man. If Abascantius was here, he would ask if you're exposed; if the Service is exposed.'

Cassius had never tried so hard to retain his composure. 'An unpleasant affair but it has nothing to do with the Service.'

'No loose ends, then?'

'None.'

Simo somehow packed all their gear into just six saddlebags. Cassius had agreed to let the Syrians keep the horses for their journey and also gave Kabir all but two of the remaining gold coins. When the mounts were delivered and the nomads took their gear downstairs, he sat in the empty room while Simo hastily stitched his wound. There would be no time later and the job would be doubly difficult aboard a ship.

With the Gaul kneeling in front of him and his hand resting on his thigh, Cassius supped from a large mug of strong wine. Despite his numerous preoccupations, it was bidding farewell to Kabir and the others that preyed on his mind. He had, however, made a single calculation that eased some of the guilt; even if he'd replied to the first of the Syrian's notes in Antioch, they would never have reached Byzantium in time to save Aikaterine.

According to Dinora, who unlike Marte could speak of her experiences, they had simply returned to their room one night and found Aikaterine missing. They asked the other slaves and even their captors what had happened but a raging Nereus dissuaded them from ever asking again.

Cassius couldn't help feeling he had let Kabir down. Perhaps he should never have promised that he would find them. The Syrian's premonition had been right after all.

Soon he was occupied only by the pain of the needle digging into already tender skin. By the time Simo tied off the last of the eleven stitches, the mug of wine was empty.

'By gods, that's sore.'

'I'll apply another treatment when the inflammation has reduced, sir.'

The Gaul tidied away his equipment then helped his master to his feet.

Cassius had asked Kabir if they could say their farewells in the room. Apart from the fact that he and Simo had to get down to the docks, he did not wish to part on some busy street.

The six Syrians came up the stairs together, the girls first. Even Marte managed a 'thank you' in Latin. Cassius did not know what else to do other than kiss each of them gently on the cheek.

Next in was Yablus.

'How's the arm?'

Simo had made a sling for the young warrior, who was clearly not concerned about the wound.

'Can't even feel it.'

Cassius shook hands with his left. 'You did well, young man. You're a credit to your family and your tribe.'

'Thank you, Cassius.'

Yablus also thanked Simo, who reminded him to change the dressing regularly and not to scratch at his stitches. Once outside, Yablus escorted the girls downstairs.

Idan came in. He now had a bruise of livid purple and yellow where Octavius's elbow had connected with his chin.

Cassius said, 'Back to that woman of yours at last, eh?'

'I can still come with you.'

It had taken Cassius quite some time to convince them – Kabir in particular – that there was now no need to honour their original arrangement.

'No, I have all the help I need. Anyway, don't you have to stay beside your chief?'

'He's freed me from the blood oath – if you need me.'

'You deserve to go home. All of you. Maybe I'll see you back in Syria. You can show me how to fire a sling.'

'You're Roman. Stick to your sword.'

Idan spoke briefly to Simo, then left. Kabir and Kammath came in together. Remarkably, other than a few scratches and scrapes, the son bore no physical trace of the fight. But there was a change in him; something in the eyes.

'I should not have doubted you,' he said. 'Without your help, we would never have even found the right city. I thank you.'

'I am only sorry that . . . we could not . . . '

Cassius fought back the emotion welling within and gripped Kammath's hand. 'You are a warrior worthy of your father.'

On his way out, Kammath offered to pick up Patch from Karolea. Simo assured him that they would do so themselves when the time came.

Kabir still looked a broken man. Cassius could hardly recall the handsome, lively figure he had known three years ago. Two bloody lines marked his forehead where he had driven it into the wall and there was lump like an egg over his right eye where Octavius's kick had landed.

Knowing how difficult this would be, Cassius had prepared some words but it was Kabir who spoke first, taking the younger man's hands in his.

'You are a true friend. I shall never forget what you did – what both of you did – for my family and me. I ask once more that you allow me to fulfil our agreement and help you find Indavara.'

'And again I say no. I won't hear of it. Get yourself back to Syria and your loved ones. Kabir, I know no words can ease your pain – it is something I cannot hope to understand. But please remember this: you did nothing wrong. There are evil men in the world, and they cause great suffering to others. They are responsible, not you. And if it's any help at all, think of those girls and the others we helped. They are free because of us, what we did.'

'It does help. A little. And do you know that I am proud? Proud that my Katia fought them. She is part of the Glorious Fire now. Whenever I look up in the hours of the day, I will see her.'

Cassius blinked but the tears came. Kabir squeezed his arm affectionately, then moved on to Simo and shook his hand.

'We will meet again,' said the Syrian to them both. 'In better times.'

XXXII

He'd lost count of the times they had bled him.

He lay on his side, freezing and unable to move. Someone had been in to give him water; he wasn't sure when. He could see the mug on the floor below the bed. He tried to move his hand but he could barely flex the fingers, let alone shift the arm. He heard scrabbling claws. The mouse perhaps? He hadn't seen it for days. The mug shimmered and blurred. He closed his eyes and put his head back on the pillow. It was more than just weakness now; there was a dull but insistent ache within his bowels, stomach and chest. It was difficult to remember anything or hold a thought.

His left arm slipped off his hip. Like the right arm it was bandaged by wrappings soaked dark with blood. Surgeon usually came in to change them but Indavara could not recall when he'd last seen him. The most recent visit he was sure of was Warty and Narrow Eyes. They had said nothing as they removed sheets covered in shit and piss. Indavara had to lie helpless on the floor watching the men change them before they lifted him back on to the bed. He thought of Corbulo and Simo. They must have given up by now. He didn't blame them; he knew they would have done everything they could. He thought of Fortuna, looking down on him, leaving him to die. He had killed so many men, perhaps that was why she had abandoned him.

He closed his eyes. He knew where he wanted to be. The forest, the village, the house with the conical roof.

A broad man; bearded and stern. A woman; dark-haired and kind. His mother and father, he was certain.

He only had one dream now; it was the same every time.

He walked inside and sat between them, in front of the fire. He leaned against his mother and she put her arm around him.

The Kingdom Simo spoke of was real. Indavara was going there. And he would stay forever.

XXXIII

At dawn, Cassius went up on deck. The ship and its captain were well known to Tarchon and they had left Chalcedon the previous afternoon. Both men appeared to still be in their cabins. The first mate was manning the tiller while another sailor bailed water from the ship's tender and four more supervised yard and mainsail.

The sky was oppressively grey overhead, mirroring the colour of the sea. Cassius did not care. All that mattered was the wind; and he was relieved to see that – though light – it was still from the north, propelling the galley south across the Sea of Marmara.

'Morning, sir,' said the first mate, whose name Cassius could not remember.

'Morning. We seem to be going well.'

'Not bad at all, though we could do with a stronger breath at our backs. You can't see Proconnesus now because of the morning mist but it's only four or five miles behind us.'

'Not far from Cyzicus then.'

'Not far at all. About fifteen miles off our port beam.'

Cassius thought of the city where he had been posted after the siege of Alauran. It was there that he had shown ability as an investigator before being recalled to Syria by Abascantius. Not long afterwards he had met Indavara: the first of many times when the bodyguard had rescued him, seeing off a gang of thuggish auxiliaries.

Despite this crucial breakthrough, Cassius again faced a journey into the unknown. He had no idea what they would find on Chios and how this man Cornelius was involved. Drinking in a long draft of fresh sea air, Cassius thanked the gods that he and Simo were at least out of Byzantium. Equally as important, Tarchon was out of there too. Whether the whole affair was covered up by the authorities or became common knowledge, it was surely too much to hope for that Abascantius would not eventually learn of the incident and connect it to his agent and the Syrians. Cassius at least had time to prepare for such an eventuality; and he had arrived at the conclusion that there was in fact little concrete proof of his involvement. The soldiers, the freed slaves and the servants he had encountered would be able to pass on little about his identity. Everyone else who could have posed a threat was dead.

He still found it hard to comprehend what he and his allies had done. But it was not the first time he had killed fellow Romans; and the last leader he'd defeated had deserved death as much as Phaedrus, Nereus and Octavius. The soldiers who had followed Octavius? That was more complicated but they must surely have been 'Earthly Gods' themselves; and they had been prepared to follow the orders of their criminal centurion without hesitation. Cassius reckoned he could have made a decent speech of defence but he was in no doubt about the outcome if charges were ever brought against him. As an officer, he could only be tried by a military court. Regardless of his enemies' crimes, he had chosen a bunch of nomads over fellow Roman officers and gentlemen. His Empire would hang him for it.

'You cold, sir?' said the first mate. 'We've some spare cloaks below.'

'I'm fine.'

'You're shivering.'

'I'm fine. Tell me, will we clear Ilium by nightfall?'

'Should do.'

From there, they would reach open sea; from there they could sail straight for Chios.

Cassius did what he could to avoid Tarchon on those first two days. Despite his usual seasickness, he stayed with Simo in the small cabin they had been provided with and tried to rest. On the evening of the third day he told the attendant all that had happened in Byzantium. He needed to do so and faltered only once: when describing how he had killed Octavius and fallen beneath the dying centurion.

'That's where all the blood came from.'

'Yes.'

The clothes had been thrown away and Cassius had insisted that Simo clean his sword, belt and mail shirt twice. All three items had now been polished and lay in a corner of the room upon a length of cloth. Cassius was sitting on the bed, Simo opposite him on the room's only chair, which fitted neatly into four holes in the floor to hold it still.

'You could never justify it of course – such violence, such sin.'

Simo did not answer.

'If there had been any other way, I would have taken it. But we had to get them out. And we had to know.'

Simo clasped his hands and stared down at the floor.

'Say something.'

'Sins are not equal,' offered Simo after a time. 'We have seen some terrible things, sir, you and I. Of the enemies you have faced, it seems to me that most of them at least had their reasons. But this . . . to treat others so cruelly purely for . . . lust and . . . '

'—entertainment.'

Simo nodded. 'I cannot condone killing, sir, not ever. But I understand it; and I cannot say that in Kabir's place I would do any different.'

'There are some forces stronger than faith, then. Even yours?'

'It is not that they are too strong, sir. It is that we are too weak.'

On the fourth morning, as the galley passed the island of Lesbos, Tarchon joined Cassius on deck. They were sitting on a bench to the right of the steering position, with only the first mate and the captain for company. The rest of the crew were manning the oars; a necessary measure as the wind had backed during the night. The galley was now fighting a strong southerly and rain which showed no sign of abating.

Like Cassius, Tarchon wore an oiled cloak with a hood.

'Need some air?'

'Indeed. I just hope we reach Chios in daylight.'

'That may be a struggle. We have been fortunate so far but they'll do well to make two or three knots against this.'

Cassius could see little of his face under the hood. Tarchon had a deep, rich voice and an accent that to Cassius sounded Greek. He also clearly favoured the language over Latin.

'You know the island well?'

'Not particularly. I was there about eight years ago, looking for some tribune who'd deserted with three chests of gold coins meant for his legion.'

'Did you find him?'

'Yes, but not there. He was holed up with his mistress in Ephesus.'

'Did he put up a fight?'

'He tried to.'

Both men turned their heads to the stern as spray arced over the bow. The captain sent the first mate forward, to where a boy was acting as lookout.

'How long have you worked for Abascantius?' Cassius asked, mainly to stop Tarchon asking him questions.

'A decade, on and off. It's been Galatia and Cappadocia for a couple of years but the Service sends me where I'm needed. Mainly the east, though I daresay I'll be headed west fairly soon. You too, probably.'

'Abascantius did mention that.'

'I don't mind a change but I'll have to brush up on my Latin.'

'It's not your first language?'

'Barely knew a word as a child.'

'May I ask how you came to be in the Service?'

'Yes.'

'Sorry?'

'Yes, you may ask.'

With a grin, Tarchon stood up and stretched then went to talk to the captain.

Though there was no chance he would see it, Cassius turned and looked south for Chios.

The island did not come into view until the following morning. Cassius knew nothing of the place other than a vague recollection of a naval battle between the Roman and Persian fleets. He wasn't sure if the incident had occurred during the first or second Macedonian War and neither captain nor crew had any idea either. What they were able to tell him was that it was shaped like a thick crescent, thirty miles at its longest, eighteen at its widest. The capital, also Chios, was situated on the far side of the island – the west – which meant there was a decision to be made.

Tarchon admitted that he could not even be sure what kind of presence the army and navy now maintained.

'Going around will add several hours,' said Cassius.

'Yes, but the sailors say the east coast is almost uninhabited and there are only two anchorages. We may not be able to find out much there; or even hire horses.'

'It has to be the capital then.'

Tarchon told the captain, who immediately consulted the first mate. The wind was light; the oarsmen were hard at work.

'Gods.' Cassius rubbed his brow and wondered how he could make the next hours pass quickly.

'You've waited weeks,' said Tarchon. 'Just be glad we're here. We can get some answers for you at last.'

The wait was as agonising as Cassius had feared. The captain could not recall precisely the location of the capital and three times they cleared a headland only for Cassius to realise they were still not there. Finally, around the ninth hour, the galley turned towards the shore.

There wasn't much to the town; the largest building Cassius spotted on the way in was a temple. Beyond it lay higher ground which virtually surrounded the settlement. It seemed unlikely that a speedy search of the island would be possible but he reckoned there was one advantage to the remote location and low population – surely someone would know Sextus Villius Cornelius.

There was no harbour or breakwater; only a large quay situated in the middle of the cove where most of the buildings were concentrated.

'Just remembered a bit of learning,' said the first mate as they approached.

'First time for everything,' said the captain, drawing a smirk from Tarchon.

'They say Homer was born here.' The first mate seemed impressed with himself. 'Homer.'

Simo came up from below. Over one shoulder was a pack containing a few essentials, over the other was Cassius's sword bag. As the crewmen shipped their oars and a towing dory came out to meet them, Cassius pulled out the sword and hung the belt from his shoulder.

Tarchon seemed faintly amused by the sight of the blade. He carried only a dagger and seemed to make every effort to appear unremarkable. His boots were of decent quality, his belt and tunic utterly average. He also carried a small goatskin bag on his back. To the casual observer, he would blend in. But to anyone who studied the man, they would soon realise that this was an individual of note.

The dark eyes seemed to take everything in but give nothing away. He only spoke when he needed to and rarely wasted a word. The physique was solid and athletic rather than overtly muscular. He looked as if he could stand and face danger or run fast enough to get away with ease. Even on the boat he moved smoothly, like an athlete.

He reminded Cassius of Indavara, and he decided he might learn a great deal from the man, given the opportunity.

Once the ship was alongside, Cassius, Simo and Tarchon jumped off. One of the men taking the galley's lines told them that the best place to ask for information was either the harbour master's or the island's assembly house. The harbour master's was closer.

As they walked past some curious boys and fishermen carrying pots teeming with shellfish, Tarchon pointed to the south. Beyond the quay were several moorings, three of which were occupied by galleys of a similar size to the one they had arrived on.

'Wonder if one of those belongs to our friend.'

'Maybe.'

Other than the plaque beside the door, the harbour master's looked like the other modest villas facing the water. At the dwelling next door, two old women sat under an awning, looking on.

Just as Tarchon reached for the door, it opened. A man of about forty stood there, a set of keys in his hand.

'Sorry, closing up for the day.'

'You'll give us a minute, though,' said Tarchon.

The harbour master inspected them, then looked at the quay.

'Did you just arrive?'

'Yes.'

The harbour master lowered his keys but remained in the doorway. 'What can I do for you?'

'We're here to visit Sextus Villius Cornelius. Can you give us directions to his home?'

'Knows you're coming, does he?'

'No.'

'Cornelius keeps himself to himself. I'm not sure he'd like me telling strangers where to find him.'

'We're army officers.'

'Where are your uni—'

Tarchon leaned forward. 'I'm already running out of patience with you, my friend. Where does Cornelius live?'

The harbour master wilted quickly under the agent's gaze. 'All right, just don't let him know I told you. Off the town square is a road leading south. After four miles you will come to a ruined temple. The next turning left takes you to his villa. It's not signposted.'

Tarchon nodded towards the moorings. 'Do any of those galleys belong to him?'

'No. He has his own dock at the villa.'

'Is there an army garrison here?'

'Just a guard officer and a squad of twelve – plus the local militia.'

'Who's the guard officer and where will we find him?'

'They'll have finished work by now. They're repairing the old barracks – apparently we're to get a half century in the spring. Guard officer is named Agapetos. He and the rest of the squad are housed in two inns. One of them is on the square, called The Octopus.

Cassius was all set to leave but Tarchon had another question.

'Cornelius – what do you know of him?'

'Same as everyone else, I suppose – not much. Except that he's very, very rich.'

They caught Agapetos in the middle of bathing. The guard officer emerged from The Octopus's bath house with a towel wrapped round his waist.

'Cornelius, you say? Who exactly are you?'

'Imperial security,' said Tarchon. 'Assemble your men – you have five minutes. Understood?'

Where Cassius often relied on his distinguished tones to convince soldiers that they should follow his orders, Tarchon clearly favoured a blunter approach.

'Yes, sir.'

Agapetos followed them back across the courtyard to the inn.

'You have horses?' asked Tarchon.

'Yes.'

'What about us? We need three.'

Agapetos darted through an open doorway, bellowed at someone, then replied.

'They'll be brought round to the front. We'll be just behind you.'

—◆—

The guard officer was true to his word. As Cassius, Tarchon and Simo guided their newly acquired mounts up a path leading out of the town, the legionaries came galloping up behind them.

His hair still wet, Agapetos reined in. 'Got six for you.'

'Good enough,' said Tarchon.

Once at the top of the slope, the narrow road continued south, occasionally passing alarmingly close to some steep drops. This part of Chios's coast was dominated by vertiginous cliffs and some pleasant-looking beaches of grey sand. They passed two men carrying a long pole, hanging from which were freshly caught squid skewered on hooks.

Tarchon waved Agapetos forward. 'Where exactly is the house?'

'Beyond the next headland at one end of what we call Long Bay. The villa itself is not that big but Cornelius owns the whole area around it.'

'And his own ship,' said Cassius, who was now riding behind the pair with Simo. He was desperate to urge his mount into a gallop but the road was neither straight nor flat enough to risk it.

'That's right,' replied Agapetos, wiping sweat from his cheek.

One of the men spoke up from behind them.

'What's that?' said Tarchon.

'Apparently the *Leontophoros* hasn't been out for a while. Some of the locals reckon Cornelius is ill – he used to take a lot of walks but he's not been seen in the town for months.'

'What else do you know of him?' asked Cassius. 'What about his employees?'

Agapetos shrugged but then turned round and questioned his men. The answers revealed that Cornelius's domestic staff still visited the town regularly. The ship's captain was also housed at the villa and kept a skeleton crew with him at all times.

As they neared the headland, the group entered an area that

had recently suffered a severe fire. The ground was covered with ash and the trees had been scorched so badly that only their blackened skeletons remained. The bitter smell was still thick in the air. Just beyond the reach of the flames, they came to the ruined temple, which was little more than a rectangle of foundation stones and rubble.

They turned off and had followed the track for no more than a quarter of a mile when the villa came into view below. Built at right angles to the shore, the dwelling had been constucted in the shelter of the headland. To the rear were numerous outbuildings plus a sizeable garden and terrace. At the front, a narrow concrete platform ran seaward, connecting the house to an impressive dock, upon which several more small buildings had been constructed.

There was no ship.

'Looks quiet,' observed Agapetos.

Cassius studied the building and the surroundings.

'I don't see anyone,' said Tarchon.

Cassius's head was buzzing.

'Sir?' said Simo.

Please no. Not after all this. I have to know. I have to know.

'Yah!'

Cassius set his horse away and took not a single look back as he followed the zigzagging trail downwards. Hands gripping the reins, his kicks kept the mount moving. As its hooves pounded the ground, the horse threw itself around each bend and in no time at all reached the bottom. Not bothering to tie it up, Cassius leaped down and drew his sword.

He marched on to the terrace and looked around. There was not only no one there but not a single sign of recent habitation. He walked up to a half-open window shutter. Inside was a kitchen. Upon a table were a few plates and jugs. As the others arrived, Cassius ran around to the nearest door. Finding it unlocked, he wrenched it open.

The house was silent. He walked across a floor of wide black and white tiles and looked into a bedroom. It was empty except for a bed and a chest of drawers. Reaching the atrium, he noted the discolouration on the walls where something – a tapestry perhaps – had been taken down. Beyond the atrium was a study, where he found a desk and a few dozen books and scrolls.

'Sir?'

Ignoring Simo, he ran out of the front door into the fading light. Scattered upon the platform were numerous wooden boxes, woven baskets and amphora. Most were empty; some contained a few bits of ironware.

Cassius walked on to the dock, only stopping when he came to the first mooring post. Around it was a coil of rope, the only line there. A single gull standing at the far end of the dock flapped into the air then headed across the bay, inches above the waves. Cassius looked down at the water lapping against the concrete.

'Sir.' Simo put a hand on his shoulder.

'I thought we would know. At least we would know.'

Cassius had no idea how long he stood there before Tarchon joined them. 'Looks like the place has been robbed. Everything portable and of value seems to have been taken. I don't know what to make of it. You?'

'What does it matter? They're gone.'

'I don't see how they could have known we were coming. Cleaning this place out would have taken time. We'll keep searching.'

Tarchon hurried back across the dock.

Cassius waited for Simo to finish his whispered prayer before speaking.

'I wonder how long we missed them by. Might have only been hours.'

Simo gazed up at the sky for some time, then walked with him back towards the house.

'Perhaps we should stop now,' said Cassius. 'Perhaps Abascantius was right.'

'This is all so strange, sir. Doesn't it suggest that this man Cornelius was somehow involved? Can't we find his ship?'

'And then what? Another moment like this? You want that?'

As they arrived in the atrium, Agapetos and the others were reporting back to Tarchon.

'I just don't understand it,' said the guard officer. 'With all the staff and the sailors there must have been at least a dozen of them. It's just been left unlocked.'

'Pirates? Slavers?' suggested one of the men.

'On Chios?' said Agapetos. 'Hardly.'

Cassius walked back into the study. The only picture left on the wall was a large piece mounted on wood. It appeared quite old and seemed to be the original architectural plans for the villa. He noted the date; the plans had been drawn up fourteen years ago. Across the top right corner was a line, and when Cassius realised what was drawn inside it, he hurried out of the atrium and towards the rear door.

'Corbulo?' said Tarchon.

'He had three more structures built. They're at the end of the headland.'

Cassius's untethered horse had wandered off. He mounted the first one he came to and set off up the path. It was not that he thought he would necessarily find something; more that he needed to be sure there was nothing to find.

It soon became clear why none of the locals had mentioned the other buildings. The dusty track that led to them was barely visible and was surrounded by thick, low bushes. It followed the increasingly narrow headland, descending past two broad, natural 'steps' before emerging on to an exposed promontory a hundred feet above the sea.

Cassius dismounted and ran up to the first structure: a miniature temple perhaps only ten feet across. On either side of the colonnaded entrance were faded murals of Jupiter. Within the shadowy interior, he could make out a marble altar and offerings of food, wine and money, all covered in a thick layer of dust.

He walked past it to the second structure. It was a viewing area; nothing more than two stone benches covered by a narrow roof.

There were three. Three buildings. Can that be it?

In front of the viewing area was a hollow tower of stone about eight feet high. Inside were some burned timbers. He had seen such things on many coastlines: it was a beacon, not a building.

Cassius walked close to the edge and looked over. The drop was vertical. Below, white spray blew up as the sea struck a cluster of dark boulders.

He turned to his left and saw it: the roof of a small hut on a flat area just below the promontory. He spun round and spied another faint trail leading downwards behind the temple.

By now Tarchon and Simo had caught up. As Simo dismounted and jogged towards him, Cassius reached the trail. He had time only to glimpse the figure outside the hut before he lost his footing and slid down on his backside. He got to his feet and descended the last few yards on to a patch of grass perhaps only ten yards across.

The man looked about sixty: he was lying on his back beside the door, head against the wall. His eyes were shut and the wind was tugging at his thin hair, which was far lighter in colour than his beard. Though he was clutching a dagger in his right hand, he appeared to be dead.

Cassius walked up to the body and tapped it with his boot. The man's head slipped down another inch.

Cassius lifted the latch, opened the door and looked inside. 'Simo. It's him.'

Cassius fell against the doorway and held on to it. He could not move.

Indavara was lying on a bed equipped with strange metal poles on either side. His arms – each covered in blood-stained bandages – were splayed outwards and his eyes were shut. A blanket lay upon his body. He seemed to have halved in size and he was not just pale, he was white.

Simo hurried past his master and knelt beside his friend. He held his wrist and put his ear to Indavara's chest. When he turned, his eyes were wet with tears.

'I can hear his heart. He's alive.'

XXXIV

Agapetos was despatched to the town to summon a surgeon. The soldiers ran back to the house and returned with more blankets. They also had fresh water but Simo could see no way of helping Indavara drink. He tried to rouse him but he simply wouldn't wake. It was as if his body had gone into hibernation, like an animal enduring the winter.

'His skin is so cold,' said the attendant, holding his hand under the covers.

'Outside, men,' Cassius told the soldiers. 'Move the body away.'

'Leave the door open though,' said Simo, 'we need to keep some air circulating.'

'So they bled him,' said Tarchon, who was leaning against the wall between two windows.

Cassius said, 'The rumours about Cornelius must have been true. He thought that a gladiator's blood could heal him.'

'He's not the first. They used to sell it right outside the arena in Ephesus.'

'It didn't even occur to me,' said Cassius quietly.

'How could it?' said Simo. 'This is barbaric.'

'Can he recover?'

'Sir, we don't know how long he's been like this; how much blood they have taken. The body can make it's own but unless he regains consciousness we can't give him food or water. He will . . . he will fade away.'

'Have you put it together yet?' said Tarchon, crossing the little room to where Cassius stood at the end of the bed.

'What?'

'Cornelius dead outside with his dagger? The empty house? The missing staff?'

Cassius had been considering little other than the torture Indavara had suffered in this foul place.

Tarchon continued: 'I think Cornelius might have had a late change of heart. He must have always admired your friend in some way. He came down here to protect him, probably when his employees realised that he was on his way out and they could do as they pleased. But there are no wounds. The effort must have been too much for him. His men just left them both for dead.'

'The surgeon – we don't have a moment to waste.'

'I'll do what I can.' Tarchon hurried outside.

'Hold his other hand, sir,' said Simo. 'We might warm him up a bit and at least he'll know we're here.'

Cassius was wary of going near him. To be so close would make the truth inescapable. But he knelt opposite Simo and felt under the blankets until his hand was on top of Indavara's calloused fingers.

'By the gods – freezing. Clammy too.'

'That may be a good sign, sir, his body has not yet dried out, though he is in great need of water.'

'His wounds?' Cassius had been unable to watch as Simo unwrapped the bandages.

'They have partially healed. Which is something.'

'Can we give him blood somehow?'

'I'm not sure that would work, sir.'

'I suppose it didn't for the old man.'

'It would also make him sick.'

Cassius looked at Indavara's face. His black hair had grown long, almost completely covering his eyes. The pallid skin made every mark and scar even clearer. The cheeks were pinched and he even seemed to have lost weight from his neck.

'I can hear his breath.'

'It is steady, sir. But the beat of his heart is not.'

'Perhaps we should just try and put the water in his mouth.'

'That might wake him, sir. But it might also be too much of

a shock for his body. I would prefer to wait for the surgeon. Bleeding is a common practice for some in his profession. He may have some other ideas.'

'Is there nothing else we can do?'

'We can pray, sir.'

'I shall. To all the gods.'

The surgeon arrived two hours later. Cassius would have preferred a military man but was glad to hear from the soldiers that the fellow had a good reputation. He was also glad to find he was middle-aged. Cassius felt that this was ideal for a physician – old enough to have acquired some experience and knowledge but not past his best. His name was Metrophanes and he concurred with Simo that Indavara should not remain in the chilly, dank hut.

Having dismissed the rest of the soldiers, Tarchon and Agapetos built up a good fire in the villa's main bedroom. A makeshift stretcher was crafted from sheets and the metal poles from the hut and – with Cassius and Simo assisting – they took Indavara to the villa. He did not stir but his saviours were relieved to find no change in his condition.

Once Simo had cleaned his wounds, he and the surgeon discussed the next course of action. Cassius was soon won over by Metrophanes: the man had a kindly way about him and lacked the arrogance of many in his profession. He was also open to Simo's contributions, though the Gaul had no formal training at all. They concluded they simply had to get water into Indavara, which meant they had to somehow wake him up.

First they shouted in his ear. Then they shook him, gently at first, then harder. Simo took the responsibility for the slap that finally drew a reaction. Indavara – who had been propped up in the bed – threw his head back. When it lolled forward again, his lips moved and drool came out. His breathing intensified and he began to cough. Only a few sharp blows on his back from Metrophanes prevented him from choking.

Indavara's eyes opened for a moment. But they were not his. There was no life in them. They rolled back in his head and he lost consciousness again.

But when Simo held his head up and Metrophanes carefully poured water from a small mug, Indavara swallowed some down. They managed to get most of the water in before his head lolled again. They watched him intently for the next few minutes but there seemed to be no ill effects.

'Thank the gods,' said Cassius. 'Do you think you'll be able to do it again?'

'We must,' said Metrophanes, eyes still on his patient. 'And then we must give him milk – if he can keep it down. I would guess they had been doing this for weeks and I doubt he would have been capable of ingesting much food.'

'He has lost at least a quarter of his weight,' said Simo. 'Maybe more.'

Metrophanes stood up. 'You said he was a gladiator?'

'Yes,' replied Cassius. 'A champion.'

'Then he is no stranger to a fight; and that is exactly what he faces.'

Though much had been stolen, Cornelius's men had at least left a few sheets, blankets and pillows. With Metrophanes and Simo taking it in turns to watch Indavara, Cassius and Tarchon made up some beds in the neighbouring room. Cassius was astonished to find he slept and – when he awoke the next day – was greatly heartened to learn that during another brief moment of consciousness, Simo had got another mugful of water into Indavara.

With nothing else to do, Cassius rifled through the cupboards and was able to prepare a basic meal of cured ham and dried fruit. Tarchon unearthed what seemed to be the last remaining flask of wine, which he watered and delivered to the others.

Once breakfast was over, the agent announced that he would be leaving. Taking an order of equipment and supplies for

Agapetos to bring to the villa, he bade the others farewell and spoke to Cassius upon the terrace.

'Apart from the fact that the hire of that ship is costing a fortune, I need to get word to Abascantius – about this and my return to Cappadocia. You must contact him as soon as possible yourself.'

'Of course. I'm sorry that you got involved in all this. And I am truly thankful for your help.'

'I just go where I'm told to. Your friend's in good hands at least.'

Tarchon untied his horse and walked it over to the road.

Cassius was still curious about him. 'You don't have any servants? Or a bodyguard?'

'Never seen the need.'

They shook forearms.

'We may well meet again,' said Tarchon.

'I hope so.'

'One last thing. You'll have noticed that I haven't asked any more questions about what happened in Byzantium. That's because I don't want to know.'

Cassius nodded.

'Abascantius will. So make sure you have the right answers.'

Waiting. Thinking.

Despite all he had endured in the last few weeks, Cassius felt as if he had done nothing else. More than ever, he longed for a life of comfort and routine: the kind of life he had enjoyed before having to join the army; the kind he wanted to enjoy in the future. After all the weeks of not knowing what had become of Indavara, he now faced the torment of wondering if his friend would survive.

Standing alone on the dock, he looked out at the dark sea. Cloud and mist had rolled in, leaving the air damp. Three large gulls were bobbing around on the water, seemingly depressed by the change in the weather. Cassius tucked his hands into his belt and wandered along the dock. Evening was approaching and he reflected on the events of the day.

Around the sixth hour, a party of soldiers and officials had arrived to collect Cornelius's body. Cassius had explained what seemed to have happened and the locals agreed that was the logical conclusion. Though all were shocked at what had been done to Indavara, they were less surprised that the old man's subordinates had turned against him. Apparently, he was known for his poor choice of staff and no longer had any family left to advise him. Cassius learned that in his time Cornelius had owned a fleet of some twenty ships and would often travel with his crews, visiting every corner of the Empire. Cassius imagined one of those trips had taken him to Pietas Julia, where he had seen Indavara fight. The man must have been truly desperate to have embarked on such a bizarre, cruel scheme. Cassius had nothing but hatred for him, despite his ultimate change of heart.

He arrived back in the atrium to the sounds of panic. Rushing into the bedroom, he saw Indavara over on his side, vomit sliding from his mouth. Simo and Metrophanes were holding him, angling his body so he wouldn't choke. Once all the liquid was out, Indavara's body spasmed twice but then became still.

Cassius came forward. 'Is he—'

'He's all right,' said Metrophanes, as they settled Indavara back into the pillows.

'Fortunately,' said Simo.

'Water alone will not sustain him,' added Metrophanes. 'Your attendant believes it is too early to give him milk. I disagree.'

'The strain on his heart from the convulsions,' said Simo.

Though Cassius would always value Simo's expertise, the surgeon was an experienced professional.

'I think we must defer to Metrophanes in this case.'

'Yes, sir.'

Metrophanes said, 'We will let him sleep tonight, then try again tomorrow. I'm afraid I must leave now – I have other patients. Shall we say the third hour?'

'That's fine,' said Cassius. Once the surgeon had departed,

he took up the chair opposite Simo, who put his hand against Indavara's heart.

'It's not beat this fast before.'

'I think his colour is a little better but that might be wishful thinking.'

'No, sir – it is. On that we agree.'

Indavara's head moved to one side. Simo used a cloth to clean away the spittle that leaked from his mouth.

Cassius looked at the ex-gladiator's arm. Once so thick with muscle and fat, it was now thinner than his own.

Simo put the cloth down then rubbed his eyes.

'You're exhausted,' said Cassius. 'We'll take it in turns tonight.'

'Very well, sir.'

It was during Cassius's second shift (from the sixth hour of night to the ninth) that he decided to talk to him. Simo was asleep – and snoring – and the only other noise came from some unsecured shutter that neither man had been unable to locate.

Cassius moved his chair close to the bed and spoke in a whisper. By then, he already had some idea what he would say.

'I doubt you can hear me. I'm sure you can't, in fact. It's strange; I've not known you even two years. I can hardly believe it. I remember that accursed tavern in Palmyra – those bloody auxiliaries who tried to strangle me. They would have too, if not for you. Asked for your money first though, didn't you, you swine?'

Cassius suddently felt stupid and remained quiet for several minutes before starting again.

'We did everything we could. In Berytus. Afterwards. I'm so sorry we didn't come sooner. I . . . I'm praying for you, Simo too. Perhaps the gods will help, I don't know. But you can help yourself.' Cassius reached out and held Indavara's shoulder. 'You are the strongest man I have ever known. You must fight, Indavara. Fight like you always have – for your life. I've pledged it before but I'll pledge it again – I'll get you home. We found *you*, didn't we? So we can find your home, your family. If it's the last thing I ever do, I will get you there. By all the gods, I swear it.'

—8—

On the next day, they made several attempts to rouse him. Simo and Metrophanes agreed that they could not risk shocking his body too much so they began with his hands: gripping them, poking them, pinching them. Nothing worked. Metrophanes administered some increasingly strong slaps to his face. Indavara murmured something but did not open his eyes.

Late in the afternoon, before Metrophanes had to leave, Simo suggested cold water. They used a little at first, dropping it on to his face. Then Metrophanes took a handful and threw it at him.

Simo tutted. To Cassius, it seemed unpleasantly aggressive. But that was nothing to what came next: a full-bodied slap that knocked Indavara's limp head to one side.

'Stop it!' yelled Simo.

'By the gods, man, you'll hurt him.'

Metrophanes ignored them. 'Indavara, wake up! Wake up!'

He gripped his jaw and shook his head.

Indavara's mouth puckered. His eyes opened. The pupils were moving around, unable to focus.

Metrophanes kept one hand on his chin; put the other on his neck.

'Indavara, can you hear me? Can you hear me?'

Cassius could hardly watch. Seeing this ox of a man reduced to such a state was more than he could bear.

One pupil stopped moving, then the other.

'Can you hear me?'

The head tilted forward slightly.

'My god,' cried Simo, holding his friend by the shoulder.

'You must have sustenance. You must drink.'

Simo passed Metrophanes the milk. The surgeon held it to Indavara's lips; he closed his eyes as he drank. He took only small sips and faded away twice but, by the end of it, Metrophanes had given him half a mug.

As they settled him down again, Indavara's right hand pawed at the air. Simo held it.

'We're here. Master Cassius and I – we're here.'

The green eyes appeared for a brief moment then were lost once more.

The wait continued. During the day, Cassius busied himself with the fire and preparing food for him and Simo. Agapetos arrived with a pot of lamb stew that his wife had made and asked if there was anything else they needed. Cassius had already realised that such gestures were not merely because of his status with the Service. Like Metrophanes, the optio was simply a kindly fellow. After all the evil bastards he had encountered since leaving Antioch, he found his faith in his fellow man partially renewed. The surgeon came as often as he could and Cassius gave him the little remaining money he had. He had no idea what would happen after; how they would get off the island. Between them, he and Simo had three and a half denarii.

On the sixth day after they reached Chios, Indavara drank an entire mug of milk and plenty of water. The surgeon noted that his colour had improved once more and that his heartbeat was becoming more stable.

On the ninth day, Indavara stayed awake long enough to ingest another mug of milk and hold Simo's hand tightly. He looked at his friend and tried to mouth a word but it was more than he could manage.

On the eleventh day, he drank two mugs of milk and mumbled a sentence that the three watchers reckoned to be, 'Where am I?'

On the twelfth day, Cassius was alone with him when he awoke of his own accord. Seeing that one of his eyes was thick with gunk, Cassius wiped it clean.

Indavara held his wrist with surprising strength.

'Simo! He's awake again!'

'Cor . . . cor . . . '

'It's me. You're safe. You're going to be all right, I promise. Do you think you can eat? They want you to eat something.'

Simo was ready with honey they had diluted with water. Indavara managed three spoonfuls and licked the last one clean.

'By Jupiter, some things never change,' said Cassius. 'He'll be asking for a roast chicken next.'

Simo cried as he laughed.

Cassius leaned forward so Indavara could see him. 'Can you speak? Can you say anything?'

'Ember . . . ember.'

'What?'

'Ember . . . em.'

Indavara held up a hand, then lay back. Only a few moments later, he fell asleep again.

Simo checked his chest and his wrist. 'It's so much steadier now. And much stronger.'

Cassius stood up. 'His body may recover, but what of his mind?'

'It's still early, sir. We'll see.'

The events of the fifteenth day eased Cassius's fears. With the surgeon present and after four spoonfuls of honey, Indavara finally spoke again.

'Thanks.'

'Ha!' Simo could barely contain himself. Even the surgeon gave a broad smile.

Indavara turned to Cassius and beckoned him forward. He held his hand and gripped it tight. 'I remember, Cassius.'

'You know who we are. That's good.'

Indavara shook his head. 'I remember who I am. Where I'm from. My mother, my father. I remember it all.'

Historical Note

Unlike most of the previous Agent of Rome novels, *The Earthly Gods* is not specifically related to the events of the time. There are, however, several notable aspects that do draw on the historical record.

What became known as 'The Plague of Cyprian' was a pandemic – probably smallpox – that broke out in AD 250 and was still a major crisis twenty years later. The outbreak claimed the life of the emperor Claudius Gothicus and spread widely across the empire.

We do know that gangs of slave traffickers existed and that there was both a legal and illegal trade. Given the predilections among certain sections of the Roman elite, I am convinced groups like 'The Earthly Gods' would have existed in some form. Men in positions of power were virtually untouchable, while slaves (especially those kept illegally) were utterly powerless.

The blood of a gladiator was believed by some to hold the power of the fighter and was used as a cure for ailments including what we would refer to as epilepsy. Given the state of contemporary medicine, I don't think it's beyond the realms of possibility that a wealthy, desperate man like Cornelius might resort to such measures.

Acknowledgements

The Earthly Gods was written between February and September, 2015. Producing a novel is a team effort. Sincere thanks to my agent David Grossman and editor Oliver Johnson for their help in developing this one. The work of Anne Perry, Sharan Matharu and everyone else at Hodder & Stoughton is also greatly appreciated. Thanks once more to all the readers, bloggers, reviewers and outlets who have supported the series since 2011.

Cassius, Indavara and Simo will return. I think Tarchon might too.